Divided Loyalties

L. K. *Malone*

kregel
PUBLICATIONS

Grand Rapids, MI 49501

Library of Congress Cataloging-in-Publication Data
Malone, L. K.
Divided loyalties / by L. K. Malone.
    p.   cm.
    1. Americans—Middle East—Fiction. 2. Middle East—Fiction. 3. Terrorism—Fiction. I. Title.
PS3613.A35 D5   2001   813'.6—dc21   2001033757

ISBN 0-8254-2796-7

Printed in the United States of America

1 2 3 4 5 / 05 04 03 02 01

To my parents
Carla, Don, Karen, and Jerry
and the rest of my family.
Thank you, all, for showing me how to live and love,
and for taking my writing seriously even when it seemed
little more than a pipe dream.

And to Mariam,
for the privilege of watching you
become a beautiful woman
and a great friend.

Acknowledgments

I wish I could thank everyone who has helped me with *Divided Loyalties,* but the names would go on forever. Having to narrow down the list to a select few was difficult, and I'm positive I will have missed someone who deserves to be mentioned. I hope those people will forgive me.

First, let me thank the Lord for giving me this story and using it to bring me into the light of his Son! To the gifted writers who mentored me—those in DeScribers Writer's Workshop and Carol Cail from the Writer's Digest School—thank you for teaching me to do something I love so much! To my dear Muslim and Jewish friends, thanks for teaching me to see a little bit through your eyes. Steve Barclift, Janyre Tromp, Paul Ingram, and the rest of the staff at Kregel Publications, thanks for your prayers, patience, and kindness as you shepherded me through this process. Captain Bill Weimer (Fleet Chaplain, U.S. Sixth Fleet), Hugh Bransford, my cousin Cleve Blouch, and J. A. Norris (Lieutenant Commander, U.S. Navy retired), thanks so much for not laughing at this poor civilian's efforts at describing military life. The details and corrections you have provided, as well as your service to our nation, are greatly appreciated.

Finally, I'd like to acknowledge the book *Princess: A True*

Acknowledgments

Story of Life Behind the Veil in Saudi Arabia by Jean P. Sasson (Avon Books, 1992). To the author, whoever you are, bless you for sharing what it is to be a woman in the land of Mohammed.

Divided Loyalties

*Chapter*One

The *Americano* was an easy target. Eloisa had spotted him ten minutes before, and the little band of *ladri* not long after. There he was on the waterfront, doling out small bills, like some great white father, to the children who were crowding around, jostling, he assumed, in their eagerness for his charity. What they were really doing was cutting the strap on his expensive digital video camera.

There! It was done, and one of the children raced away, the strap trailing like a banner behind him. The man noticed something amiss and turned, and another, still braver, thief seized the opportunity to snatch the wallet from his hand.

The man shouted after them, doing his red-faced best to follow the giggling group, which scattered, dissolving swiftly into their native streets.

Eloisa loved her little dress shop by the marina. It didn't make much money, but it had big bay windows overlooking the streets of her beloved, crowded *Napoli*. When she wasn't busy making alterations or waiting on *clienti*, she could watch the boats churning the glittering waters of the bay. In season, she could see the city afresh, through the eyes of the tourists who wandered by. And too often these days, she could also watch dramas such as this unfold before her.

Turning from the window, she whispered a soft prayer, calling on her Jesus to reach out to those children and to help them turn away from the roads they were taking in life. She prayed for the tourist, too, even though she sensed that this small loss would be no more than an inconvenience. She prayed that he would learn to love those who harmed him, as Christ had loved his tormentors, even as they crucified him.

Eloisa loved to pray, loved to spend time with Jesus, interceding for the people she saw every day. She prayed for her family, her children and grandchildren who lived in *Roma,* for her customers, who came in often, sometimes not so much to shop as to enjoy Eloisa's genuine interest in them. And she prayed for the other foreigners who came here, the tourists and the *Americani* from the Navy commands in Naples and nearby Gaeta.

There was one here today, a girl who often received her special prayers, for Eloisa sensed a shadow of sadness about her.

The girl had narrowed her selection to two blouses, but at the moment was distracted by a group of local girls who were gathered at the next rack, examining skirts and giggling about boys. If not for her slightly foreign manner, this girl was near enough in looks to be one of them, with hair the color of polished mahogany, gray eyes, and a slight stature not typical of the rawboned American women. At a new peal of giggles, she smiled softly, wistfully, as if she wished to join them. Instead, she returned to her selections, resolutely ignoring their fun.

Eloisa's heart went out to this girl, the daughter of Captain Thaddeus Hardy, the chief of staff of the U.S. Sixth Fleet. The child's life could not be easy. She had never known a home, only a series of sterile military housing facilities. She had never known true *famiglia,* the sense of belonging that came from growing up among brothers, sisters, aunts, uncles, cousins, and grandparents.

She also had never known a lasting friendship. Eloisa knew that military children quickly learned to hold themselves apart, never growing too close, never trusting too much. During her family's first assignment here, the girl, Eloisa knew, had suffered the loss of three close friendships, before learning that hard-won lesson. They had returned recently after a series of other assignments around the world, and in the time she was gone, the girl's reserve had become even more pronounced.

Eloisa rose and went to join her young customer, lifting up a prayer for wisdom in what to say. "*Buon giorno,* Giselle." She gave the name its European pronunciation: Zheezelle. "Perhaps I can help you today?" And perhaps she could try once again to share with this young woman the one Friend who would always love her and never desert her, no matter who else came and went.

"*Buon giorno,* Eloisa," the girl replied, clearly pleased to have some attention. She turned around, holding her two blouses up against her breast. "Which do you think is better, the red or the gold?"

Eloisa paused to study her, and realized with some surprise that this girl was fast becoming a woman. She remembered the day that she'd first seen her, a child perhaps eight years old, following her mother on their first shopping trip in *Napoli.* Her face still bore the same sweet innocence, with her bright eyes and soft, dimpled cheek. But her figure had matured, even since the last time she'd shopped here; this girl would soon draw men's eyes with more than paternal indulgence. Giselle had reached that glorious time in life that every woman remembers with a smile, when love is new and sweet and pure.

Eloisa softly breathed a prayer that the purity would remain. "Both blouses are lovely with your coloring," she counseled. "But perhaps the gold is best."

"*Sí, grazie,* Eloisa." Without further consideration, Giselle returned the red blouse to its place on the rack, then reached for her billfold. *"Quanto costa?"*

"For you, *cara,* I make this one a gift." Eloisa reached out to smooth the girl's hair. "You have been a good customer, and I am fond of you."

Giselle's expression of surprised pleasure was touching—she was clearly unaccustomed to gifts of affection. "*Grazie,* Eloisa."

Eloisa carried the blouse to the counter and expertly folded it with tissue to protect it from wrinkles. "What is the occasion for a blouse so special?"

"I graduate from school next week. My father's giving a party for my class."

Eloisa noted that the girl had not mentioned her mother and wondered briefly about it. Dolores Hardy seldom shopped here anymore; Eloisa had heard she was often ill. Too ill, even, to involve herself in a party for her daughter?

Eloisa thought to ask about her, but had not yet formed the question when a man entered the shop. Eloisa's gaze rose from his uniform with its Shore Patrol armband to a dark, pockmarked face that bore scabs from a hasty shaving. She recoiled from the man's eyes, which blazed with an unnerving intensity. Her spirit told her something was very wrong.

"Miss Hardy." For an *Americano,* this man spoke with odd formality. "There has been an emergency. I am ordered to escort you to the command."

The girl nodded, clearly accustomed to obedience without question. The blouse was forgotten as Giselle allowed the man to take her arm and lead her from the store. They were gone before Eloisa could collect her thoughts to pray about the worry that was rising in her heart.

❖ ❖ ❖

As they left the store, the shore patrol officer took Giselle's arm, guiding her firmly toward a waiting staff car. His face was tight, anxious, and he glanced over his shoulder as if concerned that someone might follow.

Something was wrong, Giselle realized, and it had to be something terrible. Her father had never sent for her before, not even when her mother had been hospitalized last year. She noted with increasing alarm that this guard, whose nametag read Zarid, was armed. Navy personnel didn't carry weapons among the civilian populace unless there was trouble.

"What happened?" she asked, trying to sound calm despite her growing fear. "Are my parents OK?"

Zarid shrugged, his face inscrutable. "I was told nothing." Gripping her arm more tightly, he quickened his pace. She nearly had to run to keep up.

Reaching the car, Zarid reached across her to open the back door. Giselle noticed that he positioned himself so that she was cornered between him and the car. Was he sheltering her from possible harm?

Giselle hesitated. "What about my car? Maybe I should follow you back to Gaeta."

Zarid shook his head, his jaw tightening. "It can be retrieved later. Please get in."

A sudden movement caught her eye, and she whirled with Zarid to find a stranger hurtling toward them, vaulting the front of the staff car to confront Zarid. He wore combat boots, chinos, and a T-shirt, all black. Even though he wore no uniform, his bearing was decidedly military.

The hair on Giselle's nape snapped to attention. Mercenary!

Zarid drew his gun from its holster, then caught Giselle by the waist and pulled her against his chest. Giselle stared at the weapon, thinking absurdly that it didn't look like a Beretta, the handgun issued at Gaeta.

The dark man advanced quickly. A knife appeared in his hand and flashed toward them, a terrifying blaze of steel. Giselle flinched away, expecting at any second to feel the metal slash her face.

There was a grunt, a shudder against her back; Giselle looked up to find the blade buried in Zarid's throat. She screamed as he fell, spilling warm blood down her shoulder as he crumpled to the pavement.

The assassin caught her and shoved her behind him, trapping her against the open door of the car. A young seaman in an ill-fitting uniform ran toward them, shouldering an assault rifle and looking for a vantage where the car didn't block his shot.

The dark man rushed forward as the seaman rounded the staff car, catching the rifle barrel and forcing it down. A short automatic burst ravaged the rear tire of the staff car as he twisted the weapon from the seaman's hands. Slinging the rifle under the car, the dark man's fist connected powerfully with the seaman's throat.

Giselle heard a snap as the seaman's larynx collapsed. A horrible gurgling sound came from his mouth, followed by a foamy trickle of blood.

The boy's eyes stared helplessly as he slid to the ground, struggling for air that would not come. Giselle watched in horror as he died before her eyes.

It was slow, far too slow. And painful. But she couldn't turn away. Time seemed to freeze. In the stillness of death, she could almost hear her own heart beating. She lifted her eyes to the killer, found him staring at her. The intensity of his gaze was paralyzing; she wanted to run, but couldn't. Involuntarily, her hand came up to protect her own throat.

A car pulled to the curb; a door swung open. "Hurry . . . there might be more of them!" the driver shouted.

The assassin glanced at the new arrival, and the spell between them was broken. Gathering her wits, Giselle turned and raced for Eloisa's store.

He had her before she was halfway there, catching her by the waist and dragging her back to the waiting car.

Struggling to break free, Giselle screamed at the gathering crowd. No one moved to help. Their faces were shocked, uncertain, terrified.

The man threw her roughly across the back floor of the car, and dived in across her, his body covering hers. The car squealed forward, its impetus slamming the door.

She was pinned, helpless beneath his weight, her left arm trapped between them, her right pinned against the back seat of the car. He lifted a little, staring down at her. Then, with a surprising gentleness, he reached up to brush the hair from her eyes.

A new fear welled up in her as she met his eyes. She screamed, wrenching her left hand free and raking her nails down his cheek in a desperate effort to break free.

He cursed, capturing her hand and pinning it above her head. With his free hand he covered her mouth, trying to smother her screams. "Be still," he demanded roughly. "We're not going to hurt you. . . ." He cursed again as her teeth sank into his finger, jerking his hand away as if tempted to hit her.

"You OK back there?" the driver called.

"Just drive!" the dark man growled.

"Let me go!" Giselle snarled. "If you touch me, I swear I'll kill you both!"

He appeared unmoved by her threat. "You're a regular little tiger, aren't you, kid?" His tone was casual, almost pleasant.

Furious, she spat in his face.

His look of astonished anger gave way to a slow smile, which lit his eyes with genuine mirth. The man began to laugh, his teeth gleaming white. Still pinned and helpless, Giselle raged silently.

"I don't think we're being followed," the driver said finally.

The dark man eased his weight off her, straddling her hips to keep her pinned as he stretched to peer out the rear window. Satisfied, he released her wrists and moved to the seat. "You can sit up now," he told her, offering a hand to help her. "Are you OK?"

Giselle slapped his hand away, scrambling to the far door before pulling herself up to the seat.

"Maybe I should introduce myself." He offered his hand, a sardonic grin on his face.

"It doesn't matter who you are," she snapped, ignoring his gesture. "You'll be dead when my father catches you!"

Still smiling, he withdrew his hand. "Have it your way."

She glanced out the window. The traffic light at the next intersection was changing; the car began to slow. . . .

With a sudden movement, she flung open the door and launched herself from the car.

In a flash, he had her roughly by the arm, dragging her back into the car and flinging her across the seat. Cursing, he straddled her legs. He gripped her jaw with a rough hand, forcing her to look at him, his black eyes flashing dangerously. "Don't!" he warned harshly. "Don't try it again."

When she didn't move, he cautiously reached back to his pocket.

She decided to slap him, caught him once hard across the jaw. She was going for a second strike when he caught her hand midway. Circling her wrists again with one hand, he held a card before her eyes. "Read it," he ordered, his voice a menacing growl.

It was a military ID, identifying the man as First Lieutenant Raz Chayil, attached to a Marine Corps division assigned to the Naval Support Activity facility at Gaeta.

The driver glanced back at her. "Those guys back there were probably terrorists. It's a good thing Raz wanted to swing past Eloisa's to have his new uniform altered or they'd have taken you for sure." He pronounced his friend's name "Rahz," so that it sounded kind of like "Oz."

She stared at the driver, then at Chayil, then at the card again.

His eyes laughed at her embarrassment as she began to realize what had really taken place. At her pointed stare, he chuckled and released her wrists.

He was taken by surprise when she slapped him again.

❖ ❖ ❖

Later that day, Giselle was called to her father's office, which was set up in a wing of their lovely Italian villa that sat just outside the small Naval Support Activity compound at the top of Monte Orlando in Gaeta.

She passed through the foyer, a small room with a sofa and coffee table set up for visitors, and found the door slightly ajar. She peered in curiously.

Officially, the command staff of the Sixth Fleet conducted business from offices aboard the command ship. But practically, when the ship was in its home port, Thaddeus Hardy preferred to work as much as possible from his home office. Giselle appreciated this, sensing it was his way of trying to make up to his family for his extended absences, when the flagship was touring the Mediterranean.

Dominated by an antique oak desk that he'd bought himself, the captain's office was in perfect order, with a green blotter precisely squared at the center, and a wooden work basket on the corner nearest the door. There was no mess, no clutter; as elsewhere in Thaddeus Hardy's life, everything had its place. Giselle's place was usually not here. As chief of staff, Thaddeus was second-in-command to the admiral, who commanded the U.S. Sixth Fleet, the Naval Support Activity here at Gaeta. Additionally, the facility supported a NATO telecommunications school. Much of Thaddeus' work was highly classified.

Giselle tapped on the door.

Her father glanced up and smiled, picking up a stack of papers and tapping them straight, then placing them—face down—in his work basket. "Giselle, come in."

She obeyed, crossing to his side of the desk to deliver a kiss on the cheek before moving to stand across from him.

"Sit down," he offered, gesturing to the ancient burgundy leather armchair that stood against the wall next to the file cabinet. Her father kept it for visitors, but placed it out of the way so that it had to be pulled out for use—something no one would do unless invited. Keeping visitors standing, he said, tended to keep discussions brief.

It was the first time Giselle had been offered the chair; it seemed a tremendous honor. Trying to conceal her surprise, she positioned it and sat.

The captain clasped his hands on the desk before him. He wore his most casual uniform, a crisp khaki shirt with matching trousers and belt. On his chest above his pocket, six smart rows of ribbons stood as vibrant reminders of his accomplishments.

If ever a man was meant to wear a uniform, Giselle decided, it was her father. With his deeply tanned face, authoritative gray-blue eyes and silver hair, she suspected that people didn't even need to see his insignia before they saluted. The lines at his eyes were not from smiling, but from years of sun reflected off the brilliant sea. This was a man of action, a hero, and not only in his daughter's eyes.

He gazed at her intently. "I'm told you were very brave today."

She dropped her eyes. "I didn't feel brave," she whispered. "I was scared to death." And fighting the wrong men, she almost added.

"I've never seen an act of courage that wasn't committed by someone scared to death," he assured her. "I'm proud of you."

Giselle nodded, fighting down a lump in her throat. She closed her eyes and saw the terrorists again, dying as she watched. Thinking about it made her feel sick.

"I'm sorry, sweetheart. I never wanted you to see that kind of horror." Her father's voice was strangely thick, and when she looked up, she saw that his eyes were damp. She burst into tears.

He hurried around the desk and pulled her into his arms. She squeezed his waist fiercely, wanting to lose herself in the scent of starch and aftershave. He held her so tightly that she could barely breathe, and for the first time, she began to feel safe again.

When his arms finally loosened, she realized that her forehead had been pressed against the eagle on his collar. She brought up a hand to touch the imprint.

He smiled. "Your mother complains about that, too."

Giselle laughed. "She says you even wear it to bed."

"A slight exaggeration," the captain told her fondly. It was tacitly agreed between them that her mother's resentment of his military service, like her drinking, were not to be discussed. Together, Giselle and her father pretended that all was well, and when things got so bad that pretending wasn't possible, they found things to do away from home. The shared secret had brought them closer than most military fathers and daughters.

Her father took her arms and put her away from him, giving her a long once-over. He drew in his breath and let out another sigh, his eyes growing misty again. "I hadn't realized how you've grown up. You'll be going off to university this fall, won't you?"

She nodded, suddenly wishing she could turn back the calendar. Never grow up. Never move away. The world was a terrifying place.

Her father squeezed her shoulders, then returned to his chair. "What happened today was an isolated incident—it will never happen again." He spoke as if issuing a command to the cosmos, and some part of Giselle believed it would obey. "But I want you to learn how to take care of yourself before you leave for school. Just so you'll feel safer. Report to the gymnasium tomorrow at 1300 hours for self-defense lessons."

"Yes, sir," Giselle replied automatically. He had been giving an order, not asking for her opinion.

Her father smiled and returned to his paperwork.

Dismissed, she made her way out of the office, closing the door quietly behind her.

❖ ❖ ❖

Raz paced angrily. He hated waiting. Especially for things he didn't want to do.

The gym was empty, and the walls echoed his footsteps. Basketball hoops stood at each end of the open floor, which was flanked on one side by the weight room and the other by piles of rolled-up blue practice mats.

His unit had cleared out for afternoon drills, but not before jibing him over his latest adventures. He had a reputation of being undefeated in hand-to-hand combat drills, and yet he'd come away bloodied from a scrap with a teenaged girl.

And now he had to teach her self-defense. Why didn't the captain just send her to some stupid judo class in town?

He knew the answer: Because the captain didn't have to. He had access to the best-trained fighters in the world right here on this command. Any one of them could teach the girl what she had to know. And like it or not, he'd asked for Raz.

This opportunity to do a favor for the second-in-command at this facility was supposed to be an honor, a reward for saving her life, a message to Raz's superiors that he was noticed and appreciated. But playing dojo to a little girl didn't feel very rewarding. Especially when the little girl was a self-absorbed, tantrum-throwing brat.

It wasn't an order, he'd been told. Just a request. As if he was in any position to refuse.

He crossed to the weights and began doing pull-ups to release his frustration. This assignment was good news, he tried to tell himself. It was a crucial step in the plans that had been laid out for him.

Never mind that the plans were not his own.

Never mind that the step had been taken over the bodies of two men.

His pull-ups increased in speed and fury until his muscles burned and the sweat stung his eyes. He kept going until his arms shook with the effort, then strained against his weakness, fighting to do one more.

Dropping to the floor, he looked at his watch again. She was late. The captain had said 1300—in the military, that meant sharp.

It was seven minutes past. Why didn't she show up already so they could get it over with?

His jaw tightened as he heard the outer door open. Seconds later, she came in, wearing a tight little spandex outfit that for some reason ticked him off even more. What did she think this was, ladies' aerobics class?

She dropped her matching purple gym bag and started toward him, stopping short when she realized who he was. "You . . ." The look on her face said she didn't like it any better than he did.

"You're late," he growled, looking meaningfully at his watch.

Her eyes rose to the clock on the wall. "Your watch is fast."

He made the mistake of turning to look, only to discover that she was right. Stubbornly, he shook his head. "That clock is slow. Everybody knows it."

She rolled her eyes, letting him know what a jerk he was. "I'm supposed to learn self-defense. Let's get to it."

Oh, we'll get to it, all right, he decided. The cocky little brat had just let herself in for a bit of military treatment. With luck, she'd whine to Daddy, and Raz would be off the hook. "Let's see what kind of shape you're in. Twenty laps for starters."

She stared at him. "You're kidding."

"Move," he ordered, settling on the pile of mats to watch in comfort. He could have jogged with her, but he decided this would better show her who was in charge. He would simply watch—and maybe bark a little if she set the speed too slow.

She stared at him for another long moment, waiting for him to change his mind.

He decided to accommodate her. "Make that twenty-five," he amended, meeting her gaze steadily. "Care to try for thirty?"

Muttering under her breath, she turned and began to jog.

For the next ten minutes he watched her run, round and round the room. It was boring, he decided, wishing he was somewhere else—anywhere but here.

But around the fifteenth lap, something changed. He began to notice that she wasn't tiring. That her legs were still pumping lightly as if she did this all the time. She was breaking a sweat, sure, but anyone would be by now. He became fascinated with watching the rhythm of her movements.

The twenty-five laps were over too quickly. She came to the mats beside him and flung herself down, breathing heavily. "OK?"

Very OK, he decided, watching her catch her breath. The captain's daughter wasn't hard to look at. Sleek dark hair, a cute face, big gray eyes. Not too tall—only about five-three—but built, with a neat little waist and . . .

He jerked his eyes away, cursing under his breath. He couldn't afford this kind of complication, not at this point. Besides, she was just a kid, too young to interest a grown man. He got up and busied himself dragging practice mats into place. "Take five. Then we'll start with a few basic falls."

"I'm sorry about your hand," she said, looking at the white bandage on his finger. She raised up on her arms to watch him work. "And those scratches on your face."

He ground his teeth. Was she rubbing it in?

"You should have told me who you were," she scolded.

"Is that why you hit me that last time?" he asked.

"I was scared, and you were laughing at me." Her eyes flashed accusation.

Why did he feel the need to defend himself? "I laughed because you were doing the craziest things I ever saw. If I had been a terrorist, what did you think spitting on me would accomplish, besides getting you killed?"

"I thought you were going to . . ." she stopped herself, her face reddening as her eyes dropped to the floor.

She'd thought he was going to rape her, he realized. And hopeless cause or no, she wasn't about to take it without a fight. As this dawned on him, he surprised himself by realizing he had to admire her guts.

"It was stupid, wasn't it?" she asked reluctantly.

"Maybe you just need to learn how to be more effective."

Her eyes raised at the change in his tone. "That's why I'm here, I guess." She rose and came to help him with the mats. "What was it like to kill those men?"

Raz fought off a rush of nausea at the abrupt reminder of the two dead men. He had almost forgotten them—just for a moment. Now, as he closed his eyes, he could feel the sickening crunch of the boy's larynx buckling against his fist. He could see the kid's eyes begging in vain for air. Slow suffocation was no way for a man to die, terrorist or otherwise.

He forced himself to look at the girl and saw in her horrified expression that she had glimpsed his feelings. "Let's hope you never have to find out."

She worked in silence for a few moments. Then she raised her eyes soberly to his. "It wasn't your fault," she told him quietly. "They gave you no choice. And I may not have acted like it, but I know you put it on the line for me. I am grateful."

He realized then that there was more to this kid than he had initially suspected. He had thought her shallow, senseless, and spoiled. A brat from a privileged family, who'd never had it tough. Now he could see that he had been wrong. Their eyes locked for a long moment, and he sensed she could feel his growing respect.

He clapped his hands to break the spell. "OK. Let's get to work."

❖ ❖ ❖

Giselle was curled up in the middle of her favorite room, in the upper floor of the wing of their villa that also housed her father's office. The room was empty except for a few small bookshelves, an overstuffed loveseat, and a cushioned window seat positioned beneath large uncurtained windows that overlooked most of the facility. Officially, it was a library, but no one came here anymore. No one except her. This room contained her most precious secret.

She'd discovered it when she'd played here as a child, visiting the children of the man who was chief of staff at the time. Her father, then the admiral's flag lieutenant, had often brought her here to play when he had business in the office downstairs.

Aunt Constance had sent her a Play Doctor kit for her tenth birthday. The kit had come with a real stethoscope—it was purple, but it really worked. One sunny, fateful afternoon, she'd brought the kit with her when she came to visit her friends. The girls promptly made little beds on the tile floor for each of their dolls. Crawling from patient to patient, Giselle had listened to their chests, just like the doctor at the infirmary might. The third doll's chest had spoken in her father's voice! It had been even louder and clearer when she pressed the stethoscope directly to the tile the doll had lain on. From then on, whenever her father had visited this villa, she'd asked to come along to see her friends. And every time she'd come here, she had always insisted on playing with her stethoscope.

When they had returned here years later, this time it was her father who was the chief of staff, and Giselle was delighted to learn that the villa she had once visited was now her home. She'd investigated the ostensibly soundproofed office that now belonged to her father and found the flaw. Her special tile was directly above one of the outlets for the sprinkler system. Sounds apparently carried through the space that had been made for the pipe.

Whatever the source, Giselle still cherished her secret listening place just as other only-children treasured invisible friends. She had never told anyone about it. As a little girl, she'd kept silent, knowing that if anyone found out, this access to her beloved, much-absent father would be taken away. Now, having grown older, she'd also come to realize the life-and-death implications of her father's secrets, which had grown in importance along with his rank. But that hadn't stopped her from listening. The doctor's kit was long gone, but she had kept the stethoscope as a memento of that special summer when she'd felt so close to her father. Most of the time it was hidden in plain sight around the neck of her favorite stuffed bear.

She lay curled on her side, her back to the door. She'd brought a pillow for comfort, and a book in the unlikely event that someone would come along and wonder what she was doing. She could quickly hide the stethoscope and pretend to be reading. But what she heard here was far more interesting than any book.

There was a knock at her father's door.

"What is it?" he asked. A moment later, she heard his chair sliding on the floor as he rose, then a grunt of pleased surprise. "Well, you old dog! What are you doing here?"

Giselle smiled. It could only be her godfather, Arnold Killian. Arn was the only man with whom Thaddeus Hardy was so informal. The two had been friends since their days at the Naval Academy in Annapolis. Arn had been stationed at Pensacola several years ago when he'd been offered the chance to head up a branch of the Office of Naval Intelligence.

"Nice seeing you, too, Thaddy," Arn said dryly.

The captain laughed. "Of course it's nice to see you. You just took me by surprise. I wasn't expecting this visit. So take a load off. You look great."

"The job agrees with me," Arn told him. "Yours, too, from the look of it."

There were a few muffled noises as the two men sat, but Giselle's trained ear was able to make out the voices above it. "I don't know," her father said. "I've put on a few pounds since I took on this assignment. Italian food."

"A man past fifty has earned the right to carry some extra weight. So how's the wife?"

"She's fine. I'd have her come down and say hello, but she's a bit under the weather this afternoon," Thaddeus replied, lying smoothly. In truth, Dolores Hardy was probably passed out in her bedroom, as usual for this time of day. Sometimes she woke up in time for dinner, but more often these days, she didn't.

Giselle's mother had once been a beautiful woman, a dancer, with a ballerina's slender frame and long dark hair. She had briefly been the toast of the stage and had left at the height of her career to marry a navy man. She had even named their daughter Giselle after her favorite ballet.

As Thaddeus Hardy rose in rank, his wife's skills as a hostess had become legendary, her cocktail parties as well choreographed as one of her best ballets. There was never a guest unaccompanied, never a glass unfilled at one of Dolores Hardy's events, and her effervescent, if slightly tipsy, conversation was much sought after.

The secret drinking had begun in earnest when Giselle was about six. She'd smelled it on her mother sometimes when she came home from school, and had been confused by her quickly changing moods. By the time Giselle was old enough to understand, her mother was drinking every day, hiding her bottles in bags and boxes before throwing them away, and telling people she was sick when she was really too drunk to go out. It was a well-kept family secret, since the problem could cost her father his career. The story they let out to the rest of the world was that Dolores Hardy had a chronic ailment.

"So what brings you here, Arn?" the captain repeated.

"It's good news, actually," Arn told him. "We traced the men who attacked your daughter to a Libyan terrorist operation."

"Libyans!" her father exclaimed. "I thought Muslims didn't target women and children."

"They usually don't," he agreed.

"Then what in the name of St. Peter did they want with my daughter?"

"Who knows with those guys?" Arn's voice carried a guarded tone that suggested he knew more than he was saying. "Anyway, you don't need to worry about them anymore. The operation was cleansed yesterday. I thought you should know."

Cleansed. Giselle didn't know exactly what that meant, but she could guess. The thought of more men dead because of her made her stomach turn. Still, she couldn't help feeling a little relieved as well.

Her father let out a long breath, and she realized he'd been more worried than he'd let on. The self-defense lessons should have been a clue, but he'd put on a confident face for her benefit, promised her that she was well protected; and she'd been convinced he believed it.

"Thanks," she heard him say. "That was quick."

"Yes it was," Arn agreed. "Surprisingly quick. Even if your men hadn't happened along when they did, we'd have had Giselle back in a few hours, just by tracking down where they got the car and uniforms. I'd have sworn these guys were rank amateurs if they hadn't been ducking the CIA for two years."

There was a pause. "What are you telling me?" her father asked slowly.

Giselle listened more closely. Obviously, the captain was picking up some undercurrents that she couldn't see.

She could almost hear Arn's noncommittal shrug. "Sometimes smart people do stupid things."

The words seemed to hang in the air. There was more to this. It sounded like the Libyans had been set up, and Arn wanted her father to figure it out without having to tell him.

"What else has this organization been up to?" her father asked.

"The usual—hijackings, bombings. Just last year, they took credit for downing an Italian commercial jet bound for Israel. Someone phoned in a bomb threat and the flight was canceled at the last minute, but the plane was in the air before the pilot got word. It went down over the Mediterranean—no survivors. Two members of the Israeli parliament were probably the actual targets. Actually, my next stop is a courtesy call to Mossad to let them know their troubles with this bunch are over."

"Maybe they already know," her father suggested. If the Libyans had been set up for elimination, the Mossad seemed to have a reason for doing it.

"We don't think so. This would be too indirect for the Israelis. When they decide to take out somebody like this, they handle it themselves, make a big splash—and they make sure everybody knows who did it. They want to send the message that it doesn't pay to mess with Israel. If they start letting us do their dirty work, somebody might get the idea they're going soft."

"What about the CIA?"

There was a chuckle. Giselle could almost see Arn's wry Irish face. "I doubt it. I called them earlier to let them know what went down, and let's just say they were a little peeved that we got to these guys first. As I mentioned before, these Libyans had been ducking them for a couple of years."

"So it wasn't the CIA," her father mused. "And not Mossad, either. Who's left?"

Giselle pondered this question. Arabs? But that didn't make sense! Even when rival Muslim factions fought among themselves, they still presented a united front against the West. Surely no Muslim organization would betray its brothers in Islam to the Infidel!

Her father's mind seemed to be wandering down the same path. "It couldn't have been one of their own. . . ."

Arn didn't reply.

"Sweet mother Mary . . ." Thaddeus almost whispered. He sometimes fell back on his Catholic upbringing when things got tense. ". . . the SOI?"

The Sword of Islam! Giselle had heard Arn and her father talk about them before, an organization so far underground that nobody seemed able to get a handle on them. Not even the name was known for certain. An operative had heard their leader called Seif, "the Sword," and the group had promptly been dubbed the Sword of Islam. All anyone knew was that they seemed to support certain terrorist operations, coordinating their efforts, providing money, information, and manpower as needed.

The implications of this were frightening. Terrorism was one of the primary concerns facing the United States in its involvement in the Middle East. In almost every Muslim country there were pockets of radicals, well-armed and willing to die for their cause. All of these groups had virtually declared war against the West, but their actions defied standard military response. There was no clear target against which the United States could appropriately retaliate without endangering relations with official governments in the region.

Separately, these terrorist factions were deadly, but at least their activities were disjointed, their intelligence poor, and they often worked at cross purposes. If someone managed to change that, they could become far more dangerous—an army of dedicated guerillas united for a common goal. Whoever led them could control large sections of the Middle East, and with them much of the region's oil.

"Why would the SOI betray another Muslim group?"

"Maybe the Libyans weren't coming into the fold," Arn replied. "We think the SOI may work that way. It looks like they bombed an Iranian operation that didn't follow instructions. The CIA had a man inside the Iranian group. He reported that the SOI was feeding them the flight schedule of a British negotiator who was handling some discussions between Israel and Syria."

"What happened?"

"From what we were told, the SOI was calling for a surgical strike, a simple assassination outside the airport in Tel Aviv. Their man made a big deal about not wanting to draw too much attention to this effort. But the Iranians sent in a suicide squad— killed six people besides the diplomat. The day after the hit, the

Iranian group's headquarters took an air strike from an unmarked bomber that could have come from any of six countries in the area. The CIA man was killed, too. Israel denies involvement, and, for various reasons, we don't think they're lying. The next best suspect is the SOI."

The captain gave a low whistle. "Why are you telling me this?"

"Actually, we're coming to the second reason I'm here. Our people stateside managed to get hold of some pieces of the missile. Don't ask how they got it. They're not even telling me. But it was one of ours." His voice became serious. "We got a partial serial number, and we think it came from the Sixth Fleet."

"This command," he repeated, as stunned as Giselle. "How could that be?"

"That's what we want to know," Arn told him. "We want you to run a complete inventory, and go over the records for any arms shipments sent out through this command over the past year or so. Say it's routine, involve as few people as possible. And hand pick those few." Arn paused, lowering his voice to the point Giselle almost couldn't hear. "If someone here is diverting American weapons to the SOI—or anyone else, for that matter— we want to nail the sucker."

"I find it hard to believe that someone here could be involved."

Giselle wanted to agree. There was an atmosphere of absolute loyalty on this command, augmented by the fact that it flowed both ways. The command staff here would lay down their lives for every person under his command. If someone would betray their trust . . .

"Don't be so sure," Arn cautioned. "They seem to have resources in places you wouldn't expect. That Brit who was killed? Only three people knew his flight schedule: the negotiator himself, the diplomat he was meeting, and the agent assigned to protect him in Israel."

"So the Sword of Islam has connections," her father acknowledged. "Maybe in Britain, maybe in Israel. But if they have someone here, I'm telling you, Arn . . ." Her father sighed. "It's a small command—I know most of these people. My daughter goes to school with their kids."

"Keep an open mind, Thaddy," Arn's voice was dark with warning. "Think about it: Who besides Giselle knew where she was going the day of the attack?"

Giselle considered the question. Her parents had known, of course, and she'd stated her destination to the guards at the gate as she usually did when she left the villa. . . .

A chill ran down her spine.

"Sweet mother Mary," she heard her father whisper again.

Then he took control. "I'll need a full background check on every man and woman assigned here, especially anyone who's had anything to do with weapons shipments, here or aboard our ships."

"My people are already on it," Arn agreed. "And actually, there's something you should know. We've already completed a check on one of your men. The fellow who rescued your daughter."

"Chayil!" her father exclaimed. "I should think that he, at least, would be above suspicion."

"We believe so, too. I wanted to let you know. He might be a good man to use in your internal investigation."

"I just recommended him for commendation. Why was he checked out?"

"You know that Chayil attended the academy," Arn said, knowing that Thaddeus would have seen that on his service record. "That was not long after I took this job. Anyway, we got word that the CIA had sent a man down to question him. Naturally, we were somewhat curious."

"In other words, you boys were 'scooped' again," her father jibed. The rivalry between the Office of Naval Intelligence and the CIA was long-standing and only marginally friendly, especially when jurisdictional boundaries were in question. Generally speaking, the ONI didn't like "spooks" fishing in their waters, especially if they refused to pass on what they learned, which was usually the case.

"Of course, we questioned him immediately afterward," Arn added wryly, not at all embarrassed. "It seems that he'd been contacted some days before by someone whom the CIA believed was connected with some outlaw Arab faction. When we checked Chayil out, we realized this was ridiculous. I don't know if you're aware of this, but the man's parents are Israelis. He still has family there."

"Really?"

"His parents worked at a hospital in Jerusalem until they emigrated. The kids were born shortly afterward in D.C. The older brother owns an international communications company. He moved back to Hebron after college. Chayil visits him on leave sometimes."

"What about the parents?"

"The father worked at a swank psychiatric hospital in D.C. He was visiting family in Israel when he was killed several years ago. There was a bus bombing near his sister's house. There wasn't much left to bury."

Giselle swallowed hard. She hadn't decided yet whether she liked Raz Chayil. It seemed like he got grouchy with her sometimes for no good reason. But the thought of losing her own father had always terrified her. Her eyes filled with tears of empathy.

"The mother is a press agent for Senator Howel," Arn continued. "That's how Chayil got nominated to the Naval Academy. The family is staunchly Zionist, not likely . . ."

". . . to have ties with Muslim terrorists," the captain finished.

"It turns out the man the CIA spotted with Chayil wasn't an Arab either." He chuckled. "Apparently he looked just enough like a fellow who was picked up by surveillance cameras during a terrorist action in France to fool the spooks for a while. But in fact, he was a rabbinical student, bringing Chayil a gift from his brother." Arn's voice made it clear he had enjoyed catching his archrivals in an error. "We placed him right off, but we let the spook question Chayil a few more times before we set them straight."

"I'm surprised you set them straight at all," the captain observed.

"Professional courtesy," Arn told him dryly. "Of course, everything I've said here is between us. The CIA had the file sealed, probably more out of embarrassment than for any other reason. But I wanted you to know about Chayil's background in case you needed someone you could trust."

"I appreciate that," the captain told him.

"One more thing."

"What's that?"

"Well, you didn't hear this from me, but the peace process in the Middle East is starting to take some bad turns, and a lot of people think the problem is going to get worse. For one thing, the SOI is making everyone paranoid. A lot of their hits seem to be targeting diplomats, couriers, and embassies, and they are way too effective to be going at it without intelligence. Nobody knows where their intel is coming from, so everyone is suspicious of the other guy. A few of the players have started talking about pulling out. Nobody's serious about it yet, but if it comes to it, some of the people back at D.C. want to be ready. We have been looking into ways we might keep this thing going outside the normal diplomatic channels."

"And that involves Gaeta?"

Giselle could almost hear Arn's shrug. "It involves you. Between your service as intelligence officer with the Fifth Fleet at Bahrain during the last action in the Gulf and your assignment as naval attaché at the American embassy in Tel Aviv, you have some familiarity with both sides of the issues, and you've made some connections where we might need them. I can't tell you much about the plans that are afoot, but your name came up as someone who could be useful if things go south."

There was a long pause as her father pondered the implications. Giselle couldn't begin to guess what all this might mean. Finally, she heard her father's chair slide on the floor again as he rose. "Arn, thanks for dropping by. I'll keep you posted on the investigation. Can I buy you dinner while you're here?"

"Maybe next time, Thaddy. I'm eating kosher tonight, remember? In fact, I'd better hustle if I'm going to catch my flight to Israel."

"I'll walk you out."

"Next time I'll call ahead, and we can make some plans. I haven't seen Dody and Giselle in ages," Arn remarked.

Giselle heard the door open; then the two men's voices faded from her hearing.

❖ ❖ ❖

Lieutenant Commander Samuel Gilchrist, the chaplain at the small Naval Support Activity at Gaeta, was working on his sermon when he heard a knock on his office door. Rather than call for the visitor to come in, he rose and opened the door himself. He liked to greet people personally when they came to see him.

He was pleased to find that his visitor was Giselle Hardy.

By one of the odd coincidences that were part of navy life, he had been privileged to serve with Thaddeus Hardy in the naval home port at Manama, Bahrain. During that tour, Samuel had come to like and appreciate Giselle's father as a strong leader with a compassionate heart. He had been pleased last year when Thaddeus Hardy had been promoted to this command.

Back in Bahrain, Giselle had taken one of Samuel's classes in conversational Arabic. Her facility for languages was impressive, and soon she had outpaced the class and he was tutoring her independently. During their sessions, he'd come to enjoy her keen and curious mind. She was fascinated with many subjects, from politics to philosophy. Also, he'd sensed that she had a fledgling spirituality that might take wing if encouraged.

Since moving here, Giselle had taken to visiting him now and again, ostensibly to keep up her Arabic. In truth, he knew that the girl found in him a feeling of belonging, a sense of continuity that was often absent for military children. Her visit today was probably at least in part inspired by the fact that the command ship, with her father aboard, had been touring the Mediterranean for two weeks. She had no one home to talk to.

"*Marhaban,* Giselle, what can I do for you?" he asked in Arabic.

She came in and accepted the seat he offered her, her eyes roaming around the sparsely-furnished office, seeming to notice everything new: the swivel chair behind his cheap metal desk, the recent photo of his niece back in Kansas. "Chaplain, I'm curious about something." She was speaking English, a sign that she didn't want to practice today.

Samuel took the hint. "That's not unusual for you." He smiled, taking his seat behind the desk. "What is it this time?"

"What do Jewish people believe?"

He tried not to look surprised. "Are you thinking of converting?"

She shook her head. "I'm only curious."

There was more to it than that. He raised his eyebrows. "May I ask . . . ?"

"Did you hear what happened last week?" He nodded, and she went on. "The man who rescued me, Raz Chayil—now he's teaching me self-defense. I heard that he's Jewish, and I wondered . . ."

"I take it you like this man," Samuel observed.

She shrugged, but her eyes wouldn't meet his. Samuel bit back a knowing smile. Giselle was a lovely girl and long overdue for her first crush. He didn't know this Chayil, but he hoped the man was a decent fellow, the kind who wouldn't abuse her innocent interest.

"I guess he's nice," she admitted. "Most of the time. But then he gets all gruff and irritable again." She shrugged. "When I found out he was Jewish, I got to thinking that maybe I say or do things that offend him."

Samuel chuckled. "I doubt that very much, Giselle. Jewish people aren't so very different from anyone else. And if your friend made it through basic training, his sensibilities can't be that fragile." More likely, he decided privately, Chayil found her perfectly engaging but was trying to maintain an appropriate distance.

"But Jewish people believe differently than Christians do, don't they? I mean they don't believe in Jesus—not as the Son of God, anyway." She paused for a moment, fixing him with her stare. "Does that mean they go to hell when they die? Or that they think that we go to hell?"

He was tempted to smile at her bluntness, but clearly, the question mattered to her. Unfortunately, his answer wasn't likely to please her. Samuel sat back, his eyes turning as they often did to the cross that hung on the wall next to his sole window. It was not a crucifix, the symbol favored by Catholics. He preferred the empty cross, which to him represented the Resurrection.

After a brief prayer for guidance, he turned his gaze back to the girl. "I can't tell you what Jews think of Christians in terms of eternity, Giselle. Maybe you should ask your friend, once you know him better."

"What do we think of them?"

She wasn't going to let him off the hook. Samuel sighed. "I'm going to tell you what I firmly believe, OK? A lot of people will tell you it doesn't matter, that all beliefs are just different ways to God. But that doesn't work for most of the young men and women who come to sit in that chair because life is crashing around them. Catholics, Protestants, Jews, atheists, they want to know that there is something that is true and solid. As a Catholic, you've been taught to look to the foundations of the church and the Bible for your faith. As a Protestant, I believe the bottom-line authority has to be the Bible and what it says about Jesus Christ.

"If you believe what the Bible says, I have some bad news, if you want to look at it that way, and some good news. Jesus said, 'I am the way, the truth, and the life. No one comes to the Father but through me.' That's in John 14:6."

She stared at him. "But what does that mean, 'through me'? Unless a person becomes a Christian and goes to church, he goes to hell? Do you really believe that?"

He took a long breath and let it out slowly as he composed his answer. The captain's family attended Catholic Mass every Sunday, he knew, but he sensed it had little to do with any strong religious conviction. It was more a matter of setting an example, connecting with the personnel, and presenting a strong familial front. While not required by military protocol, that sort of thing was still tacitly encouraged.

Despite Giselle's chapel attendance, and her use of "we" as if including herself as a Christian, Samuel Gilchrist was fairly certain that she was not yet truly among the faithful. She observed the sacraments of her church, and she'd listened to the things Samuel tried to teach her as well. But he sensed that her acceptance of Christian teaching was merely in the abstract.

He prayed that some word he spoke today would reach her.

He rose and crossed the room to the window, appreciating again his magnificent view of the azure waters of the Mediterranean and the ships below. From here he prayed for the mercy of God upon sailors each time a ship was deployed. And from here, he thanked God each time a ship returned safely.

"Going to chapel is a good thing, Giselle, because it strengthens believers to come together in worship. It's good because we can help each other at times of need and pray for each other and build one another in faith. Those things are important. But going to chapel won't get you into heaven."

She frowned. "How *do* you get to heaven, then?"

"A lot of people think that we can all go to heaven if we're good enough. Is that what you believe right now?"

"I guess so."

He had expected that answer. "How good do you think you'd have to be to be 'good enough' for heaven, Giselle?"

"I don't know. . . . Maybe enough that the good things you do outweigh the bad?"

"OK. . . . But what kind of place do you think heaven would be if it was full of people that were 70 percent good? Wouldn't that mean that heaven was about 30 percent bad?" He didn't wait for an answer. "Does that sound like heaven, the place where God dwells? Or wouldn't heaven be perfect, without any corruption or evil or sadness?"

She thought about it, then nodded.

He smiled. She seemed to be taking the conversation seriously. "I believe heaven is perfect, Giselle, because I know that God is perfect, and his dwelling must be a place that radiates his goodness. Does that make sense to you?"

"Yes."

"Good. So if you want to enter a perfect place, and be with a perfect God, don't you think you would have to be perfect, too?"

She pondered the question, frowning. "I don't know. . . ."

"In Matthew 5:48, Jesus told us, 'Be perfect, therefore, as your heavenly Father is perfect.'"

"But nobody is perfect," she protested.

"That's right, Giselle. No one is perfect. Paul taught that everyone, whether Jew or a Gentile, is caught up in sin and unable to save himself. He said, 'For all have sinned and fallen short of the glory of God.' Do you think that's true of you, Giselle? That you've fallen short of God's glory?"

Giselle nodded, more, he sensed, to keep him talking than because she had any real conviction about the point, so he pressed the issue. "When you go to confession, don't you have things to talk about?"

She shrugged. "Everyone does."

"That's right. Everyone sins. And if everyone sins, then no one deserves to get into heaven based on their own goodness, do they?"

She considered his point. "I guess not. . . ."

"It's like sin has raised this insurmountable barrier between us and God. Have you ever had someone in your life, someone you loved and wanted to be with, who kept doing things that hurt you and pushed you away?"

Samuel saw Giselle's eyes cloud and suspected she was thinking about her parents. Over the years he'd picked up enough subtleties to have some idea what was going on in their home. He would never breathe a word, and he'd never judge, but his heart went out to this girl, who obviously needed someone constant, someone who wasn't too busy or too sick to spend time with her. The best someone Samuel knew was Christ. He prayed that she'd meet him today.

"That's how God feels about us, Giselle" he continued gently. "He loves us and he wants to be with us. But when we sin—and we all do—we build up this barrier between him and us. If we die with that barrier separating us, we will be separated from God for all eternity in hell. And we'll know that it was our doing, our choices that put us there. Every time we choose to do something that we know is wrong, we build up that barrier of separation even more.

"But that's not what God wants. He loves us even though we don't deserve it. That's why he sent Jesus to tear down that barrier." He paused for a moment, considering a way to make this point more real to her. "Do you have a crucifix at home, Giselle?"

"Yes, over my bed."

He smiled. "When you look at it, do you see how much Jesus suffered? Can you imagine what it must have been like to have those huge nails driven through your hands and feet, how the pain must have radiated through his whole body? Can you imagine what he must have felt while he was hanging by those nails, barely able to breathe because his chest was filling up with fluid? The very people he came to save were jeering and spitting on him. He had received thirty-nine lashes from a whip that was imbedded with bits of metal, so his back was ripped to shreds. He had been beaten, too, so his whole body must have been bruised and bleeding. He probably couldn't see because of the blood that flowed into his eyes from the crown of thorns they'd smashed down on his head. This was God's only son, dying to take away our sins! Do you think God would have done that to Jesus if there had been any other way?"

Giselle stared at him, not responding. But he sensed that she was seriously considering what he was saying.

He pressed on. "No, Giselle. Being good is not enough. But God did make a way for us. He made a way for us to be perfect, just as he himself is perfect. He sent Jesus, his beloved, innocent son, to take each one of our sins upon himself and put them to death on that bloodstained cross two thousand years ago. When you look at those outstretched arms on that crucifix, that's how much he loves us. That's how much he loves *you*, Giselle."

There was a long silence. Samuel let it do its work, praying silently that Giselle would receive this truth.

Finally, Giselle stirred, brushing back her hair and looking at him soberly.

"But doesn't God love the Jews too?" Giselle asked. "Didn't he give them their religion too?"

Samuel's heart ached; he wanted so much to see the light dawn in her eyes. "Yes, Giselle, of course he loves them too. In fact, Jesus came to the Jewish people first, and he perfectly fulfilled the law that God gave them through his sinless life, his sacrificial death, and his victory over the grave through resurrection. The first people who believed in Jesus were all Jewish, did you know that? Did you know that Peter, the man the Catholic church names as the first pope, was Jewish? Most of the New

Testament was written by Jewish followers of Jesus. These men did not reject their Jewishness. In fact, the book of Acts shows that they continued to worship in the synagogues and in the temple, that they were zealous for their Torah, viewing Jesus as the completion of their faith."

She stared at him. "Then why don't the Jewish people believe in him today?"

"There are a lot of things that come into it, Giselle. For many centuries, Gentiles who called themselves Christians attacked and persecuted the Jewish people. A lot of Jewish people died horrible deaths with a cross being the last thing they saw. Jewish people look at that history and believe that the New Testament must teach hatred for the Jew, and that the Christian Lord Jesus could not have been their Messiah."

"I don't blame them," she remarked.

"Nor do I. But what it really proves is what I've been telling you—that people are unworthy of God's favor. It should tell everyone, Jew and Gentile, that we all need God's mercy and his forgiveness. The gospel seems like an insult to most people, Giselle. It tells you you're not good enough. It says that even if you kept God's law in every respect, but broke it just one time, you have broken the entire law. It says that the only way to be reconciled with God is to stop trying to earn your way and trust entirely in something that you've never seen. The gospel asks you to believe in faith that Jesus' bloody death on the cross was entirely sufficient for you, and that his empty tomb brings you the promise, not only of eternal life, but of the power of the Resurrection, which builds you up every day to live for God. The gospel tells us that we cannot live to please God until we put to death our own strength and our own wisdom and our own desires and receive the life of Christ, his lordship over everything we do from now on. The gospel offends many people, Giselle, because it says there is no other way."

Giselle was staring at him, her brow furrowed earnestly. "But if God is so compassionate, how could he punish someone just for not understanding all this? Would he send a righteous Jew to hell just because he was taught all his life not to believe in Jesus? Would he send Ghandi to hell for being a Hindu?"

They were going in circles. Was there a better way to explain it? Samuel decided to try bringing it closer to home. "Let's look at this another way. Suppose there was a tiny nation that was being taken over by a larger country. Suppose America committed troops to rescue the little nation, and we fought our way through at the cost of many lives." Samuel returned to his desk. "Now suppose we reached the last stronghold of that little nation, where the last of its people were surrounded and fighting a losing battle, but when we got there, they told us, 'No, thanks, we want to handle this our way.' What should we do—go in as conquerors and force them to take the help we have offered? Or should we pull out and leave them, even though it means they will be slaughtered by their enemy?"

Giselle pondered the question. "I guess we should pull out."

Samuel nodded. "That's how it is with God. He sent the help we need. He sent his son, Jesus, to break down that barrier of sin and take away the power of death. But we have to let him save us his way. If we insist on doing things our own way, then God will honor our decision, even though it means we go to hell. Does that make sense?"

She looked at him doubtfully. "But there are people all over the world who never even heard about Jesus. And what about the people who heard, but never really understood?"

Samuel smiled. "I believe that God puts truth before everyone at some point in his life, Giselle. Maybe he does it a little at a time, first showing us that the path we're following is not the right way. Maybe if a person is Hindu, God gives him the truth that the deities he is worshiping are just statues made by men. If he responds to that, then God will see to it he receives more truth. But if that Hindu won't respond to that first truth, Giselle, then it doesn't matter whether he ever hears about Jesus, because he would reject the greater truth as well." He gave her what he hoped was an encouraging smile. "Maybe when it comes to your friend Raz, God put you in his life to bring him a little truth."

"You're saying that I should try to convert him?"

Samuel shook his head. "God is the one who changes people, Giselle. It's not your responsibility. I'm just saying that you might find this friendship gives you an opportunity to share Jesus with your Jewish friend."

She thought for a moment, then shook her head slowly. "I'm not sure, Chaplain. It seems too narrow-minded. Too . . . one-sided."

Samuel's heart sank. He loved Giselle; her soul was precious to him. And he could feel her slipping away even as he watched. "Giselle, would you at least study the question before you decide what you think?" His eyes fell to the notes for the sermon he was writing. He was planning to present Jesus and his mission using prophecies from the Old Testament. It occurred to him that the Scriptures he'd be quoting might help Giselle and her Jewish friend. He tore the page out of his notebook. "Giselle, if I give you this, will you read it?"

She nodded and took the page, but he could see that, at least for now, it was an empty promise.

As she left, he felt his eyes well up. All he could do now was pray.

❖ ❖ ❖

Giselle found herself looking forward to her daily self-defense lessons. Raz was a good teacher, chewing her out when she slacked off, forcing her to focus and work hard. She was starting to feel that she could handle herself. She hadn't wanted anyone to know it, but since the attack the mere thought of leaving the compound left her palms sweating and her mouth dry. Raz was helping her get past that.

She arrived at the gym at 12:50, only slightly out of breath. She had done her half-hour jog around the track by the pier before coming to the gym. That way, they would have more time for training.

Raz was waiting. No matter how early she got here, he was always waiting, and never patiently. She wondered if he, too, was beginning to look forward to their sessions. Despite his gruffness, she sensed that he liked her.

A couple of SEALs were leaving as she entered; they were wearing sweats, but she knew them by their attitude—SEALs thought they owned the place. One of them whistled as she walked by. She ignored him.

Raz saw her and nodded. He seldom smiled, and when he did, the smile disappeared as quickly as it came, leaving only a glimmer in those dark eyes of his. "I saw you on the track earlier. How many miles are you running these days?" he asked, all business, as usual.

She shrugged. "I don't pay attention. More than when I started."

"Start keeping track," he said. "And I've signed you up for the obstacle course twice a week, starting tomorrow."

"You want me to climb ropes?" Giselle grumbled, annoyed at his high-handed way of giving orders.

"You could use some work on upper-body strength. The obstacle course will give you a better full-body workout." He didn't give her a chance to argue. "Need a break before we start in?"

She shook her head, blotted her face with a towel, and crossed to the mat. "Ready when you are, Captain." Her father had just promoted him last week. It felt strange to call him by the same rank as her father. In reality, a captain in the Marine Corps was still lower in rank than a naval captain.

He drew her to the center of the mat, using his hands to position her. "Head up, knees slightly bent. Feet shoulder-width apart. Good. We're going to try something new today. Are you ready?"

She nodded, watching him.

He circled her, keeping his eyes on her as she turned. "Keep your weight centered. That's better."

As she moved again, he rushed her. Quickly she shifted to one side, grabbed his arm, and began to flip him, using her body as a fulcrum, just as he had been teaching. But this time he side-stepped, and her efforts to throw him failed miserably. Before she could react, he'd pulled her off balance, swept her feet out from under her, and dropped her to the mat.

She landed hard, knocking the breath from her lungs.

He came down on one knee above her, grinning at her distress as she gasped for air. "What did I teach you about falling?"

"I know," she wheezed irritably. "You don't have to enjoy . . . it so much when I forget."

He offered her a hand and pulled her to her feet, his dark eyes still smiling. "Did you see what I did?"

"I think so," she told him. "You shifted . . . center of gravity . . . no leverage."

"Good," he agreed. "Now you try it."

"In a minute." Giselle doubled over, hands on her knees, waiting to catch her breath.

"The bad guys aren't going to give you a minute," he reminded her, moving in suddenly. She let him come, then met his rush with a quick kick at his groin.

He turned at the last moment, catching her ankle, then letting it drop. "Good try."

"Not good enough, or you'd be talking funny," she retorted.

He chuckled. "You'd like that, wouldn't you, Gili?" Sometimes he called her that, pronouncing it Hebrew-style—Geelee. Giselle didn't know what it meant, but she'd decided that she liked it.

She grinned. "You bet I would, you big jerk."

"Come on," he challenged. "Try to take me down."

"Do you really thank God every morning that you weren't born a woman?" she asked, and knew from his startled expression that she had broken his concentration. Taking advantage of the moment, she rushed him, trying to mimic the movement he'd given at the very last moment. It worked, more or less. He wasn't able to throw her, although he still pulled her off balance, sending her face down to the mat.

"Where did that question come from?" he asked.

She half sat, meeting his gaze. "I read in a book that Jewish men did that."

"How did you know that I was Jewish?"

She shrugged cautiously. "I heard it somewhere. So do you?"

"Would it offend your feminist sensibilities if I said I did?"

She laughed. "Probably."

"Good." He gave her a sly grin and dropped to his knees on the mat beside her. "And since we're getting into personal questions, I have one for you."

She raised her eyebrows, waiting.

"Why are you going off to college this fall instead of enlisting or trying for a nomination to the Academy? I mean, your father's got some pull—and you obviously worship the ground he walks on. Don't you want to follow in his footsteps?"

"My parents don't think it's a good idea." She shrugged, remembering the fight they'd had over the issue.

"Why not?" he asked, seeming genuinely interested.

She considered glossing over the subject, but surprised herself by deciding to tell him the truth. "My mom hates the military. It keeps Dad working all the time, and she thinks he doesn't have time for us."

He nodded, his eyes gentle on her face. "I can understand that. Your dad's a very busy man." He settled into a comfortable sitting position. "You said both parents didn't want you to join. What was your father's reason?"

She watched him closely, wondering if she was doing the right thing. If word got out, it could damage her father's reputation. "This stays between you and me."

Raz nodded solemnly. "Not a word."

She believed him; somehow she felt she could tell him anything. It was a new feeling, and she realized she liked it. She watched Raz shyly, enjoying this momentary closeness. "Dad doesn't think women should be serving in the military."

He tried not to look surprised. "That's not exactly the approved attitude. The Navy is doing all it can to bring in female recruits and promote the ones already in service."

She sighed. "I know. Daddy said that the Navy does what it has to do to keep the purse strings open. But he still thinks a seaman's bunk is no place for a lady."

He watched her face, and felt oddly pleased by her apparent ignorance of the double-entendre. "So you're going to be the dutiful daughter and go off to college, even though that's not what you want?"

She shrugged again. "It's not that important."

She could see he was considering an argument, but after a moment, he just nodded. "I guess we all have to make sacrifices for our families," he mused.

"What's yours?" she asked.

There was a long pause. "It's not worth talking about." He rose, offering his hand again, and as she came to her feet, he assumed a ready stance. "Try it again. You're doing fine—some of the guys don't pick up that move for three or four tries."

Trying to conceal her disappointment at his sudden change of mood, she nodded her thanks for the praise. As she rushed him this time, she kept her weight lower and moved just another inch to the side at the last moment. This time he had no leverage, and she managed to keep her feet—and to break his grip on her arm as well.

He nodded, impressed. "One more time," he told her. "But this time, I'm going to show you the counter."

She moved back to the starting position. "What do you know about the Sword of Islam?" she asked, hoping to catch him off guard again. The question had been floating around in her mind ever since she'd overheard her father's conversation with Arn.

His face registered astonishment, followed by wariness, probably due to the secret assignment he'd received after Arn's visit. "What do *you* know about them?"

"I've heard the name. It's a Muslim group, right?"

"That's what they say." It was his turn to shrug with a forced casualness. "I've heard that they eat nosy kids like you for lunch."

The words struck her like a slap in the face. She had trusted him, confided in him, and now he called her a nosy kid? Hurt and angry, she flung herself at him, shoving him down to the mat.

She stepped back, but not quickly enough, and he caught her ankle, pulling her down beside him. Before she could react, he rolled and pinned her. "You let me get to you," he told her as she struggled to free herself. "That's the quickest way to lose a fight. You've got to keep your wits about you—keep thinking, Gili."

Ignoring him, she kept fighting, grunting with her efforts to force him off. Then, slowly, she became aware of something else—the muscular arms pinning hers to her sides, the slow, vaguely alarming warmth that was spreading from her cheeks.

She looked up into his eyes, and what she saw there drained the fight from her. Even if she had wanted to, at that moment, she couldn't have moved away.

He felt it too; somehow she knew it. The realization made her smile.

He stared at her for a long moment. "Are you flirting with me, little girl?" he asked, as if amazed at her audacity.

She laughed to cover the sting. "Now it's little girl, is it? Maybe you haven't noticed, Captain, but I'm old enough to vote." Before he could react, she lifted her head abruptly and kissed him.

For a moment she thought he was responding, thought she felt his lips part against hers, thought she felt his breath catch. . . .

And for a moment, just a moment, Raz was tempted. Her lips were sweet, as sweet as he'd imagined them when his mind got away from him. Would she soften in his arms if he let himself draw her in?

What was he thinking?

He pushed away, furious with himself. What? Would he ask her for a date, maybe hold her hand at the movies? Go to her father's place for dinner? This was insane. This girl was a ticking bomb. She could ruin everything! He looked around the room, praying that no one had walked in. Then he returned his gaze to Giselle.

She was flushed, her lips still far too inviting. She watched him curiously, looking as if she hoped he'd return her kiss.

And for a crazy minute, he almost did.

Instead, he forced himself to move away, sitting with his back to her until he regained some control.

"Raz?" Her voice was a whisper, half temptress, half frightened little girl.

"I was wrong," he murmured almost to himself as he fought to calm the sudden warfare within him.

"About what?"

"About you." He rose and moved away. "You're not a little girl anymore."

❖ ❖ ❖

"Sir, I've been teaching your daughter self-defense for six weeks," Raz began. He stood at parade rest before the captain's desk, fixing his eyes on the painting of a sailing ship on the wall above the old man's head. The captain obviously had a sense of humor; the ship's half-furled flag was a pirate's "Jolly Roger," and the man in the crow's nest was drunk. But these were subtle details that most people wouldn't notice.

"You're doing quite a good job with her, son," Captain Hardy agreed. "I've had her show me some of the things she's learned."

Raz felt a slow heat creep up from his collar as he remembered what she'd learned today. "She's the one doing a good job, sir," he managed over a catch in his throat, glad the captain didn't look up from his paperwork just then.

The captain nodded, as if he expected nothing less of his only offspring. "Thank you, Captain. Is that why you came here?"

"Sir, I want to be relieved of this duty," Raz told him, keeping his eyes on the wall above the captain's head. He was nervous, but his discipline wouldn't let it show.

"Why is that?" the captain asked, still not looking up from his work.

"I'd prefer not to give a reason, sir. I just think it's best for all concerned that I no longer teach her."

That brought Hardy's eyes up sharply, and he stared hard at Raz over his reading glasses. "I'm sure you realize that I asked you to do this as a personal favor. It was never an order. You're free to drop out anytime you'd like."

"Thank you, sir."

"I'm assuming you have a good reason for pulling out," the captain added, his expression revealing his annoyance.

"Yes, sir," Raz responded smartly.

"I'd like to know what it is."

"Yes, sir," he repeated. He'd figured the old man would play hardball, but had hoped to get through this without any uncomfortable moments. Now it was inevitable. "Permission to speak freely, sir."

The captain nodded.

"Your daughter is a very . . ." Bad start. He cleared his throat and began again. "I'm afraid I'm becoming interested in your daughter, sir."

"Romantically interested?" Hardy watched him closely.

"Yes, sir." Raz fought the urge to shift his weight, remaining still under the other man's gaze.

"Well." The captain paused for what seemed an eternity, then cleared his throat. "You were right to come to me. I'll ask someone else to take over, effective tomorrow."

"Thank you, sir." Raz wasn't sure whether he felt relieved or sorry, even though he knew it was for the best.

There was a long, uncomfortable moment as he waited for the captain to dismiss him. Instead, the man let Raz stand there, his steely eyes studying him keenly. Finally, he nodded.

With relief, Raz turned to leave.

"Son?" the captain said as Raz reached the door.

"Yes, sir?"

"I appreciate your telling me this. It took guts."

"Thank you, sir."

The next question brought Raz up short. "How old are you, son?"

He winced, knowing what Giselle's father would think. "Twenty-seven, sir."

The old man nodded grimly. "I hope you understand, Captain. That's far too old for my daughter." There was an edge to his voice; it wasn't an order to stay away from the girl, but it might as well have been.

Raz met his gaze steadily. "I agree, sir."

"I'm glad we understand each other." The captain returned to his paperwork.

❖ ❖ ❖

The captain's villa was situated on a hillside that rose majestically from the bay. From the library window, Giselle could see most of the NSA compound, the comings and goings of the people under her father's command. As a girl, she had once felt like a fairytale princess, watching her kingdom from the windows of her tower.

Today, she watched as Raz left the house, heading back toward the compound. His stride was long and smooth, the walk of a man used to long marches and hard runs.

He stopped abruptly as the loudspeakers began the first few notes of Retreat. This ritual took place at sunset, every day, at every American naval command around the world. Everyone stopped, no matter where they were, no matter what they were doing. Raz raised his eyes to the flag that waved near the compound's gate, saluting smartly as the banner was respectfully lowered and retired for the evening.

Giselle, too, watched in reverence as the ceremony took place. She could see most of the buildings in the compound, and the men on the ships in the waters below, all still for this one moment.

This was what brought soldiers together, united them heart and soul behind their country. This was the reason for every sacrifice made by military personnel and their families. This was the reason she barely knew her grandparents and cousins, the reason her daddy was always too busy and her mother too angry to have any other children that she might feel close to. This was the reason that, at eighteen, she'd never had a date or a best girlfriend.

It was reason enough, she told herself. It had to be.

As the last note died over the rooftops, Giselle looked at Raz again and found him staring back at her. Their eyes met for a moment, then he slowly turned and walked away.

He never looked back.

She watched, her wet cheek pressed against the glass, until he was out of sight.

"I hate you," she muttered as she wiped away a tear with her fingertips.

Chapter Two

"With things the way they are in the world these days, Rome is the last place I'd want to be. Just add the Antichrist, stir, and set the timer for Armageddon."

Giselle smiled, remembering her college roommate's apocalyptic warning just a few months ago as they'd said their good-byes. She'd gotten used to Judith's dire prophecies. She almost missed them.

What would Judith say if she knew about tonight? Probably something dark and foreboding. Then again, Giselle decided, if all the secrets in this room were told, the world might very well come to an end.

With its demure sounds of strings and chat and the scents of rich food and expensive perfumes, this ambassador's reception might, on the surface, seem to be just another stuffy affair for the pompous and powerful. But Giselle knew its secret. What was taking place here in Rome tonight—if it worked—could lay a foundation for world-changing accords between nations. And if something went wrong, well, anything might happen. It was terribly exciting—perhaps even more so because she wasn't supposed to know.

There, near the majestic balustrade that swept down to the dance floor, a cardinal from the Vatican was talking quietly with an Israeli journalist named Tovia Rachamim. And there, next to the da Vinci, stood Marie Von Varner, the widow of former Prime Minister Gilbert Von Varner. Handsome in a floor-length silver gown that matched her perfectly-coiffed hair, the grande dame was chatting with a bespectacled Syrian businessman. And by the doors to the grand marble balcony, Giselle's father, now Vice Admiral Thaddeus Hardy, in formal dress uniform with white gloves and tie, enjoyed a cigar with a Saudi prince, an old friend from his days in the Arabian Gulf.

In many ways, little had changed in the six years since Giselle left for university. But in other ways, everything had changed. After his assignment here ended, her father had spent two tours stateside; few people knew that while serving there, he had quietly received training and briefings through the State Department to position him for an unprecedented assignment. During that time, too, he had handpicked most of the personnel now serving at NSA Gaeta and aboard the new Sixth Fleet command ship, the USS *Lamar.*

His selection to return here last year was ostensibly to replace Vice Admiral Earnest Watt, who had abruptly retired due to health concerns. But in truth, the time had come to make good on the connections Arn had spoken of in her father's office so long ago.

Only a few people knew there was a connection between the conversations taking place here tonight and others happening elsewhere: The first was August Renauld, the American ambassador to Italy and the host of this reception. The second was her father, in whose office some of the plans had been discussed. And the third was Giselle, who had listened in on the discussions from the room above her father's office.

Giselle had been surprised—and delighted—to discover that their old villa, after some interior renovations that had made it a more desirable property, had been redesignated as housing for the COMSIXTHFLT. She had been even more delighted when she confirmed that the renovations had not affected her secret tile.

As Arn had predicted years earlier, the peace talks in the Mideast had almost completely broken down a few years ago. As far as the public was concerned, the discussions now amounted to little more than threats and saber-rattling. Many of the international pundits warned that it was just a matter of time before the region dissolved into all-out war.

But through her old listening post, Giselle had learned that, behind the scenes, a few committed leaders and their most trusted negotiators were still hard at work. To protect the process, they were no longer using normal diplomatic channels. Instead, they were relying on a few, specially-cleared individuals and facilities in the U.S. military, people like Giselle's father and commands like his at Gaeta, to transmit communications, arrange plans, and provide security at negotiations. Military dispatches went around the globe almost daily, thus providing a handy means of communication between global leaders. Command ships like her father's, which occasionally hosted VIP tours, could easily transport an envoy or host a quick meeting far from listening ears. A warship, with all its defenses, made a difficult target for terrorists.

The military wasn't the only unconventional channel being used. A number of international business leaders had quietly been cleared to act as couriers, carrying communiqués back and forth between world leaders under the pretext of discussing trade matters. Even a journalist, a reporter whose credentials allowed her to be cleared, was occasionally used to carry information.

There was precedent for covert diplomacy using nondiplomatic channels and personnel, but nothing on this scale before. The more untrained people who were involved, the greater the risk of exposure. But the SOI and other terrorist groups had clearly derailed all efforts at traditional negotiation, and with the specter of all-out war in the Middle East an increasingly fearsome likelihood, desperate times called for desperate measures.

The embassy in Rome was one of only two U.S. embassies worldwide that had any involvement in the process. Ambassador Renauld, who had served in many delicate negotiations in the Middle East, was acting as advisor and facilitator, helping to quash any tensions and level any bumps that might arise, stepping in when appropriate with the authority to negotiate for the president. Most of the people here were kept in the dark—but a handpicked few, who had been specially cleared, were in the loop.

Meanwhile, the rest of the world's embassies and diplomats continued with business as usual, in the hope that all those opposed to peace would remain unaware of the plans that were being made.

And now, if things went as anticipated, there would be an accord between most of the nations of the Middle East within just a few months. It could mean an end, at least at a national level, to animosities that had begun with Ishmael and Isaac, the biblical sons of Abraham. And in this era of third-world nuclear proliferation, the rest of the world could breathe a little easier as well.

If only she could tell Judith! Of course, her friend would probably have nothing positive to say about it. She'd probably mutter some dark reference to prophesies about one world government, false peace, all that. Living with Judith for the past two years while at Georgetown University, Giselle had learned enough about Bible prophecy to have some idea of the gist.

And it wasn't all wrong, she supposed. Of course, there was a tremendous danger involved anytime someone tried to take bold steps to change things. There would always be people who had a vested interest in continued hostilities. And there would always be those who could accept no peace unless it came through the total destruction of the enemy. It was hoped that if a peace accord could be presented as a *fait accompli*, these factions would pause to regroup, buying time for the authorities in their respective nations to step in and break them up.

But if the nature of these talks became known too soon, extremists and fundamentalists on all sides would redouble their efforts to fan the ancient fires of hatred and stop the process before it was completed. Terrorist acts would certainly increase, both in frequency and violence, at a time when the diplomatic efforts could least withstand the pressures that would arise from them.

The Sword of Islam was by far the most worrisome of these groups, the more so because little progress had been made in discovering the organization's sources of information and weapons. Her father's investigation into the possible theft of a missile six years before had come up empty, and, from a conversation between her father and Arn last week, Giselle knew that the intelligence community's activities elsewhere had yielded similar results.

Tonight's efforts were aimed at reaching some crucial agreements in principle. Once this was accomplished, representatives would be chosen to attend a summit held somewhere in Italy, under the protection of a Marine detachment under her father's command.

Giselle was enormously proud of what her father was achieving. If everything worked as planned, one day the whole world would see him as the hero she knew him to be.

Enjoying her secret knowledge, she let her eyes wander around the room, wishing there was some way to move close enough to one of those mysterious conversations to overhear what was being said. Her eyes came to rest on the one other person in the room who might know what was happening: Gregory Benedetti, Ambassador Renauld's chargé d'affaires. Though he was the ambassador's second-in-command at the embassy, Gregory wasn't on the eyes-only list for what was happening tonight. However, if Arn and her father were right, he had his own sources, as an undercover CIA operative.

Every embassy had at least one spy, and guessing his or her identity was a favorite pastime among diplomatic personnel. Everyone had his favorite candidate; some even placed bets on their choices. And, too, other countries were always trying to place their own spies inside these heavily secured doors.

No one could be trusted; everyone was suspect. It all seemed so deliciously mysterious!

Gregory was a lot more handsome than the other men in the room, Giselle decided. He had a strong, square jaw, blue eyes, and thick, sandy hair that seemed always to look both boyishly rumpled and perfectly in place. Tonight, he wore a black tie and tails, which lent elegance to his lean, athletic physique.

Giselle decided she hoped he was the CIA operative. Any man that good-looking, cloaked in an aura of mystery, would be almost impossible to resist.

Ensign Arlene Riley, the wife of Vice Admiral Hardy's flag lieutenant, followed the direction of Giselle's gaze and smiled. "He's gorgeous, isn't he?" She twirled her curly red hair around her finger. "Don't tell Riley I said that. I'm not supposed to notice these things anymore."

Giselle laughed. Though she was a Christian, Arlene was refreshingly down-to-earth; Giselle had never felt she was being preached at. Instead, she was often surprised by her new friend's frank remarks. Arlene was just a few years older than Giselle and only newly married. She hadn't yet forgotten what it was like to be single.

Giselle was glad she was here. Everyone else in the room was well over forty, except Gregory. He looked to be somewhere around thirty-five.

Just then, his eyes lit on their table. He saw the two of them staring and winked rakishly. Caught, the two women glanced at each other and laughed.

Moments later, he made his way through the crowd and presented himself at their table. "Would either of you lovely ladies care to dance?" He gave a little bow, extending a white-gloved hand.

Arlene sighed, her eyes sparkling as she repressed the urge to flirt. "I can't. My husband wants me to behave myself for once. But you go on, Giselle; give him a whirl."

Giselle hesitated, uncertain what was expected of her. Her father had brought her here tonight in lieu of her mother, whose "illness" prevented her from appearing in public very much these days. After a few introductions, he'd wandered off for a quiet chat with his Saudi friend, and she had eventually drifted to the military wives' table. She hadn't anticipated being asked to dance. What would her father want her to do?

"Go on," Arlene urged again. "At least one of us should have some fun at this clambake."

Giselle gazed up into Gregory's clear blue eyes that seemed to see everything and decided the opportunity was too good to miss. Taking his hand, she smiled and allowed him to lead her to the dance floor.

"Your studies at Yale and Georgetown University paid off," Gregory commented as he led her through several complicated dance steps. "You follow flawlessly."

"Thank you," Giselle murmured, forcing a smile. Surely he didn't mean to imply that her tenure at two prestigious universities was successful only in terms of her having learned to dance. "Between dance lessons, I also managed to pick up a bachelor's degree in Near Eastern Languages and Civilizations from Yale, and a master's degree from Georgetown," she added sweetly.

"So I've heard," Gregory affirmed.

After hearing Arn discussing the peace process with her father that afternoon six years ago, Giselle had designed her degree program to position herself for some involvement. She had begun her language studies hoping to serve as a translator for the United Nations.

Then one day during her senior year at Yale, Arn had come to visit, and Giselle had found a way to hear part of the conversation that took place in her father's den. That was when she'd realized the ramifications of her father's assignment at the Pentagon. After that, she had applied for the graduate program in Foreign Service at Georgetown University. This program, she had hoped, would complement what her father was preparing to do. When asked, she'd said she wanted to work in an embassy, and she would, but in fact, she had hoped that she would be in a position to assist her father's involvement with the peace effort when the time came.

Now, to her disappointment, it looked like everything would be coming together too quickly, before she finished her mandatory initial tour as a junior Foreign Services officer. A junior officer could never be cleared to serve on any truly sensitive assignment. Still, she knew that even after the initial peace agreements were nailed down, there would be a myriad of details and further negotiations that would probably go on for many years. There would be enough going on when she was ready that she could still make a difference.

"How did you know where I went to school, anyway?" Giselle asked Gregory. After her near-miss with the terrorists, her father had made a point of keeping the location of her university under wraps. Maybe this was proof that Gregory was the spy!

He chuckled as if reading her thoughts. "One of my good friends is acquainted with your mother. She mentioned your school at one of their afternoon teas."

It sounded reasonable, if a bit disappointing. Dolores Hardy and her few remaining friends were known to get together for an occasional tea party, and considering her mother's favorite "flavoring" for her tea, her slipping up would come as a small surprise.

"Speaking of your impressive résumé," Gregory remarked, leading her through another turn on the dance floor, "I happen to know that your bid for assignment in our consular office is being looked upon with great favor. Ambassador Renauld himself commented on your qualifications."

"Might my father have anything to do with that?" Giselle watched his face closely. She had extracted a promise from her father that he would refrain from acting on her behalf. He and the ambassador were old friends, and she knew it wasn't beneath him to pull strings.

He raised a wry eyebrow. "As far as I know, he hasn't. I take it you'd prefer to get the job on your own merits."

"Exactly," Giselle agreed.

He smiled. "In this business, all of us must occasionally ride on another's coattails, my dear. Be thankful that your father's are so long."

Glancing around, Giselle realized that Gregory was leading her to the outer fringes of the dance floor. Where was he taking her? She followed his gaze to a small, darkened balcony, whose doors were open to admit the cool night breeze.

"You're very beautiful, Giselle." He stared into her eyes a long moment, then allowed his gaze to drop none-too-subtly to her décolletage.

She hesitated ungracefully, wondering how to handle this sudden turn of events. Gregory Benedetti had a reputation as a terrible womanizer.

On the other hand, Giselle decided, it might be interesting to see just how far he'd try to take this. She'd fended off the libidinous efforts of more than a few classmates in college—and one or two professors as well. She could handle herself.

As she let him dance her through the open French doors, he gave her a gratified smile. "For a moment, I thought you might run off," he told her, leading her to the shadows just behind the doorway.

"I considered it," she admitted, stepping quickly away from the wall to avoid being cornered.

"But you didn't." He smiled knowingly, pursuing her along the balcony rail as she moved into the light from the doorway. He caught her hand. "Don't be coy, Giselle. Let's enjoy the evening." He glanced skyward. "The moon is almost as brilliant as your eyes."

Giselle followed his gaze. "It is beautiful," she agreed, wondering whether she should be impressed by the transparent flattery.

She realized her mistake almost immediately, ducking Gregory's kiss at the last moment. She moved away, reassessing the situation. Maybe coming out here had been foolish. She hadn't expected he'd be so aggressive.

Gregory caught her again, this time gripping the rail on either side of her so that she couldn't escape. He smiled at her flustered expression, then bent down once again, trying to claim a kiss.

She turned away quickly, pushing aside his arm to move away again. He laughed and gave chase.

She held up a hand. "I think we should go back inside," she suggested sternly.

He smiled at her quelling glare. "You knew why I brought you out here, Giselle. Why the halfhearted protests now?"

"Maybe because she wants you to stop," a new voice cut in.

Giselle knew the voice instantly, even after all these years. She froze. "Raz!"

He was leaning casually in the doorway, his arms crossed over his blue evening dress jacket, a smile in his dark eyes as he looked at her. "It's been a long time, Giselle." He fixed Gregory with a coolly assessing gaze, a wariness in his expression that belied his relaxed stance. Then he extended a hand to Giselle. "Why don't I escort you back inside."

"You're interrupting," Gregory said curtly. "The lady and I were enjoying a private moment. If you don't mind . . ."

"It's all right." Grateful to be spared an awkward scene, Giselle cut him off by accepting Raz's hand. "I enjoyed the dance, Mr. Benedetti, but Raz is an old friend, and we haven't seen each other in years. I'm sure you understand."

Gregory paused a moment, as if seeking a way to persuade her to stay. Finally, he gave a reluctant nod, offering a handshake. "As you wish." When she gave him her hand, he bent to kiss it, turning it at the last moment so that his lips pressed lingeringly against her palm. The intimacy of the gesture sent a shiver up her arm. Then he straightened and gave Raz a brief challenging look. "We can finish our business another time."

Raz watched him walk away, then turned his attention to Giselle, his eyes assessing her warmly. "Why is it that whenever we meet, I'm coming to your rescue?" With a soft smile, he reached out a finger to slide her dress strap up to her shoulder.

Giselle flushed, wondering when the strap had slipped down. Raz seemed to be mocking her. She suddenly remembered that she hated him. "I see you still think I'm some naive little girl who can't take care of herself," she told him coolly. "As it happens, I knew exactly what he had in mind when we came out here."

He raised an eyebrow. "Maybe I should apologize for intruding."

"Maybe you should," she agreed.

"Do you want me to bring him back?" He turned as if preparing to do so.

"No." Hastily, she caught his arm. Why did he always manage to put her off balance like this? "I just meant that I could have handled him."

"How many men like him have you handled?" His dark eyes briefly traced her figure, then returned to her face. "Maybe that's a stupid question. Look at you. I bet those Ivy League boys were beating down your door."

The reference to them as "boys" grated. "I guess that's supposed to be a compliment," she snapped, then remembered her manners and gave him a too-sweet smile. "If so, thank you. And thanks for the interruption as well," she added grudgingly. "As I said, I could have handled him, but I might have had to make a scene."

He returned her smile warmly. "You're welcome. On both counts."

He hadn't changed much in the past six years, she decided. He was still devastatingly handsome, his elegant, gold-trimmed dark-blue trousers and jacket rippling over muscular legs and powerful shoulders with a red satin cummerbund emphasizing his narrow waist. His close-cropped but still-curly dark hair bore a slight ring where his cap had pressed; he was not a man to fuss about his appearance. There was still something enigmatic about him, too—something she could never quite put a finger on. Maybe it was those fathomless dark eyes.

She realized she was staring and dropped her gaze. The last thing she needed was to let him get to her again. "I should get back to the others. Arlene's probably looking for me."

"Let me walk you." He extended his arm.

"I'm sure I can find my own way. Good evening." Ignoring his arm, she tried to step around him.

Raz countered quickly, blocking her way. "Listen, you don't have to be embarrassed. Benedetti tries that with every woman he meets. He even gets away with it—more often than you might think."

"I'm not embarrassed." The suggestion that she was one of Gregory's many attempted conquests annoyed her. Stepping around him again, she reentered the room, walking briskly along the rim of the dance floor in the hope that he might be dislodged from her side.

"OK, then I guess you're not happy to see me," he concluded, remaining doggedly beside her.

"Oh, I'm very glad to see you," she disagreed, using a tone that made it clear she was lying.

"Bingo," he decided. "Well, since I haven't had time to make you mad in the last three minutes, that leaves the last time I saw you. What could I have done six years ago that you'd still be mad about?" he asked, as if he really didn't know.

She stopped walking and stared at him. "Try cowardice."

He stared at her, astonished. "Cowardice?"

Giselle touched the tip of her nose. "Bingo." She started walking again.

He took her arm, pulling her up short. "Cowardice? I don't get it."

She glared at him. How could he have forgotten? "Well, I don't know what you call it, but what happened between us must have been more than you could handle, because you ran straight to Daddy and asked him to get you off the hook."

He shook his head as if he couldn't believe what he was hearing. "It was inappropriate for me to continue teaching you after what happened that day. And if you don't understand that, then you are still pretty naive," he added pointedly.

"Oh, I understand just fine," she told him through gritted teeth. "You didn't even have the nerve to say good-bye, or to explain why you didn't want to see me anymore." The emotion that threatened to choke off her voice surprised her. She swallowed it down, jabbing her finger at the medals on his chest. "What was the matter, Marine? Were you afraid of a teenaged girl?"

He caught her hand. "OK. I probably should have come and talked to you. I didn't think it through. I'm sorry."

"Not good enough." Not by a long shot. She realized with astonishment that her feelings hadn't diminished over the last six years, and she hated the revelation that he'd mattered that much to her.

"Not good enough," he repeated agreeably. "OK, then, how can I make it up to you?" He sounded sincere, but his eyes were too bright. Was he laughing at her again?

She wanted to slap him. "You can't."

He seemed to be suppressing a smile. "Have it your way. But it's going to be awkward working together if you're avoiding me."

"You're working here?"

"When I left Gaeta, I was transferred to the Marine security detachment at the embassy in Austria. As of last year, I took command over the Marines securing the embassy here in Rome and at the consulates around Italy."

She glanced at his collar insignia and realized that he'd been promoted again since she'd last seen him. He was already a major, and obviously her father's choice to oversee the Marines who would provide security for Ambassador Renauld. "I see you've done all right by yourself. Kissing up to Daddy probably gave you a good start, didn't it?" She turned and started walking again.

"Ouch," he said, hurrying to catch up with her. "OK, Gili . . ."

She stopped short at his use of the nickname. Then she realized something else he'd said. "You said we're going to be working together. What makes you so certain?"

"Your clearance came through from the State Department this morning. I mentioned it to your father. I assumed he'd already told you the job was yours."

She glanced at her father, who had joined the conversation with the Syrian. "He probably has too much on his mind just now, with all that's going on."

His expression sobered abruptly, and he took her arm to keep her from leaving. "What would you know about that?"

She lowered her eyes. She'd nearly slipped. Raz was throwing her concentration. "I just assumed that he would be rubbing elbows with a lot of VIPs tonight. That's what these shindigs are for, isn't it?"

He smiled, but his eyes were deadly serious. "Yes it is," he agreed. "But that's not what you were talking about, was it? Gili, you'd better tell me what you know, or you'll find yourself in a world of trouble." He lowered his voice. "And maybe your father, too, if he's talking where he shouldn't."

"He isn't," she nearly shouted. Then she stared at Raz again. How had he known she was lying? She looked around, realizing that her outburst had drawn attention from people around them. Her eyes dropped again, focusing on her suddenly trembling hands. "I'd better go."

"No," he decided. "I think you'd better dance with me while we talk a bit."

❖ ❖ ❖

If she was hard to resist as a girl, Giselle was magnificent as a woman. Raz had spotted her almost as soon as she'd come in the door.

She'd lost the vestiges of baby fat that had softened her figure six years ago and had gained, instead, that careless beauty that models spent hours trying to duplicate. He studied her face closely, but could see no hint of makeup. Instead, her skin seemed translucent, reflecting the sheen of her red satin dress, a simple sheath that fit her all too well, emphasizing eye-popping curves that had commanded Raz's attention even before he'd realized who she was. . . .

He cursed mentally. Forget the dress. Right now, he had more important things on his mind—or should have. "Tell me what you think is going on here tonight, Giselle," Raz urged, drawing her into his arms and moving into an open spot on the dance floor. She moved with him easily, seeming to anticipate his lead. "I need to know what you know."

She glanced at him, then her eyes dropped again. She was about to tell a whopper, he decided. "I can't say I know anything. . . . I just figured that the ambassador was working on some kind of business in the Middle East. Maybe I overheard someone talking about it." She raised her eyes up to his, her face earnest. "But Daddy didn't tell me anything, OK?"

He nodded. That last part, at least, was true. He relaxed a

little. If her father wasn't talking, how much could she possibly know?

Enough to think she might be in trouble, he realized, or she wouldn't be on this dance floor. She was still mad at him, after all.

"Be straight with me, Gili," he pleaded. "Look, I don't want to make trouble, OK? But you have to talk to me."

She looked miserable, but her chin jutted out defiantly. "I don't know anything."

She didn't know when to admit defeat. What was it about her stubbornness that made him want to smile?

Get serious, he admonished himself. This little lady had almost tripped him up before—Hardy would have had his stripes if he'd lost control with her. He'd sidestepped that and moved ahead, and now he was where he needed to be. He couldn't let her sideline him now.

He decided to try a new approach. "Gili, I pulled strings to help you get this job. I want to know that I did the right thing."

"You pulled strings?" She stopped dancing, jerking her hand from his grip. "Who asked you?"

He stared at her, surprised again. "I take it that was the wrong thing to do."

"Bingo." She was roasting him alive with her eyes.

"Explain," he suggested. "Why shouldn't I help an old friend?"

She looked at him as if he was an idiot. "I worked hard for my degree. I wanted it to count for something."

He had always loved her temper, he realized. The fire behind her eyes made him feel alive. "Your degree did count, Gili. I wouldn't have helped you if I didn't think you were qualified."

She shook her head, still glowering. "I wanted to get the job because I earned it, not because someone I know had pull. I want to be taken seriously, and your interference won't help!"

She was incredible! "If it makes any difference, I thought you were the most qualified. Knowing what I know about you, I thought you were a perfect fit for the business going on here," he told her.

"And just what could you possibly know about me?" she challenged.

People were looking. He pulled her back into his arms and began dancing again. "I know that you're a gutsy woman, or you wouldn't have put up such a fight the day we met. I know that you're smart—bachelor of arts and master's degrees in six years, and *magna cum laude,* wasn't it? And I know you can take care of yourself, thanks to what you learned from me." And now, because she was angry about this, he also knew that she had integrity.

If she were some kind of mole, she would have been grateful for any help in getting her in place. Besides, when would anyone have had the chance to turn her against her country? Raised on Navy facilities, practically cloistered, the only time she'd really been exposed to people who might be less than true blue was back in the States. And even then, the way she worshiped her old man, somehow, he couldn't picture it.

So what was she hiding? He had to know what he was dealing with. And looking at her determined face, he knew she wasn't going to tell him anything.

He was going to have to find out for himself.

❖ ❖ ❖

The next day, a quiet little Italian maid worked in the Hardy home while the family was at chapel.

Two days after that, Raz left the embassy for his morning jog and stopped to make a call on a pay phone across town.

"J.C. Penney's." A receptionist answered from a phone somewhere in Texas, from the sound of it.

"House and garden," Raz replied.

After a brief pause, he could hear clicks as the call was switched to a secure satellite uplink. A heavily-accented voice came on the line. "How may I help you, please?"

"I need a garden hose, at least three hundred and twenty-five yards long."

Computer keys rattled as the man calculated Raz's age, one inch per day. "Identity accepted, Major. What is your message?"

He gripped the phone tightly. "I've detected a potential flaw in Admiral Hardy's security. The sprinkler system in his office may have been installed improperly," he replied. "It looks like there could be open space surrounding the pipes."

"We will have someone look into it at the next opportunity," the Arab said. "We thank you for your cooperation, Major. We have long wished to learn what is known by the admiral and certain of his friends. This information may prove most helpful in that respect."

Raz rubbed his eyes, suddenly weary. He speculated about what they were going to do, but he didn't want to know about it. Close one keyhole, open another. The world was a complicated place.

"What caused you to learn about this situation?" the Arab asked.

"Nothing specific," Raz lied smoothly. "I saw the possibility the last time I was with him."

"Good, fine," the man said. "Thank you, Major. Please do business with us again."

Raz hung up the phone, feeling the sudden need of a shower.

❖ ❖ ❖

It was Giselle's first day on the job. Her supervisor, Amory, seemed nice, if a bit harried. He showed her to her office—a garden-level closet with just one opaque window high up on the wall—then hurried off. She was working already, dictating a reply to a routine citizen inquiry.

There was a knock at the door. "Come in," she called, shutting off her dictation recorder.

Raz let himself in.

She let her eyes trail coolly over him. "Good morning, Major. Yes, I'm settling in just fine. No, I don't need anything. Thanks for asking." Dismissively, she flicked on her recorder again.

A muffled laugh brought her eyes up again. Irritated, she hit the pause button. "What's so funny?"

"You." He stepped around her desk and sat on her paperwork. "We need to have a talk."

"Talk away." She shrugged, pulling the document from under his leg and turning on the recorder again.

"Not here. You're just about due for a lunch break, aren't you?"

She glanced at the clock on her desk. "Not for twenty minutes."

He picked up the clock and adjusted it, then set it down with a shrug. "Time flies."

She frowned at him and readjusted her clock. "Look, this is my first day, remember? The last thing I need is to get in trouble."

"I'll clear it with Amory before we leave."

"If I go, then will you leave me alone?" she asked.

He crossed his heart with false sobriety. "If that's what you want."

She turned off her recorder again, retrieved her purse from under the desk, and stood, gesturing toward the door. "Lead the way."

He held the door for her, then joined her, taking her arm protectively as she walked down the hall.

She pulled away. "Keep your hands to yourself, Major."

He put his hand in his pocket and kept pace with her, his eyes bright with humor. "You're a pistol, you know that?"

"And don't patronize me," she warned, glaring at him dangerously.

He raised his hands, signaling surrender, but his eyes were still laughing.

Wanting to slap him, she turned on her heel and continued walking.

At her supervisor's office, he paused, ducking his head inside. "I need to borrow Ms. Hardy for a couple of hours. A few details with her clearance."

Amory nodded, obviously too busy to care.

Raz led her outside, then down the drive toward a row of parked cars. They reached his car, a shiny green two-seat convertible—nice, but old, the best he could afford. He cranked down the roof before getting in.

"Where are we going?" she asked, hesitating.

"You'll know when we get there," he told her, holding the passenger door for her.

She glared at him, refusing to get in. "What's this about?"

His expression darkened. "Your stethoscope," he said sharply. "Get in."

He knew. Heart in her throat, Giselle slowly obeyed. Would he really recommend that her clearance be revoked? That would mean she'd lose her job. Her father would be so embarrassed!

He got behind the wheel and pulled out, his face still deadly serious. The gates of the embassy opened, then closed serenely behind them as they pulled out into the streets of Rome.

❖ ❖ ❖

Guiding the car along the narrow, tree-lined roads, Raz glanced at Giselle. Some soft, low clouds were drifting in, threatening rain, and he wondered if he should put the top up, but she seemed oblivious.

She'd been grilling him for over an hour now—what was this about, what did he want. Now, as she saw where they were going, she was quiet. Her face was pale, and her eyes were getting wider by the minute.

Good. She was scared. That was exactly why he'd brought her here.

He turned on the street that would take them to the compound—or to her father's villa.

She turned to him suddenly, putting a hand on his arm. "Look, why does my father have to be dragged into this?"

He stopped the car, stared at her intently. "What are we dragging him into?"

Her eyes pleaded with him. "You're going to revoke my security clearance, aren't you?"

He kept his face expressionless. "Why would I do that?"

Realizing what he was doing, she shrugged, her eyes shuttering themselves to him. "I don't know. You tell me."

She was going to make it tough. He sighed and put the car in gear again.

She looked surprised when they continued on past her father's driveway. "Where are we going?" she demanded again.

He pulled in at the compound, flashed his ID, and was cleared to enter. "I want to show you something I'm pretty sure you've never seen," he told her. Something she would never want to see again, he hoped.

He kept driving until they reached the far end of the facility. There, hidden behind a large, utilitarian office building, stood a sturdy little concrete structure that was fenced off from the rest of the small compound. Giselle, if she'd ever noticed it, had probably assumed it was some kind of mechanical building. It wasn't big. Didn't have to be. Few people ever came here.

If anyone had been inside, there would be guards, but there were none today. Good. He wanted them to be alone. Raz parked the car by the gate and escorted Giselle inside, gliding his magnetized card through the reader and punching in an ID code at the gate. It swung open automatically.

Inside was a dark, stuffy little office, with a tiny metal desk and a row of cheap video monitors. Behind a locked steel door was an even darker and more stuffy row of three small, steel cells, which smelled of old sweat and tobacco. The air in here was decades old.

He took Giselle's arm and led her into one of the cells. He wanted her to have a good look.

It was clean, white, almost sterile, with room enough for a cot, a toilet and sink, and a little square of floor where one could pace about a stride and a half. There were no windows and no light except one bare bulb recessed deeply in the ceiling; it was protected by a steel mesh. He closed the door behind them, allowing the sound to reverberate through the cell.

She watched him, a spreading panic on her face. "What are we doing here?"

He let his eyes travel slowly around the room. "This place is called the Security Unit. Prisoners accused of treason are held here until they can be shipped back to the States for trial."

"Treason?" She swallowed hard. "What are you talking . . ."

He rounded on her, his voice harsh. "What you did could have endangered lives!"

She shook her head. "I don't know what you're . . ."

He grabbed her arms. "Stop pretending, Gili. What if someone had seen you? What if someone had learned your little secret and had done the same thing you did? You could have gotten people killed!"

Her face went white as his words sank in. Then, slowly, she began to shake her head. "No one ever saw. I'm sure no one . . ." she stammered.

"I saw," he cut in. "Someone else could have."

"You?" She said sharply, magnificently angry for a moment. Then her eyes filled with tears. "I never realized . . ."

He made her sit on the bunk, then took a seat beside her. "How long have you been eavesdropping on your father, Gili?" he asked, taking a handkerchief from his pocket and handing it to her.

It took her a moment to control her voice. "Since we moved back. I discovered the tile the first time we were here, when I was a kid."

"And you're sure no one ever saw you?"

She shook her head. "Mom might have once, but she was . . ."

"Drunk," he finished for her. There was no kind way to put it.

She looked up at him in surprise. "How did you know?"

He didn't answer. "How much do you know about what was going on at the embassy the other night?"

Her eyes dropped. She obviously knew a great deal. She obviously wasn't about to talk.

"I have to know, Gili," he told her. "If you don't tell me, I might as well leave you here."

She raised her chin, suddenly defiant again. "Then do it, because what was said in my father's office was his business. As far as I know, you don't have clearance to hear it."

He smiled soberly at the irony of her statement. "Did you?"

She ignored him. "In fact, maybe I should be asking how much you know about what's going on," she said. "Only Daddy and a few others were supposed to know anything was happening. Where do you fit in?"

"I command the embassy detachment, remember? They tell me what's going on so I can assign appropriate security." Then he smiled, realizing that she'd just managed to put him on the defensive. "That was pretty good, Gili, but let's get back to what you know. Did you ever see anyone else in the library, anyone who might have been doing what you did?"

Again she shook her head. "I'm sure it never happened. I'd go in there at all hours. Sometimes in the middle of the night when I woke up and needed . . ." She pulled at her lip with her teeth. "Daddy was the only person I felt that I could talk to, and he was always working. I wanted so much to be part of his life." Her eyes filled again, and this time, she began to cry.

He put an arm around her and pulled her against him, resting his chin on her head. "It's OK, Gili," he soothed. "I'm not going to tell anybody about what you did." He realized as he said it that he'd made the decision long before they arrived here. This woman was going to get him in trouble no matter how hard he tried to avoid it!

He should change his mind, he told himself, do what was expected of him. If anyone found out that he'd held this back, they might start digging into some of his other activities. He couldn't afford that.

But the feel of her against his chest, the sense that she trusted his word, outweighed all the danger.

She pulled back and looked at him, her eyes suddenly soft with gratitude. "Thank you," she whispered.

"But if you ever do anything like this again . . ." He tipped up her chin and stared into her eyes, making his expression hard. "No kidding, Gili, you'll end up here for real."

❖ ❖ ❖

They were halfway back to the embassy when Giselle's mind stopped spinning long enough for a few realizations to sink in. She turned and looked at Raz.

"Do you have a question?" he asked, keeping his eyes on the road. He didn't seem to be angry with her. She wondered why not. She was so stupid!

"You should turn me in," she told him. "If anyone finds out, you're in trouble, too."

He didn't answer, but she could see his jaw working, the muscles tightening like bands. He should, but he wasn't going to. She almost asked why, but realized she might not want to hear his answer.

Her mind moved to another subject. "You said you watched me. Were you there?"

He smiled as if he'd known she'd eventually get to that.

She couldn't help noticing how deep his dimples were. "Not exactly."

"What, exactly?" she asked.

"Cameras."

She felt a sudden chill, a sudden sense of being exposed. "Cameras where? Just in the library, or . . . ?"

He shrugged, too casually. "Not just in the library."

She stared at him, mortified. "You mean you . . ."

He pulled the car over and looked at her seriously, his dark eyes penetrating hers. "Gili, this wasn't a game, OK? And I'm not some sick pervert peeking through windows for thrills. I had to know what was going on, and you weren't going to tell me."

She couldn't meet his gaze. "I know, but . . ." She clutched her purse, embarrassed.

He turned his eyes away as if to respect her modesty, and ran his fingers through his short black curls. "I won't say that I didn't see and hear some things you probably thought were private. Conversations with your parents, phone calls to friends." He glanced at her again. "But I didn't have them place the cameras where you might be too exposed. And I didn't dwell on anything I didn't have to see, OK?"

She nodded uncertainly.

"Good." He started the car again and slipped it into gear, pulling smoothly into traffic. A few minutes later, he glanced at her again. "Gili?"

"What?"

"A purple stethoscope?" He threw back his head and laughed. He didn't stop for a very long time.

❖ ❖ ❖

When they got back to her office, Gregory Benedetti was waiting. He seemed annoyed at seeing the two of them together.

"That was quite a long lunch break," he told Giselle as she entered her office.

"We had to settle a few matters regarding her security clearance," Raz explained.

"Well, see that it doesn't happen again." Gregory dropped a file on her desk. "I need you to handle this visa application by next week."

"And you waited all this time to hand it to her personally instead of dropping it in her work basket."

Gregory gave Raz a sour smile, then turned his attention to Giselle. "I also wanted to see how you were settling in," he told her. "And . . . I wanted to be sure there are no hard feelings about the other night."

"How about that, Gili?" Raz asked sardonically. "What a guy."

Giselle gave him a quelling look, then turned back to Gregory. "I appreciate it."

Gregory smiled, pleased with her attitude. "I also had another matter to discuss with you. . . ." He glanced at Raz. "That is, if your business with the major is finished."

Raz raised an eyebrow at Giselle. When she nodded slightly, he shrugged. "I guess I'll see you later." Turning, he left. Giselle noticed that he didn't close the door.

Gregory noticed, too, and quickly remedied the situation. "Is something going on between you two?"

Giselle shrugged. "Why do you ask?"

He smiled. "I wanted to let you know, Gili . . ."

"Don't call me that," she said firmly, surprised that it mattered.

His smile tightened. "I wanted you to know, Giselle, that I'm not always so forward as I was the other night. I'm afraid I lost my head. You're quite beautiful, you know."

"Thank you." Giselle bent to put her purse in a desk drawer. "And I'm willing to forget the other night. Now if you'll excuse me, I should get back to work." She sat down and picked up the visa application, scanning it briefly. Everything looked to be in order—assuming the applicant was available to be interviewed in the next day or so, the request should be adjudicated fairly quickly. It didn't look like anything that required urgent handling.

He waited for her to look at him again. "I am rather intrigued by you," he told her, moving around her desk and sitting on the corner. His blue eyes played warmly on her face. "Were you playing hard-to-get the other night or were you serious?"

She gave him a tight smile. "I don't play games."

"All right," he agreed smoothly, flashing her a rakish grin. "I can respect that. I'll take it slower, go the traditional route. It's been awhile since I've done that—it might even be fun." Still smiling, he gave her a courtly little bow, clicking his heels together as he reached for her hand. "Perhaps I might call on you sometime, Miss Hardy?"

She shook her head firmly. "I'm sorry, Gregory, but I don't think that's a good idea. We're going to be working together, and I don't want things getting awkward."

"You needn't worry. I can be most discreet. Why don't you think about it for a few days?" He smiled again, reaching out to trace her jaw with his finger.

She pulled back. "Mr. Benedetti, . . ."

"Such formality is completely unnecessary," he cut in smoothly before she could finish her protest, pressing his finger against her lips. "I believe we're going to know each other very, very well before too long." Smiling at her dumbstruck expression, he moved around her desk. At the door, he turned back. "By the way, I mentioned to your supervisor that we expect you to do great things here. Amory was quite pleased to know that you'd already made such a positive impression."

"I appreciate the vote of confidence," she told him.

"By way of thanking me, consider saying yes the next time I invite you to dinner."

He let himself out of the office before Giselle could respond.

Staring at the door, she found herself wondering whether she should be angry or alarmed. She let out a long, slow breath before returning to her work.

❖ ❖ ❖

Raz was waiting by her car that evening. "How was your day?"

She shrugged. "All right." She hadn't gotten to know any of her coworkers. She guessed that would come later, once she had settled into the job.

"Good." He took her keys and opened the door for her. "Listen, Gili, I didn't get a chance to finish that talk with you earlier."

"Oh?" It seemed to her he'd said plenty. She had considered that maybe she should resent his intrusion on her privacy. And his hardball tactics in getting her to confess. On the other hand, he could have turned her in—and he was probably risking his career by not doing so. She wasn't sure how to feel.

He watched her face carefully. "I just want to say that what happened today is behind us. I don't want you to think you owe me anything, OK?"

"I don't," she replied calmly.

A smile dashed across his face at her unexpected bluntness, a flash of white against the tan of his cheeks. "Good. But not everybody's that way around here. Take Benedetti—if he does you any favors, he will expect a return."

"Well, then, I guess he'll be sadly disappointed."

"One other thing—just because your door is closed, don't assume your conversations are private."

She stared as his meaning sank in. "My office is bugged, isn't it?"

He shoved his hands into his pockets, looking casually for eavesdroppers. "That would be a safe assumption. There are probably only a few in this complex that aren't."

She almost laughed. "Let me guess. Yours and who else's?"

He leaned against her car. "I can't even be sure of mine."

"Do people know?"

"It's assumed."

"Why are you telling me this?"

"I figured I owed you one." He shrugged, dropping his eyes to the pavement. "Maybe more than one."

She bristled at the implication. "Listen, if you want to make me happy, just take the cameras out of my father's house."

He grinned, giving her a noncommittal nod. "I'll think about it."

"Raz . . ." She glared at him.

He laughed. "It's already done."

"Thank you."

"About Benedetti." He kicked at an imaginary stone, then glanced at her again. "I'll have a talk with him."

She glared at him. "Raz, I'm not a teenager anymore, and I don't need your protection. I can handle him, OK?"

"No offense, Gili, but there's more to this guy than you know."

"If you mean that he's the CIA man here at the embassy . . ."

His expression momentarily registered astonishment, then just as quickly masked itself. "I wouldn't know about that—and neither should you," he added pointedly. "All I'm saying is that Benedetti isn't some sweaty-palmed adolescent like the guys you're used to."

"Sweaty-palmed . . ." She stopped herself. Why did he always push her to the point where she wanted to slap him? Why did she let him? She slowed, speaking deliberately for emphasis. "And all I'm saying, Major, is that I want you to leave Gregory alone. And while you're at it, leave me alone, too." She slammed her car door, then started her car and put it in gear, forcing him to move away.

When she glanced in her rearview mirror, he was still standing there, watching her drive away. He seemed to be smiling.

Chapter Three

"I believe we're finished here, Major." The admiral closed his file and set it aside. "This plan's about as tight as we can get it without more details from the White House."

"Yes, sir," Raz agreed. If this thing came off, it was going to be big—*very* big—and in more ways than the admiral was expecting.

He yanked himself out of his reverie. He couldn't afford to think about that, not with the admiral's sharp eyes watching him. He placed his copy of the file back in his briefcase and rose. "Will that be all, sir?"

"Actually, there is something else I'd like to discuss with you. Something of a more personal nature."

Raz left his briefcase on the chair and came forward, standing attentively before his desk. The admiral had aged some since that day six years ago. But his eyes were still hawklike, his bearing very much that of a seasoned commander. There could be no underestimating admiral Thaddeus Hardy.

"I saw you talking with my daughter the other evening at the reception," he said. "It was quite an animated discussion."

Raz thought about the transmitter, sitting like a spider just above their heads. He considered asking the admiral to step outside, but that would only raise suspicions on both ends of the device. No, this would have to play itself out in range of listening ears. He nodded reluctantly. "Yes, sir."

"She seemed to be angry with you. Would you mind telling me why?"

"I believe it has something to do with the way we parted company six years ago, sir," Raz told him.

The admiral looked surprised. "After all this time?"

"Yes, sir."

The admiral paused to consider the implications of this. Then he leaned forward, his blue-gray eyes as hard as polished steel. "And do you still have feelings for her?"

A growing sense of inevitability began to fill Raz. Those listening to this conversation would have their own ideas about what they heard. They would want to use this information, and Raz himself, even more than now. He felt himself becoming trapped in yet another of their webs, but knew of no way to avoid it, short of lying. And he didn't want to lie.

He settled his weight and cleared his throat. "Would you have any objection if I did, sir?"

Hardy gazed at him for a long moment. "She's still nine years younger than you."

"Yes, sir." Raz hesitated, then decided that, bug or no bug, it was time to have this out. "But she's not eighteen anymore, sir."

"I'm well aware of that, Major," the admiral snapped. Then his eyes dropped, and he took a deep breath. It was the first time Raz had ever seen the old man blink.

The admiral cleared his throat. "I am concerned about this, Major, partly because you'll have some influence over Giselle's work at the embassy. Her career advancement will depend partly upon her security clearance, and you have some input in that decision."

"We just file reports, sir," Raz reminded him. The real decision was made by the State Department. "And I've already asked my second to handle her file." He'd done it for more reasons than the one the admiral was concerned about, though that would be his explanation. The truth was, Raz wanted zero authority over Giselle Hardy. There were too many ways some people might want him to use it.

The admiral nodded slowly, digesting this information and what it seemed to mean. "What does Giselle have to say about all this?"

"You'll have to ask her that, sir," Raz told him.

The old man stared at him for several moments, then he seemed to come to a decision. "Sit down, Major. I have a few questions for you."

Raz set his briefcase on the floor and brought the chair closer to the desk. "Fire away, sir."

"How serious are you about this?"

Raz winced, thinking about the bug again. "The fact that my feelings haven't changed in six years should tell you something, sir."

The old man nodded. "I've expected this moment. Not necessarily you, but someone. I'm actually surprised it didn't happen sooner, but I'm glad of it, too."

"I understand, sir," Raz said, hoping he wouldn't elaborate. No need to parade the old man's feelings before the roomful of calculating bloodsuckers who would soon be hearing this. Hardy had already said enough.

"She's seen a few young men over the years, but nothing serious. And they have been intimidated by me." He smiled at Raz. "At least until now."

Raz didn't reply. Giselle's past was another subject he didn't want discussed.

The admiral's eyes were still fixed on him. "I've gone over your background thoroughly, Major. Several times over the years, in fact."

Raz nodded. "I expect that you have, sir."

"Your service record is exemplary. Your behavior, both on and off duty, has been unimpeachable. And nothing in your personal history would raise any red flags. But I'd like you to fill in a few details for me, if you will."

Raz almost smiled. The admiral had already concluded that he was good enough to serve his country in the most delicate matters imaginable and had recommended that he be cleared for certain top-secret information. But now Raz was treading on even more sacred ground. He nodded. "If I can, sir, I will."

"You were questioned by various intelligence agencies while you were studying at Annapolis. For several days, I understand. Tell me about the situation that precipitated their interest."

Raz hesitated a moment, digesting what the admiral had unwittingly revealed. The only way the old man could know this was from his old friend, Arnold Killian. It should probably come as no surprise that the two had spoken of him. Still, the file on his interrogations had supposedly been sealed, and this gave rise to the question of what other secrets the admiral's friend might have spilled behind these doors. Those listening would be taking note, and they would expect Raz to draw him out. He did so reluctantly. "What exactly do you want to know, sir?"

"Start at the beginning. How did you happen to meet this rabbinical student?"

"Actually, that was the first time I'd seen him." Raz kept his answer short, forcing the admiral to ask another question.

"How did your brother meet him, then?" Another nugget of information. It seemed Killian hadn't left much out.

Slowly, the story came out, the admiral not realizing that he told more of it than Raz did. The old man seemed to know all of the details, even down to a description of the "present" that had been sent to Raz, a gold charm popular among Jewish people.

"You're Jewish yourself, aren't you?" the old man asked.

"I am." Officially, anyway. In truth, he wasn't particularly religious. It was hard to believe in a God who could allow his people to suffer so much. "I understand that your family is Catholic. Is that going to be a problem, sir?"

The old man thought about it, then shook his head. "It might be different for Mrs. Hardy, especially if things get serious. But we'll deal with that if the need arises."

"Understood." His own family, if it came to it, would probably be more of a problem. They were serious about their religion, especially his uncles. But why was he thinking that far ahead? He hadn't even asked Giselle out yet.

Hardy seemed satisfied. "All right, Major. I appreciate your honesty." He rose, and Raz followed quickly. "Despite the difference in your ages, I see no reason to object to your seeing my daughter." His eyes lit briefly with humor. "Provided that she agrees."

Raz smiled. "That might be a bit of a problem, admiral. Your daughter has some strong opinions about me at the moment."

The admiral nodded sagely. "I know Giselle's moods, Major. She wouldn't be angry if she didn't care. Give her time."

Dismissed, Raz retrieved his briefcase and left the study, pondering the inferences that could be drawn from the discussion. It was obvious that the admiral liked him, trusted him almost as a son. Those listening would be pleased.

The thought churned in his stomach like a bad meal.

❖ ❖ ❖

He received the expected message a few days later, coded in a dispatch from Syria. Obediently, as soon as his shift was over, he took a nice, leisurely evening drive along the coast, stopping only briefly to grab a sandwich and make a quick call from another public phone.

"Air Britain." A new receptionist, another location. Her voice was softer. More melodic.

"I'd like to book a flight to Scotland," he told her. There

were other ways to do this, better technologies. But there were problems. What if he were caught carrying the equipment? What if the technology were traced to its source? His handlers (how he hated that word!) had decided to keep it simple, work the old-fashioned way. It would be far easier to explain using a public phone, if it came to it, so long as it was never clear to whom the call was made.

"Right away, sir, just let me connect you."

Again the clicks. A moment later, the familiar accented voice came on. "Which place in Scotland would you care to visit, sir?"

"How far is it from Zanzibar to Nome?" he asked.

There was a moment while the distance was checked on the map. In inches, it would be his Social Security number. "Yes, Major. We have instructions for you."

Raz waited, feeling himself growing angry. He knew what was coming. The admiral had revealed his weak spot, and the vultures were moving in to exploit it. Just as they had done with Raz.

"We wish to encourage your relationship with Giselle Hardy."

Raz closed his eyes. He felt like a swimmer being pulled out by the tide. "What if she's not interested?" He almost hoped she wasn't. Almost.

The question was expected. "Then you will find a way to compromise her. The admiral may be in a position to learn our secret. We must have leverage, in case it is needed to gain his cooperation."

Before he was even aware that his hand had formed a fist, it had connected violently with the phone. The astonishing explosion of pain only served to fuel his anger. *"Yichrebetak!"* he shouted, no longer caring if he was overheard. The word was a curse uttered between Arabs and Israelis for many decades. "Is there anyone you wouldn't use?" He followed with a stream of curses, venting years of fury over the line.

"Please try to relax, Major," the voice urged calmly, unaffected by his show of temper. The man waited until Raz's breathing slowed, then continued in a soothing tone. "We are aware that you are under great strain, Major Chayil. But you must remember what is at stake. This is a game we must win. Your personal concerns are of little matter."

Raz ground his teeth. They would think of this as a game. This was the kind of people he was dealing with. "With people like you moving the pieces, I'm beginning to wonder if I care who wins," he muttered.

"If you continue to wonder," the voice grew hard, "then I urge you to remember the personal consequences. If you fail us, you will be responsible for the destruction of your family. How will you live with yourself after bringing such pain to your mother?"

One day, Raz promised himself, he would meet this man, this Arab, face-to-face. And only one of them would walk away. He cursed again, but he knew that his voice reflected his defeat.

"There is another matter of consideration, which may make this assignment somewhat more palatable. We believe that our mutual friends also have plans for Giselle Hardy—plans that are not nearly so pleasant for her or for her father. By cultivating her interest, you will be in a position to protect her."

He realized his knuckles were bleeding. Taking out a handkerchief, he wrapped it tightly around his hand before he replied, his voice shaking with repressed emotion. "I'll handle it." Then, with exaggerated calm, he replaced the receiver and walked away.

❖   ❖   ❖

Raz passed her office without looking in. It was the third time that day. Giselle sighed and continued recording her dictation.

She had known about her father's discussion with Raz last

weekend; in fact, she'd seen him come in, and had paced off her frustration in the library until he left. She'd even tried her stethoscope, even though she'd promised herself that she'd never do it again. But she could hear nothing. She'd cried as she realized her precious connection with her father was irrevocably broken.

She'd tried to hate Raz for that, but couldn't.

That night, at dinner with her father, she'd mentioned that she noticed the major had been by, hoping that he might elaborate. But the admiral had only smiled and asked for the salt.

Well, at least they hadn't been talking about her eavesdropping. Her father wouldn't have smiled if he knew that, would he? Giselle didn't think so. It wasn't funny.

She felt so awful about it! She'd even gone to confession last week, hoping to get it off her conscience. But in the end she couldn't bring herself to mention it. Instead, she'd made up a few sins and accepted a mild penance, knowing that it was not enough to assuage her guilt. And on some level she did blame Raz for that. She hadn't thought it was a sin before he came along.

There was a knock on her office door. She looked up to find Gregory Benedetti leaning against the doorframe.

She forced a brief smile, touching the stop button on her tape recorder. "Thank you for the flowers, Gregory. Although it was quite unnecessary."

The roses had been arriving daily, just a single blossom at a time—one lying on her desk when she arrived for work, another on her car windshield when she left the building. At first, she hadn't been sure who was sending them. She'd found out by questioning one of the Marine guards stationed near the staff parking lot.

Then she hadn't known what to do about it. Had he sent her an entire bouquet, she could have returned it, explaining that she preferred not to accept gifts from professional colleagues. But to return a single flower seemed petty. So she'd kept them, each time wincing at the implied encouragement.

Gregory smiled and stepped inside, closing the door behind him. "I've been waiting for your response, Giselle."

She extended a hand. "Thank you, Gregory."

"There are better ways to show gratitude." He bowed over her desk, kissing her palm as he'd done the night they met. The intimate gesture sent the same uncomfortable shiver up her arm. He seemed to sense her reaction, because he smiled knowingly. "I understand you're an old-fashioned girl. You like for the man to make the first move, is that it?"

She wondered if Raz was listening. If so, this was a chance to show him that she could handle herself. Assuming he cared. She straightened her back, facing Gregory with determination. "I think you've already made the first move, Mr. Benedetti."

His smile widened. "I'm pleased you noticed."

"And the fact that I haven't responded in kind should be taken as an indication that I'm not interested," she told him coolly.

His eyes narrowed. "Now, that's no way to be, Giselle. I thought I made it clear that I could do a great deal for you, and not just personally."

"Are you offering promotion in exchange for favors, Mr. Benedetti?" Giselle asked, pushing back her chair and standing up.

He raised an eyebrow with almost comic innocence. "Of course not. That would be sexual harassment, a no-no even on this side of the Atlantic. I'm merely pointing out that, were we to spend time together, I could help you make contacts that would take years to develop on your own." He moved around her desk to stand beside her, his eyes gliding over her in a way that made her flesh burn as if touched. "A person's first tour in a foreign country can be a bit overwhelming. Why not tap into friendships that can help ease the way?"

She held her ground. "I don't mean to be rude, but I don't know too many more ways to say no. You're not my type, Gregory."

He smiled tightly, his eyes now an icy blue. "And what is your type, Giselle? I've noticed that you seem to have quite a thing for uniforms. But I've also noticed that a certain major hasn't given you the time of day for at least a week."

Giselle shrugged, trying not to show that it mattered.

"If you're looking for a way to get over him, trust me—I can make you forget he ever existed." He stepped closer.

He was about to try to kiss her again. Quickly picking up her coffee cup, Giselle positioned it between them, barring his further advance. "You may want to back off a few paces, Mr. Benedetti. This coffee is fresh, very hot, and very black." She gestured with the cup, tipping it dangerously toward his light-gray silk jacket.

Heeding her warning, he stepped back slightly, his smile taking on a pained tightness. "My dear, this is becoming tiresome. I enjoy the chase as much as the next man, but my patience is limited."

"Don't let me keep you," she retorted, gesturing toward the door.

He hesitated as if tempted to push the issue, then remembered the coffee cup and decided to retreat. At the door, he turned back. His expression this time was one of mock concern. "You're new here, Giselle. Perhaps I overestimated your ability to understand the nuances of your situation. Let me suggest . . ."

He was cut off by a knock at the door.

"Come in," Giselle called. Glowering, Gregory opened the door.

A secretary stepped in, brandishing a thick pile of envelopes. "Citizen inquiries, hot off the presses. Amory says to try to get responses drafted before you leave tonight."

"Thank you. And, please, stay for a moment. I have some outgoing correspondence for you." Giselle smiled at the woman, then returned her attention to Gregory. "I believe we were finished, Mr. Benedetti."

He forced a stiff smile. "Not quite. But I believe you understood what I was getting at?"

"I'm sure I did," Giselle affirmed. She glanced at the recorder on her desk and raised a hand to her cheek in mock astonishment. "Oh my gosh, will you look at that! I thought I turned off my tape recorder when you came in, but I guess I didn't. It's been running this whole time."

Gregory froze, staring at the recorder until he had verified that, indeed, the machine was running. Then he returned his gaze to her, his eyes helpless—and furious. For a moment she was taken aback by a menacing look in his eyes. But then his expression shifted, leaving her uncertain whether she'd read him correctly.

She gave him a disarming smile. "Don't worry—I'll see that our conversation remains private." She gave him a meaningful look. "But I will have to archive the tape in case there's a question later."

He stared at the recorder again, as if tempted to smash it to pieces. Then, glancing at the secretary, he gave her an abrupt nod and turned to leave. At the door, he turned back and gave her a hard smile. "Giselle, you're just beginning what looks to be a very promising career. Trust me when I tell you that in this business, you can never have too many friends. The day will come when you need an assist, and when it does, I just hope that you don't feel you've made a terrible mistake today."

The secretary watched him go. When he was out of earshot, she turned to Giselle. "I lied about Amory wanting the work done before you left—there's nothing urgent there. I just figured that you might want an excuse for Gregory to leave."

Giselle gave her a grateful smile. "Thanks, uh . . ."

The woman shrugged. "Call me Monica."

"Thanks, Monica."

"No problem." She turned to go, then stopped again, making way for Raz to pass down the narrow hall heading toward the ambassador's wing. As he passed, he glanced at Monica, and their eyes met briefly.

Returning to her desk, Giselle glanced through the new material, sorting it according to task. Each of the manila envelopes was stamped "Routine Documents," meaning the material inside required the lowest security clearance. Perfect for a minor functionary like her. Her job as a consular officer was tedious work, very uninteresting. And she deserved nothing better, she told herself.

At the bottom of the pile was a manila envelope stamped "Top Secret." The envelope listed the names of those who could see the file. One of those cleared to see it was Raz.

Monica had obviously made a mistake.

Giselle wondered what was inside the envelope. Something far more interesting than what she was reading, probably. But she wouldn't look. She wasn't even tempted.

Picking up the envelope, she carried it down the hall.

❖ ❖ ❖

Raz looked up as Giselle entered his office and tried not to smile at her apparent surprise at finding him there. So she'd seen him go by in the other direction. She was paying attention.

She dropped the envelope on his desk, her gaze catching on the bandage around his knuckles, then dropping away. "This was put in my work basket by accident."

He opened the envelope. The dab of glue he'd put inside popped as he tugged out the contents. They were old security documents, nothing important, but she didn't know that. She'd learned her lesson.

"Thank you," he said.

She started to go, then turned back. "Raz?"

He looked up.

She glanced at the floor, then the wall, then him, then back at the floor. The words, when they came, were timid. "Are you avoiding me?"

He smiled. She'd noticed his absence. "I'm doing what you asked me to do."

She frowned. "What do you mean?"

"You said to leave you alone."

"Oh." She looked at the floor again. "Thanks." She didn't sound thankful. She paused for a moment, as if tempted to say something, then she started to go.

"Gili?" He watched her stop, her back still to him. "If you have a minute, stick around. And close the door."

She did as he asked, then turned hesitantly to face him.

He rose and came around to lean against his desk. He didn't want to sit formally across a desk from her as he said this. "Have a seat, if you'd like."

She nodded and took the visitor's chair, appearing to be a little uncomfortable, but obviously curious.

He leaned back, enjoying her presence here. It made an otherwise cheerless office far more interesting. With her in this room, the possibilities seemed endless. Even though he was about to do what was expected of him. Even though there might be a transmitter, undetectable, in this room, too. Gazing into those quicksilver eyes, he could almost believe that this was entirely his idea.

He waited until she finally looked at him before speaking. He wanted to see her eyes as he said it, to know what she was thinking. "I don't want to leave you alone."

She digested it slowly. "What *do* you want?" She never ceased to surprise him. Whatever was happening in that head of hers, for once her expression didn't show it. He nearly laughed at her inscrutability. Then he sobered again, afraid his grin might annoy her.

He decided to lay out a few ground rules. Never go anywhere without a map. "First off, Gili, I want you to know that no matter what happens between us, if you tell me to back off, I'll back off. No hard feelings."

She nodded soberly, her face still unreadable.

"Now, you asked, so I'll tell you what I want. I want the same thing I wanted six years ago, when you were still a kid and I was under your father's command."

She was watching his face, and he wondered if she could read his expression. He was beginning to feel uncomfortable. What was she thinking?

He cleared his throat. "Well, now you're a grown woman, and I'm a little more my own man." The irony of the statement almost caught in his throat. He paused, dampening his lips. "So now, if you say yes, I want us to pick up where we left off back then and see where it goes." He watched her eyes. "Is that OK with you?"

Her eyes dropped and her hands, tugging at the hem of her skirt, seemed to tense for a second. But then she gave a little nod.

He realized he'd been holding his breath. He let it out, smiling, and reached out his hand. "Come here."

She rose slowly, accepting his hand with a shyness that pleased him. He brushed his thumb over her knuckles, then slowly drew her hand up to his lips. Gazing down into her eyes, and seeing the blush that rose to her cheeks, it was almost as if the past six years had never happened. Suddenly he was back in that gym, wanting to kiss her, wanting to . . .

". . . Compromise her." The remembered words splashed through his mind like cold water. He released her hand abruptly, remembering the lack of privacy.

Deliberately, he put her away from him and stood. "If you're not doing anything tonight, I'd like to take you to dinner."

❖ ❖ ❖

A few weeks later, Giselle was eating dinner at home for the first time in several days. Both parents had joined her, an increasingly rare event, and one she no longer cherished. She desperately missed the family meals of her early childhood, when clinking dishes and happy chatter had floated over the table like music. Over the years, her mother's drinking had changed things. The simplest comment, even the clatter of a spoon against good china, could set off a tirade. Tonight they ate in painful silence.

The admiral cleared his throat. "You seem to be out a lot at night these days, Giselle." It was the first time in weeks that he'd left the office before midnight, so she was surprised that he'd noticed.

They'd had so little time together that she was considering taking an apartment in Rome. The drive from Gaeta to the embassy was over an hour and a half each way. But she was used to long commutes—being bused to high school in Naples as a girl had taken almost as long. Besides, what little time she did get with her father was far too precious to give up.

"Is it someone special?" he asked, his blue-gray eyes inquisitive.

"You have a boyfriend?" Her mother leaned forward attentively, and Giselle's heart sank. Nothing good could come of this.

She nodded reluctantly, more to her father's question than her mother's. She felt guilty for ignoring her mother, but it was almost impossible to really talk to her.

The admiral nodded. "You have a certain look about you. I'm not so old that I don't remember." He glanced at his wife, his face softening in memory of better days.

Her mother smiled briefly, and for a moment Giselle remembered that, before all the anger and the pity, her parents had loved each other. It made her sad to see what that love had become.

She wondered again if there was any way to help her mother. They'd tried once, confronting her with her drinking in hopes that she'd be willing to enter a rehab clinic. She'd left home in a drunken rage that night, threatening suicide. She had not returned for several days, leaving Giselle and her father beside themselves, worried that she'd been hurt—or worse.

"Why don't you ask this man to come for dinner one night next week?" her mother asked eagerly. "I'd like to meet him."

Giselle looked at her father apprehensively, wanting him to come up with a reason it wouldn't work.

Her mother caught the signal. "I promise," she said as she crossed her heart, "I'll be good. I won't even have my evening cocktail."

"I'll make sure of it," her father promised.

Giselle considered it. Was Raz ready for this? He might take this sort of invitation as a desire to advance their relationship, a hint that she wanted more than he was ready to give. Maybe she would scare him off again by asking.

On the other hand, her father seemed to want this, and she hated cutting him out of any part of her life. And she trusted his promise; her mother wouldn't embarrass her.

She nodded. "I'll ask him."

❖ ❖ ❖

Raz found the Hardy family dynamics more than a little daunting. The old man was obviously the linchpin of the household. Giselle clearly doted on his every word. His wife, on the other hand, seemed to all but detest the admiral. Raz had noticed the glaring look at her husband before dinner when he'd offered to "freshen" her tea, taking away the cup she'd been holding and filling a new one. Her hands shook now as she sipped her water.

Dolores Hardy was slipping fast. Raz had known there was a problem, but he hadn't realized that she was this bad. Her body, still slim as a dancer's, was no longer firm. The skin sagged, with fine, crepey wrinkles at her neck and the folds of her arms. Her eyes, heavily painted to hide as much damage as possible, were suffused with an unmistakable pink tinge.

He watched the admiral now, making subtle efforts to cover for his wife, and wondered how the man had let things get so far out of hand. Alcoholic spouses were nothing new to the military—the stresses of military family life could push anyone over the edge. But as a man rose in rank, his family problems could shipwreck his career. Surely the admiral's family had been thoroughly investigated before he was selected for this assignment. He could only assume that somehow Arn Killian had kept this problem from becoming an issue with the brass.

Giselle, too, was covering for her mother, filling her water glass only halfway so that her shaking hands wouldn't splash water. Far from feeling embarrassment or pity for her, Raz found his heart swelling with pride. She was a tough little nut, his Gili. He had heard once that one had only to look at the mother to see how the daughter might age, but in this case, it just didn't fit. Giselle was too much her father's daughter to surrender to anything, even her family's dysfunction.

He realized again, as he had many times in recent days, that he loved her. It came to him in surges, like the sea. It was always there, drifting beneath his thoughts, but then some small thing would happen, and it would rush up to wash over him, drowning all denial.

"What exactly do you do at the embassy, Raz?" Mrs. Hardy asked, her tone making it clear that she didn't care to call him by his rank. She sipped her water slowly, watching him with catlike eyes. It was obvious that she didn't approve of him. She apparently preferred that Giselle steer clear of men in uniform.

"I'm in charge of security, ma'am."

"Call me Dolores," she said sharply, unhappy with his formality.

"Dolores," he repeated.

"And your last name—what sort of name is Chayil?"

"It's Hebrew," he answered. He didn't want to add that the name meant "soldier."

"You're Jewish, then," Mrs. Hardy deduced, frowning. "Our family is Catholic, you know."

Raz glanced at the admiral and noted the pained expression on his face as he tried to think of a way to salvage the situation. Before he could speak, Raz set down his fork, deciding to meet the problem head-on. "I'm aware of that, Mrs. Hardy. Giselle and I have discussed the issue, and frankly, we don't think it's a problem."

"Neither do we, Major," the admiral put in quickly, his hand gripping his wife's tightly as a signal that she wasn't to disagree. "In any event, our daughter is old enough to make her own decisions."

"Thank you, sir," Raz replied.

"What about your family?" Dolores put in, ignoring the painful squeeze the admiral gave her fingers. "How will they feel about your involvement with a Christian girl?"

"I'm sure that some of them will be unhappy," Raz admitted. "But my mother and brother won't object, and they're the ones who matter."

"You won't expect our daughter to convert if things get serious?"

He shook his head. "Nor would I be willing to convert, in case you were wondering. I can tell you what my ancestors were doing four thousand years ago, Mrs. Hardy. I've always been proud of my heritage. I won't turn my back on it."

She was silent for a moment, seeming impressed by his firmness. Then, helped not a little by another nudge from the admiral, she nodded. "I suppose I can respect that."

"So, Major, how are you coming with that new security setup for the embassy gates?" the admiral asked, changing the subject quickly before the momentary peace could be broken.

"A few bugs, sir, but we're working on it," Raz replied gratefully. "The system still isn't accepting the magnetized cards. We may have to call the manufacturer and have them send out a technician." He gave more detail than requested, wanting to dally on this neutral subject.

"It seems to me that we had a similar problem here at Gaeta. I'll ask around—maybe one of the men who handled the problem here can help."

"I'd appreciate it, sir," Raz told him. "We've just—"

"Is the embassy unsafe?" Mrs. Hardy cut in.

"I have Marines at all of the access points, ma'am . . . Dolores," he corrected himself. "No one's getting through without being checked out."

"I should hope so," she replied. "After that terrible bombing at our embassy in Greece last year . . ." She shot her daughter a worried look, as if only now realizing the possibilities.

Gili's safe with me, he wanted to tell her. But like so much about his life, it wouldn't be true. How could he protect Giselle when he was probably her greatest threat?

His latest orders had come in yesterday, this time direct from the heart of the Middle East. For the first time, Raz had heard the voice of the most dangerous man in the modern world. The man known only as Seif—the Sword.

The voice had come from the back of a limousine, with Raz riding next to the driver. Like all but a select few in the organization, Raz never saw the man's face and would be unable to identify him if questioned. To protect their discussion from unwanted listeners, the two men spoke quietly, rapidly, using a language little known in the modern world.

"What may I do for you?" Raz had asked.

"I am about to ask much of you, my young friend. More, perhaps, than you are prepared to give." The man's voice was that of an old man, but aged like a fine wine, resonating just the proper mixture of fatherly concern and authority. "But I would have you bear in mind that what I ask is for our sacred homeland, for the restoration of our people to the greatness promised us in the days of our fathers."

"I am willing," Raz had replied, feeling at once a welling of dread and a grudging respect for this man because he was delivering the request himself. He began to understand why so many followed Seif willingly. Here was a man who understood the worth of loyalty.

And along with those first emotions, there was also a tiny swell of hope. Raz's heart beat faster as he waited, thinking this might be it, what he had worked for all these years. And if so, God willing, he and his family might finally be free!

"You must marry this woman." The words had sounded like a knell, signaling the death of hope. Seif had delivered, not freedom, but further bondage.

They wanted Giselle to be easily accessible, the man had explained, in case a hostage was needed. And they wanted to maximize Raz's influence, his position of trust with the admiral, so that when the time came to execute their plans, he would be in an optimum position to control those who might stop them. This marriage would achieve both ends.

The marriage would also give them one more piece of Raz. The last, most precious, piece. If he gave them this, everything he had would have been twisted to serve their cause. His career, his honor, his loyalty, and now even his love. There would be nothing left that was uncorrupted. Every triumph, every joy he managed to extract from his life would be tainted with guilt, tarnished by betrayal and lies.

And when it was over, even if he managed to come through this with a hard-won freedom for himself and his family, there would be nothing left of Raz Chayil worth saving.

Surfacing from his bleak thoughts, Raz discovered the Hardys watching him curiously. Had he missed something? He couldn't afford to let his thoughts drift like that!

"Major, if you're finished eating, why don't you join me in

the living room?" the admiral suggested. "Giselle will probably want to freshen up before you two go for your drive this evening."

❖ ❖ ❖

Giselle's mother retired to her room after dinner, pleading a migraine. Giselle was relieved, knowing that she'd already stretched her limits. She'd actually dropped a fork full of food on her lap during supper. Giselle was thankful that Raz had missed it.

She hurriedly checked her hair, not wanting to leave the men alone too long. Then she hurried down to the living room, expecting to find Raz getting the third degree. Instead she found him chatting amiably with the admiral about their plans for the evening.

She frowned. This wasn't like her father. Usually, when a date came to pick her up, he was suspicious, even borderline rude, making every effort to intimidate. But this time, it looked as if everything was already settled between them. She wasn't sure she liked it.

She let Raz help her with her jacket and followed him outside. As he opened the car door for her, she put a hand on his arm. "Have you talked to my father about us?"

"A little."

She glared at him. "I don't believe it! Don't you remember how angry that made me before?"

He braced himself, one hand on the roof, the other on the car door, facing her. "Gili, your father is still my C.O. I can't afford to offend him. He asked what was happening between us. I told him what he had a right to know."

"What did you tell him?"

He shrugged. "The same thing I told him the first time, when you were probably upstairs listening. I told him I'm interested in you."

"And what did he say?"

"He asked a few questions about my family and background. Once he decided I was on the level, he gave me the go-ahead to ask you out."

She glared at him. "This was before you even asked me out? I was barely speaking to you, and you and my father were already mapping out my future?"

"You could put it that way," he admitted, stepping away so that she could leave if she wanted to.

Angrily, she threw herself into his car. "The next time you talk to my father about me," she snapped, pulling in her skirt so that he could close the door, "I expect to be in the room."

As he rounded the car, she thought she heard a muffled laugh.

❖ ❖ ❖

The car slowed, grumbling to a halt at a walled overlook. Giselle looked around, realizing with surprise that they were driving along the steep ocean-side mountains south of Pompeii. She had ridden for over an hour in silence, staring out the window but seeing nothing they passed.

Abruptly, the splendor of the view struck her. The narrow ribbon of road that had brought them here clung to sharp and jagged rocks high above the sea. The stone retaining wall gleamed white in the moonlight, and beyond it, the earth dropped away to reveal the Gulf of Naples, which reflected the bright light of the moon—and the shadow of Vesuvius. The beauty of it made her momentarily forget her anger. She got out of the car and moved to the wall for a better look.

Raz shut off the engine and set to work cranking down the roof of his convertible. Abstractedly, she watched him, her eyes drawn to the powerful but controlled movements of his arm. He had taken off his jacket before getting into the car, and in the moonlight she could see the outline of his shoulders beneath his crisp khaki shirt.

He caught her looking and smiled. "Are you through being mad at me yet?"

"No," she replied stubbornly, pulling her gaze away and turning to look at the moonlit Tyrrhenian. He hadn't apologized yet. He owed her that, at least.

She heard something that sounded like a strangled chuckle, and when she glanced at him, he was trying not to grin.

"I'm glad you're having a good time. Why don't you enjoy the rest of the evening alone?" she snapped, and spun away, starting off the way they'd come.

He abandoned the car and hurried to catch up. "Where are you going?"

"Home."

He laughed again. "It's sixty-five miles at least, Gili, and that's as the crow flies. Get back in the car and I'll drive you home, if that's what you want."

She turned on him angrily. "Why are you always laughing at me?"

He sobered abruptly, caught her arms so that she had to look at him. "I'm not laughing at you. Never at you," he swore earnestly.

She pulled away. "Well, you're not laughing with me, because I don't see the humor." She turned, continuing down the road.

"Giselle, hear me out," he pleaded.

She ignored him and kept walking. He followed her a short way, then moved around her so that he blocked her path, mirroring her as she tried to move around him once, twice, and a third time.

Finally, he took her hand and held her still. The firmness of his grip was at once comforting and maddening. She tried to pull free, but he countered easily. "Shall I show you how to break this hold?" he offered.

She stopped fighting and glared at him. "Red light, Major," she snapped, using the Navy words meant to warn that a situation was crossing the line into harassment.

He quickly dropped her hand. "I'm sorry."

Brushing past him, she started walking again, ignoring his footsteps at her side.

They walked a long way, silently, and she wondered if he meant to stay with her all the way back home. The whole thing suddenly seemed like a stupid idea. She slowed, wondering if there was a way to back down gracefully.

His voice came out of the darkness. "I'm used to being able to read people, Gili, but for some reason, I never could read you. I can never guess what you're going to do. Back at your villa, I figured you were going to walk back inside and slam the door in my face. Instead, you got in the car. Now, more than an hour's drive away, you're mad enough to walk all the way home." His teeth flashed whitely in the moonlight. "You astonish me, Gili. You surprise me." He shrugged, gazing steadily into her eyes. "I like it."

She backed away stiffly. "I don't like being laughed at, Raz— especially when I'm upset. It feels like you don't take me seriously."

"I'm sorry," he told her solemnly. "I never meant to make you feel that way." He paused, then moved closer, his eyes watching her face. This time she didn't move away. "I laugh because you thrill me, Gili. Every time you do something I don't expect, I want to smile, even when I shouldn't want to smile. I love the fact that I can't figure you out. I love the fact that there's one thing in my life that isn't going by the books."

She wondered if he could see the way his words affected her. Those bottomless eyes of his always seemed to see everything. "How can I surprise you? You know everything about me."

His eyes didn't leave her face. "Not everything, Gili. Not a lot of things." He stepped forward again, closing the distance between them. The expression on his face was tender. Sweeter than she'd ever seen it. She didn't want to blink for fear it would disappear. "Not half of what I want to know."

"You probably even know my favorite color," she challenged.

"I'd guess purple—from the stethoscope." A smile flicked across his face, but was quickly suppressed.

"See? I have no secrets." She wanted to hang onto her annoyance. Anything to keep her mind off the things he could make her feel. He'd break her heart again, if she let him. "I don't know that about you."

His eyes caressed her. "My favorite color is whatever color you're wearing. Or maybe gray, for your eyes, or pink, for your lips."

She closed her eyes, feeling the warmth of his breath on her face. Then, impulsively, she went up on her toes, kissing him hard. He grinned against her lips, then kissed her back.

He hugged her tight, then tighter, as if he couldn't get enough of her.

As she raised her arms to circle his neck, a part of her ached to urge him on, to feel the things she sensed he could make her feel. But . . .

She didn't have to stop him; on some level he seemed to sense her hesitation. An almost-growl escaped him, and he pulled away.

"I'm sorry," she murmured.

"It's OK." He took her hand, studied it, then let it go, taking a deep breath. "Gili, I need to tell you a few things before this goes any further. I brought you out here because I wanted to get away from all the bugs and eavesdroppers."

She tensed at the last word, and he smiled an apology. "If you're with me, Gili, you're in deep. There are things I can't tell you, a whole part of my life I can't share. There are people who will want to use you to get to me. You might even be in danger."

"I know," she said. "I've lived with Dad all these years, haven't I? And I was in danger then, too, or have you forgotten how we met?"

He paused for a long moment, his expression suggesting that he was tempted to tell her something. But finally he shrugged, and his face became unreadable. "With me, you may get more than you bargained for."

"Are you trying to warn me off?"

"Maybe that's what I'm doing," he agreed, almost to himself. Then his eyes returned to her face. "Gili, you might not be happy with me. Look at your mom, what your father's secrets are doing to her. That's why she hates the military so much, isn't it?"

Giselle winced. She hated thinking about her mother's condition. Could she one day be like that? The thought terrified her.

Raz was watching her as if he knew what she was thinking. She turned away. "I'm not like her. I've lived with Dad's secrets, too, haven't I?"

"You knew your father's secrets," he reminded her. "You won't know mine."

She paused, thinking about what he said. How would it be, knowing that Raz might be asked to put himself in danger, but not knowing how or why or when? How would she like it when, like her father, Raz spent long hours closeted away, where she couldn't see him, hear him, talk to him? Lonely, maybe. Frustrated. Probably sometimes frightened. Was this really what she wanted?

He was reading her thoughts again. "Gili, there are a lot of guys at the embassy who'd grab you in a flash if you'd let them. I've heard them talking about you, seen them looking. Maybe you'd be happier with one of them."

She shook her head. The other guys at the embassy weren't men—at least not next to Raz and her father. They were like the guys she'd dated in school. She'd liked them, but there was something missing. "They're just thinking about what Daddy could do for them."

"It's occurred to me, too," he admitted.

She stared at him, shocked and hurt.

He shrugged. "I want to be honest with you. What I feel for you, what happens when we kiss, that's real. And I'd be standing here with you even if your dad was Joe Blow, even if . . ." He cut himself off abruptly, dropping his eyes. After a long pause, he continued. "Like it or not, Gili, your father's influence is going to factor into every relationship you have over here. If you don't want that, you might do better stateside, away from the military and the politics." He paused again, then turned away. When he spoke again, his voice was strangely tight. "You'd be a whole lot safer there."

Frowning, she caught his arm, turning him back to face her. "Raz, what are you saying?"

For a moment, his eyes frightened her, piercing her with a fury she didn't understand. Then, abruptly, they emptied, and their hollowness was nearly as terrifying as the rage. "I'm saying that you'd be better off without me, Gili." He spoke hoarsely. "I'm saying you should get out while you can," he added in a whisper.

She stared at him, her backbone prickling with a sudden sense of danger. "Something's wrong, isn't it?" Giselle whispered. "Tell me."

Raz looked at her for what seemed like an eternity. Then his face masked itself, a sober, calm expression taking hold. "No." He shook his head. "Nothing's wrong, Gili. Everything's normal. I just want to give you an out in case you need one."

She stared at him, disbelieving his words. "Normal" wasn't what she'd seen in his eyes, was it? No, she was sure she'd sensed something more, something terrible.

Her mind flashed back to the day they met, to the violence she'd seen him commit before her eyes. She'd seen that look on his face then, too. A look of rage, of suppressed violence. A look of fear, like a trapped animal. Her hand rose to her throat as it had when she'd watched that young boy die. Was Raz capable of hurting her?

Her mind protested furiously. What a ridiculous thought! This was Raz, she reminded herself. What happened that day was done to save her life. Every soldier was capable of killing in such situations, and any man with a conscience would feel guilty afterward, no matter how just the cause.

No. Raz would never hurt her, not intentionally. Even during the self-defense training, even when things got rough, he'd never put a bruise on her, never a mark. Raz was always perfectly controlled, always carefully gentle.

No. She was just imagining things. Her mind was making up monsters in the moonlight, just as it had when her father had taken her camping as a kid. That was all. That was all.

Summoning a smile, she bravely took his hand. "I'm still here, Raz. You're not going to scare me away, if that's what you meant to do. This is what I want. You're what I want."

He smiled, but it was a pained smile. He squeezed her fingers—gently, she noticed. "You're sure?"

She nodded. "I'm sure."

He brought her hand to his lips and pressed it there for a moment. She could feel his stubble scrape her skin. Then he nodded soberly. It was almost a surrender, as if to confirm something he'd already known, something inevitable. "Then let's do it, Gili. Let's set the date."

She stood there watching him, wondering if he was serious. When she realized he was, she pulled her hand away. A part of her wanted to be angry again, but she couldn't. "I don't believe you, Raz Chayil! I've been waiting all my life for this moment, and you just asked me to marry you as if someone had a gun to your head! You really know how to sweep a girl off her feet, you know that?" When he didn't respond, she gave him a challenging look. "What's the matter, marine? You don't want to dirty your uniform by going down on one knee?"

A grin flashed across his face, but before she could take offense, he caught her in his arms and silenced her with a kiss. "You have a way with me, Gili." Pulling away, he smiled tenderly, brushing her cheek with a knuckle. "I hardly ever smile when you're not around, did you know that? But you can make me laugh for pure joy—*Gili meod*. Even when everything else has me pinned against the wall, when you do something unexpected, somehow, I feel free."

Releasing her, he stepped back and dropped to one knee. "Marry me, Gili. Let's grab what happiness we can find together, for as long as it lasts." He paused, a brief shadow crossing his face. "And promise me that you'll never regret it," he added softly.

"For as long as it lasts? You'd better mean for the rest of our lives, marine, because for me marriage is right up there with God and country. 'Til death do us part, no kidding."

He smiled poignantly, rising and pulling her into his arms. There were tears in his eyes as he pressed a kiss to her forehead. "From your lips to God's ears, Gili. To God's ears."

❖ ❖ ❖

"Marriage is a solemn vow, not to be entered into lightly," Samuel Gilchrist pronounced solemnly as they stood before him at the altar. The Catholic chaplain had declined to marry an interfaith couple, so this was a non-denominational Christian service, agreed upon to satisfy Giselle's mother, since Raz's family was unable to attend. Reverend Gilchrist, now retired from the Navy, had flown in to officiate over the ceremony.

"In a moment, I will ask each of you to give yourself to the other as to the Lord, wholly and without reservation, for as long as you both draw breath. Both Jews and Christians believe in the marital union as a metaphor for God's covenant with us, through which we can begin to understand his love for us. Solomon's Song of Songs, to some, depicts our Lord as the Bridegroom and his people as the bride. The covenant is one of intense joy and passion, but it also is eternal and unshakable. This is the model for our earthly unions, a total and irrevocable giving of ourselves, one to the other. Raz, Giselle, before you enter this earthly covenant with each other, I ask you each to take a moment to consider the importance and solemnity of your vows."

Raz could feel Giselle's hand tremble. Was she having second thoughts? She had plenty of reason. Her mother had not let up about the difference in their religions, even though it seemed obvious that the woman's true objection was to his career. And then the Catholic chaplain had joined in, counseling her strongly not to marry outside her faith. There were, it seemed, dozens of questions that couldn't be answered. How would they celebrate the holidays—and which holidays would they celebrate? What faith would they instill in any children they might have? In fact, those questions only scratched the surface.

Every issue they'd brought up had chipped away at Giselle's confidence. He had begun to think she might call it off until Reverend Gilchrist, out of fondness for the family, had agreed to officiate.

Raz, meanwhile, had never felt less in control of his life. The religious issues didn't bother him. He had a growing conviction that it was unlikely that their marriage would last long enough for any of it to matter. But that itself was the problem. Since their engagement, a new guilt had crept into each growing intimacy between them, a silent voice in his mind whispering that with each caress, with each kiss, he was betraying her.

Gili would never have agreed to this if she knew about Seif, about the deception that Raz was living. How dare he ask her to give herself to him without knowing the danger? And how could he promise her his undying fidelity when he knew that what he was doing was worse than cheating on her? A part of him, the greater part, belonged to others, to people listening in the distance—people with no honor, people who controlled his every move. And one day, those people would demand that he turn his back on her love and hurt her in ways she could never imagine. In ways she would never forgive.

The reverend continued, as if reading his desperate thoughts. "If anyone has reason why this marriage should not take place, let him speak now or forever hold his peace."

Raz turned to Giselle, wondering if he should raise his hand and stop the wedding. She wore pure white, a gown of simple pearly satin, and he was certain that with her it was more than empty tradition. All this meant something to her, and one day she would look back on it and regret it. What right did he have to do this to her? What right did he have to place his family, his personal interests, above Giselle's happiness, above her safety?

He had no right at all. Clearing his throat, Raz began to lift his hand.

But then, Giselle's mist gray eyes came up to meet his gaze, and the love he saw there shattered his resolve. Suddenly he knew that there was no way he could let her walk away from him, no way he could bear it if he saw her wearing white for someone else. Giselle was for him. Maybe the fact that others said so too only made it more true.

"Do you, Giselle Ruth Hardy," the reverend intoned, "take this man, Raz Chayil, to have and to hold, from this day forward, for better and for worse, for richer and for poorer, in sickness and in health, and forsaking all others, cleave only unto him for so long as you both may live?"

"I do," she said softly.

Then it was Raz's turn. He nearly choked on the vows, managing to say them only in a whisper. He thought he saw a tear on Giselle's cheek and nearly cried himself.

And then it was done. He took her hand, turning to face the guests, and shattered the cloth-wrapped glass that was placed by his foot. A few voices in the congregation, led by the admiral himself, called out, *"Mazel tov."* Raz felt a knot in his throat.

Giselle turned to give a quick hug to her bridesmaid, Arlene Riley, whose pregnancy was just becoming visible under her formal dress uniform. Raz's marines moved quickly to stand at attention on either side of the aisle. At a command, they bared their swords, raising them to form an arch. Then, glancing at each other and almost simultaneously taking a deep breath, the two caught hands and marched beneath the archway to greet their guests.

When they reached the end, the last man dropped his sword, swatting Gili's rear with the flat of it. "*Semper Fi.* The Corps is a jealous mistress," he announced loudly.

And not the only one.

❖ ❖ ❖

The reception at the villa was over before Giselle knew it. One minute she was dancing her first dance with Raz, the next, she was giving her father a tearful kiss and receiving a hug from her mother. Dolores Hardy had managed to pull herself together for the event, sticking to club soda and even putting on a cheerful face, although her disapproval of Raz still was evident.

The couple raced out to Raz's car, decorated by his marines with everything from infirmary bedpans to a bawdy phrase in shaving cream, from which Giselle turned her gaze in embarrassment. Seeing her blush, Raz quickly rubbed it out and glared good-naturedly at a grinning lance corporal. "A little respect for my bride, men."

The drive to Rome was over before Giselle really felt prepared, and then Raz was carrying her across the threshold of his quarters, a secured apartment on the embassy grounds. They were alone.

There would be no honeymoon, only a weekend. Too much was going on, Raz had explained. She didn't mind. In fact, forty-eight hours alone with her new husband suddenly seemed more than a little daunting.

Raz let her down inside the suite, then shut the door and locked it.

"Are you sure you don't want dinner first?" She tried not to sound as nervous as she felt. "You barely ate anything at the reception."

"I had other things on my mind," he told her, tossing off his cap. Slowly, he unfastened his sword from its sling, laying it on the chair by the foyer. Then came his gloves, finger by finger.

She realized she'd moved away, to the center of the living room.

He watched her, unbuttoning the collar of his dress jacket. When it was loose, he slipped a hand inside, rubbing his neck where the stiff cloth had irritated his skin. His eyes smiled at her, teasing her for what she'd been thinking.

Calming, she glanced around the room, wondering what she should do to busy herself. The room was big and airy, painted a light gold. The furniture was a little threadbare, but truly antique, in shades of ivory, sage, and rose. It was nice enough, but Raz's military fastidiousness made it look unlived-in. She applied her mind to finding ways to correct this. Maybe a few paintings, and a china knickknack or two on the tables . . .

Her eyes caught on the open French doors at the far side of the room. Those doors had always been closed before when she was here. Through them, she could see a large Queen Anne bed. She froze.

"That's the bedroom," Raz told her solemnly, catching the direction of her gaze.

Giselle nodded, not moving toward it.

He was beside her when she turned back. She flinched, then held herself still with effort as his hand came up to touch her cheek. He laughed. "You look like the sacrificial lamb."

She dropped her eyes. "I'm sorry."

He took her hand and brought it to his lips. "Gili, I'm not going to demand my husbandly rights, or whatever else might be going through that crazy mind of yours. Nothing will happen here tonight that you don't want to happen."

She looked up, found those dark eyes gazing at her, waiting for her reply, so patient, so disciplined, so restrained. "I think you're always doing what someone else wants you to do," she observed, the sudden insight surprising her. Forgetting her initial anxiety, she managed a smile and moved closer. "Tonight, all those other people are outside that door. In here, it's just you and me. And whatever you want, I want that too."

She had seen passion in his eyes before, but she was totally unprepared for what her words evoked. It was as if she'd set a match to tinder. He caught her in his arms, pulling her against him and holding her so tightly that she thought it should hurt, but it didn't.

She held nothing back. He wouldn't let her. His lips came down on hers and his arms squeezed as if he wanted to pull her inside of him, to make them one body.

She could barely breathe. It didn't matter. Her arms were around him, squeezing as fiercely as his were.

"Gili, I love you," he whispered against her lips as he drew her into the bedroom. "I can't believe how much I love you. . . ."

❖ ❖ ❖

As the night progressed, Giselle began to understand what her priest had once told her about marital relations being a sacrament, the husband and wife becoming one flesh. She realized now why she had waited for this, her wedding night, and this man, her husband. It couldn't possibly have been this right, this perfect, at any other time, or with any other man. She had never felt this close to anyone before.

Suddenly, the weekend didn't seem long enough, and she found herself wishing for a honeymoon after all. Couldn't the Marines do without Raz for a few days?

The thought of his job gave her pause. "Raz?"

"Mmm?" He watched her face attentively, as if trying to read her thoughts.

"You said most rooms here at the embassy are bugged. What about this apartment?"

He kissed her forehead. "I'm sure the spooks have better things to do than eavesdrop on us when we're alone."

She stiffened. "No kidding, Raz. Is it?"

Staring down into her eyes, he slowly shook his head. "The CIA is not bugging us here."

"Are you sure?"

He shook his head again, this time more firmly. "Trust me, Giselle. You have to trust me."

Something about the tightness of his lips told her that Raz knew more than he was saying. But she knew better than to press him.

It was the first of a multitude of secrets that would lie unspoken between them, just as he had warned her. She forced herself to shrug off the frustration and smile, snuggling into his arms with a contentment she'd previously only imagined. "I do trust you," she sighed, her fingers tracing the contours of his arm.

He whispered something against her hair, so quietly that she couldn't hear. She thought of asking him to repeat it, but decided it was unimportant. They had better things to think about over the next two days.

❖ ❖ ❖

Giselle slept fitfully, unused to sharing her bed with someone else. Raz, equally accustomed to solitude, slept not at all. But it was all right. He needed little sleep, and he enjoyed watching her. It especially pleased him when she would bump into him and wake, and a slow smile would dawn upon her face as she realized where she was.

As he thought of her, he found that he began to understand

the passion of Solomon's florid prose. Her lips were like new wine, and her scent was intoxicating. Her smile like the trembling of fresh blossoms in the morning breeze. Her timid touch was like the caress of meadow grass, and her eyes were as changing as the clouds.

She had come to this bed a virgin. He felt both honored and strangely devastated. It was painful to know that she had given herself so completely to him, when he could not repay her trust in kind.

She was so beautiful. So trusting. So unsuspecting. He swore to himself that he'd find some way to protect her, whatever the cost to him and his family. Somewhere around midnight, he realized that he would give his life for her.

His life, but not his soul. He had sold that long ago.

Chapter Four

It was almost midnight when Raz's keys rattled in the door. The sound woke Giselle, who had been dozing on the sofa. She stretched and rose to greet him. "Your dinner's in the 'fridge. Why don't you take a shower while I heat it up?"

He accepted her kiss, then continued past her to the bedroom. "Not hungry."

"You're sure? I made custard for dessert." She followed him into the bedroom and watched as he removed his uniform and changed into a pair of sweat pants. Then he sat on the bed, elbows on his knees. He didn't bother to reply.

She sighed. In the three months since their wedding, Raz had not had a day off. He worked every day, and often long into the evening. He frequently came home tired, or worse yet, moody. She was trying not to take it personally.

Taking a deep breath, he pressed his palms over his eyes and lay back. When he opened his eyes again, they lit on the crucifix Giselle had installed over her side of the bed earlier that evening.

His expression darkened. "What's *that* doing here?"

"I had it over my bed as a kid," she explained. "When I visited my parents yesterday, I decided I wanted it."

He glared at it. "Take it down."

She went rigid at his tone. She didn't like it, but she didn't want to fight. She turned away, reaching into her dresser for a nightgown. "Let's talk about it tomorrow."

"I said take it down," he repeated, anger resonating in his voice.

She froze, took a deep breath, then turned around deliberately, struggling to keep her voice calm. "I'm not one of your marines, Raz, so please don't give me orders. And I pray here just like you do. If you can put up your *mezuzah,* why can't I put up my crucifix?" Giselle referred to the gold box he'd mounted on the doorpost of their apartment, a wedding gift from his brother. The box contained a parchment inscribed as commanded by God in Deuteronomy: *"And thou shalt write them on the doorposts of thy house and upon thy gates. . . ."* Jews touched the *mezuzah* each time they entered or left their homes, remembering God's commandments for his people.

"The *mezuzah* isn't incompatible with your faith," he retorted, his voice tight with anger. "It isn't the last thing your ancestors saw before their throats were cut by Crusaders."

She stared at him. What was wrong with him? He was usually very open-minded about her religion. He'd even attended Mass with her last Sunday.

He glared at her, seemingly determined to press the argument. "How would you feel if I was a Muslim and I kept throwing Muhammad in your face?"

"I wouldn't be as intolerant as you're being," she retorted before she could stop herself.

"I don't want to be looking at that *thing* every night before I go to sleep," he snarled. "It's morbid."

She stiffened. "It's not morbid! That *thing* depicts God's greatest expression of love for humanity. You may not believe that, but I do, and I have a right to have it in my home."

"You can have whatever you want, but don't impose it on me." He rose. "I'll be sleeping on the sofa until it comes down."

She stared after him, watching as he took a pillow and a blanket from the bed and headed for the living room. "Oh, all right!" She removed the cross from the wall, putting it in her nightstand drawer. "There. You have your way."

He glanced back at her, then slowly forced himself to return.

Giselle watched him as he returned his blanket to its place across the foot of the bed. He sat with the pillow across his lap, resting his elbows on it and staring off into space.

Well, whatever it was, it looked like he wanted to be left alone. Giselle decided to take a shower. She stripped and put her clothes in the hamper, crossing naked to the bathroom. He didn't even look up.

She sighed, closing the door behind her. Married life was taking a lot of getting used to. On one hand, the good times with Raz were the best she'd had in her life. She loved waking up in his arms every morning, looked forward to resting in his arms every night. If anything, the passion between them had intensified.

On the other hand, he was gone too much of the time. As an only child, she was independent enough to find ways to entertain herself. Still, she couldn't help missing him and resenting the amount of time he spent away from her. Her mother had warned her of this, she reminded herself, and she'd argued that she could handle it. But she hadn't realized how neglected she would feel.

And she'd been totally unprepared for his black moods, the nights like tonight when he came home exhausted and angry. He'd just sit on their bed, wrestling silently with his demons, the problems he could not talk about. Lately, it was getting worse, manifesting itself in flashes of temper that surprised and sometimes frightened her.

Whatever was on his mind, she decided, it was something dark, something painful. And she hated not knowing what it was.

Her life with her mother had taught her to detach, to walk away and let the other person's problem be their problem. When her mother drank or got nasty, Giselle would just leave the room and do something else. But she'd come to see that her withdrawal had probably only fueled her mother's loneliness, the root of her drinking problem. It was a vicious cycle, Giselle realized, that had ended with the two of them feeling like strangers.

It was not a pattern she wanted to continue with Raz.

She finished her shower and went back into the bedroom. He was still sitting on the bed, but the cross was back in its place on the wall. The sight of it tugged at her heartstrings. Rounding the bed, she quickly donned her nightgown, then climbed up on the bed behind him and wrapped her arms around his shoulders. "Can you talk about it?"

He shook his head, and the silence stood between them like a wall.

"All right." She began kneading his tense shoulders. "Do you have to think about it right now? Why don't you lie down and let me give you a back rub?"

He reached up and squeezed her fingers, then pulled away.

That hurt. But it hurt worse to see him in pain.

She came around in front of him and knelt on the floor between his feet, looking up at him. "Tell me what you want me to do."

"There's nothing you can do," he told her, his voice sounding as if it came from inside a long, dark tunnel.

"Daddy would sometimes be depressed when he had to make a hard choice," she mused. "But never anything like this."

"Your father never had to make this kind of choice." His gaze bored into her eyes, and she realized he wasn't just angry. He was furious.

Maybe he just needed to vent. She decided to play along, give him an avenue of release for his anger. "How would you know?" she argued, provoking him deliberately. "He had to order ships into combat once, and he knew he was sending some of those men to their deaths. I know, because he talked about that when he signed the orders."

A new look came into his eyes—almost like fear. He rose abruptly, heading for the living room. "I don't want to talk about your father."

She followed him. "I heard him agonizing about it for hours after the decision was made. What could possibly be worse than that?"

He turned to face her, and his eyes were haunted again, full of that frightening, hollow look. "You can't begin to imagine."

He started to turn away again, but she caught his arm. "What do you mean?" She was terrified by the look on his face. Something was very wrong. "Raz, what's going on? Tell me!"

He pulled away from her, and with a wild movement, swept a china flower vase off a nearby stand. It struck the wall and shattered. He spun to face her, catching her arms so that she was forced to look into his terrible black eyes. "Your daddy never had to pretend to be something he wasn't!" he shouted, his face red and terrifying. "He never had to choose . . ." He broke off, choking on the words he couldn't say.

She stared at him, her concern for him erupting into fear. "Raz, what's going on? What could possibly be tearing you up like this?"

He released her suddenly and took a deep breath, as if realizing he'd said too much. His eyes shuttered themselves, and he turned away, heading for the front door.

She raced ahead of him, blocking his path. "Don't walk away from me!"

"Get out of my way." His voice was clipped, tightly under control.

She stood fast, defying him to force her. "You're my husband, Raz Chayil. Whatever you're into, I'm into with you. If you can't tell me what it is, I'll live with that. But you're not going to shut me out."

He took her by the shoulders, gently but firmly pushing her out of his way. In desperation, she threw out the only card she still held. "If you walk out this door," she warned, "I'll walk out right behind you. I'm sure your marines will love the show."

He stopped. "You wouldn't."

She looked him squarely in the eye, daring him to disregard her. "I most certainly would." She was wearing only a filmy negligee, so the threat carried some weight.

He stared at her, speechless, for a long moment. Then, finally, his mood broke and he began to laugh. Relieved, she laughed with him.

He tipped up her chin and kissed her. "I don't think you'll ever cease to amaze me, Mrs. Chayil."

Late that night, when she was asleep, Raz pulled her into his arms, curling his body around hers and savoring her satiny warmth against his skin. Her hair smelled like warm honey; he buried his face in it and breathed deeply.

No matter whose idea it was, this marriage was the best thing that had ever happened to him. And the worst. Gili was a constant distraction. Too many times during the day he was tempted to march down the hall to her office and lock the door, shutting the world out and them safely inside. He couldn't get enough of her voice, her eyes, her smile, her touch.

She was his Delilah; more and more, he found himself wanting to let down his guard, to tell her things she mustn't ever hear. And there were many who might try to use her to find his weaknesses. The thought terrified him, because it just might work.

"I'm walking a tightrope, Gili," he whispered into her hair, too quietly to be heard. "Sooner or later, I'm going to be pushed off. Will you forgive me when I fall?"

She didn't respond, only mumbled something in her sleep and pressed against him.

❖ ❖ ❖

She found it hidden among a row of classics on Raz's book-shelf, tucked in so deeply, it was all but invisible: The *Epic of Gilgamesh*, an ancient poem believed by some to support the Bible's account of Noah's Ark. It had English footnotes, but the text was printed in the original Akkadian, an ancient language that was grandfather to most modern Semitic tongues. The language was interesting in that, even though for centuries it had existed only on cuneiform tablets, enough was known that linguists today had discerned how to speak it.

From the condition of the book, Raz had read it more than once. The dog-eared pages had notes in the margins and lightly penciled numbers beside each line. Written Akkadian looked like a series of scratches and arrows—most people would mistake it for doodles if they saw it on a piece of paper. Giselle was surprised Raz knew the language; as far as she understood, it was dead to all but a few thousand dedicated linguists and archaeologists scattered at various universities around the globe.

She'd learned Akkadian on her own at Yale by auditing a few classes. At the time, she'd intended to use it in her master's thesis. But then she decided to attend Georgetown University, instead, so she'd never put the knowledge to any use.

But now she could! The thought of sharing a secret language with Raz pleased her immensely. They could whisper to one another without fear of being overheard. Exchange intimacies in public without worry of embarrassment. Gossip without a thought of being caught.

She resolved to surprise him that night by whispering an endearment to him during a quiet moment.

But she was asleep before he got home, and it had slipped her mind by morning.

❖ ❖ ❖

It was Raz's first day off since the weekend of their wedding, and Giselle had the day all planned. They'd spent most of the morning sleeping in, a much-needed recharge for Raz's spent batteries. After a relaxed start to the day, they were now off for a quick shopping trip to pick up a birthday gift for Giselle's mother; next, they would catch a ferry to the Isle of Capri. They would have lunch near the Blue Grotto, then spend the night in a hotel at the foot of Monte Solaro. It sounded perfect.

The only problem was that they were being followed.

Raz had noticed the car just after leaving the embassy, then again several blocks later, when they turned toward the shopping center. He glanced at Giselle, but she wasn't paying attention. Her mind was on other things.

"Maybe she'd like a locket," she mused. "No, let's wait on that until we can put a picture of a baby inside." She smiled at him warmly.

He couldn't help smiling back. "I like the thought, Gili, but let's not rush things," he told her. "I want you all to myself for a while."

On the pretext of looking for the perfect space, he circled the parking lot twice. The car was still with them, laying back, patiently waiting for him to stop. He turned down a row of cars, driving slowly until the car came up behind him. When he recognized the driver, he relaxed slightly and pulled into a vacant parking space. He gave the man in the other car a slight nod as he passed.

"Go on in," he told Giselle. "I'll meet you in the jewelry store. I need to pick up a few things over at that men's store."

"Why don't I go with you?" she suggested. "I kind of like the idea of shopping for my husband."

There was no way to turn her down without hurting her feelings, so he took her hand. "Let's do the jewelry store first, in case we don't have time for both."

Inside the store, he let her take the lead, following her to a counter and glancing at the items she pointed out to him. A saleslady came toward them, and Giselle asked her to bring out several pieces for closer inspection.

Once she was thoroughly engrossed in her project, he edged away, pretending to be browsing. The man had come inside, taking a position at another counter close to the front window. Raz casually glanced around. No one in the store seemed to be paying attention.

He started at the end of the counter and worked his way toward the man. A saleswoman approached, smiling. He shook his head slightly, and she turned her attention to another customer. Raz moved closer to the man, as if curious about the object of his attention.

"It's a beautiful piece, is it not?" the man asked for the benefit of a passing customer.

Raz nodded, waiting until they were alone. "What is it?" he asked quietly, no longer speaking Italian. Anyone who might overhear them would still not understand.

"It is good to see you, too," the man told him wryly. "I was sent to bring you warning. We have information that you are under investigation. ONI," he added in English. Office of Naval Intelligence.

So the wheels were turning. Raz felt a sense of inevitability overtake him. It was too soon, too soon. He'd hoped to have a few more months of relative peace with Gili before the betrayals began.

"It is standard practice to investigate a man to whom they intend to assign a particularly sensitive duty." He spoke calmly, despite the tide of desperation that lapped at him, threatening to pull him down. "It is as we've hoped."

"So we believe as well," the man agreed. "However, I must ask. Have you done anything recently that may have aroused suspicion?"

"No." Raz answered with certainty. If anything, since his

marriage, he had been even more cautious. The fear of Giselle discovering his activities was even greater than his concern of being caught by his superiors.

"We will not contact you again until the investigation is concluded," the man said, then turned to meet his eyes. "Please be cautious."

❖ ❖ ❖

Giselle settled on a garnet tennis bracelet. While the saleswoman was wrapping it, she looked around for Raz.

There he was, at the front of the store, talking with another man. She could only see part of the man's profile, but he looked like someone she knew. She tried, but couldn't place him. If only his thick beard didn't obscure so much of his face.

Accepting the package from the saleswoman, she headed toward them, intending to slip in beside her husband and wait for an introduction.

Raz glanced up and saw her approaching. He seemed startled by her nearness. He spoke softly to his companion, who broke off and hurried away, never looking back.

Raz smiled at Giselle, holding out his hand. "What did we buy your mother?"

"A tennis bracelet." She gave his fingers a squeeze. "Who was that? He looked familiar."

His shrug was far too casual. "He's a friend from my tour in Austria," he told her, watching her reactions closely.

"No he's not," she whispered, stopping in the middle of the sidewalk. It hurt that he had lied to her. Worse, he had done it so easily. Had he told other lies without her knowing?

He closed his eyes, and an anguished furrow creased his forehead. "I'm sorry, Gili. The man's an informant. He occasionally gives us information about terrorist activity. Please forget that you ever saw him. It's very important that he remain anonymous."

She nodded, reluctantly accepting what he'd told her. "I didn't really see his face anyway."

"Good." He reached for her hand again. "Are you ready? We have to hustle if we want to catch the next ferry."

❖ ❖ ❖

The afternoon was idyllic. Several times, Giselle caught Raz staring at her, his eyes lingering over her features as if memorizing her expressions. He touched her often, his caresses drawn out, his hugs too long, too tight.

She found herself catching his mood, wanting to save each moment as if on film, to be replayed again and again at a later time. Their time alone was too precious, too infrequent, to be treated casually.

And that night, as he held her, she could almost feel his heart echoing inside her own chest, like waves beating against the walls of the *Grota Azzura* that afternoon.

She was drowning in him; he was filling every empty part of her until she thought she'd explode. They were becoming one.

❖ ❖ ❖

The feeling lasted all the next day as they returned home. Their eyes would meet, and it was as if she knew what he was thinking. She could feel his love for her, the joy he took in being with her. When she mentioned children again, she could see that he wanted them, too.

But beneath it all, something was desperately wrong. It was there behind his eyes, behind that smile that haunted her from the other side of a line she couldn't cross.

When they reached home, she found that she couldn't ignore it any longer. She stared at him as he unpacked his suitcase. "What's going on, Raz?"

He glanced at her. "What do you mean?"

"You know what I mean. Something's wrong. And don't say it's nothing, because I can see it in your eyes."

"Gili, we've talked about this," he pointed out. "There are things I can't tell you. It goes with the job." He turned away, taking a shirt to his dresser.

She moved between him and the drawer, pushing it closed with her hip. "I'm not talking about your job, and neither are you," she accused. "This is about us. I can see it on your face when you tell me how much you love me."

He stared down at her, his face slowly becoming as hard and blank as stone. "Don't push this, Gili. I love you. Isn't that enough?"

"No," she whispered. "Not when I know you're afraid that something will come between us. Are you in danger?"

He stood there, not answering, and she could almost see the link that had joined them stretch, then snap. Suddenly she was alone again. She hugged herself, suddenly feeling cold.

He reached up and touched a tear from her cheek, then pulled her against him. "I do love you," he repeated. "Whatever else you might come to believe about me, please always believe that."

She resisted at first, then slowly wrapped her arms around his waist, crying against his shoulder.

❖ ❖ ❖

That night, Giselle was awakened from a troubled sleep by the sound of urgent whispers. Sleepily, she reached for Raz and found his pillow vacant.

She opened her eyes cautiously, half expecting to be blinded by the bedside lamp, but finding it was still dark. In the next room, illuminated by a small table lamp, she could make out the dim figures of her husband and another man. They were talking rapidly, their voices hushed but animated.

Fully awake now, she rolled quietly to her side and tried not to eavesdrop. But she couldn't help it; the voices came too clearly through the silence of the bedroom. Besides, surely it wasn't classified or they wouldn't be talking here, with her in the next room.

". . . scheduled for 1300 on the eighteenth," the man was saying. "You'll be in charge of security."

"The terrorists will be out in force if they know about this," Raz commented.

"Count on it," the man agreed. "We need you to develop a plan for every contingency. Select several potential meeting places. Map out various possible routes to each location, and arrange for decoy cars. The actual route and destination will be chosen just before Air Force One touches down, at which point you will dispatch the decoys and coordinate the activities of your marines with those of the Secret Service."

Air Force One! The Secret Service! The president of the United States was coming to Italy! Giselle had to fight to keep from sitting up in bed. It could only mean one thing. The Mideast peace talks were about to begin in earnest!

She was too excited to hear any more of the discussion. Her husband was in charge of security for negotiations that would take the human race into the next age. The honor implied by the assignment made her heart swell with pride.

Then Raz was closing the door and coming to bed. She tried to feign sleep, but he laughed when he saw her face.

"How much did you hear?" he asked.

"Only that the president is coming," she whispered, trying to sound nonchalant. "And that my husband will be protecting him."

"I'll expect you to keep that little tidbit to yourself." Climbing into bed beside her, he gathered her against him in preparation for sleep. He squeezed her tightly, his chest expanding against her back as he gave a long, contented sigh.

Or was it contented? His muscles were rigid, his arms a band of steel around her. She wished she could see his expression. Did whatever was wrong have something to do with this upcoming visit? No. It couldn't. After all, Raz hadn't known about it until tonight.

Or had he?

"Is this what you couldn't talk about this afternoon?" she asked. "Is the president in some kind of danger?"

"It's a dangerous job," he answered cryptically.

Was there something ominous in his tone?

She started to ask another question, but he pressed a finger against her lips, brushing a kiss to her cheek.

"Shhhhhh. . . ."

❖ ❖ ❖

In the following days, the embassy was a flurry of activity. The number of dispatches and communiqués had increased beyond NSA Gaeta's capacity, and the embassy was quietly taking up the slack. Envoys hurried in and out, and telephone traffic nearly quintupled.

Only those with the highest clearance—and Giselle—had a clue what was really about to happen. The story widely given to explain the sudden rush was an upcoming visit from the secretary of state. Important enough to justify a lot of fuss—even an increase in security, since such a visit would likely draw protestors. But it wasn't anything to attract the interest of the SOI.

Giselle found herself working overtime, handling most of the routine documents to free the ambassador and his core team to deal with the upcoming meeting. It was frustrating, knowing that important things were happening, and being stuck with the scut work.

Worse, she missed her husband desperately. He spent nearly twenty hours a day closeted with members of his hastily-assembled security team. And when he did come home, he was exhausted, moody, and uncommunicative, either falling into a fitful slumber as soon as he touched the bed, or staring silently into the darkness until the time came to rise. If he spoke to her at all, his words were clipped, and his anger flared easily.

Maybe it was just the tremendous responsibility that had been conferred upon him. How must it be to know that the president's life depended on his making no mistakes?

"The terrorists will be out in force," Raz had said on learning of this assignment. And he and his team would be expected to lay down their lives, if necessary, to stop them. That was it, Giselle decided. That must be what was bothering him.

And rightly so. There were dozens of terrorist groups who would move heaven and earth to stop these meetings. Any one of them alone would be troubling, but coordinated by the Sword of Islam, they posed a terrifying threat.

And God alone knew what information the SOI had already gained and passed along its network. They seemed to have sources everywhere, even in the Pentagon. According to the last conversation she'd overheard between her father and Arn, it was now believed that they were connected with the government of a country with resources. Their intelligence was just too good to have come from moles and informants.

But who? The SOI seemed to have access to information-gathering equipment and technology that was beyond the reach of most countries in the Arabian Gulf. Some former Soviet nation, then? But what would they have to gain? If the aggressions in the Middle East continued, it was just a matter of time before there would be all-out nuclear war, right on Eastern Europe's doorstep. Surely no one wanted that.

The upshot was that, after years of trying, nobody seemed to know who was behind the SOI, or how they were resourced. Even the investigation at Giselle's father's command had come up empty. While it was certain that the missile had been issued to the Sixth Fleet, no one could say how it ended up in the wrong hands. All records had disappeared without a trace. The source, whoever it was, must have known exactly how to cover his tracks.

But how?

Even after six years, the only thing that was certain about the SOI was that they had to be stopped before they brought the world to its knees.

With each day that passed, Giselle became increasingly fretful. Nothing of any magnitude had happened at the embassy in years, and since no one was aware of the upcoming summit, adherence to security protocol was far too lax.

Already among the documents Giselle had handled, she'd found a mention of the peace summit in a memo that was not properly classified. When she'd shown the document to Raz, he'd tracked the error to its source stateside, and recommended that the man's clearance be revoked.

But the damage may have already been done, if not by someone here, then elsewhere, by any number of people involved directly or indirectly in the upcoming meetings. Giselle was beginning to imagine minions of the Sword of Islam everywhere, listening behind doors, tapping the phones, reading even the most sensitive coded documents.

Raz and his security team had only three weeks to make Italy safe for the meeting. It wasn't enough time.

❖ ❖ ❖

"Don't come back to the apartment for the rest of the day," Raz told her apologetically one morning as they dressed for their respective duties. "The conference rooms are all booked, so my team will be working here today. I'm sorry for the inconvenience."

"I don't mind. Just let me know me when it's safe to come back." Giselle slipped a comfortable dress over her head, then crossed the room to Raz and straightened his ribbons. Her fingers lingered over the Navy and Marine Corps ribbon, representing the medal her father had conferred upon him for saving her life. The real medal was displayed with the others in a glass case above his chest of drawers. Except on formal occasions, ribbon bars were worn instead.

Raz smiled, dropping his hands to her waist. "I'm also sorry we haven't had much time together lately," he murmured, drawing her in for a kiss.

Giselle sighed, enjoying the warmth of his gaze, the pang of longing at the feel of his kiss. She gave him an impish look. "I haven't missed it a bit."

He laughed. He was already late for inspection, but his marines could wait a few minutes.

"When this is over, I want us to take at least a week off and go away somewhere where nobody wants anything from you."

"I'd like that too." He managed a smile. When this was over, he fully expected that she'd either hate the sight of him or be a widow.

"I don't know if I've told you this, but I'm so proud of you."

His heart clenched at the sweetness on her face. He picked up her hand and kissed it, fighting the tears that pricked behind his eyes. "I love you, Gili. More than I ever thought possible."

"Isn't it exciting?" she asked, a childlike eagerness in her voice. "What's about to happen will change the world, and you're going to be right in the thick of it. Your name might go down in history."

"Exciting," he agreed, but without much feeling.

Suddenly, she was quiet—too quiet. He turned to find her watching him closely. And again, she'd seen too much.

"We've never talked about how you feel about this," she observed slowly, cautiously drawing him out. "What do you think about what they're trying to do?"

He saw a trap opening and tried to sidestep it. "There's nothing to talk about," he said simply. "I have my assignment. It doesn't matter what I think."

"It matters to me," she said, still watching his expression. "I'd like to hear your opinion."

He winced, wishing there was a way to avoid this discussion. Not here. Not now. But she wasn't going to let this go. He shrugged, picking his words carefully. "I think it's a mistake."

She was shocked. "Why?"

"What they're about to do won't work. Remember the last peace negotiations? More people died during that time than during the Intifada. This will be no different, and who knows how many innocent people will die before anyone admits it," he told her. "Arabs and Jews will always be enemies, no matter how many treaties the governments sign. It's dangerous to pretend otherwise."

"I never knew you felt that way."

He took her hands. "I wish you could come with me to the West Bank, Gili, to see how the people live. The homes have sealed rooms to protect the families from toxic gas. Even the babies have their own gas masks. You can't walk down the street or get on a bus without thinking that around the next corner there might be someone waiting to kill you, just because you're there." He stared at her, willing her to understand. "You've never lived that way, Gili, and neither have I, but I have family who live with it every day."

She wasn't sure what to make of this. "I'd think you'd be happy about this, then. It's a step toward ending that violence. It's a step toward finally making peace."

He shook his head. "It's naive to think Arabs and Jews could coexist peacefully. How can they share holy ground when each feels the other is defiling it?" He paused, considering his words. "Anything that brings the lion together with the lamb can only end in slaughter."

He saw from her expression that he'd worried her again.

"Maybe you should have refused this assignment," she considered. "If you feel so strongly about it." Then her eyes met his, and the doubt he saw there made him almost physically ill. "You'd never do anything to . . ."

He cut her off. "I'm a soldier. I follow orders," he assured her. "What else can I do?"

❖ ❖ ❖

It was past midnight. Giselle waited patiently in the embassy library, wondering when it would be all right to slip into her quarters. She wanted nothing more than to kiss her husband and slip into a nice, hot bath.

She wanted, too, to continue her discussion with Raz, to understand the things he'd tried to tell her. Their talk had ended abruptly, with Raz realizing the time and rushing off for inspection.

She'd been late for work as well, and Amory had glared at her when she arrived. "Of all times to be late. . . . We're swamped today."

"Something came up at home." She'd tried to look apologetic, but managed only to blush profusely.

He'd sighed and shrugged theatrically. "Next time, remind me not to hire a newlywed."

Giselle had turned away to hide her embarrassment, promising to work late in order to make up for her tardiness. And she had, putting in four extra hours after the evening meal.

They'd finally closed up shop two hours ago, and she'd drifted over to their quarters, pausing at the front door and wondering whether to knock. Just then, her father had come out.

"Sorry, sweetheart, but it looks like your husband will be busy for at least another hour," he'd told her, giving her a kiss on the forehead. Then he checked his watch and lowered his voice. "Listen, the *Lamar* is deploying tonight. I should be back in several days. Check in with your mother a few times while I'm gone, won't you?"

Giselle had nodded and sent her father away with a kiss on the cheek, though some part of her had wanted to protest that he should be here, where he could help if there was trouble. What could draw her father away from Italy at a time like this? Wasn't he supposed to be involved in the summit?

She didn't want to admit it, but part of her sensed that something was about to go terribly, desperately wrong.

She forced the worry from her mind, and turned her attention to the shelves of books. But a long day of responding to public inquiries made the thought of reading unappealing. Unable to find anything that grabbed her attention, Giselle finally decided to wander back toward the apartment, hoping that by now the meeting was breaking up.

When she got to the door, she rapped loudly. Hearing no answer, she slowly opened the door. No one was inside.

A few minutes later, she was in the tub, her feet propped up by the faucet as she settled into the steaming water. She dripped in some of her favorite bath oil, enjoying the way it spread over the water and clung to her skin. Soaking a large natural sponge, she wrung it over her legs, wondering if she had the energy for a shave. She decided against it and sank back until the water soaked the hair at her nape.

She hoped Raz would be home soon. She needed to put her arms around him, to hear him reassure her that everything was fine. Her husband was an honorable man; surely there was no reason to doubt him. It was just the stress of this important assignment that had made him so edgy lately.

She realized abruptly that Raz was probably out looking for her, wanting to let her know that she could come back to the apartment. She should phone the guard station and ask them to find him and let him know she was already here.

The thought of leaving the warmth of her bath made her

groan, but she pulled herself out of the water. Donning a robe, she headed for the phone.

Raz's desk lamp was glowing from the far side of the living room. She crossed to his desk and sat, picking up the phone and dialing the number of the guardhouse.

A scrap of paper lay beneath the beam of the lamp. It bore a handwritten list of numbers: 10 2 5, 8 18 14, 78 15 1. . . . It seemed like some sort of mathematical equation or puzzle, Giselle decided. Or maybe map coordinates. . . .

On the other side of the desk, she noticed the *Epic of Gilgamesh,* propped up, along with a few notebooks, between two bookends. Waiting on hold, Giselle picked up the book, thinking she'd read a few pages just to stay in practice. She was flipping through idly when a passport dropped onto her lap.

A guard came on the line, and Giselle explained the situation. He told her politely that he'd see what he could do. Thanking him, Giselle hung up the phone.

The passport was Raz's—at least the photo was his. But the name was different. Rashid ibn Kasim, it said. A Palestinian from Jordan. She frowned. Why would Raz have such a document? A false name, a false passport . . . What was going on?

She flipped through a few more pages of the book, noticing again that each line was hand-numbered in the margin. She had done the same for study in her foreign language texts at Yale. It allowed her to reference a page, line, and word in her scholarly papers.

Her eyes dropped to the piece of paper Raz had left on the desk. That's what the numbers were! It was a code! She started deciphering, intending to check a couple of words, just to see if she was right.

The first word was a greeting: "Brother." She went on, re-peating each word aloud as she found it, translating to English as she went along. The first phrase stunned her.

"The leaders we wish to kill . . ."

Swallowing, she read on. ". . . will be delivered into our hands in eight days." Eight days! That was the day of the meeting!

"You must contact Seif. . . ." Giselle paused. The name meant "sword."

A chill swept over her. What was she reading?

Unable to stop herself, she kept reading. ". . . so that he may be ready." The missive went on to give the potential locations of the meetings and the various possible routes, concluding, "I myself shall disarm the guards and assist Seif as I may. For the Glory of Allah, Rashid"

Stunned, she took a long deep breath. "Raz, no. . . ." They were going to assassinate the delegates—and the president! And Raz was going to help them do it! How could that be?

Her hands shook as she put away the passport, replacing the book and paper. She pushed away from the desk, backing across the room. Raz would be here any minute. She couldn't let him know what she had seen.

A sound made her jump. Turning, she discovered a shadowy form near the door.

"Raz, . . ." she started, trying to look glad to see him. "I was just calling around trying to find you."

He emerged into the dim light of the living room. He looked exhausted; his dark eyes had bags under them, and his uniform jacket was stained with perspiration. "Playing spy again, Giselle?" he asked, his voice more tired than angry. "I thought you'd learned your lesson."

Deny, her instincts told her. "What do you mean?" Giselle tried to sound calm, as if she hadn't read a thing.

He sighed. "Don't lie to me, Gili. You were reading aloud."

For a moment Giselle was ashamed, feeling like a child caught doing something wrong. But then she remembered what she had read. "How could you help someone kill the president? How could you . . ." She stopped herself, not wanting to voice the rest of the questions reeling in her mind. How could the man she loved be a traitor? How could he betray everything she believed in? How could he have deceived her, deceived her father, deceived everyone who believed in him?

He stepped slowly toward her, his eyes the same unfathomable black she'd seen before—that hollow, haunted look. Only now, they were cold, so very cold.

"What am I going to do with you?" he asked, a hardness she'd never heard before thickening his voice. He gripped her wrist roughly.

A chill shot through her as she realized what he was thinking. She twisted away, the slick film of bath oil on her skin making it easy to break his grip. She was halfway across the living room when he tripped her from behind. She hit the floor with a stunning force.

He had her pinned before she could recover, his insignia pins raking her skin through her robe. "Don't fight me, Gili," he whispered rapidly. "Trust me, I won't hurt you." But even as he said it, his hand began to close around her throat.

As she fought to break his grip, part of her considered the situation with a surreal dispassion. How would Raz explain her death to her father? An assault? Her body would be found in a ditch somewhere, strangled by an unknown attacker.

"No!" Heart thrashing, she struck his arm, breaking his leverage. She forced her gaze to meet his, searching for a hint of the sweet, gentle man she'd thought she married, even as she fought to keep his fingers from regaining their hold on her throat. "Please. . . ."

His eyes were darker and more frightening than she'd ever seen them. "What choice have you left me?" With those words, his fingers tightened on her windpipe, squeezing off the air. She gasped convulsively, but couldn't get a breath.

He was killing her, just as he'd killed those men six years ago. In a moment, the darkness would close around her, and . . .

No! Something inside of her snapped, and with a final effort, she managed to pry his hand away. Quickly, she crossed her hands over her neck as he'd once taught her, protecting her throat. Air flooded into her lungs, burning all the way down.

He caught her wrists, encircling them with one rock-solid grip and pulling them up over her head. She thrashed, twisting her body to block his hands with her shoulders, but she was still pinned and helpless beneath his weight. She knew that in a moment, he would have her throat again. And there was nothing she could do to stop it.

Unless . . . The only weapon she had left to her was persuasion. It seemed unlikely to work, but she had no other options.

Suddenly she stopped struggling, going limp in his grasp. "Wait." She forced her voice to sound calm. "You don't have to do this. I won't turn you in."

Her words caused him to hesitate. She seized the opportunity and kept talking, hoping that something she said would somehow get through to him. "There was a time when you could have turned *me* in, remember? When you found out I was eavesdropping on Daddy? But you risked everything to protect my secret. I owe you one."

Still gripping her wrists tightly, he stared at her for a long moment, as if uncertain what to do.

"I won't turn you in," she repeated desperately. "I love you, Raz. You're my husband, and I believe in you. You're the most honorable man I know. I have to believe you're doing the right thing, even if I don't understand it."

He paused for a moment, searching her eyes as if he wanted to believe her. But then he shook his head and brought his hand to her throat again. "I'm sorry."

This time she didn't fight him. She lay still, fighting all her instincts to struggle, feeling her body slowly growing heavy. As darkness began to shroud her, she mouthed the words, "I believe in you."

Just as she was about to black out, he let go, releasing her hands and throat and rolling away. Her throat flamed again as the air surged in, and she rolled helplessly to her side, coughing so violently that she retched, still desperately unable to get a breath. She nearly passed out before she finally managed to fill her lungs.

It took several moments before she was finally able to move again. When she turned, he was sitting beside her, his hand solicitously on her hip. "Are you all right?" he asked, his voice shaking with emotion.

She nodded slowly, and he pulled her into his arms, rocking her back and forth. She tugged her robe more tightly around her, but didn't resist him.

She let him hold her for what seemed like a long time, felt his tears drop on her face, and wondered just what kind of man she'd married.

He pulled her up until she was sitting beside him. He looked deep into her eyes, and she was again surprised at how little she could read of what he was thinking. "Did you mean it?" he asked quietly. "You won't turn me in?"

She nodded again, and this time he slowly bent to kiss her. His lips quivered against hers. "Thank you," he whispered, almost too quietly to hear, "for trusting me."

Trusting him? The sheer craziness of the thought made her want to laugh. And yet she had trusted him—implicitly—and only a day ago. She nodded again.

Gently, he took her hand, kissing each finger. His eyes suddenly seemed warm again. "You don't know what this means to me, Gili."

Rubbing her bruised throat, she nodded again, responding as he seemed to expect.

He saw her gesture and reached out, gently running his fingers over the marks he'd left just moments before. It took effort for Giselle not to flinch away.

"Everything has to seem normal, do you understand?" he

told her. "If you disappeared it would raise suspicions, and that's the last thing I need right now." He paused. "You're doing the right thing. I swear it—trust me."

She nodded again.

"Are you sure you're all right?" His eyes searched hers, and she had to fight the urge to draw away, to run from the man who knew her better than she knew herself. Seeing bruises darkening at her wrist, he lifted it slowly to his lips. As he kissed her she stared at him—at the dark, curly hair that she'd loved to comb with her fingers, at the hard, firm jaw that made him look so powerfully handsome. She held her breath as he brushed her cheek with his knuckle.

The Raz she knew could never use his strength to hurt her. Who is this man? she wondered.

Rashid! The passport, the signature on the coded document . . . Suddenly, she didn't even know her own husband's name! A chill swept over her, filling her with waves of nausea.

He felt her shiver, and before she realized what he was going to do, he lifted her and carried her to the bedroom. Feeling herself on the verge of hysteria, she gripped his shoulders to keep from screaming as he lay her on the bed. If he tried to make love to her, she knew that all pretense of cooperation would be over.

But then he did something he'd never done before. Drawing the covers up around her shoulders, he moved away, taking a blanket with him and settling into a chair by the door.

❖ ❖ ❖

The next morning, Raz dressed as usual—as if nothing at all abnormal had happened the night before.

She watched his movements. His muscular body was as graceful as a wolf. And as deadly.

He saw that she was awake and came to sit beside her. "How are you feeling?"

She nodded, wincing as her aching muscles protested when she tried to sit.

He saw the bruises on her wrists and neck and reached out as if to stroke away the marks. She quailed inwardly, but remained still, even managed to smile at his touch.

"Make sure you wear something that covers those," he said. "They might be hard to explain."

She nodded, hoping the fury she felt didn't show in her eyes.

He caressed her cheek, then bent toward her and kissed her gently. "Gili, I'm so proud of you," he whispered. "And I'm so honored that you trust me. I've never loved you more than I do right now."

She stared at him, then nodded slowly. "I love you, too," she whispered, finding her throat too sore to speak.

He winced, then forced a smile. "I'm due at the guard station right away—no time for breakfast," he told her. "Bring me a cup of coffee and a sweet roll before you go to work." The request was casual, almost offhand, but there was an edge to his voice. He was giving her an order.

Giselle stared at him as he left, wondering again just who it was she'd really married. Last night, he'd nearly killed her, and today he was ordering her around like a servant. She wondered if she'd ever really known him.

As soon as she heard the front door close, she let out a long breath. Her hands were shaking, and she felt sick.

Her father . . . he'd know what to do! She rolled out of bed and hurried out to the desk. But the phone was gone. Raz had hidden it.

She didn't have time to find it. She crossed to the front door, peering between the curtains. It took a moment to find him, but there he was, waiting in the doorway of the apartment next door. This was a test. He had left her alone, and now he was watching to see if she would try to betray him.

She returned to the bedroom and dressed quickly, a plan

forming in her mind. She picked up her purse and ran to the kitchen. Over the sink there was a small window, more for ventilation than sunlight. Raz would have thought of this and dismissed it, believing it too small to serve as a viable exit. All of the other windows were in plain view of his hiding place.

The window opened by crank, and Giselle turned it frantically, cringing at the groans it made as she opened it wider than it had gone in years. Dropping her purse out the window, she climbed up on the counter and went out feet first. The window frame was painfully tight around her hips. She nearly got stuck, but she braced her knees against the wall, and with a desperate push, managed to get through. She hung by her hands for a moment, then dropped, as silently as she could, to the ground.

Picking up her purse, she hurried off, moving behind the apartment building, then the barracks where Raz's marines were quartered.

Pausing at the corner of the second building, Giselle carefully peered out at Raz. He hadn't gone in to check on her yet, but she could see that he was growing impatient. He checked his watch, then stared at the door again.

While he was looking the other way, Giselle hurried across the open lot, ducking behind cars until she reached her own.

❖ ❖ ❖

It wasn't until Raz heard the engine start that he realized what Giselle was doing.

Cursing, he raced toward her car, slamming a hand down on the windshield as he tried to wrench the door open.

She jerked the stick shift into reverse and peeled out, with him running alongside the car. Then she forced it into first and squealed forward, spinning the steering wheel so that he had to leap out of the way to keep from being hit.

She was out of the compound before he could get to a radio and give the order to close the gates.

Furious, he commandeered a passing humvee, and went screeching out of the compound, trying to pick up her trail.

When he couldn't see her car, he located a pay phone and dialed quickly. He gave a code and waited for the accented voice to come on. Then, urgently, he explained the situation.

"You made a grave error, not taking care of it last night," the voice replied. "You knew what had to be done."

"It would have raised suspicions if she had disappeared at a time like this," Raz argued. "She said she was going to cooperate. I thought she understood."

"And you foolishly believed her! Now our operation is in jeopardy," the man said angrily. "She must be stopped before she tells anyone what she has discovered."

What had he done? He felt sick. "She'll be headed for Gaeta. Do what you have to do."

*Chapter*Five

Giselle was halfway to Gaeta before she realized that if Raz was looking for her, her father's villa would be the first place he'd go. It probably wasn't even safe to be on this highway. She turned off at the next exit and drove to the first town she found. Parking next to a pay phone, she got out and dialed her father's number.

"Admiral Hardy's office, Lieutenant Riley speaking."

"Riley, this is Giselle." Her voice was hoarse. She cleared her throat, but it made no difference.

"Miss Hardy—or Mrs. Chayil now, isn't it?" Riley corrected himself.

Was she Mrs. Chayil? She didn't even know her own name! She rubbed her burning eyes. "Listen, I need to speak to my father."

"I'm sorry, but he's not available."

Giselle sagged. She'd forgotten what her father had told her the night before. Fighting to keep the tears from her voice, she said, "Please, Riley, it's urgent. Can you at least get him a message?"

He hesitated. "You sound upset. Are you all right?"

She wanted desperately to tell him, to just hand over this

problem and let someone else take care of it. But she didn't dare. She wasn't even supposed to know about the meeting, let alone risk mentioning it over an unsecured telephone line. She took a long breath. "I can't tell you, Riley, but trust me, this is important enough that Daddy won't mind your contacting him."

Another pause, then a sigh. "OK. I'm not supposed to do this, but I'll get a message to him. Where are you?"

She looked around, her eyes taking in the hillside village. She had been here once or twice before. "I think it's Frosinone."

"This may take awhile. Why don't you come on out here?"

"I don't think it's safe, Riley. There are people who might try to stop me."

"Stop you? Giselle, what's going on?" Riley asked urgently.

She closed her eyes, leaning against the wall beside the phone. "Please, Riley, just get my father for me."

"I'm sending the *Carabinieri* to pick you up," he decided. "Where exactly are you?"

Carabinieri! The Italian military police who served as the admiral's bodyguards when he left the facility—they would protect her, even against Raz! Relieved at the suggestion, Giselle glanced around, looking for a street sign. "I don't know the street name, but it's fairly busy," she told him. "It's probably the main street. I'm next to the first pay phone."

"Stay put," Riley instructed. "I'll have someone out there ASAP."

Giselle thanked him and hung up.

Not knowing what else to do, she paced the sidewalk near the pay phone. How difficult would it be for Riley to contact her father? What would she have to say to get him to come home?

She paced some more, composing in her mind what she would tell him. "Please, Daddy, you have to come home. Raz is in trouble." No. "Raz and I are in trouble."

No. He might not come for that. Even a family emergency would take back seat if what he was doing was important enough.

She had learned long ago that the Navy—the nation—had to come first.

"It's a matter of national security, and I can't talk to anyone else." It sounded melodramatic, but it might work if her father believed her.

She didn't see the car until it pulled up to the curb nearby.

Two men in civilian clothing got out. One was tall, dark, with piercing foreign eyes. He looked angry, frighteningly so. The second man, a black man, caught his sleeve and pointed in her direction. Uneasy, she turned and started to walk away.

"Mrs. Chayil?" the Arab called in thickly accented English. "We must ask you please to come with us." Giselle glanced back to see the black man striding toward her.

Gripping her purse against her body, Giselle bolted, racing out onto the busy street. Cars honked, tires screeched; but miraculously, she wasn't hit. On the other side, she glanced back to see the two men gesture to a second car, pointing in her direction.

She broke to her right, racing toward the next street. Reaching it, she slowed, trying to hail a passing taxi. But the cab already had passengers; it passed without slowing.

Before she could move on, the Arab appeared at her side, catching her arm. "Mrs. Chayil, you must please come with us," he repeated as he pulled her toward a waiting car. The second man hurried up, catching her other arm.

Giselle dropped to the ground, making it impossible for the men to do anything but drag her. *"Aiuto!"* she screamed to the people watching. "Help! These men are trying to rape me!"

A heavyset woman stepped forward, gripping a cane firmly and shaking it at Giselle's captors. *"Lasciare la signora solo,"* she ordered, shaking her meaty fist. "Leave the lady alone."

Giselle jammed her foot into the Arab's kneecap, breaking his grip on her arm. Twisting free of the other man, she scrambled to her feet again, racing out into the street. "Help!" she shouted, flagging the cars that swerved to avoid her. *"Aiuto!"*

A weatherworn VW pulled up next to her, and a dark-haired man with a bushy beard pushed open the passenger door for her. "Get in!"

Giselle hesitated. When he'd pulled up, for an instant she'd thought he might be someone she knew. But nothing about his face looked familiar. Was he one of them? Uncertainly, she glanced over her shoulder.

The Arab was only a few feet away. He was reaching inside his jacket, and she saw his shoulder holster plainly.

She dived into the man's car. *"Fretta—adesso!"* she shouted. "They have guns!"

The car lurched forward, nearly stalling, but then the gears caught and they sped away.

Giselle stared out the back window, breathing a sigh of relief as they pulled out of sight of the two men. *"Grazie,"* she told the driver in Italian.

"Don't thank me yet," the man said in English. "We're being followed."

She looked again, this time seeing the second car, the one the two men had run toward as she'd made her escape. It was several cars back, but gaining quickly. "Hurry!"

"It's floored already. We don't have enough car to outrun them," the driver told her.

Moments later, the other car was drawing up alongside them. As the car veered in threateningly, one of the men leaned out the window, leveling his gun at her rescuer as he gestured for them to pull over. Giselle screamed in fear for him.

Abruptly, the driver slammed on the brakes and veered onto a side road. The VW fishtailed wildly, nearly rolling onto its side. Giselle quickly fastened her seatbelt, too frightened to do anything but pray.

Moments later, the other car was behind them again, but at least the move had bought them some distance. As Giselle watched, the man with the gun leaned out the window, gesturing for them to pull over, then leveled his weapon again.

"Look out!" Giselle shouted, ducking down behind the seat.

"There's a gun in my glove compartment," the driver said grimly. "Get it out."

Hastily, Giselle complied, drawing out a military-issue Colt. She turned it in her hands. "Where did you get this?"

"Careful—it's loaded."

Giselle gripped the weapon as her father had taught her, her finger outside the trigger guard, the gun's muzzle pointed toward the floorboards.

"Do you know how to shoot?" the man asked.

Giselle's mouth dropped open. "You want me to . . ."

"It's not hard," he told her, reaching over to chamber a round. "Just aim out the sunroof and pull the trigger."

Giselle stared numbly at the weapon in her hands. She'd fired a gun before, but never at a person. Could she?

"Do it!" the man shouted. "You don't have to try to hit anyone—just give them enough of a scare to make them back off." He glanced at his rearview mirror. "Look, they're catching up again. If you don't shoot, it's all over."

With shaking hands, Giselle complied, bracing her arms against the roof of the car and squeezing the trigger. The kickback was bruising; she nearly lost her grip on the weapon. But the shot had the desired effect. Immediately, the other car slowed, giving them some much-needed distance.

Moments later, however, they sped up again. A shot rang out, shattering the rear window and burrowing into the dash. Giselle screamed as shards of glass rained down around them.

"All right," the man muttered. "If they want to play hardball, we'll drive this thing straight down their throats. Get down."

Giselle gripped the dashboard as the man executed a bootleg turn, doubling back the way they had come. A new shot glanced off the front of their car. The other car turned sharply, coming to a halt broadside, blocking the road. Both men got out, bracing their weapons, ready to fire.

"Get down!" the driver ordered again, pushing Giselle's head between her knees. He grabbed the Colt from her hands before she could react and fired two shots in rapid succession.

Seconds later, Giselle heard an explosion and peered over the dash. A fireball rolled above the other car. The two men lay on the ground several yards away. As she watched, one of them came to his knees and crawled over to help the other.

The man put the car in gear and stomped on the gas pedal, the tires spitting gravel as they picked up speed. He veered off onto the shoulder to avoid the burning car. As they passed, one of the men scrambled for his weapon, which lay on the pavement several feet away. Giselle's rescuer fired again, and the terrorist dropped to his belly, the gun still spitting bullets that tore through their car. Giselle ducked again and held her breath until they were out of range.

The driver watched his rearview mirror for a long moment, then seemed satisfied. "That should give us some breathing room."

She sighed, settling back in her seat. "I don't know how to begin to thank you."

"Start by telling me what I just got into. Who were those men?"

"Terrorists," she murmured, too numb to think better of it.

"Terrorists!" His voice registered his shock. He paused, then glanced at her. "What do they want with you?"

She glanced back at the burning car, now issuing a rolling cloud of black smoke into the sky. "My husband sent them."

The man frowned. "Why would your husband send those men after you?"

Giselle stared at him numbly as the likely answer filled her mind. He had sent them to kill her. Before she could stop herself, she was sobbing into her palms.

❖ ❖ ❖

"What are you telling me?" Admiral Hardy bellowed into the telephone.

"I don't know what happened, sir," Riley said. "She said that she was in some kind of trouble and couldn't talk to anyone but you. She was afraid to drive to the villa, so I sent *Carabinieri* to pick her up. When they got there, she was gone, and some of the locals said two men with guns had tried to drag her into a car. They seemed to think she might have gotten away."

The admiral gripped the telephone receiver tightly. *Not Giselle. Mother Mary, don't let her be a hostage!* "Have you contacted the major?"

"Yes, sir, just a few moments ago. He's on his way out here."

"I want to talk to him as soon as possible." The admiral hung up the phone and, for the first time in years, began to pray.

❖ ❖ ❖

"Maybe it's not what you think," the driver told Giselle softly, a kind expression on his face as she dried her eyes. "Why don't you tell me about it? What makes you think your husband sent those men?"

"I can't explain," she answered miserably. "The only person I can talk to is my father."

"Who's your father?"

"Vice Admiral Hardy, U.S. Sixth Fleet."

"Vice admiral?" the man repeated. "You run with the big dogs, don't you? Who's your husband?"

"He's a major," Giselle said. "Marine Corps."

"So, Mrs. Major." He offered her a hand. "My name is Mared. What's yours?"

"Giselle." She stopped short of saying her last name. The less Mared knew, the better, she decided.

"Well, Giselle, I'd say the first order of business is to figure out where we're going."

"Listen, Mared, I think you should just pull over and let me out," Giselle told him. "This is my problem. I don't want you getting in any deeper."

"I'd say I'm already up to my armpits," he pointed out. "One of those men had a cellular phone. I saw him take it out of his pocket when we were driving away. By now, he's probably relayed my license plate number and a description of this car to whomever else is out there. So they're looking for me too. From what you say, I don't think I want them to find me."

"I'm sorry." She touched his arm apologetically. "I didn't mean to drag you into this."

"It's not your fault. Anyway, we should get off this road before reinforcements show up." He made a turn, heading north, the opposite direction from Gaeta.

"Where are we going?" Giselle asked.

"Sora. I have a friend there," he said. "We can lie low at his place until we figure out what to do."

"But . . ." she started.

"Look, your husband knows all of your friends and family here in Italy, right?"

She nodded reluctantly.

"Well, he doesn't know mine," he pointed out. "You'll be safer playing this my way."

Would she? Giselle was suddenly uncomfortably aware that this man was a stranger. She didn't know him, didn't know anything about him.

Except that he'd just saved her life.

❖ ❖ ❖

The trip to Sora was uneventful. Mared's friend, Dusan Bogomir, came out to meet them in the driveway. He was a tall, sober-looking man with silver temples and finely manicured hands that betrayed him for the dignitary he was. Few people knew that this distinguished Serbian emigrant, an ostensibly retired diplomat who had helped to engineer the fall of the Soviet Union, was still actively consulting for the United Nations on negotiations in several world hot spots.

Giselle turned her astonished eyes to Mared, as he greeted their host with a warm familiarity. "Apparently you also run with the big dogs," she commented.

Bogomir looked at her in surprise. "You know me."

She nodded. "I've admired your accomplishments for years, sir. You're one of the reasons I studied languages in college. I kind of hoped that one day I might get a chance to translate for you."

Bogomir accepted the compliment with grace. "I am very flattered. But, of course, you are aware that I've been retired for several years. Surely that was well before you entered the university?"

Giselle dropped her eyes. She had almost slipped again. She would have to be more careful. "Of course. I meant to say that I had decided what to study before you retired." To change the subject, she turned to Mared. "How do you know each other?"

Mared smiled. "Dusan helped me with a negotiation for my company a few years ago. What surprises me is that *you* know him. Dusan's been keeping a low profile the last few years."

"Certainly long enough for most people to have forgotten me," Dusan agreed amiably.

Giselle shrugged, keeping her expression carefully casual. "Chalk it up to being the daughter of an admiral. I guess I've gone to enough diplomatic receptions to have a fair idea of who's who."

Dusan nodded, exchanging a glance with Mared. "Well, I'm pleased to be recognized by someone so young and attractive. Please come inside." He took Giselle's arm and escorted her through the door.

It was a large home, very nicely decorated with antique cherry finish around the doors and windows. The walls were painted a cheery shade of pale yellow. Giselle noticed a few children's toys, stored neatly in a corner of the living room. "Children?" she asked, a little surprised, considering his age.

Dusan followed her gaze and smiled. "My daughter and her family stayed with me recently. I am still finding various items they left behind." He glanced at Mared, then back at Giselle. "May I get you some refreshment?"

"No, thank you," she replied.

"Actually, I'm a little hungry," Mared put in. "Why don't we go into the kitchen and put something together? Perhaps Giselle will change her mind when she smells our cooking."

Dusan chuckled. "I doubt that very much." He turned to Giselle. "Please, have a seat. There is a television, if you'd care to watch something, or there are magazines you might read."

"Why don't I come help you?" she suggested.

Dusan appeared shocked at the thought. "I cannot allow a guest to work in my home. Please, just sit and find some pleasant occupation. We'll return shortly."

Giselle did as he bade her, feeling awkward as she realized that Mared and Dusan wanted to speak privately. Alone in the living room, she wandered aimlessly, inspecting the antique furniture, including some very lovely pieces. But what she found more interesting was a grouping of framed photographs on the wall nearest the entry. Each of them showed Dusan Bogomir shaking hands with a different head of state. King Fahd of Saudi Arabia, Prime Minister Netanyahu of Israel, President Bush— nearly every part of the world was represented.

The men were still in the kitchen; she could hear the low hum of their conversation, and the occasional clink of plates. She wandered to a handsome rolltop desk near the far wall, its cover closed. Giselle saw a telephone wire leading into the desk and sat down, opening the desk just enough to bring out the phone.

Dusan hadn't invited her to use his phone, but surely he wouldn't mind. Besides, the sooner she spoke with her father, the sooner this would be over and everyone would be out of danger.

Sitting on the wooden office chair, she dialed Gaeta again.

"Lieutenant Riley."

"Riley, this is Giselle again. . . ."

"Giselle, where are you?" he demanded. "Your father is frantic."

"Can you put me through to him right now?" she asked.

"I'll try. Hold on." Riley put her on hold.

Moments later, there was a series of clicks, then her father's voice came over the line. "Giselle where are you? Are you all right?"

"I'm fine," she told him, nearing tears at the sound of his voice. "Please come home, Daddy. I'm in trouble. I need you."

There was a pause, the kind Giselle had become too familiar with over the years. Wherever he was, whatever he was doing, he couldn't leave. "What's going on, honey?"

"Daddy, I swear it's really important." She spoke urgently, allowing her desperation to creep into her voice. "I promise, this is more important than whatever you're doing. It's a matter of national security," she added, remembering what she'd decided to say.

That got his attention, at least. "What do you mean?"

How could she convince him? She thought quickly. "I can't explain on the phone, but it has to do with what Raz has been working on." A sob caught in her throat at the mention of her husband's name. "Please, just come home."

"Giselle, I want you to go to the villa, and I'll be there as soon as I can. There are some important things—"

"I can't go to the villa," she interrupted miserably. "I'm sure it's being watched."

"Giselle, listen to me." Her father spoke with the practiced calm of a commander in the heat of battle. "We'll get you to Gaeta, and you'll be safe there until I can get home. Just tell me where you are, and I'll have Riley send an armed escort to pick you up."

She was about to agree when she remembered that Riley was the only person who'd known where she was the last time, in Frosinone. Was he in on this? No, he wouldn't have put her through to her father if he were trying to stop her from telling what she knew.

That meant the phone lines were tapped! A chill ran through her at the realization. She'd already said too much, maybe enough to put her father in danger, too.

"Giselle, are you still there?"

"Daddy, I just realized that someone could be listening to this conversation."

"Listening? What are you talking about?"

Classified or not, this might be the only chance she'd have to tell her father what she knew, she decided. He had to act before they found a way to stop him. "Listen, Daddy, there's a man named Seif who's going to . . ." She stopped. The line had gone dead. "Daddy?"

She stared at the receiver for a long moment before realizing that her hand was shaking. She hung up the phone slowly, too terrified to think.

Mared and Dusan entered the room, Mared carrying a tray of food and looking worried. He saw her hand still on the phone. "Who were you calling?"

"My father," she replied. "But the phones are tapped. They cut us off before I could tell him anything."

He glanced at Dusan. "We have to leave," he said quietly.

"Take my car." Dusan took keys from a ring by the door and handed them to Mared. Crossing to his desk, he flipped open a hidden drawer and withdrew a substantial roll of money. "Take this as well; you'll need it."

Mared nodded, accepting both. "What about you? They'll know we were here."

"Do not concern yourself. Just go, before they find you here. I will take your car and try to lead them away. Then I will simply disappear." He smiled. "I have been planning this for a long time."

"I'm sorry," Giselle said as Mared led her to the door. "I didn't mean to cause you any more trouble."

"The Lord works everything for his own ends." He smiled soberly, reciting part of a biblical proverb that Giselle recognized. Giselle opened her mouth to say the rest, but somehow the words evaded her. Accepting his extended hand, she took her leave.

❖ ❖ ❖

The car their host had loaned them turned out to be a brand-new Volvo. "Mr. Bogomir must think a lot of you," Giselle commented.

Mared shrugged. "He's glad to help a friend in need." He glanced in the rearview mirror. They'd been driving for nearly an hour, moving northwest on deserted country roads, where other cars would be easily noticed. His Colt was on the seat between them, along with several boxes of ammunition that he'd retrieved from his own car before leaving. Giselle wondered briefly how he'd managed to get the weapon into this gun-controlled country, but she had too much on her mind to ask about it.

They were coming to a small town that was bustling with tourists. Mared pulled over near a little street-side café. "Why don't we grab a bite while we consider our options?" Bending, he stowed most of the ammunition under the seat, keeping one clip and tucking the Colt into his belt. He pulled out his shirt to cover the weapon. "I'm going to run over to the store across the street and pick up a few things we might need." He pulled out the roll of bills Dusan had given him and handed a few notes to Giselle. "Get me a dish of pasta and fresh vegetables, no meat or cheese. Order everything to go. We want to stay near the car. And no more phone calls, right?"

Giselle nodded and headed for the café. The smells inside made her realize that she was hungry. At the last minute, she decided to pay for the meal herself and give the money back to Mared. It was the least she could do after he'd saved her life.

She was waiting on a little bench outside the café when he came back with two large bags.

"What did you get?" she asked.

He sat down beside her. "Odds and ends. A change of clothes for both of us. Sweats. I might not have gotten your size right."

"It's OK," she told him. "You didn't have to get me anything."

He glanced at her between bites of pasta. "We both need to change the way we look—make it harder for people to match our descriptions."

She nodded. "I hadn't thought of that."

They ate in silence for several minutes, watching the locals and tourists wander by. When he finished his pasta, Mared tore off half of a warm loaf of bread and used it to sop up the leftover sauce from his paper plate. Chewing thoughtfully, he turned to her. "Giselle, it would be easier for me to figure out what to do if I knew what we were running from. Are you certain your husband sent those men after you? Have you seen him with any of them before?"

She sighed. "I'm sorry, Mared, but I really can't talk about it. I know this isn't fair to you, and if you want to just leave me here, I'll understand. Maybe if they know we've split up, they'll concentrate on finding me and leave you alone."

He shook his head resolutely. "I consider myself a pretty good judge of character, and those guys don't seem the type to leave loose ends." He shrugged. "If you know something they don't want spread around, then anyone you've talked to is also a target. I think we should stick together."

Giselle considered his assessment of the situation, then nodded slowly. "Maybe so." The thought of being on the run with a virtual stranger was unsettling, but still, it was better than being alone. She had no idea what to do next, but Mared seemed to have a lot of ideas. She was actually a little relieved.

He grinned. "OK. We know that your father's phone lines are tapped, and we can assume that the compound is being watched. I don't see any point in sticking around. Unless you have a better idea, I think we should head north. I know someone in Switzerland who might be able to help us."

"Who?"

Mared shrugged. "She's nobody, but her father's a bigwig in the British Royal Air Force. Maybe he can get a message to your dad."

"It sounds reasonable," Giselle agreed.

"Meanwhile, why don't you go find a rest room and put these on? And do something with your hair. I bought you a pair of scissors." He handed her one of the bags. "Just don't leave anything that would clue them in that you've changed your appearance."

Giselle did as he suggested. The sweat suit was nice, but much too large. She cinched the drawstring at the waist, then rolled up the excess at her ankles and wrists. Finally, she reluctantly picked up the scissors and went to work on her hair.

At first she snipped carefully, but she decided it was taking too long. Impatient, she doubled over, brushing her hair until it hung straight down. Then she caught it in one hand and used the scissors to cut it all a few inches from the top of her head. The result was uneven, but she was able to remedy that fairly well. In a few minutes, she sported an acceptable-looking layered cut that ended just above her shoulders. She looked at the formerly waist-length hank of hair in the sink and felt strangely bereft.

Remembering Mared's last-minute instruction, she put her old clothes and the hair in the shopping bag and carried it out with her.

Mared was nowhere to be seen when she returned to the car,

so after stowing her old clothes under the seat, she jogged over to the store and picked up a pair of tennis shoes. She'd look funny wearing sweats and oxfords.

She stepped back outside the store, passing a man who was leaning against the outer wall. He whistled as she walked by, but she ignored him, looking for Mared. It wasn't until he moved in front of her that she recognized him. He'd shaved his beard and trimmed his hair to just below the ears. He wore a dark-blue baseball cap that shaded his eyes, accentuating their darkness and the deep hollows around them. Once again he seemed oddly familiar, but the feeling passed quickly.

He grinned at her astonishment. "You didn't recognize me?"

"You look like an American tourist," she told him.

"So do you," he pointed out. "We should blend in fairly well this time of year." He glanced over her shoulder and froze. "We have company."

Giselle followed his gaze. The car had just pulled up, parking at the little café. As she watched, the Arab got out and went inside. The other man stayed outside, studying passersby with more than a casual interest as he spoke on a cellular phone.

"How did they find us?" she asked, letting him draw her back into the doorway of the store.

He thought for a moment. "Did you use the cash I gave you to buy our lunch?"

She shook her head, her eyes widening. "My credit card! How did they—"

"Did you use it in this store, too?" he broke in urgently.

She nodded, feeling trapped.

"Then they'll be coming here next." He kept his eyes on the man across the street as he spoke. "We have to get moving. I want you to wander casually down the street. Act like you're window-shopping. Maybe try to blend in with those women over there."

Giselle nodded, glancing at the little group of women he was talking about, down the street they'd come in on. They looked friendly. It shouldn't be hard to strike up a conversation, make it seem like she was with them. "What are you going to do?" she asked.

He shrugged. "We won't get far without a car. I don't think those men got much of a look at me back in Frosinone, so I'm going to try to get past them. I'll pick you up at the far end of town. If I don't show up in ten minutes, that means they recognized me and I'm leading them away from here. I saw an old, deserted stone cottage about half a mile back. Make your way there and hide, and I'll get there when I can."

"Be careful," she cautioned.

"You too." He nodded grimly. "Now go, before they see us together."

❖ ❖ ❖

Putting on a pair of dark glasses, Mared moved toward the Volvo. As he neared it, the man glanced at him, then looked at him again, this time a little harder. Mared gave him a casual nod and kept walking.

As he was unlocking the door, the Arab came out of the café, carrying a receipt. He said something to the waiting man, then glanced at Mared.

If anyone was going to recognize him, this man would.

Fighting his tension, Mared got in the car and settled himself. He forced himself to take his time, using his right hand to adjust the rearview mirror and fasten his seat belt. As he did so, his left hand slowly crept under his sweatshirt, withdrawing the Colt from the leather belt he'd fastened around his bare waist as a holster. He slid the weapon under his thigh. Then he started the engine.

He had just slipped the gearshift into reverse when the Arab stepped up to the car and rapped on his window. Mared looked up into the other man's face, his hand easing toward the gun. But there was nothing aggressive in the man's expression, so he reluctantly pressed the button for the automatic window. He left the car in gear in case he needed to move in a hurry. "May I help you?" he asked, giving his Italian a heavy American accent.

"*Sí,*" the man said. "Yes," he added in English. "Do you recognize this woman?" He pulled out a picture of Giselle beaming into the camera, holding up a hand with an engagement ring. "She might be with a man." He produced another photo.

Mared stared at the second photo. It was about five years old and not very good—a typical American driver's license photo. He slowly looked up at the man, thanking God that he'd had the foresight to shave. He felt indecently exposed, but it was obvious that this man had no idea who he was talking to.

"The lady's long hair looks kind of familiar," he said, wanting to keep their focus on her previous hairstyle. "Maybe it was her I just saw in that store over there," he pointed to the store they'd just left. "She bought a few things, then left, but she rushed back in a few minutes later and asked if they had a back door." He shrugged. "I hope that helps."

"Thank you." The man turned to his partner and gestured toward the store. The two of them moved toward it in unison, one of them going around back to look for a rear exit.

With a deep breath of relief, Mared pulled away.

Giselle was standing in front of the last store, trying to seem interested in a set of souvenir spoons on display in the window. He pulled up and popped the door for her. "We have to get out of here. They've got pictures of both of us."

❖ ❖ ❖

They doubled back toward Rome, keeping to dirt roads when they could to make sure they weren't followed. When they reached the city, Mared surprised Giselle by making a detour through one of the major tourist centers. He drove slowly past the Colosseum and watched the crowds for a few minutes.

Then he glanced at Giselle. "Give me your purse."

She handed it to him without question, thinking even as she did so that it was strange she should trust him so easily. It was almost as if they'd known each other before today. Maybe nearly being killed together tended to make for fast friendships.

He pulled out her wallet and took out most of the cash, leaving only a small amount. He handed the money to her. "Keep this in your socks or bra, in case you have to leave your purse somewhere. Is there anything else in here that you can't live without?"

Giselle reached for the wallet, thumbing through it until she found what she wanted: a wedding photo of her and Raz. Her eyes filled again as she saw his beaming face.

Mared gently took the photo. "Your major looks like a pretty great guy," he commented.

"I thought he was," she agreed quietly, her fingers coming up to rub the bruises at her throat.

He watched her for a moment, then pulled her hand away, examining the marks. "He did this to you?"

She turned away. Part of her wanted to protest that Raz would never do such a thing. But he had.

Mared watched her for a long moment, then took the wallet gently. Putting the car into gear, he moved in closer to the tourists, then opened his window and threw the wallet into the crowd.

"Hey! What are you doing?" Giselle cried, watching as two teenagers in threadbare clothing grabbed it and raced away.

Mared put the car in gear and drove off. "Those kids are going to have a ball maxing out your credit cards, and our friends will be chasing the receipts all over Rome. It should buy us several hours before they figure out what we've done."

❖ ❖ ❖

"What's going on, son?" the admiral asked, his voice sounding hollow over the speaker phone.

Raz closed his eyes, pausing to gather his thoughts. More lies, and more and more. If questioned, some of his marines might say they'd seen him chasing her, so he had to come up with a compatible story. "We had an argument this morning. Giselle's not very happy about being kept in the dark." He knew the admiral would understand that. "She left the embassy before I could apologize. I assumed she was coming here. Then I got the call from Lieutenant Riley."

"Do you think that her assailants might be terrorists?"

"I don't know, sir," Raz repeated tiredly. "The *Carabinieri* questioned the witnesses in Frosinone, and I haven't had a chance to debrief them."

"The witnesses seemed to think that the men were rapists, sir," Riley put in.

"Rapists . . ." the admiral breathed.

Raz winced. He could hear the anguish in the old man's voice. "She might have just said that to get someone to help her," he said. "It's the kind of thing she would do."

"I want every single law enforcement agency in Italy—ours and theirs—on this," the admiral commanded.

"Yes, sir," Raz agreed. He was sure those giving him his orders would prefer to keep the Italians out of it, but there was no way to sidestep this without raising the admiral's suspicions. They'd just have to finesse the authorities as best they could.

"I want you to contact me hourly with updates."

"Yes, sir."

Raz was hanging up the phone when Dolores Hardy stepped into the room. From the look on her face, she'd been listening just outside the door for several minutes. She walked toward Raz, none too steady on her feet, and gripped his collar with hands that smelled of bourbon. "What have you done to my baby?"

❖ ❖ ❖

Mared was getting tired, Giselle realized. He'd been driving almost nonstop since this morning. "Do you want me to take the wheel?" she asked him.

He shook his head. "You need rest, too. Anyway, they're probably still chasing your credit-card trail in Rome. Let's stop for the night. Florence isn't far ahead."

They arrived just before nightfall, cresting the last gentle hill in time to see the city's ornate amber buildings glowing in the last, fiery rays of the sunset—sparkling jewels against the darkening sky. Even had she not known that *Firenze* was the birthplace of the Renaissance, Giselle felt she would have guessed simply from its beauty.

Staying near the highway that skirted the city, Mared bypassed several popular-looking *penziones* in favor of a much older hotel, an L-shaped two-story former apartment building with ground-floor units that opened directly onto the parking lot. Only two older, run-down cars were parked there. The place had definitely seen better days.

"Why here?" Giselle asked.

"We want outdoor access," Mared explained. "In case we need to get away in a hurry." He circled the building several times, checking it out from all angles. Then, satisfied that everything seemed normal, he circled back to the entrance. "Get down on the floorboards and stay out of sight," he ordered.

"Why?"

"They're looking for you, or for both of us together. If they start calling hotels, they might not ask about men registering alone." He waited until she was out of sight, then pulled into the hotel drive. "I'll be right back," he told her.

A few minutes later, he was back. He put the car in gear and drove into the parking lot. "I'll go open the door first. Then I'll come back, and when the coast is clear, I'll open your door. Run into the room. I'll be right behind you."

Moments later, Giselle was inside a small but clean-looking suite. She couldn't decide which she wanted more, a bath or to crawl into the double bed that dominated the room.

She turned back just as Mared was coming in with his pack. "What's wrong?" he asked.

"There's only one bed," she told him.

He laughed. "I couldn't exactly ask for two, could I? Don't worry, I was planning to sleep on the floor."

She shook her head, eyeing the hard tile floor. "I can't ask you to do that, not after everything you've done for me," she said. "I'll take the floor."

He rolled his eyes. "Call me old-fashioned, but I'm not going to sleep very well if you make me feel guilty. You take the bathroom first." He rummaged in his pack, pulling out a gray T-shirt and a pair of cotton boxers. He tossed them to Giselle. "You can sleep in these—they'll be more comfortable than the sweats."

❖   ❖   ❖

Mared knew by the tightness of her eyes that Giselle was feigning sleep when he emerged from the bathroom. She was still afraid, still a little distrustful of him. It wasn't hard to understand. After all, he was a complete stranger, and she'd just discovered that she couldn't trust her own husband.

She stiffened almost imperceptibly when he approached the bed, and he could feel her relief when he merely took a pillow. He slipped the spare blanket off the foot of the bed and folded it into a mattress of sorts. Reclining on it, he settled in quickly, allowing his breathing to deepen, to even out into the relaxing rhythm of near slumber.

He felt her eyes on him, knew that she was watching his face, counting his breaths, slowly coming to realize that she was truly safe—at least for now. The silence drew out until he was almost sure she was asleep. Then, in the darkness, he heard her muffled sobs.

They were private tears, not meant for him to see. And any attempt to comfort her might be misunderstood. Mared needed her trust, her cooperation, for at least a while yet. So he kept his eyes closed, his breathing even, and listened as she cried herself to sleep.

❖ ❖ ❖

Giselle woke with a start, catching herself just before she started to scream. She turned, expecting to find Raz asleep beside her, wanting to draw his arm around her, to feel his whiskers scrape her forehead, to breathe deeply and fill herself with his scent. But the space beside her was empty, and the room was strange.

It wasn't a dream.

Reality struck her like a fist. She sat up, drawing her knees against her chest, and rocked slowly, trying to make sense of what had brought her here.

Yesterday, she'd been a woman wildly in love with her husband. Now here she was in a strange room with a strange man, on the run from that same husband.

And the men he'd sent to kill her.

It wasn't real! Something was wrong! Raz loved her! Everything in her wanted to deny what had happened in the last twenty-four hours. But it *had* happened. When she closed her eyes, she could still feel Raz's hands tightening around her throat.

"Trust me. . . ."

Those same hands had shaken with emotion as he'd slipped the wedding ring on her finger. Those same hands, only hours before, had caressed her with something bordering on reverence.

How she wanted it all to be a dream! She wanted to wake up in Raz's arms and smile at the absurdity of all this. It made no sense! Raz could never hurt her! Raz could never betray his country! He wouldn't betray his family—his brother in Israel, his mother, an avowed Zionist—by collaborating with Arab terrorists!

Or was all that a lie? She remembered his passport, the name on it that she had never seen before yesterday. Was there any other way to interpret that letter? Any other way to explain his fingers tightening on her throat, closing off her breath?

The man she'd married wasn't Raz Chayil. He was Rashid ibn Kasim—traitor, assassin, and terrorist. And if she didn't stop him, he was going to help the Sword of Islam strike a lethal blow against the United States, and against peace in the Middle East.

If she didn't stop him. The responsibility bore down on her like a weight. She was the only one who knew, the only one who could stop him. If she didn't find a way to tell her father . . .

How could she turn in her own husband? No American court would require a woman to do it. But if she refused, many leaders would die, including the president of the United States. She would be a traitor, too, as guilty as Raz.

An image flashed unbidden through her mind, of the look on Raz's face in the security unit, when he'd decided not to turn her in for eavesdropping on her father. He'd risked his career—and, she realized now, his cover—to protect her.

He could have killed her last night, too, but he hadn't. Instead, somehow he had believed her words of love and faith in him, and he had spared her life. He had somehow believed that she loved him even above the interests of her country.

"I do love you," he had said. "Whatever else you come to believe about me . . ." And suddenly, she knew that it was true. Whatever else he was, whatever else he was capable of doing, Raz—Rashid—the man who'd shared her bed, whatever his name was—loved her. Too much to harm her, even to protect himself.

Could she betray him?

She wanted to cry again, but she had no more tears. All she had was a sick feeling, a nausea that burned in her chest, by her heart.

Quietly, Giselle got out of bed, gathered up her clothing, and went into the bathroom to dress.

❖ ❖ ❖

She'd been walking for almost an hour when she came upon a small church—not one of the tourist attractions, but a place that looked like people really worshiped here. Its graceful spire formed a ghostly shadow against the glowing clouds. A statue of Jesus stood benignly over the doorway, his palms outstretched in benediction or welcome.

Giselle mounted the stairs and tried the door. It was unlocked. She went inside, dampening her fingers with holy water before entering the chapel. Genuflecting toward the altar, she slipped into the last pew.

"Chi è là?" an aging voice came from the front of the chapel. "Who is there?" A small, gray-haired man in a bathrobe that looked out of place with his hastily-donned Roman collar, peered through a door to the rear of the sanctuary.

She rose quickly. *"Perdono l' intrusione, padre,"* she said. "I didn't mean to disturb you."

"It is nothing," he told her. "I was awake. I had just finished my morning prayers when I heard you come in." He opened the door wider, beckoning her to join him. "You are in need of a priest?"

She moved forward, obeying his gesture. "I came to ask for God's guidance," she told him. "I have a problem."

He smiled softly. "Those who come to church in the hours before dawn are seldom untroubled. Please, come back to the rectory and let me hear about it while I prepare for the day's duties."

She nodded, following him down a long hallway to his living quarters. She noted that his breakfast was on the table. He reached into a cabinet for an empty bowl, intending to share with her.

I'm not hungry." She raised her hand. "But please, eat. I don't mind."

"Thank you," he said, gesturing for her to sit beside him. "How may I help you?"

"Father, I have a problem, and I don't know what to do about it. I just got married a few months ago."

"And you are unhappy with him?" he asked, sipping from a glass of milk and watching her face with kind eyes.

She shook her head, then nodded, then shrugged. "I love him, at least I thought I did. But he's going to do something awful."

"Is there another woman?"

She shook her head. "My husband wouldn't do such a thing." She was surprised at her certainty.

"Perhaps I should be silent and let you tell me your problem," the priest said.

"My story involves important secrets."

He nodded soberly. "I will consider this a confession. I will keep your trust."

"My husband is involved in a conspiracy," she told him. It was still hard to say, even though she knew that the priest wouldn't tell anyone. "I found out and ran away. He has to be stopped, but I don't know if I can turn him in."

The old man stopped eating. "This is a problem," he agreed. "What has he conspired to do?"

Giselle's gaze dropped slowly to the table. "He's going to help terrorists kill a number of important people."

The priest tried not to look astonished. He turned his gaze to his food and took a bite, chewing slowly as he considered what to say. "Did you try to dissuade him?"

She nodded. "He nearly killed me to keep me from telling anyone." She rubbed her throat, imagining that she could feel the bruises Raz had left there. "I managed to convince him that I loved him too much to turn him in."

"And then you ran away." He watched her face as she nodded, then he stared off into space, chewing slowly. "Normally, I would admonish a wife to return to her husband, to counsel him and then trust that he will do the right thing. I do not think that is what I should say to you. Do you fear him?"

She nodded again, swallowing back her tears.

"And you fear also that he might also become responsible for the deaths of others." The priest spooned up another bite of his cereal, then turned to Giselle. "To whom would you tell your story if you decide to turn him in?"

"My father, if I can reach him."

"He has the power to deal with the situation?"

"Yes," Giselle told him.

"What would happen to your husband then?"

Giselle thought for a moment. "He would be arrested and taken to this terrible little prison at Gaeta." The image of Raz sitting in one of those tiny cells in the security unit made her feel desperately unhappy. He had saved her from one of those cells once. How could she forgive herself if she sent him there?

"And then he would be tried, I am sure," the priest prompted. "And if convicted?"

"It would depend on the charges, I guess." She shrugged. "I don't know that much about military law. Giving comfort to the enemy, maybe, or trea—" she broke off, bringing her hand up to her mouth. "Treason is a capital offense!" She rose suddenly, feeling herself teeter on the brink of hysterics. "Father, I can't turn my husband over to be executed!"

He stood, taking her arms to still her, and staring gently into her eyes. "And will you be able to live with yourself if you do not turn him in, and he commits murder?"

Suddenly she could no longer control her tears. She felt his arms go around her as her body shook with deep, wrenching sobs. "Help me, Father. I don't know what to do."

He held her until the tears subsided, then drew her back to the table and sat with her, keeping hold of her hands. "The Bible directs wives to obey their husbands as the Lord," he told her. "But God also commands us not to kill. If your husband intends to break God's law, you must do whatever you must to stop him."

She sobbed once more, bringing a hand to her mouth. "I don't know if I have what it takes to do this."

He squeezed her fingers. "Let us pray together for the Lord's counsel. He will give you the strength to do his will, and peace with your decisions."

❖ ❖ ❖

Dawn was just a rosy gleam on the horizon when she left the chapel, calmer, if no more comfortable with her options. The night sky still twinkled above her as she made her way back to the hotel.

She halted abruptly as she rounded the corner. A dark sedan was parked next to Dusan's car, and two men were getting out. Her heart racing, she backed into the shadows beneath the stairs and watched as one of them turned his attention from the car to the hotel room. He cautiously peered through the window, then drew a weapon and signaled to his partner. A handgun appeared in the second man's hand as he moved into place next to the door. With a swift kick, the first man ripped the door from its frame.

"Don't move! Stay down!" she heard the first man shout as he entered the room. The second man hung back for a moment, then moved in as well. Giselle could hear the sound of fists striking flesh.

She hurried forward and peered inside. Mared lay prone on the floor, his face bleeding where someone had struck him. The first man straddled him, a beefy fist poised above his face. The second man stood above them, his weapon trained on Mared's head.

"Where is the woman?" the first man asked.

"I don't know!" Mared answered.

The man brought a knee hard into Mared's groin. "Tell us where she is!"

Mared groaned, rolling to his side and curling up in agony.

Giselle could stand no more. She stepped into the doorway. "Were you looking for me?" As soon as she had their attention, she ducked away and crouched just out of sight beside the door.

"Get her!"

Giselle put out her foot, sending the man sprawling as he raced out to catch her. She scrambled toward him, twisting his gun from his grasp before he realized what was happening. She rose quickly, aiming the weapon at his head.

"On your face," she ordered quietly, not wanting his partner to hear. "Put your hands behind your head." As he reluctantly obeyed, she circled him gingerly, looking for a way to tie him up.

She heard a crash inside the room, and seconds later, Mared raced out, having somehow freed himself from his captor. He skidded to a halt, astonished at the sight that greeted him. Then he laughed. "Don't ever let me underestimate you again, Giselle."

"Are you all right?" she asked, worriedly scanning his bruises.

He nodded briefly, stepping forward to take charge of her captive. He marched the man back into the room at gunpoint.

Inside, the man glanced at his partner, who lay unconscious on the floor, and his mouth tightened grimly. "Mrs. Chayil, you—"

His words were cut off as the butt of the gun struck his skull, and he sank slowly to the floor. Mared glanced at Giselle's astonished face, and in answer to her unspoken question, bent to retrieve a second, small-caliber revolver from a holster on the man's arm. He held it up for her to see.

Returning to his work, he found a billfold, and a wallet-sized kit containing a syringe and a vial of clear liquid. Mared examined the label before setting it aside. The other man's pockets yielded a set of handcuffs, keys, and a small can of mace. Mared deposited all but the handcuffs on the dresser, then dragged the two men over to the bed, where he cuffed them together through the iron railing.

The fear was catching up with Giselle. Numbly and with shaking hands, she examined the items on the dresser.

"Giselle, we have to go," Mared told her gently. Noting her confused expression, he explained. "These men probably called in our location; reinforcements will be on the way."

Giselle stared at him blankly for a moment, then gathered her senses and nodded. Picking up his pack, he dug out his sweat suit.

Giselle dropped her eyes, suddenly embarrassed. She hadn't realized until that moment that he was wearing only a pair of dark-blue cotton boxers.

Mared noticed her discomfiture. "Check the bathroom," he suggested, and Giselle hurried to obey.

When she returned, he was repacking his knapsack. She stopped him to add his razor and toothbrush, and before he closed it, he walked over to the dresser. Examining the items from the men's pockets, he pocketed a knife, the mace, and after a brief consideration, the little medical kit. He opened the billfold, examining the contents.

The billfold had a plastic window, and under it, Giselle saw what looked like an identification card. "Who is he?" she asked.

Mared glanced at her, then returned the billfold to the dresser. "His ID said he was attached to the U.N. Security Council."

Giselle's mind reeled at the implications. If the SOI had infiltrated the Security Council, ". . . that explains where they get such detailed intelligence! And the weapons, too!" she mused aloud.

Mared was staring at her. "Intelligence? Weapons? Giselle, what are you talking about?"

Giselle turned away quickly, horrified that she'd spoken her thoughts aloud. "Please forget what you just heard, Mared. It'll only put you in more danger."

He caught her arms, turning her to face him. "Giselle, those men were going to kill me. How much more danger could I be in? Please tell me what you know. I need to know what we're up against."

She dropped her eyes. "You said we had to get going."

"All right." Reluctantly, he released her and bent to shoulder his pack. "But I'm going to ask again once we're on the road."

She followed him to the car. "How did they find us?"

"They must have caught Dusan," he told her grimly. "Once they knew we had his car, all they had to do was start calling hotels and asking the managers to check their parking lots for his license plates." Mared opened the driver's door, waited for Giselle to slide in, and got in behind her. "I should have thought of that and dumped the car yesterday," he berated himself. Then he turned to her, his eyes angry. "Where on earth did you go, anyway?"

"I needed to think," Giselle told him. "I went for a walk to clear my head. Then I found a church and made confession."

"You talked to the priest?" He hesitated, then nodded. "I guess that's safe enough." He glanced in the rearview mirror. "I don't think we're being followed. So our next order of business is to find some new wheels."

❖ ❖ ❖

They stopped once more in Florence with Giselle waiting nervously in the Volvo while Mared hot-wired an older Fiat, whose owners had painted it in abstract layers of chartreuse, red, and blue.

"I don't think this is going to do a lot of good," Mared mused as they drove away. "They know we're headed north now, so it's going to be harder to avoid them."

"Well, if you're so worried that they'll spot us, why'd you pick such an eye-catching car?" Giselle asked.

"If you were looking for someone who wanted not to be noticed, you wouldn't expect this, would you?" he pointed out.

"And it only has to get us as far as the mountains. We'll cross the border on foot."

This took her by surprise. "Over the Alps? You mean we have to hike?"

"They'll have people watching for us at all the check-point stations. I don't want to take the chance of being spotted. Do you?"

She shook her head slowly. "You know, if it wasn't for you, I'd have been caught by now. How do you know all this stuff?"

He shrugged. "I read a lot of spy novels. If we get through this, maybe we should write thank-you notes to Tom Clancy and Robert Ludlum."

Giselle laughed.

He smiled. "You have a great laugh, Giselle. A great smile, too. I'd like to see them more often."

She blushed. "Thank you. I'm sorry I've been so morose. It's just . . . hard, you know?"

"You love your husband, don't you?" he asked.

"I thought I did," she said slowly.

"Now you're not so sure?" he asked.

"I don't know what to think." She looked out the window at the tree-lined hills north of Florence. "Let's change the subject before I start crying again." She glanced at him. "Let's talk about you for a change. I don't know anything about you."

"What do you want to know?" he asked.

"Where are you from?"

"You mean where was I born, or where do I live?"

"Both."

He smiled. "I was born in the States, but I've lived abroad since I got out of college. I travel most of the time."

"What keeps you on the road so much?" she asked.

"I'm a consultant. I work with organizations all over the world, teaching them to share resources and operate more efficiently."

"It sounds interesting," she commented politely.

He chuckled. "That's nice of you to say, even though you don't mean it. I don't imagine anything beyond the military holds much interest for you, does it?"

She shrugged. "I guess I hadn't thought about it."

"And yet you're a civilian. Why didn't you enlist?"

"My parents didn't want me to. And now we're talking about me again," she pointed out. "Tell me more about what you do. What's your favorite place?"

He smiled. "Bethesda, Maryland. My mother lives there. I try to spend the holidays with her every year."

"That's not far from Washington. Were you there last year when the terrorists bombed the Israeli embassy?" It had happened at the start of Hanukkah. The blast had killed twenty people and injured dozens more. The terrorists responsible had been tracked down, and their headquarters were bombed the next week by the Israeli government, almost starting a war with Lebanon.

"I knew some of the people who died," he affirmed soberly. "My job takes me to Israel now and then."

"Do you think the violence there will ever end?"

Mared glanced at her, then returned his eyes to the road. "Why do you ask?"

She dropped her eyes to her lap. "My husband says it won't. No matter what anyone tries to do. The extremists won't let it happen."

"There are those who would agree with him," Mared said, watching her from the corner of his eyes. "What do you think?"

She sighed wearily. "I don't know anymore. But I think they should try."

"Do you have any ideas on how it would work?" Mared argued good-naturedly. "Even if the leaders come to an agreement, there are too many individuals who won't live by it. There is a lot of very personal hatred between Arabs and Jews in Israel, and it grows every time someone gets killed or maimed. Parents are afraid to send their children to school because some nut might want to blow it up. How do you not take that personally? And that's even before you get to the religious issues. Jerusalem is sacred to both Jews and Muslims. They both lay claim to the same block of land. The religious Jews dream of a day when they can rebuild their temple. The Muslims riot every time they try. How are they going to coexist peacefully?"

"But why should it be so hard? Jews, Christians, and Muslims all worship the same God, don't they?" she protested.

"Do they?" he asked. "Take a look in the Qur'an sometime. You'll find that Allah bears little resemblance to the biblical God."

"Isn't it possible that God manifests himself in different ways to different people? Isn't it possible that he wants us all to live in peace, despite our differences?"

"That may be what he wants, but how do you live at peace with people who hate the very sight of you?"

She sighed. Maybe she was being naive. Maybe you had to spend time in Israel to understand the depth of the enmity between Jews and Arabs. Hadn't Raz said as much? Maybe you had to be Jewish.

But Raz—Rashid—wasn't Jewish. The passport she'd found had said he was a Palestinian. Everything she'd thought she knew about him was just part of his cover story. The part about being from an Israeli family was a brilliant touch, she saw now. Who would suspect a Zionist Jew of conspiring with Arab terrorists?

That was exactly what Arn had said when he'd told her father that Raz was above suspicion! She suddenly realized that Raz had probably been the man who had diverted weapons to the SOI six years ago. And then, placed in charge of the investigation, he had been able to cover his own tracks with ease.

A new thought chilled her. Arn had also said that naval intelligence believed the attack on her was somehow connected to the Sword of Islam. It had occurred to her now and again what a coincidence it had been that two off-duty marines were there just as everything was happening. She'd wondered, too, how Raz had known something was wrong, when she herself had noticed nothing unusual. But why would the SOI send the Libyans to kidnap her, then send Raz to stop them?

The answer came to her now. After the rescue, Raz had been promoted rapidly, trusted with progressively complex and sensitive assignments. Assignments that had put him more and more in a position to help the Sword of Islam. And now, with his help, they were preparing to deliver the *coup de grace*.

"Oh, Raz . . ." she whispered. Had he been using her from the very start? Had even his saving her life been a lie?

"Is something wrong?" Mared asked, a concerned expression on his face as he saw her sudden pallor.

"It's nothing. Just another little revelation about my marriage." Giselle turned away, staring out the window until her eyes were dry again.

❖ ❖ ❖

They drove steadily for the next several hours, stopping only for gas and to pick up supplies from a camping goods store in Brescia. Another few hours of mountain driving got them to Campodolcino, a small town near the border with Switzerland.

Finding a deserted road, Mared drove for a few miles before he pulled off into a meadow and parked behind a thick clump of bushes. He got out and stretched. Giselle did the same, becoming aware as she did so that the long drive and the tension had stiffened her limbs and joints. It hurt to move, but it felt good, too.

The mountain air was crisp, too chilly for Giselle's tastes. But it smelled so sweet that she didn't mind. She pulled a brand new jacket from her pack and drew it on over her sweats.

"Let's do what we can about the tire tracks," Mared told her. "Then we'll hike from here."

"How far will we have to walk?" No matter which direction

they took, it was going to be a hard climb. They were surrounded on all sides by mountains so steep that even the trees clung precariously, seeming to know that the next spring melt might take them down. And the peaks of the mountains were invisible, disappearing into the clouds as if they ascended forever.

Mared grinned as if he knew what she was thinking. "Think of it as boot camp. Assuming there's no trouble, we can stop after we've crossed the border, then go on to this town I know in Switzerland tomorrow morning."

"Why can't we sleep in the car tonight and start out tomorrow?" she asked for the fourth time. "I hate camping."

Mared sighed with exaggerated patience. "Those men might be right behind us. We don't want to risk another night in Italy."

"Speak for yourself," Giselle grumbled. "The last time I went camping, I woke up with a snake in my sleeping bag."

"Was it poisonous?" he asked, as if that was the only thing remotely disturbing about finding a reptile on one's pillow.

"Does it matter?" she retorted. "It was enough to put me off camping for life."

"Well, there aren't any snakes at this altitude," he assured her.

"I'm not crazy about bugs, either."

Mared chuckled, then pulled a long, leafy branch from a nearby bush and offered it to her, tearing off another for himself.

"What do we do with these?"

"I'll show you." Gesturing for her to follow him, Mared walked back to the road along the tracks left by their car in the grass and damp earth. Then they retraced their steps, with Mared showing her how to use her branch to brush away the trail as best they could. When they were finished, it was still clear that a car had been there, but the imprints no longer looked fresh.

"Where did you get the idea for this?" Giselle asked, impressed with his resourcefulness. Or was it resourcefulness? It occurred to her to wonder whether Mared was more than he seemed. All these things he seemed to know so conveniently . . .

"ROTC," he replied. "They sent us out on a reconnaissance weekend with Army instructors my last year of high school. One team tracked the other, and we also learned ways to avoid being tracked. Besides that, we learned how to avoid tripping mines." He laughed. "Who'd have thought any of that would ever come in handy?"

"Who'd have thought?" Giselle echoed. The Army did do more of the type of training Mared was talking about. After all, they were ground troops. It would also explain where Mared got his Colt. Frankly, that branch of the service had never appealed to her.

"That's as good as it's going to get." Mared returned to the car, opened the trunk, and drew out his pack. He'd bought one for Giselle, too, and he helped her shoulder it.

"Hey, this is heavy," she said, surprised at the weight. "You expect me to carry this over the Alps?"

"I do. And it may be all there is between you and a cold, hungry night, so take care of it." He closed the trunk and started walking. "Use your branch to cover your footprints as you go, at least as long as we're in soft dirt. We're going to be above timberline for a good part of the way, so keep it with you in case you need it again."

She followed him reluctantly, swishing the branch awkwardly along behind her. She wasn't convinced that it was necessary, since the trail was mostly rocks, but every time she tried to stop, Mared barked at her to keep using it. She continued obediently until a splinter lodged itself in her thumb. "I'll probably need a tetanus shot by the time we're through," she grumbled, using her teeth to pull it out. She sucked at the sting. "I hate camping."

"So you've said already—five or six times, in fact," Mared reminded her dryly.

"Oh, I'm sorry, am I boring you?" she challenged.

"So far in the past two days I've been shot at, beaten, and

chased all over Italy." He snapped his fingers. "That's my problem—I'm bored."

"Very funny!" Giselle muttered, annoyance rising in her voice. Why was he making fun of her after all she'd been through?

He grinned and kept walking. After a few minutes, he began to sing an old hiking song Giselle had learned as a child. She was almost tempted to hum along, but his determined cheerfulness annoyed her. She satisfied herself with occasionally correcting his lyrics.

They climbed to timberline, rested briefly, then began the more dangerous effort to traverse the increasingly barren moonscape that was the mountain peak. Mared kept a brisk pace, using his hands to grip whatever he could, then reaching back to pull Giselle up behind him. The thin air made it all the harder. Giselle found herself growing breathless and dizzy, surprisingly so, since she still made a habit of working out on the obstacle course at least four times a week. She struggled to keep up, but Mared insisted that they were too exposed to slow down. The thought of being seen, of possibly having weapons trained on their backs as they climbed, persuaded Giselle to keep trying. It occurred to her to appreciate the colors they were wearing; their gray sweats and dark-blue packs and coats blended well against the mountainside. From a distance, they would be difficult to spot with the naked eye.

By the time they reached the top of the trail, Giselle had a pounding headache that threatened to attack her stomach as well. They made their way between two jutting crags, dwarfed between monoliths that time had forgotten. They were in the clouds now, and everything was a whitish gray. Above them in the mist, Giselle could see a blurred line separating peak and sky. Looking down was dizzying; through the thinning clouds, she could see where they'd left their car, but it was tiny, smaller than a child's toy. It seemed that if she fell, she would keep falling for miles.

She was standing at the top of the world, but she didn't care. "I think I'm sick," she panted, looking for a place to sit.

"It's the altitude," Mared told her, and she was gratified to hear strain in his voice as well. He caught her arm and propelled her forward. "Stopping here won't help. You won't feel better until we reach a lower elevation. But the worst is over. It's all downhill from here."

But going down had its own problems. The loose, chipped rocks on the steep mountainside made their footing uncertain, and Giselle's dizziness didn't help. She fell and slid nearly twenty feet, coming to a halt with a thud against a boulder.

Mared scrambled down to her, setting off a small rockslide that nearly buried her. "Are you all right?"

Winded by the jarring fall, she picked herself up slowly and gingerly tested her arms and legs. "Nothing serious. Just a few more scrapes and bruises for my collection."

"Are we feeling a little sorry for ourselves?"

"Are we getting a little patronizing?" she snapped, sick of his stupid grin. "Let's just trade places, and see how you'd feel in my position."

"Just a little bit farther," he promised. "When we get below timberline, we'll find a place to camp for the night."

"The sooner the better." She stumbled after him, suddenly sorry for snarling at him. "I'm exhausted."

He stayed ahead of her the rest of the way down, catching her when she started to slide again.

The descent went more quickly, and soon they were below timberline. Giselle noted the passing of her headache, but she was too exhausted to care much.

They left the trail, Mared insisting again that Giselle use her branch to cover her tracks. After a mile or so, he found a well-wooded gully and set down his pack. "This is probably as good as we'll find," he told her. "I'm sorry, but we can't risk a fire."

"I'm warm enough in this jacket." She shrugged off her pack and plopped down on the ground.

"You won't be for long. Once darkness sets in, sleeping on

the ground won't be at all comfortable." He sat down, too, his back against a fallen log. "At the moment, though, it does feel good to rest." He pulled his pack over beside him, and rummaged through it for the food they'd bought that afternoon.

Giselle's stomach was still threatening to revolt, but she reluctantly accepted a sandwich. As she nibbled, the nausea began to subside, and she discovered that she was really hungry. Using an arm to pillow her head, she stared into the darkening sky as she ate. The stars began to appear, one by one, glittering like tiny diamonds through a veil of moonlit mist. For some reason, she was reminded of Raz again.

Where was he now? What was he doing? Surely, since those men hadn't caught her, he would realize that the conspiracy was about to be exposed. Maybe Seif would call off the assassination attempt. Maybe Raz would disappear, using his alternate passport to leave the country quietly.

The thought that he might leave before she could turn him in gave her comfort. He'd be a wanted man, but better that than a dead one.

She might never see him again. The thought left her feeling bereft and unspeakably alone.

She glanced at Mared and found him watching her. For a moment, the expression on his face was enough to give her pause. She had noticed it before, a few times when he thought she wasn't looking. There was warmth to his gaze, a fondness that seemed to go deeper than his carefully casual expression. Was he becoming attracted to her?

She dropped her eyes quickly, looking away into the trees. She had never loved anyone but Raz, never been seriously attracted to anyone else. She remembered her dates in college. She had liked all of them, but not one had inspired the feelings she had at the mere touch of Raz's eyes.

And now she was terrified of him. How could everything have changed so quickly?

She glanced at Mared again and found him busy with a bottle of juice. In the moonlight, she realized, he even looked a little like Raz. He was dark like her husband, taller and leaner, but the muscular thickness of his legs and arms, the breadth of his shoulders, seemed a little bit like Raz. Even the way he laughed at her was Raz-like, more fond teasing than ridicule. Maybe it was these little familiarities that had made her feel as if she'd known him before.

A sound brought her gaze to Mared's face, and she realized that he'd caught her staring. She felt a slow flush creep over her face and was thankful for the darkness.

He rose and untied his sleeping bag from his pack, spreading it out next to the log. "Let's bed down before it gets any colder." He gestured to a space beside him. "Spread your sleeping bag next to mine. We'll need to stay close for the warmth."

She hesitated, suddenly uncomfortable. "I'm not sure . . ."

His teeth flashed at her in the moonlight. "Giselle, you're another man's wife, and you're going through enough trauma without any complications from me. I've decided to think of you as a little sister."

She dropped her eyes, embarrassed by her concern. Then she nodded and rose, spreading her sleeping bag where he'd suggested.

When they were safely zipped in, she smiled at him. "Thank you, Mared. I'm sorry I was such a pain earlier. It's nice to be able to trust someone right now."

He gazed at her soberly for a long moment. "Go to sleep, little sister. Tomorrow will be another long day."

Despite her exhaustion, it seemed to take half the night for Giselle to fall asleep. She lay awake, watching Mared sleep. She found his nearness comforting, and somehow that made her feel guilty. She lay there uncomfortably, watching him doze, until she finally drifted into a troubled half-sleep.

She was awakened by a hand pressed over her mouth and an arm pinning her down. Raz! A momentary panic filled her, and she struggled until she recognized Mared's eyes.

"Shhh," Mared whispered. "Someone's coming."

He let go of her, and they quickly got out of their sleeping bags and rolled them up, retying them to their packs. He was right. There were men's voices, several of them, coming from just beyond the ridge.

"Come on. We've got to get out of here before they get any closer." He helped her shoulder her pack, then set out in a slow jog.

She followed him numbly for what seemed like a long time, turning first one way, then doubling back, until it seemed they were back where they started. Every so often, Mared would stop and look up. She realized he was using the stars to guide his movements.

Finally, he found a hiding place in a tight little thicket of brush and drew her in, gesturing for her to be quiet as he listened to the breeze. She waited, fighting her own breathlessness to listen too.

They were closer now, and Giselle heard the baying of bloodhounds now as well as the men's shouting.

Mared heard them, too. "We're not going to be able to lose them, not with those dogs on our scent." He pulled off his sweatshirt. "Take off your clothes and wipe down with them. We're going to switch."

She stared at him. "Why?"

"They've probably trained the dogs on your scent rather than mine. I don't think I've left anything for them to use. We'll split up. That bright star there is the north star." He pointed until she saw which one he was talking about. "Keep it on your right until you see the highway, then follow that south to the first town. I'll go north, and I'll rub up against everything I see to draw the dogs away from you."

"What if they catch you?" she asked worriedly.

He grinned. "I've still got a few tricks up my sleeve. There's a little delicatessen in Mesocco, on your right as you enter town. Wait for me there at noon tomorrow. I'll be there as soon as I can."

Giselle caught his arm, realizing that she didn't want to let him leave her. "Please, Mared, let's just take our chances together. I don't want to put you in any more danger."

The baying of the dogs was growing louder.

"There's no time to argue," he told her. "Just do as I say."

She refused to move, still looking for a way to dissuade him.

"If you don't get out of those sweats, Gili, . . ." he warned, reaching for her determinedly.

She scurried into the bushes then, neatly ducking his hands. As she undressed, she heard a rattling in the branches above her and looked up to find his sweatshirt waiting for her. She wiped down with her own clothing, then tossed them out to him.

Moments later, she emerged from the bushes, wearing his outfit, which hung on her like a tent. He was just pulling her sweatshirt over his head, inside out to expose as much of her scent as possible. It was a snug fit, the material stretching tightly over his shoulders, chest, and arms. The outline of his gun showed clearly beneath the waistband of the pants.

"It's a good thing you did such a poor job of guessing my size when you bought those sweats," she observed. "There's no way you would have fit into them if they were any smaller."

Something in his responding grin made her consider the possibility that he'd chosen the size intentionally. But how could he have expected a situation like this? She hadn't even agreed to head north until after he'd bought these outfits.

He took her arms and looked seriously into her face. "Whatever you do, Giselle, don't come back this way, even if you think I might be in trouble, all right?"

She nodded reluctantly. "Please be careful, Mared. I don't want anything to happen to you."

He smiled. "You take care, too, little sister. I'll meet you at the café tomorrow at noon." Chucking her chin, he turned and jogged back the way they'd come.

Turning, Giselle began walking, striking a pace she knew she could maintain. She wasn't sure how far she had to go, and she wanted some reserve in case she had to run.

The sound of the dogs grew increasingly close, then began to fade. They were following Mared. Trying not to worry, she kept on walking.

A few minutes later, she heard gunfire in the distance.

ChapterSix

It was almost dawn when Giselle spotted the little Swiss village Mared had told her about, tucked in a pocket of the Alps. Even in late spring, the area had the feel of a winter resort. It was vintage Switzerland, with quaint little buildings facing narrow, tree-lined streets; even a medieval castle perched prominently on the hillside. She could see an abandoned rail station at one end of town, the buildings, painted a uniform ivory, bearing signs of wear. She stayed in the trees, moving cautiously around the perimeter of the town, hoping for signs of Mared. Finding none, she found a vantage point and settled in to wait.

The sounds she'd heard the night before still echoed in her mind. One moment, she had herself convinced it was only distant lightning, or the backfire of a car. The next, she was sure that Mared was dead or injured, that she should go back and help him.

But back where? She had no idea where those sounds had come from.

Still, she felt like a coward for not doubling back. What if Mared had been hurt? What if he was dead, or dying out in those woods?

The thought of Mared dying tormented her. He had not asked

for this. He had simply tried to help a stranger. She owed him more than she could repay.

And more than that, strangely, she would miss him.

What about his family, she wondered. If Mared had died because of her, the least she could do was contact them and let them know what had happened. But she had no idea how to reach them, or where to start looking. Bethesda, that was all she knew. She didn't even know his last name. It surprised her to realize that she'd been so involved in her own situation that she'd never thought to ask. She should pay more attention, she admonished herself.

The hours stretched out until, finally, it was nearing noon. Giselle rose anxiously and headed for the town. "Please, God," she whispered, "let him be there waiting for me."

She quickly found the delicatessen that he'd told her about. It was a small café; through the storefront window, Giselle could see a few tables decked with flowered cloths in the dining area. There were only two people sitting in the dining room. Neither was Mared. Giselle swallowed her disappointment. Mared had said to wait for him. Perhaps he was somewhere nearby, making sure she wasn't being followed.

Opening the door jangled a small bell that attracted the attention of the customers. Giselle ducked her face away from them and quickly found a seat. In a few minutes, a woman appeared at her table. She had dark blond hair shot with gray, and a full figure encased in a crisp white apron. In her hands were two menus, and after giving Giselle an appraising look, she set one of them before her. She said something in Swiss, then returned to the kitchen.

Giselle wasn't hungry, but she knew she should order something to justify taking up a table. With an anxious glance toward the door, she opened the menu.

A folded slip of paper dropped into her lap. Assuming it was an old receipt, Giselle was about to set it aside, when she saw the words "Little Sister" written on the outside. She wanted to shout with relief. Only Mared could have written this!

Quickly, she unfolded the paper and read:

"Be careful! Our friends are in town. By now they've probably seen you," the note warned. Giselle glanced at the other customers again. An elderly gentleman nibbled on his sandwich, calmly reading a newspaper. The other, a lady, sipped her coffee and studied a tour guide. Giselle looked out the window, but nothing seemed unusual there either. A middle-aged man sat on a bench outside his store, awaiting customers. A young couple was ambling hand in hand down the sidewalk, headed in the other direction.

She returned her attention to the note, now being careful to keep it hidden in the menu. "The owner of this deli is a friend of mine. She'll help you avoid capture until I can come for you. When she returns, order something and ask where the rest room is. Go where she tells you, and do what she asks you to do."

As casually as she could, Giselle closed the menu and set it down, again glancing at the people she'd seen before. The couple was farther down the street and had stopped to share a kiss. The shopkeeper had gone back into his store, and Giselle could see him working behind the counter. And the old man was now dozing over his newspaper. None of them appeared to be particularly interested in her or this place.

As if on cue, the matron returned, pen in hand, ready to take her order. Giselle gave her an anxious smile, which the woman did not return. "I'll have a hot turkey sandwich and a cup of coffee." As the woman wrote, Giselle added her request for directions to the rest room.

"I will show you." From her inflection, Giselle guessed that these words were practiced, that the woman spoke no English.

Obediently, Giselle followed her from the dining area into a narrow hallway. On the right, there was a wooden door with a sign that Giselle guessed said "rest room" in Swiss. Glancing over her shoulder, the woman took Giselle's arm and hustled her through a swinging door on the left, into the kitchen.

The room had an almost military utility, with a steel walk-in refrigerator, an aging iron stove, and pristine countertops with perfectly aligned knife caddies and spice racks. A young girl with short-cropped, light brown curls stood next to the sink, half-heartedly washing dishes. She stopped when they came in and smiled at Giselle, her eyes taking on a strange excitement.

The matron gave the girl a worried frown, then turned to Giselle. "You are to exchange clothing with my daughter." Again the words came with an odd inflection, as if rehearsed rather than understood.

Knowing it would do no good to question the bizarre order, Giselle obediently turned away and began removing her sweat suit. Moments later, she was wearing a comfortable pair of jeans and a white shirt that was too tight across the bust. Next, the woman drew out something from beneath a counter. It was some sort of harness. Giselle obediently held still as the woman fastened it around her.

Then the woman turned to her daughter, who had taken a cloth napkin and was making a scarf of it. The matron eyed her briefly, then reached out and caressed her daughter's face, speaking quietly in Swiss. The girl nodded soberly, but her eyes were still bright, her expression eager. She spoke words that sounded reassuring, then, with a shy smile at Giselle, she turned and left the kitchen.

The woman watched the door close behind her daughter, a look of inexplicable fear on her face. Then she briskly took Giselle in hand, showing her the back door. Giselle took her hand, hoping to convey her thanks. The woman nodded again and opened the door for her, gesturing to a ladder that would take her to the roof of the building. "Go up," she ordered emphatically. "Go up."

Giselle didn't understand the order, but because it could only have come from Mared, she obeyed, quickly climbing the ladder and crawling up the sloping rooftop. Cautiously, she made her way to the peak, finding a vantage point where she could see the street below without being seen.

Below, she could hear the bell announce the opening of the deli's front door. The girl wearing the too-loose sweat suit raced up the street. The couple abruptly broke their embrace and gave chase, the woman shouting into a handheld radio.

Giselle sat up, intending to give warning. But her cry died in her throat as a helicopter materialized from behind a ridge and swooped toward the town. Giselle didn't recognize the model, but knew instantly that it was military, built for speed and silence. Its third rotor allowed it to move more quietly than its two-rotor cousins, and it was almost overhead before anyone below realized what was happening.

Shouting, the couple dropped their pursuit of the girl as the chopper continued its course. A rope dropped from its cargo door and trailed behind it. As it came nearer, a man stepped out and was lowered on a second rope.

It was coming for her! Giselle scrambled down the roof, intending to drop to the ground and run. A shout stopped her, and she looked up to see that the man on the rope was Mared!

The chopper dipped, bringing him nearer, and he stretched out his hand to her. "Grab on!"

She froze, staring dumbly at him, her hair whipping her face in the wind from the rotors. It all seemed so surreal. How could this be happening?

A car screeched up to the deli, disgorging several men with automatic rifles. As Giselle hesitated, they assumed a firing stance, aiming their weapons at the chopper.

Mared glanced at them, then swung toward her again. "Come on, Giselle! This is no time to be afraid of heights. Grab on!"

A shot whizzed past him, and a second struck sparks off the tail section of the helicopter. Giselle glanced down to see a second car pull up. The Arab stepped out, his arm raised as if to order his men to fire again.

"Me or them, Giselle!" Mared shouted.

Giselle launched herself at him, wrapping her arms around his neck. He quickly hooked her harness to the second rope and signaled the man above. The chopper lifted off and raced away, trailing the two of them behind.

❖ ❖ ❖

The helplessness was killing him. Raz stared at the walls of his living room, wishing that he could do something—anything—to right the wrong he had done Giselle. The guilt was like a storm raging through him, hurling emotions like lightning bolts through his heart.

He should have told her. The knowledge was his damnation. He had no right to marry her without telling her what she was getting into. She would have thrown his proposal in his face, of course. That would have been agony, but far better than what was happening now.

Now, because of him, Giselle might die.

He was on his feet before he knew it, clearing his desktop with a sweep of his arm. The shattering of glass brought him to his senses, and he looked down to find the remnants of a glass paperweight Giselle had given him. As he bent to pick up a fragment, he heard a voice coming from the telephone receiver, which lay uncradled amidst a pile of papers on the floor.

It was the admiral. Raz snatched up the phone. "I'm here, sir."

"Is everything all right?" the old man asked.

"Fine, sir. I just dropped the phone," Raz answered quickly. "Is there any news from Riley?"

There was a pause. "Nothing good. He was in touch with Arn Killian over at the ONI, and they're still tracking a few leads, but so far, they're coming up empty. I had hoped the authorities might have contacted you."

Raz slumped. "No, sir. Nothing here."

"Well." The admiral was trying to sound calm, but there was a quiver in his voice. "Keep me posted, son."

"I'll do that, sir." Raz squeezed his eyes closed. Should he tell the admiral—come clean and hope it would do some good? He would be arrested, maybe even worse, but if there was a chance it would help Gili . . .

"Sir?" he spoke quickly, before the admiral could hang up.

"Yes?"

"I'm . . . sorry. I know this must be very difficult for you."

There was another pause, then a long sigh. "No more than for you, son. But thanks for your concern."

Raz hung up the phone gently, then bent to pick up the items that had fallen from his desk. Among them was Giselle's Bible. Her father had given it to her for her catechism, she'd said. She kept it, obviously treasured it, but the gilt edges of the pages still shone like new, testifying to the fact that she rarely read it.

He found himself opening the book, hoping, he guessed, to find words of comfort.

The Bible opened to a place marked by a sheet of note paper. It was folded neatly, yellowed around the edges. Unfolding it, Raz saw that it contained a list of Scripture references. Were these Gili's favorite quotes? It didn't look like her handwriting, but for some reason she'd kept it.

All of the quotes seemed to be from the Hebrew Scriptures. The books of Giselle's Old Testament, he knew, were the same as the Hebrew Tanakh, though not organized in the same order.

Referencing the first note on the page, he turned to a psalm. The first verse seemed to speak his heart. *"My God, my God, why have you forsaken me? Why are you so far from saving me, so far from the words of my groaning? O my God, I cry out by day, but you do not answer, by night, and am not silent."*

Raz was surprised. He had always believed that the Bible was nothing but stories of holy men, people who had an "in" with God. Instead, this was something he could relate to. Whoever wrote this seemed to be going through something like what he was experiencing.

He kept reading. *"But I am a worm, and not a man, scorned by men and despised by the people. . . ."* There it was. His guilt, his unworthiness. He deserved to be despised.

"Dogs have surrounded me; a band of evil men has encircled me, they have pierced my hands and my feet."

Stunned, Raz stared at the passage, reading it again and again. What on earth?

Abruptly he rose, taking the book with him into the bedroom. Retrieving Giselle's crucifix from the wall, he stared at it, then back at the words he had just read: *". . . pierced my hands and my feet."*

The note page had a bulleted section that described the agonizing details of death on a cross. Each point referred back to a passage in this psalm. It spoke of thirst, quenched by gall. A heart being strangled in its own fluids. The taunts of the onlookers. *"They divide my garments among them and cast lots for my clothing."* Hadn't he read somewhere that the Romans had cast lots for Jesus' clothing?

If he remembered his Hebrew culture studies correctly, this psalm had been written by King David, hundreds of years before the birth of Jesus. And yet it seemed to foretell exactly what would happen to this man depicted on Giselle's icon. *How had David known?*

The question jarred him.

Raz continued following the Scriptures on the notepaper. The more he read, the more perplexed he became.

In Daniel 9, Raz read about the Messiah-King arriving *before* the destruction of the temple, which he knew had taken place in A.D. 70. The passage said he would be cut off—didn't that mean executed? Jesus, he knew, had been crucified around A.D. 32.

Isaiah 53 spoke of an innocent man who suffered and died a criminal's death, receiving the punishment for the sins of others. If Raz had read it anywhere but in the Hebrew Scriptures, he would have thought it was a Christian poem.

Why had his teachers never told him about this Scripture?

The men who wrote these prophecies had lived between four hundred and seven hundred years before the birth of Jesus. Their writings were on parchment no later than 200 B.C., when the Septuagint, a Greek translation of the Hebrew Scriptures, was written. He remembered from his Bar Mitzvah studies that the accuracy of the modern texts was verified by the Dead Sea Scrolls, themselves dated nearly one hundred years before Jesus Christ was born.

How had they known?

Isaiah 46:9–10: *"I am God, and there is no other; I am God, and there is none like me. I make known the end from the beginning, from ancient times, what is still to come."* Had God foretold the life and death of this man Jesus? Was all of it real after all?

Like a tree cut at the trunk, he felt himself crumpling, dropping to his knees. His face was wet, his eyes blurred with tears, as he whispered, "God, please, I beg you. Don't let Giselle die. You've never answered my prayers before, but I beg you, answer this one. I know I don't deserve for you to hear me. If you want me to pay for what I've done, I'll pay any price you want. But not her. Don't let her die because of me."

It was as if a dam had broken. The words kept coming, as if from the depths of his soul. "Je . . . Jesus, I don't know if you're who Giselle thinks you are. But if you are, I'll pray to you, too. Please keep my Gili alive. Please bring her home safe. I'll die. I'll go to prison—I'll do whatever you want. Just let me see her one more time."

He slumped, weeping. "Please . . . !"

❖ ❖ ❖

Giselle's heart was still drumming against her rib cage when the helicopter set down in a field several miles away.

The pilot handed a set of keys to Mared. "Wait at the condominium until you receive word," he said in English. "We'll arrange your flight as quickly as possible."

Mared nodded and jumped to the ground, then turned and helped Giselle out of the helicopter. She followed him at a distance as he hurried to a car that was parked near the side of the road.

Mared inserted the keys in the passenger door and opened it for her, not realizing until he turned toward her that she was hanging back. "What's wrong?"

She eyed him warily. "Who are you, Mared?"

"What do you mean?" His face registered bewilderment, but the expression seemed contrived.

She gestured to the chopper, which had achieved flight altitude and was speeding away. "That's a military helicopter—special ops. We're talking millions of dollars. Who were those men, and how did they get it?"

He shrugged guardedly. "They're friends of mine. . . ."

"You and your 'friends!'" she exploded. "I'm sick of being lied to, Mared!"

"Giselle, we don't have time for this." He spoke urgently. "If the chopper was tracked by radar, our pursuers will be here in minutes."

Giselle was stunned. "Radar? What makes you think they'd have radar? Who do you think those people are?"

Mared's expression closed abruptly. "Giselle, please. I'll tell you what you want to know, but first let's get out of here." His voice was earnest, but his eyes were measuring the distance between them.

Giselle backed away several paces, realizing abruptly that she shouldn't have confronted him here. The area was deserted. There was nowhere to run, no one to help her if he tried to force her into the car.

Mared nodded toward an approaching cloud of dust. "That's a car coming up the road. If those are our friends, we have one minute. Maybe less." He stepped forward, reaching for her arm.

"Don't!" Giselle snapped, automatically dropping into a ready stance, feet apart, weight distributed evenly, knees slightly bent. She probably couldn't fight him off, but she could slow him down.

"OK." He raised his hands and backed off. "It's up to you, Giselle. We can stay here and argue or you can trust me. Make up your mind quick, though, because that car is getting closer."

"The military-issue Colt, the clothes, the way you drove the car back in Frosinone, the way you've always seemed to know just what to do—you're no amateur, Mared. Tell me who you're working for."

He gauged her determination, then nodded reluctantly. "All right. I'm sorry for the lies. I'm supposed to be undercover, or I'd have told you right away. I'm with Naval Intelligence."

One of Arn's agents! If it was true. She wanted badly to believe him, but part of her was still wary. "Show me some ID."

"Giselle, I said I was working undercover," he reminded her. "Carrying ID can get a man killed."

She eyed him skeptically. "Why should I believe you?"

He glanced at the dust cloud, then back at her. "Giselle, who do you trust? Me, or the men who almost shot us down a few minutes ago? Because here they come."

Noting the nearness of the approaching car, Giselle realized she had to acquiesce. She nodded. "OK," she said, "but I'm driving." She held out her hand expectantly.

Seeming relieved, he tossed her the keys.

She didn't budge. "The gun, too."

He hesitated, then shrugged and withdrew it from his belt. For a tense moment, Giselle thought he might point it at her, but then he turned it, offering it to her butt-first. She took it, emptied the clip and chamber, then tossed it through the open rear window.

She hurried round the car to get in, hoping that he wouldn't overpower her before she could start the engine. Once the car was moving, he'd have to find a way to control both it and her, and she gambled that he wouldn't try it.

The other car followed them for almost a mile. Giselle drove as quickly as she dared, noting with relief that it quickly fell behind and eventually turned onto a side road.

Mared sat quietly until she pulled onto a crossroad, then leaned back in his seat, a calm expression on his face. "Keep going in this direction and we'll end up back in Italy," he told her.

She hesitated, then turned the car around.

"Do you really think that your driving is a good idea?" he asked her. "If our friends do start chasing us, you don't know these roads well enough to shake them."

"You prove you're who you say you are and I'll think about letting you drive," she told him, noting with relief that he appeared to have no intention of trying anything. "I'm sick of being lied to, Mared," she repeated. "First my husband, and now you."

"I understand," he told her soberly. "But this goes a lot deeper than your hurt feelings, Giselle. Those men in that chopper, the woman back at the deli, their lives are in danger. You must understand that."

She pondered this, then glanced at him. "I'm beginning to understand a lot of things, Mared. You didn't just happen to be in Frosinone the other day, did you?"

He stared at her, then shook his head with a rueful grin. "You're too smart for your own good, you know that?" He paused for a moment, then continued cautiously. "I can tell you this much. We think there's a leak at the embassy. I was assigned to watch the comings and goings from the dry cleaner's shop across the street. When I saw you tearing out of there with your husband chasing you, I decided to follow. Then I saw those men try to grab you."

She nodded. "Who do you answer to?" she asked, as casually

as she could manage. It was a simple question, and almost anyone who paid attention to the ONI would know the official answer. But a true insider might say something she could verify.

"Killjoy Killian." Mared grinned, using a friendly nickname that had followed Arn since his days at Annapolis. "He's OK, for brass. I've been answering directly to him ever since Gersham's libido got him bounced back home several months ago."

Giselle felt herself relaxing. Only a few people knew the circumstances of Ira Gersham's abrupt "retirement." The man Arn had placed in charge of operations in Italy had been relieved when it was discovered that his mistress was an agent for the Mossad. And Mared was right about another thing as well—Arn probably hadn't sought a replacement yet. During one of the last conversations she'd overheard between him and her father, he'd said that the times were too sensitive to be training a newcomer. At the time, Giselle hadn't understood his meaning, although it had become clear enough in recent weeks.

"Listen," Mared broke into her thoughts. "Now that this is out in the open, it's time you answered some of my questions. I've been trying to find out what you knew for days without arousing your suspicions."

She hesitated. Was she ready to incriminate Raz? Once done, it couldn't be undone. Slowly, she shook her head. "I need a little time to digest this first, all right?"

He sighed. "All right, but you'll have to open up pretty soon, either to me or to my superiors." He paused for a moment, watching her intently. "Giselle, if there's a way to get through this without anyone you care about getting hurt, I want to help you. But you're going to have to trust me."

Trust me. She sighed wearily. "It's nothing personal, Mared, but trust doesn't come all that easy to me these days."

"Understandable," he noted soberly. "Meanwhile, why don't you let me take the wheel? No offense, but we'll be safer if I'm driving."

❖ ❖ ❖

Mared glanced at Giselle, wondering what she was thinking. She had been unusually quiet for the past several hours, barely seeming to notice his cautious maneuvers, his frequent turns off the road to make certain they weren't followed. Her silence worried him. He hoped it didn't mean she was reassessing her decision to trust him.

They entered Bern at twilight, the skylight dominated by a cathedral's spire, a black spear against the golden sunset. Mared drove to a newer row of condominiums that had been constructed near the airport for late-arriving holiday skiers. He parked before a first-floor unit and circled the car. Opening the trunk, he drew out a large suitcase.

"What's in there?" Giselle asked as he unlocked the front door.

"Just a change of clothes for later," Mared told her, relieved at her conversational tone. Perhaps his concerns were unfounded.

The condo was a single-room unit with a utility kitchen and a foldout sofa bed. Still, it was larger and more luxurious than it appeared from outside, with a glass door at the rear that opened to a patio, complete with hot tub, overlooking the common gardens.

"Grab a shower if you want," he said. "There should be towels and soap in the bathroom. I was told this place would be fully stocked. I'm going to check the kitchen and see what there is to eat."

Half an hour later, they were sitting comfortably on the sofa, their feet up on the coffee table, sharing a pot of chicken soup. Giselle was wearing an oversized terrycloth robe that she'd found in the bathroom. "There's even a towel warmer in there," she told him. "I'm surprised the ONI would put us up in such a high-rent place."

Mared wanted to smile at her astute observation, but kept his face straight. "These were probably the cheapest digs available on short notice."

She rose and stretched. "I think I'll take a cat nap, if that's all right with you."

"I was planning to shower next," he said agreeably, coming to his feet. Before she could turn away, he caught her shoulders, gazing at her earnestly. "But when you wake up, we need to talk. It may be a matter of life and death."

She nodded slowly and busied herself with the foldout bed. Mared watched her for a moment, then headed for the bathroom.

He had received new orders from the men in the helicopter this morning. Initially, the plan had been for him to keep her busy for a few days, let things run their course. But now he was to bring her in.

This was not good news. Not at all.

It was more urgent than ever that he find out what she knew.

❖ ❖ ❖

Giselle was half asleep when Mared reentered the room wearing only his sweat pants. He paused, apparently considering the open side of the bed, then walked over to the reclining chair. He sat in it, watching her intently, then leaned back and closed his eyes.

She watched him silently as his features settled into the unguarded expression she was beginning to find dear. A gleam caught her eye from the thatch of black hair that curled over his chest. It was a square gold charm, hanging from a chain around his neck. It reminded her of something, but she couldn't decide what. Curious, Giselle squinted at it, trying to determine what it was.

Finally, her mind fixed on the *mezuzah,* the box that Raz had affixed to the doorpost of her home. Mared's charm reminded her of that. All it lacked was the traditional Hebrew letter "shin" for *Shaddai,* the Almighty God of Israel, which was inscribed on all the *mezuzot* she had seen. This must be something else. Still, the charm reminded her of home, of the warmth and security she had known just a couple of days ago. Looking at it, Giselle felt a need to trust someone. Could she trust Mared?

He liked her. She could tell by the way he looked at her. And he wanted to help her. He'd even told her as much. Maybe if she explained her dilemma, he could find a way to help her protect Raz as much as possible. Others—even Arn and her father—weren't likely to be so sympathetic.

"Mared?" she whispered, not wanting to wake him if he was asleep.

His eyelids fluttered. "Mmm?"

"I'm ready to talk whenever you want to listen."

His eyes opened, and he looked at her. "Go ahead."

She steeled herself, then launched in. "There's a plot to assassinate the delegates." It was her final test. If he asked what delegates, she'd know she could say no more.

But he nodded. "We expected it. What can you tell me?"

"Only that someone called Seif—his name means Sword—will have access to the delegates once they arrive in Italy." She was leaving out Raz's part in it, but she could fill that in later. She needed to work up to it.

Mared nodded again. "Tell me what you know about the Sword of Islam."

She paused, realizing that most of what she knew came from sources she couldn't reveal. "I know that they're a terrorist organization," she told him guardedly.

He frowned. "Giselle, you must realize how important it is that you tell me everything you know."

"All right." She shrugged. "I know that they've been working with other terrorist groups, offering arms and information in exchange for cooperation with their goals. And they're probably linked to some government agency, because their intelligence is too good to come from civilian sources. They seem to have connections almost everywhere."

A slow astonishment spread over his face. "Where did you learn all that? Did Raz tell you?"

She shook her head. "It wasn't him."

"Then where?" he insisted.

She shook her head. "I can't say."

He saw the resolve on her face and sighed. "Let's back up a few steps. How deeply is your husband involved?"

She hesitated for a long moment, then dropped her eyes, swallowing hard. "I found a letter in his desk." Blinking back tears, she told Mared the contents.

He waited for her to look up again, then caught her eyes in a gaze so intense it almost frightened her. "Do you think your husband is capable of doing what he says?"

She hesitated, then nodded miserably.

He smiled grimly, his eyes unreadable. "What about those men who have been chasing us? What makes you think your husband sent them?"

She shrugged. "Who else would have sent them?"

"But it's just an assumption?" His expression had a surprising urgency.

Giselle nodded, wondering at his intensity. "Yes."

He leaned forward. "Have you ever seen your husband with any of those men? Think about this. It's important that I know whether he's been contacted by them."

She thought briefly, then shook her head again. "No. Never those men. I did see him once, talking with a man in a jewelry store. . . ." She drifted off, her mouth going dry. A slow horror dawned on her as she realized where she'd seen Mared before. The jewelry store!

His eyes hardened as he saw her expression change. He closed the distance between them and caught her arms before she could get away. "You were saying?"

Her heart was thrashing against her ribs like a caged animal. Swallowing, she shook her head. "It was nothing. I don't remember."

He smiled sadly at her obvious lie. "I'm sorry, Giselle. I wish there was some way to reassure you that this is for the best." Just as she opened her mouth to scream, he clipped her on the jaw with his fist.

❖ ❖ ❖

When Giselle regained consciousness, she was prone on the foldout bed. Groggily, she looked for Mared.

He was on the phone, speaking rapidly in Akkadian. When he glanced at her, Giselle averted her eyes, pretending not to understand what he was saying.

"I was forced to subdue her. She will not come with me willingly now. It matters little, except at the airport. . . ." The word "airport," spoken in modern Arabic, sounded strange intermixed with the ancient tongue. He paused, listening to his instructions, then added, "It will be as you say."

Hanging up the phone, he turned to her and spoke in English. "I'm sorry I hit you. Please don't make me do it again." He sat next to her on the bed, looking frustrated when she pulled away from him. "I wish it didn't have to be like this, Giselle. Please believe me, the last thing I want to do is hurt you."

When she still didn't respond, he backed away, crossing to the suitcase he'd brought inside earlier. "You can use the bathroom if you want," he said. "I'd suggest that you do so now, because this will be your last chance for several hours." He handed her a large parcel from the suitcase, something wrapped in tissue as if newly purchased. "Put these on while you're in there."

Giselle glared at him, but obediently rose, heading for the bathroom. There were no windows in the bathroom. She'd noticed that when she'd showered earlier. But maybe if she locked herself in and pounded on the wall, she might draw a neighbor's attention.

As if he was reading her thoughts, Mared shadowed her and braced a hand against the door when she tried to close it. "I'll stand away and give you some privacy, but if you try to close the door or scream, I intend to kick it open," he warned.

Giselle glared at him, closing the door as far as he would allow.

Inside the tissue was a pair of soft black slippers, black gloves, stockings, and to her shock, an *abaaya,* the hooded black cloak that covered women in many Arab countries from wrist to neck to foot. With it was a *shayla,* a scarf that covered the hair completely.

So Mared meant to take her to the Middle East—but which country? Giselle quickly donned the robe and slippers, leaving the gloves on the sink. Then she flushed the toilet. Mared would be getting impatient, and she wanted to keep him outside as long as possible. Checking the crack in the door to make sure he wasn't looking, she silently opened the shower door and, grabbing a tube of toothpaste, scrawled a message on the shower floor:

"Kidnapped! Airport—Middle East."

She had just put away the toothpaste and was closing the shower door when Mared called out. She had just enough time to turn back to the sink, when he entered the bathroom.

Mared, too, had changed clothing, donning a white *thobe* and red-checked *ghutra,* the traditional male attire in many Arab countries. He wore them as if born to them, and she found herself startled by his appearance. How could she have thought she knew him? She had trusted him even after she had caught him in a lie. How could she have been so stupid?

Gripping her arm, he gave the room a quick visual search, but miraculously, he missed her message. Seeming satisfied, he picked up the gloves and pulled her into the main room, positioning her next to the bed. Taking each of her hands, he forced the gloves over her rigid fingers. Then, he picked up something new—a black, gauzy veil.

Attached to a cap that was anchored by the *shayla,* the veil would cover Giselle's face completely, rendering her unrecognizable. With a growing sense of helplessness, Giselle tried to back away, but she tripped on the hem of the *abaaya* and fell. He straddled her quickly, discarding the veil long enough to bind her wrists with a strip torn from the sheet. Keeping her down, he reached for the veil and arranged it over her face, pulling the hood of her cloak in place to help anchor the cap. Then he turned, binding her thrashing legs with a short length of sheet between them.

Finally, he rose, drawing her up after him. He straightened her clothing to cover his handiwork, then pulled her with him to the door. She stumbled twice, the sheet bringing her up short when she tried for a normal stride.

It was worse in the darkness outside. Giselle couldn't see anything through the veil, except the ghostly outline of Mared's white form as he led her to the car. He held the back door for her and reached down to tuck in her robe. When he closed the door, she realized for the first time that the rear doors had no interior handles. She was trapped.

"Where are we going?" she ventured as he got in the driver's side.

"Riyadh," he told her.

"Saudi Arabia!" she exclaimed. "But they're our allies! They don't harbor terrorists there!"

He smiled humorlessly. "That's the official story. But it's a bit naive, don't you think? Arabs are a passionate people, and Saudi Arabia is not divorced from the concerns of its neighbors."

They rode in silence the rest of the way. When they reached the airport, Mared got out of the car and climbed in the back next to her. He drew a roll of tape from a pocket, and before

Giselle realized what he was going to do, he leaned across the back seat, lifted her veil and pressed a strip firmly over her mouth.

Watching her, he withdrew the little medical kit from a pocket in his robe. He checked the label on the vial, then quickly attached a needle to the syringe and began to fill it. Realizing what was about to happen, Giselle lunged over the seat, hoping to make it to the front and out the door, but he caught her leg and she was trapped, bent over the seat. As she struggled, he pinned her legs against the seat and got on with what he was doing. He tugged the needle from the bottle, tapped the syringe several times, and depressed the plunger until liquid squirted out. Then he reached down and drew up the skirt of her robe. Giselle thrashed helplessly as he injected the fluid into her bare thigh.

"It's nothing dangerous," he assured her, tugging her robe back down. "Just a strong sedative. It should take effect quickly."

Mared stayed close to her inside the terminal, keeping an arm around her for support as her legs grew heavy. They drew a few curious stares, she noticed, but most people seemed accustomed to seeing the occasional Arab and his wife, dressed in traditional garb.

A security officer was coming toward them. Mared's arm tightened around her waist, his hand gripping her arm in warning. Ignoring him, Giselle managed to work up the skirt of her robe. She accentuated her hobbled stride, hoping to draw the man's attention to her feet, where he might see the bindings and realize what was happening.

But Mared noticed first and yanked her to a halt, pulling down the hem of her robe and cursing her roundly in Arabic. The guard continued past them, giving Mared a contemptuous glare.

"Don't try it again," Mared warned, this time in English, before pulling her along with him again.

Giselle felt herself growing groggy, stumbling more and more, her head tilting to Mared's shoulder. He was nearly carrying her by the time they reached the gate. Mared handed two passports to the gate attendant, who barely looked at them before waving them through.

Within minutes, they were aboard a small private jet. A male attendant closed the hatch as Mared deposited Giselle in a seat and belted her in. With barely a look in their direction, the man moved to the cockpit and rapped sharply, then took a seat next to the door. After a brief wait, the jet began making its way toward a runway.

Unable to lift her head away from the window, Giselle watched as the lights of the terminal drifted hazily from sight. A feeling of despair flooded her as she lost her battle with unconsciousness.

❖ ❖ ❖

She awoke as if rising through murky waters. Someone was shaking her shoulder. "Wake up," the voice said. "Giselle, wake up." Then, before she was fully conscious, someone was pulling her to her feet. She staggered dizzily, disoriented in a hot, heavy darkness that seemed far too close, thickening even the air she breathed. She sank back to the seat, certain she was still asleep, but an arm firmly hauled her up and forced her to move again.

Gradually, as she walked, her surroundings began to make sense. It wasn't night; the veil over her face only made it seem dark. Mared was half-carrying her down a set of steel stairs, across the tarmac, and then she was inside the terminal of the King Khalid International Airport near Riyadh.

Filtered through the thin black gauze that clouded her vision and the drug that still fogged her mind, she recorded a scene that seemed almost surreal. The airport itself was fairly new, clean, and as modern as any she'd seen in Europe. But the people!

An almost toothless old Bedouin passed by in dusty robes, hawking and spitting directly on the polished tile floor as if to show he had no more regard for tile than sand. A man close behind him slipped in the spittle and nearly fell. To either side of the walkway, women, formless black shadows in their *abaayas,* sat in clusters on the chairs, their luggage and children scattered around them. Their white-clad husbands stood detached at the perimeters of the groups, chatting easily with one another while seemingly ignoring their families.

Giselle turned her head and the world spun wildly. She tripped over something and nearly sank to the floor, but was hauled to her feet again by Mared's strong grasp.

They were caught up in a stream of people that carried them outside again. After only a few moments beneath the powerful desert sun, she was sweating profusely under the heavy black robe. The combination of the heat and the remnants of the sedative made her feel ill. Ignoring Mared's efforts to move her along, she stopped short, bending forward to ease the cramping in her stomach.

"Yallah! Emshu!" Mared barked at her. "Come on! Get moving!" He started walking again, pulling hard on the skirt of her robe until she had to follow him or be pulled off balance. She wanted to argue, but the tape that was still over her mouth made reply impossible.

She staggered after him, stubbing a toe painfully on a crack in the sidewalk. The sweat was pouring from her forehead, stinging her already half-blinded eyes. She reached under the veil to blot it away, wishing she could bare her head to the desert breeze and see where she was walking. But such an act might get her arrested if she bumped into the wrong people.

Arrested! Some dim part of her mind said that might be just what she wanted. She allowed her sluggish steps to lag and positioned herself behind Mared, just out of his line of sight. Keeping up his appearance as a disdainful Saudi husband, he ignored her, merely keeping a grip on her robe so that she had to keep moving.

Cautiously, Giselle reached up with her bound hands, tossed back the hood of her cloak, and pulled off her *shayla* and veil, baring her face and hair for all to see. That turned a number of heads, but didn't provoke the desired response. Dropping still further out of Mared's line of sight, she again worked up the skirt of her *abaaya* to reveal the bindings on her legs.

The reaction was astonishing. Men stopped dead in their tracks and stared as if transfixed by the view of a forbidden woman. Murmurs of shock and disapproval followed them, and Giselle was afraid that Mared would realize what she was doing before someone in authority saw her. But it wasn't long before she caught the attention of a *mutawa,* an official keeper of the public morals, whom she recognized by his red-stained beard.

He came after her, screeching angrily and waving a fierce-looking camel whip. A small crowd of men followed him, some of them furious, others staring with such fierce lust that Giselle felt naked before them. A man reached out to touch her, and she cowered away, realizing suddenly that she'd made a very dangerous mistake.

Mared stopped short and turned, realizing the cause of the excitement. He stared into her eyes with a dangerous anger.

Gathering her courage, Giselle turned to the *mutawa.* She tried to speak before she remembered Mared's gag. Hastily, she reached up and ripped the tape away. "Please help me, sir," she said, her Arabic thickened by her drug-sodden tongue. "I'm an American. This man is a terrorist, and he has kidnapped me from my family." When the man stared at her skeptically, she again lifted the skirt of her robe to reveal the lengths of sheet that bound her ankles.

The crowd gasped, and the *mutawa* stepped back several paces, horrified by this glimpse of a woman's limbs. Then he rushed forward with his whip, thrashing her legs painfully and shouting at her in Arabic. When she dropped her skirt, he shook the whip in her face, threatening to strike her there as well if she failed to replace her veil.

"*Min fadlak*—please!" Desperately, Giselle stared at each of the men in turn, tearfully begging one of them to intervene. "Someone help me!"

Mared turned to the *mutawa*. *"As-salaam alaykum,"* he said respectfully. "Peace be upon you, sir. A thousand apologies for this disturbance. This woman is indeed half-American," he said, explaining her accent and appearance. "But her father is Saudi. She is my wife, but she has dishonored herself. I am returning her to her father's house, where I intend to divorce her. She will say anything to avoid the certain punishment that she knows awaits her."

To Giselle's horror, many of the men uttered sympathetic noises, and reached out to clap Mared on the back supportively.

The *mutawa* nodded benignly. "The word of a woman is always suspect, especially that of an adulteress. And I have no doubt of that after seeing her display herself so immodestly! She is a threat to Islam, and should be stoned."

Many of the men agreed, some of them even bending to pick up rocks from a nearby garden. Terrified, Giselle cowered behind Mared.

Mared shrugged. "It is nothing to me. But her father wishes to kill her himself, and so remove the dishonor she has already brought his name."

The old man nodded sagely, gesturing to the others to move away. "It is his right."

"Please," Giselle tried again. "I beg you—my father is an American—he knows one of your princes. His name is Vice Admiral Thaddeus Hardy."

Before she could protect herself, the old man abruptly raised his whip and struck a vicious, slashing blow across her cheeks. "Cover yourself, harlot! It is good you should die today before your vile immodesty causes another man to offend Allah with impure thoughts!" So saying, he raised the whip again.

The blow fell this time on Giselle's shaking hands as she

hurriedly replaced the *shayla,* veil, and hood. The crowd muttered its approval, satisfied at seeing her brought to heel.

Turning to Giselle, Mared took her arm roughly, and began to walk rapidly, forcing her to run, and dragging her when she fell. Behind her, Giselle could hear the *mutawa* beseeching the crowd to return their thoughts to holy things and go about their business.

Mared stopped and let her regain her feet once they were out of sight of the men. "That was a stupid thing to do, Giselle. Those men would have stoned you to death if I hadn't stopped them."

"Am I supposed to thank you?" she snapped, cursing him in Arabic. Her hands were still shaking.

He turned and started walking again, leaving the sidewalk for the open parking lot. The heat coming off the asphalt struck Giselle like a new assault, blistering her feet through her slippers, and surging in waves under her robes.

"Isn't someone picking us up?" she asked.

"Flight schedules in this part of the world are iffy at best," Mared told her. "It's easier to just leave a car and let us drive ourselves." He led her to a black sedan and opened the back door. Shutting her in, he quickly entered through the driver's door.

The car had been left in the sun all day. The intensified heat inside was even more brutal than that of the parking lot, dehydrating her quickly before Mared finally got the air conditioner going. She turned in her seat and held her veil over the vent, letting the cool air billow under it.

Mared watched her in the rearview mirror.

She ignored him, letting the cold air revitalize her. It seemed to clear her mind even as her sodden muscles began to regain their strength.

A sand-beaten truck careened from a side road into their path, forcing Mared to stand on the brakes. As the car came to a near stop, Mared quickly locked the door, but his precaution was unnecessary. Giselle knew better than to try to get away again. Back at the airport, her mind must have been dulled by the sedative, she realized. What she'd done was more than stupid.

Her actions had flown in the face of every Saudi propriety— not to mention a law or two. Speaking to strange men—and worse, revealing her body—was considered an alarming breech of the public morals in a country where immoral behavior could be punished by anything from public whippings to execution. Saudi women risked beatings if they dared to walk through the streets with short sleeves, and harassment if they were without a male relative to protect them from unacceptable contact with unrelated men.

A woman's *ird,* her chastity, was a matter of honor for the men of her family. Should she lose it or even appear to lose it, her nearest male blood relation was considered within his rights to kill her in order to erase the stain on his reputation. In a country where the births of females went unrecorded, their desert graves unmarked, no one knew how many women had been executed by their fathers, uncles, brothers, or even sons.

She had just entered what could be the most dangerous country in the world for women—and the most difficult country for a female hostage to escape.

As they entered the bustling city of Riyadh, Giselle watched out the window, trying to keep track of their route. Most of the streets were unmarked, making this difficult—especially when Mared made a complex series of turns, seeming to double back a number of times before finding another major thoroughfare. She fixed it in her mind as best she could by focusing on land-marks and counting the streets they passed.

Finally, they arrived at a splendid palace near the heart of the city. Its outer walls, painted a sun-reflecting white, gleamed in the daylight as guards opened the gates to allow them to pass through. A row of palm trees lined the long drive. As Mared pulled up to the head of the drive, servants hurried out to greet them. One of them took the car keys from Mared, promising, with an accent that Giselle couldn't place, to drive carefully to the garage. Others hurried forward to usher them toward the palace, seeming unsurprised at their lack of luggage.

Mared handed Giselle over to three female servants. "Take her to the room you have prepared," he instructed. "See to her needs, but do not engage her in conversation." Then he turned to her. "Do as they say, Giselle, and you won't get hurt." So saying, he walked away, unconcerned with her response.

Knowing it was hopeless to resist, Giselle followed the women as they led her to a separate entrance. One of them paused at the doorway, touching her breastbone, then kissing her fingers, murmuring some kind of blessing. Giselle strained to hear the words, but couldn't make them out. In all her studies of Arab customs, she had never heard of this tradition, and she wondered at its significance.

Immediately inside the doorway, there was a narrow and steep set of stairs that led up to the *hareem,* the place where Arab women lived apart from their men. Giselle understood that this living arrangement was a practicality in this society, protecting the unveiled women of the household from accidental contact with male visitors. Likewise, female visitors could come and go without bumping into the men who lived here.

At Yale, reading about this, she had struggled not to see this practice through Western eyes, judgmentally, but to consider it in terms of its context within a culture where her own ways would seem equally shocking. As a woman, she'd found it almost impossible not to feel somehow insulted by such profound segregation. But now, after standing unveiled before a crowd of Arab men, she saw it in a different light. In this place, where contact between men and women was severely restricted, the men had never learned to control their baser instincts. A woman alone, a woman uncovered, was in serious personal danger.

The servants led her past a lavish living room that opened out to a rooftop garden, where the women of the home were entertaining. Without the prying eyes of men to see them, the ladies had shed their *abaayas* in favor of what could only be described as fairy-tale dresses. Giselle knew that the best designers in Europe made millions of dollars designing such gowns for Saudi women, who seemed to prefer lavish ornamentation and dramatic appeal over the simpler garments worn by women almost everywhere else in the world.

Servants fanned incense toward them so that their clothing and hair would catch the scent, while they chattered excitedly about their latest purchases at the *souq,* the marketplace. The discussion went silent as she was led past the open doors.

"Who is that?" Giselle heard one of the guests asking.

"That's Chardae. Her husband is my brother-in-law. She's from the eastern province."

"Will she join us?"

"No. Hashim tells me she has been disobedient and must stay in her room while she is here. We are not to speak to her."

Beginning to sense what her stay was going to be like, Giselle reluctantly followed the servant down a long hallway to her apartment.

❖ ❖ ❖

"*Alahu akbar*—Allah is great. I testify that there is no god but Allah! Come to prayer!" Five times a day, the words echoed from loudspeakers all over the city, calling all Muslims to prayer at mosques erected in every neighborhood.

Giselle had been here three days, marking the hours by prayer calls, which came at dawn, midday, midafternoon, sunset, and one hour after sunset. Other than brief visits from a servant charged with bringing her food, she'd had no contact with anyone. Her guards had told her, in no uncertain terms, that she was not to leave the room, and in any event, the heavy door was bolted from outside.

She paced the elegantly tiled floor of her apartment for what seemed like the thousandth time, passing without notice the canopy bed with its delicately tapestried pillows. She ignored, too, the posh European designer furniture, the Arabian knick-knacks, and the carefully painted desert scenes on each of the room's walls. These things had already been analyzed until they were burned into her mind. They had ceased to distract her from her predicament, and from the growing realization of the danger she was in.

There was a small television in the sitting area, but it held no interest for her. She'd watched a few hours this morning, hoping to catch some news that might tell her what was going on at home. But Saudi TV was dominated by bearded Islamic teachers giving verbose sermons on every aspect of Muslim life, and informational offerings on such topics as the good reasons for obeying traffic signals and the proven dangers of eating pork. There was one channel for Western viewers, offering family-oriented television shows from the United States, but the news was so heavily censored that the stories and pictures made little sense.

She stilled, hearing the women of the household chattering excitedly at the head of the hallway. They were coming this way! Giselle hurried to the door, pressing her ear to the wood in hopes of hearing something. But, as if they knew she was listening, a hush dropped like a veil over the conversation as they passed.

Frustrated, she wandered back toward the room's sole window, which she had thrown open earlier in hopes of hearing something from below. During the day, the breeze that blew in from the desert was stifling, especially since she still had nothing to wear but the sweat-stiffened *abaaya*. But at least she could see what was going on below.

Her room overlooked an inner courtyard, near the center of

the palace. The window was covered with a decorative screen so that the woman who lived here could look out without being seen. The purpose was to protect the honor of the woman peering through, but to Giselle, the iron bars, however ornamented, drove home the extent of her confinement.

Shaded by overhanging awnings and cooled by fans and lush green plants, the courtyard was usually dominated by men. But sometimes, when there were no guests or outsiders in the palace, the women came down and joined them, mingling freely, laughing and arguing, behaving almost as equals to the men.

And yesterday, Giselle had seen something that she'd found even more curious. Normally, the call to prayer elicited immediate and automatic response. But yesterday, when the men and women of the house had been mingling in the courtyard, not one of them even raised their heads at the sound of the *muezzin's* cry. Everyone stayed where they were, continuing to read or talk as if the all-important Muslim devotions meant nothing to them. If these were Islamic fundamentalists, their actions when no one was watching certainly didn't show it.

There was no one outside now; it was still daytime, too hot to sit in the courtyard. Giselle rose and crossed the room, flinging herself on the bed.

But it was impossible to rest. Every time she stilled, her mind began to agonize over her helplessness. She wanted to believe she would be rescued, but how would anyone find her here? What was going to happen to her? Were they going to kill her? Torture her? What did they want from her?

Her own predicament aside, what about the diplomats? Would they be killed?

Would her father be with them?

What about Raz?

She sprung from the bed, feeling like a caged animal. She had to do something—anything—but what?

Pray.

The word came to her almost as if someone had spoken it. She tried to shrug it off. But it seemed to echo in her mind.

Pray.

What else *could* she do? After pacing a few more minutes, Giselle turned and went down on her knees beside her bed, just as she had done as a young girl at bedtime.

The words came hesitantly. "God, I don't know what to say. . . . I guess I don't talk to you very much. . . ." Even as she said it, she realized that she actually talked to him all the time. Didn't she whisper prayers whenever she felt afraid or stressed? This was different, though. Those little prayers were just habits, sort of like knocking on wood for luck. But now she was really trying to talk to God.

How ridiculous! She rose to her feet and resumed pacing.

What was the point in praying if she wasn't even all that sure she really believed in God? And if he did exist, why should he listen to her? She certainly didn't deserve it. It's not like she went to church or confession or any of the things she was supposed to do.

What if she died here? The possibility had become increasingly real to her over the past few days, because she suddenly had little else to think about.

If she died, would that be the end? Somehow she sensed that it wouldn't. What if all the things they told her about heaven and hell were true? Was she good enough to go to heaven? She had a sinking feeling that she wasn't.

All her life she had called herself a Christian. All her life she had taken God for granted, reciting Bible passages by rote for catechism, but never even trying to understand their meaning. She had been focusing on her own selfish ambition and need for adventure.

Those pursuits had brought her to this place, to a foreign country, held hostage by terrorists who would kill her without hesitation. And for what? If she died tonight, what would she

leave behind? All of it, everything she'd once thought important, everything that she'd poured her life into, was without
meaning. She had done nothing with her life that really mattered or that would last beyond her time. She had occupied her
mind with the temporary when she should have been thinking
about the eternal.

If there really was a judgment day, Giselle was terrified that
she would be found lacking. All the rebellion, the harsh words
and flashes of anger, all the critical and hurtful things she had
said—even enjoyed saying—these things came back to haunt her
when she thought of dying.

What had she done to redeem herself? Maybe a few things
here or there. But nothing really important. Nothing that would
matter in eternity.

But hadn't Chaplain Gilchrist said that *nobody* deserved to be
accepted by God; that this was why Jesus had come and died? If
that was true . . .

Suddenly, knowing God, being sure about Jesus, was more
important than anything else that had been on her mind before.

She returned to the bed and tried again. "God, if you're real,
I have to know. I need you. I need to be able to trust you like my
friend Judith does." The words came easier now. "Please, God,
show me if you're real. Show me if Jesus is real. God, I need
you!"

When she heard the midafternoon call of the *muezzin* some
hours later, Giselle was still on her knees, but now her prayers
were no longer so desperate. Instead, she was enveloped in a
strange peace that was beyond understanding. Something had
changed—permanently, she sensed—in just this last hour or so.
Somehow, deep inside, she now *knew* that everything Samuel,
Judith, Eloisa, and Arlene had been telling her was true. God
was real! And he did love her.

And somehow, knowing that made everything she was facing
all right. Even if these people killed her—even if she suffered—

somehow, knowing that she would go to heaven and that God was with her here on earth, somehow that made all her worries fade. It didn't make sense, but it didn't have to. All that mattered was the joy that was filling her heart, and the knowledge that, somehow, she'd touched the face of God today.

She continued praying. "Lord, Jesus, thank you so much for what you've done for me. If I'm about to die, at least I know that because of you, I'll go to heaven. Lord, I give you my life, and trust your will. With you, I know I'll have the strength to face whatever comes."

As if in answer, her thoughts were interrupted by the sound of the bolt lifting. Hastily, she struggled to her feet, just as a man entered her room. He was younger than her father, with gray-flecked hair, a long beard, and dark eyes that seemed to burn through her. Something about this man was truly ominous.

"My dear." He addressed her in English, with an accent that seemed out of place for some reason. "I regret that I was unable to speak with you sooner. I'm afraid I had business elsewhere." He crossed to her side, gestured for her to sit on the bed, and pulled up a chair. "As you may have guessed, we have many questions for you."

Beneath his soothing tone lurked the presence of terrible danger—a wolf crouched in the shadows, ready to spring. Giselle sensed a real possibility that she might not live through this conversation. She sat facing him, lifting up a silent prayer. Immediately, a fresh flood of peace came over her. She was amazed that God would so quickly answer her prayers, and was grateful for receiving the strength she needed to face this man calmly. "I'm here against my will, sir. I want to go home," she said firmly.

The man smiled with false sympathy. "I'm afraid your wishes are inconsequential, my dear. I am certain you are well aware of what is at stake here. In fact, we are very interested in learning where you got your information. Perhaps if you give us a name, we will consider sending you home to your husband when this unpleasantness is over."

"My husband is a traitor. But then you'd know that, wouldn't you?" Giselle replied. The man's eyebrow raised slightly, and she wondered why her opinion of Raz interested him.

He paused, as if hoping she'd elaborate. When she didn't, he took a deep breath and sat back, watching her closely. "Perhaps another incentive would prove more effective. If you tell me what I wish to know, I will allow you to continue taking breath."

He said it so casually, so matter-of-factly that Giselle almost believed she had misheard. Her heart skipped a beat when the threat sank in. She prayed again as her mind searched for an avenue of escape. She had to think, had to buy time. "What . . . what do you want to know?"

The man took her question for acquiescence and smiled in triumph. "It is quite simple. I wish to know everything you know—about our organization, about our plans, about your father's military command, and about the security for the upcoming meeting. And I wish to know the source of your information."

Her hands were growing clammy. "What makes you think I know about any of those things? My security clearance at the embassy is low. You probably know more than I do."

The man laughed humorlessly. "Your own words betray you. If you knew nothing of our organization, you could hardly be so assured of the superiority of our intelligence."

"I don't know anything," she repeated, realizing helplessly that it would do little good. This man knew that she had information. The question was, how did he know? Had Raz . . .

"That is untrue," the man's voice asserted, cutting off her thoughts. His eyes were those of a charmed cobra, unwavering and deadly. Giselle was afraid to take her gaze from them, sensing that if the charm were broken, he might strike. "Would it surprise you to learn that we have recorded conversations, during which you discuss these issues with your husband?"

"Recorded!" Giselle watched him warily, looking for some suggestion that he was bluffing. How could they have recorded her and Raz talking about such things? They had barely had time to speak to each other since the night she had learned about the meeting, and what little they had said to each other had been in the privacy of . . .

Their home! Her mind flashed on her wedding night, and the terrible expression on Raz's face as he'd promised her that the apartment wasn't bugged. Not by the CIA . . .

"Oh, Raz!" she whispered, trying to remember what she said that might have compromised her father's secrets. She recalled instead the quiet intimacies that had passed her lips as she had learned to open herself to her husband. She had bared her soul to Raz as to no one before him. She had trusted him with her most private thoughts, things she'd never even spoken aloud before.

A sense of betrayal surged through her. Raz had carried her knowingly into a world of hidden cameras and secret tapes, where men like this had listened, marking the secrets of her heart, her most private thoughts! It all seemed so depraved, so . . .

The man was staring at her, smiling as if he knew what she had been thinking. "You see, you have no secrets from us."

Fury filled her as she stared at his smug, smiling face. She wanted to strike him. "I hope you enjoyed those tapes, you sick little man, because these are the last words you'll hear from me," she whispered, her fingernails sinking deeply into her palms.

He smiled with feigned sadness, and withdrew a syringe from the folds of his robe. "I had anticipated that a degree of force might be necessary. It is sad that you proved me right, as this drug has been known to have unfortunate side effects. Guard!"

The door opened, and a large man entered the room. Giselle scrambled away, but she was quickly captured and dragged back to the bed. The man pinned her down, baring her arm for the needle. As the old man approached, Giselle screamed, trying desperately to push the man off, but he braced himself, keeping her arm still.

"Jesus," she cried, "help me!"

And suddenly Mared was there, catching the old man's hand. "What are you doing?"

"I am questioning our hostage," the man replied, his voice clipped with annoyance. "This does not concern you."

Mared positioned himself between the old man and Giselle. "You know well that it does concern me, Talman." He spoke rapidly in Akkadian. "Giselle is my responsibility. If any harm befalls her, I will answer to my brother."

The old man snorted derisively. "I should have known that you would prioritize your family concerns over those of our nation."

Giselle stopped struggling and stared at the men. "Family concerns? What are you talking about?"

Talman glanced at her briefly, then raised his eyes to Mared again. "You see? She speaks Akkadian. That is why I believe she knows far more than she has seen fit to tell you. She may even be an American agent! It would explain a great many things."

"Giselle is no agent," Mared countered angrily. "My brother has known her since she was a girl."

His brother! The implication finally sank into Giselle's mind. That explained why Mared had seemed so familiar to her, even though they had never met! Raz and Mared were brothers!

Talman glared at him fiercely. "You may leave or you may stay, but do not interfere. If I must, I will call in additional guards." He brushed past Mared without waiting for a reply, advancing on Giselle with the needle. She shrieked and began struggling again, but the guard kept her pinned, her bare arm stretched out from her side. She tensed helplessly, waiting for the sting of the needle.

It never came. Instead, the door opened again, and a young

woman stepped inside. Catching Talman's attention, she beckoned for him to go with her. "He has arrived," she said softly in Akkadian, her awed tone of voice suggesting that whoever she was speaking of was quite important. "He requires us all to join him for the evening meal."

Everything seemed to stop. Talman's lips tightened, and he nodded at the girl, who glanced at Giselle and left quickly. He turned to the guard and waved him away, then watched Giselle as she struggled to sit and pushed herself to a corner of the bed. "We will take this up again tomorrow, my dear. You may wish to use this time to reconsider your options. If you cooperate voluntarily, perhaps the drug will not be necessary." So saying, he recapped the syringe and left the room.

Mared stayed behind, his head bowed, and his back to Giselle. Turning, he glanced at the guard, who waited by the door for him to leave. Then he looked at her, his expression helpless.

She glared at him, tearing the rubber strap from her arm and flinging it at him. "I'm so very pleased to meet you, brother of my husband," she spat in Arabic.

He shrugged unhappily, as if the guard's presence prevented him from saying all that he wanted to say. "I'm sorry," he whispered, then hurried after Talman.

Her pulse still pounding in her throat, Giselle watched the door close and heard the bolt slide home.

❖ ❖ ❖

It took several moments for Giselle's numbed mind to start working again, but finally, she began to formulate a plan of escape. The only problem was that it required something that she might not have—time. Silently, she searched the room, looking for items she might use as tools.

There was little to be found; most of the things she thought of would have been removed from the room as potential weapons. But she was able to locate some bath oil capsules and a pair of tweezers. Taking these, she hurried to the window.

The trellislike iron screen was held in place by four bolts; fortunately, they looked fairly new and the threads were clean. Even so, it took some effort to get the tweezers to grip tightly enough to turn the nut. Finally, the first one began to turn, slowly, painfully. She squeezed a bath capsule onto the threads, hoping to lubricate them. Then she slipped her arm through the trellis, using her sleeve to hold the bolt while she continued twisting the nut from inside.

The first bolt was almost free when she heard voices coming. Pulling her hand inside quickly, she ducked low, peering out as a group of men passed below her. Mared walked with a number of men about his own age, preceded by Talman and another man, one whom Giselle had never seen before.

The newcomer was quite old, with white hair and a silvery beard. There was a quiet air of confidence about him, and the other men, including Talman, clearly deferred to him. Giselle studied his features as he passed below her. She wondered who he was. Then it dawned on her—this man could very well be Seif, the notorious leader of the Sword of Islam!

She held her breath, pressing her cheek against the trellis and trying to hear their words as they passed below her window. But although their voices continued to drift up from the room below, their words were lost to her.

The men had taken seats directly below her, in a room that opened onto the garden. Occasionally, one of them would step outside, drawing casually on a cigarette as he listened to the conversation. She hesitated, wondering what to do next; if she continued working on the window, she ran the risk of being caught.

Then she thought she heard her father's name, followed by her own, and she realized that she had to know what was being said.

Lying flat on the floor, she pressed her ear to the tiles, but still couldn't quite make out what was being said. Frustrated, she looked around, trying to think of something that might amplify the sound.

She tried a water glass, which improved things, but only minimally.

If only she had her stethoscope! Perhaps she could fashion something similar to it, she decided. After all, she'd taken her toy one apart several times, and she understood what made it work.

First, she needed tubing and an earpiece to carry the sound. Her eyes darted around the room, fixing quickly on the *shisha*, the gaily-colored water pipe that stood in the corner by the door, probably more for decoration than actual use. A narrow rubber hose led from an opening on the pipe up to a metal mouthpiece. That would work, she decided excitedly. She carefully twisted it until it came loose.

Now for something to catch and concentrate the sound. This proved more difficult. She considered and rejected the water glass, as it had no opening to which she could affix the tubing. She tried a metal pill box, but it didn't work. Finally, her eyes settled on a small silver bell with a wooden handle. She rushed toward it, plucking it happily from its shelf.

It rang sharply, and Giselle barely had time to slide the tubing under her bed before the guard appeared.

"What do you wish?" the man asked, his bulky frame firmly blocking the doorway.

Giselle hesitated, then shrugged. "I was only looking at the bell. I did not realize it would summon you here," she explained.

The guard nodded and closed the door again, bolting it loudly behind him.

Carefully, Giselle examined the bell. The body was of finely-pounded silver, the pewter clapper dangling by a wire from a round hook affixed to the wooden handle. She learned with satisfaction that the handle screwed onto the body of the bell. Unhooking the clapper, she removed the handle, then attached the rubber hose to the place where the handle had been. It fit almost perfectly.

She pressed the bell to the floor, putting the pipe's mouth-piece in her ear. There! That was much better, although the sound still wasn't as distinct as she'd like.

What she needed was a diaphragm, something to stretch tightly over the mouth of the bell; that would amplify the sound vibrations from the floor and allow them to resonate inside the bell.

Her own stethoscope had been covered with a thin membrane of rubber. A condom! She almost laughed at the thought of it; an item that she had been taught was anathema to her Catholic religion might now prove useful. But a thorough search of the dressers unearthed no such treasure. She realized that in Saudi Arabia, where a woman's value was determined almost exclusively by the number of sons she produced, birth control was probably not in great demand.

Then she remembered something. In one of the bathroom cabinets, she had seen a hair-coloring kit. Henna, a plant-based dye common in the Middle East, was used for many things in countries like Saudi Arabia. Women used it to paint intricate designs on their palms before their weddings, and to dye their hair a lovely black or red if they didn't come by it naturally. The red beards of the *mutawain* owed much to henna, too. And even the men used it to cover gray, though that was a well-kept secret in this part of the world.

Thanking God for the plant, Giselle ran and got it, ripping open the box and dumping its contents on her bed: a plastic mixing bowl, a packet of black henna, and—yes—a pair of thin latex gloves to protect the hands!

Taking one of the gloves, Giselle used her teeth to begin a tear, then tore out the palm and stretched the latex tightly over the bell's mouth, pulling it until it stuck to the rim by itself. She smiled at her handiwork, and, sitting cross-legged on the floor, pressed the bell to the tile.

Much better! She could make out most of what was being said. She slid around the floor, looking for a tile that might carry sound better than others. She found one quickly.

"The men who followed you," a man was asking in Akkadian. "Did the woman give you any explanation as to why they would be interested in her?"

There was a pause, then Mared spoke. "She did not know who they were. I can only guess that they saw her leaving the embassy and decided to follow, just as I did."

Giselle frowned, wondering why he was lying. Why hadn't he repeated her belief that Raz had sent the men who'd chased them? A moment later, the answer dawned on her. If the Arab and his companion were not with the SOI, that meant they were probably from some intelligence organization. If Raz *had* sent them, then Talman and the others would have every reason to believe that he had betrayed them!

She wanted to shout aloud. Instead, she bit her lip and listened all the more closely.

"Is it possible they are aware of her husband's activities on our behalf?" a new man asked.

"If so, they would have arrested him," Mared replied.

"Perhaps," the man agreed. "Unless they have allowed the scout to pass in order to lie in wait for the general."

"That has already been considered and precautions taken," an older man—Giselle guessed it was the man she'd seen coming in—informed them.

"Or unless," Talman spoke up, his nasal voice easy to recognize, "her husband is in league with them."

"Why would you suspect such a thing?" Mared asked, sounding shocked and outraged.

"It is my job—as it should be yours—to prepare for all possibilities, no matter how painful," Talman replied. "Your brother appears to have fallen in love with his wife. Many men wiser and more loyal than he have done foolish things in the name of love."

"What are you saying, Talman?" Seif inquired.

"Merely that, since his marriage, the major's loyalties have seemed somewhat divided. He has been slower in responding to our orders, and the information he has provided has been far less detailed."

"He's had to be more cautious," Mared argued. "My brother could not afford mistakes with the admiral's own daughter living under his very roof!"

"Perhaps," Talman agreed, but his tone implied that he was unconvinced. "There is, however, the additional question of how your pursuers knew to place the delicatessen in Switzerland under surveillance. Only a few select operatives were told of its availability as a safe house, including you and your brother."

There was a stunned silence, then Giselle jumped as Mared struck something sharply. "My brother is no traitor!"

"We will know soon enough. Let us hope your loyalty is not misplaced," Talman said too calmly. "In the meanwhile, tell me, has the woman said anything to you about our organization that suggests she knows more than she should?"

It was a test, Giselle realized. Talman already knew the answer. A negative reply would bring Mared under suspicion as well.

There was a brief pause, then Mared spoke in measured tones. "She said very little. She believed that I was a civilian during most of our time together, and she believed she was protecting me by withholding information. But there was one thing that troubled me. She said it was believed that we might be connected to a government, because our intelligence was too detailed for us to be independent."

Seif grunted. "That *is* disturbing. If this is known in the American intelligence communities, then they are closer than we believed to learning our secret."

"Perhaps we have been incautious in some way," another man commented thoughtfully.

"Perhaps," the leader agreed. "But it will not matter after our business in Italy is finished. If we succeed there, we will destroy with a single stone most of our enemies, those leaders who are strongest in favor of these peace efforts." He almost spat the words. "And all of the trails we lay will lead to the doorstep of the house of . . . the royal family itself. The resulting loss of Western support should destabilize this government, and many factions will rise up for control of Mecca."

Giselle pondered this. Saudi Arabia was a Sunni country, and the Shiites had long disputed the Sunnis' claim to Mecca. Were these men Shiites, then, hoping their plan would both destroy the peace talks and bring Islam's holiest city under their control? It made some sense, although the minority Shiites were second-class citizens in Saudi Arabia, hardly likely to command such fabulous wealth as she saw around her now. And then there was the infamous Saudi secret police, known for their harassment of Shiites and other minorities. It would be impossible for Shiites to conduct operations at this level without being noticed.

"What if the Americans already know who truly controls our operation?" Talman asked.

"That would be unfortunate for us, but it could still work in favor of our cause," Seif replied. "If it is learned that we have infiltrated our enemies' most powerful organizations . . ."

". . . They will crumble like a house of sand!" Talman nearly shouted in glee. "Who among their leaders will they trust? Any one of them may be one of us! How they will hate that!"

"Either way, in the end, we will have crippled most of the terrorists that plague us. And after our nation's traitorous leaders die in Italy, the men we have chosen to replace them will move swiftly against the legitimate armies of our enemies—where we have operatives as well. The war will be short, and with our nuclear weapons, we will be victorious," Seif concluded.

Giselle frowned. Something here didn't fit her earlier deduction. Something. . . .

"What about Giselle?" Mared asked, interrupting her contemplations.

"For now, we will treat her well. But after what Talman has said, I too have concerns about your brother."

"Our holding his beloved wife should assure that he does what is expected," Talman put in. "I will send a message to the major, telling him that she is under our protection. He will understand my meaning."

"Is this how we treat our own—with threats and hostages?" Mared asked.

"Your brother may no longer be one of our own," the leader replied quietly.

"And if he isn't?" Talman asked. "He knows far too much about our organization—and the upcoming operation."

"I agree," Seif answered grimly. "But we will not pin the success of our operation entirely on him. The men who will use the access he creates will be members of *Hamas.* The major does not know my face and will assume that I am among this group. If they are arrested, his treachery will be exposed."

"Only those here are aware that you will already be inside, among the delegates," Talman added. "But if he fails us, what can you do alone?"

"I will carry enough plastic explosives on my person to level whatever building we are in and kill all inside."

There were shocked protests. "But that is suicide!"

Seif chuckled. "Our enemies have always stood ready to die for their cause. If we are to fight them, we cannot do less."

There was a stunned pause, then Talman spoke again. "If you must take this course, rest assured your traitor will follow you to the grave!" His voice turned into a vicious growl. "Our man at the embassy, and those at Gaeta, will have orders to bring him here, where he will see his wife die slowly in front of his eyes before he dies."

"Do not kill an innocent woman for my sake," Seif interjected. "She is the daughter of a man who can give us much. Use whatever means you must to question her, but do not kill her. Use her instead to bargain with the admiral."

"This is all unnecessary," Mared told them furiously. "My brother is loyal. He will follow your plan."

"I hope you are right," Talman said acidly. "If he fails us, we will be without our leader."

"I, too, hope you are right," Seif added. "Not for myself—I am old, and martyrdom might better serve our cause. But the immediate gains will be greater if our original plan comes to fruition."

"You have not told us this original plan," Talman said. "We understand and respect your secrecy, but if you were to die, it would be well for us to know the whole of it so that we may follow through."

"I agree. It is time," Seif replied. "If the terrorists enter undisturbed, all but the Arab delegations will be taken hostage. Under my direction, the drama will continue for days. In Israel and the West, all eyes will watch in horror as Muslim terrorists kill their leaders—these peaceful lambs slaughtered one by one in the name of transcendent Islam." He paused for effect. "After this, there will be no more talk of peace. The world's passions will be inflamed, and all will cry out for *jihad,* for holy war."

Giselle frowned. What Seif was saying was probably true, but didn't he realize that in such a war, the West would surely side with Israel? His plan's success would be no victory for Islam— more likely, it would be the key to its defeat. After the world saw its leaders killed, no Muslim would be safe anywhere in the world. Surely someone would see that!

There was a long silence as the men pondered his words. Then a man spoke. "Mared, perhaps you should return to Italy and speak with your brother. Tell him what is riding on his cooperation."

"Promise him one million American dollars in exchange for his efforts," Talman added.

"Enough of your insults!" Mared responded angrily. "My brother's loyalty will not be greater for your money!"

"Then tell him that his wife will die if he fails us," Talman said flatly.

"Your willingness to turn on a comrade disturbs me, Talman," Mared said coldly. "It makes me wonder whether any of us should trust you."

"Enough of your brother!" Talman shouted. "Our leader may give his life to bring us victory. What are your brother's concerns next to that?"

"And if we are on the threshold of victory, it is my brother's doing!" Mared argued heatedly. "He has lived undercover for nearly twelve years. He has risked prison or even death to supply us first with weapons that could not be traced to our country, and then with classified information. He has been isolated, without true friends, unable to let down his guard at any turn. You even asked him to marry for the cause! All this he has done without question, and you doubt his loyalty? A man so distrustful of others should himself be watched, Talman, for we usually seek in others the failings we harbor ourselves!"

"Remember those words, for you will regret them," Talman snarled.

"Enough!" Seif cut in. "Save your hatred for our enemies. Let us review our plans once more to see if anything has been overlooked."

The discussions continued, but Giselle was only half listening. Her mind was reeling with what she had learned. It was no longer a suspicion. Raz—Rashid—her husband was truly a traitor. He had supplied these men with information and weapons to be used against America's interests, against the interests of peace. And now he was going to help them precipitate what might be World War III!

She had to get away—she had to tell someone!

Brushing the wetness from her eyes, she disassembled her stethoscope and returned to the window.

ChapterSeven

"Just . . . one . . . more," Giselle grunted, making headway with a stubborn bolt that was one of the last two holding the iron trellis over her window. She'd been working at it since the final prayer call, and by her best guess she had about two hours of darkness left. She had to be far away by sunrise, when the amplified *"alahu akbar"* would wake the household and draw attention to her absence.

She took a quick break to massage her cramping hands, then resumed, slipping one hand out through the ironwork vine pattern to grip the hexagonal bolt head while she turned the nut with the tweezers. Her fingers were bruised, and two of her nails broken to the bleeding quick, but she ignored the pain. She had to keep going.

She had realized sometime during the night who these men were. Her mind had played over all she'd seen, homing in on the way the servants had touched their breastbones on entering the building. Then she'd remembered Mared's gold charm, and things had begun to come together like pieces of a puzzle. The SOI was not part of the radical Islamic movement. The men plotting war in the room below were radical Israelis!

Now it all made sense. That explained all of the odd statements she'd heard through her makeshift stethoscope. By posing as Muslims, they were able to divert Western attention to their enemies and cause friction between America and its Arab allies. And if caught, they would still win. If it became known that Jews had infiltrated any Islamic organization, the organization would lose support and crumble.

Seif, whatever his true name was, had conceived an ingenious plan. But it could also turn against him, she realized. If the peace delegates could be saved and his organization exposed, the resulting destabilization of terrorist groups would be a giant step toward peace. And once Israel's mainstream learned that a radical faction had sacrificed Jews in the name of their hatred, there might very well be a greater commitment to the ending of hostilities.

There were still missing pieces to the puzzle. For example, Seif himself—who was he? Saudi society was closed to the world outside. Alliances and connections were made by relationships between families. A man who was rich enough to own a palace such as this, and connected enough to be numbered among the Saudi delegation at the upcoming peace conference, could not stand alone. He would have a traceable ancestry—perhaps even as far back as the days of Muhammad himself. There would be marriages between his family and families of powerful Saudis. Giselle was certain that no outsider could set up a cover like this without raising suspicions here. But if Seif was an Arab, why would he side with Jews against his own people?

One more painful twist, and the nut came loose. Giselle had been pulling on the other side, and the abruptly-freed bolt slipped through her numb fingers, rattling down the tile roof and out into the courtyard.

Giselle ducked out of sight as a man stepped out into the courtyard and looked up. Breathlessly she prayed that he wouldn't see the bolt and realize what she was doing. With trembling hands, she quickly gathered the rest of the loosened nuts and bolts and hid them under her pillow, lying down on the bed in case someone came to check on her.

After a few minutes, when there were no sounds from the courtyard or outside her door, she slipped out of bed and peered out. The man had returned to wherever he'd come from. She sighed in relief and started to work on the last bolt. This one was at the top left corner of the screen, and the instant she managed to get it loose, the screen swung to one side with a terrible creak.

Heart pounding in her throat, Giselle straightened it and ducked out of sight, holding the screen in place. This time, if anyone decided to investigate, she would surely be caught, since the minute she left the window the screen would swing askew again. She held her breath as she heard the footsteps below, silently praying that the man would somehow decide it was the wind.

It seemed to take forever before she heard quiet, unhurried footsteps moving away. Another few minutes, and she dared to move, standing up on the ledge and using a foot to hold the screen as she worked the bolt looser, so that the screen would swing more quietly. Instead of removing the bolt entirely, she decided, she would swing the screen aside, step out, and then move it back into place, slipping a second bolt through another hole to help anchor the iron screen. That way, no one would see what she'd done from the courtyard, and they might not miss her until someone brought her breakfast.

When the bolt was loose enough, she swung the screen quietly aside, then dropped to the floor, letting it hang. She prayed that the single bolt wouldn't break, sending the screen crashing into the courtyard as she prepared to leave.

Gathering her gloves, slippers, and veil, she tucked them into her voluminous sleeve and knotted it at the wrist. Then, retrieving a bolt from beneath her pillow, she peered out the window once more and slipped out of her prison.

The tiled awning below her window was still warm from yesterday's sun. Giselle elected to remain barefoot; she would risk slipping to her death in the smooth-soled slippers Mared had given her. Cautiously, she secured the screen, then tiptoed down the sloping roof at an angle. Lying on her belly, she peered into the courtyard.

The man was almost directly below her, smoking a cigarette and reading a book by a dim light next to his chair. Giselle watched quietly for several minutes, reassuring herself that he was alone. Then, carefully, she crawled to the far edge of the awning and quietly let herself down until it was a short drop to the tiles below. Crouching, she quickly donned her slippers and pulled up the hood of her cloak to shadow her face so that she would blend into the darkness.

She edged quietly toward the other doorway on the far side of the courtyard. Glancing back at the reading man, she silently opened the glass doors and slipped through.

She found herself in another sitting room, similar to the one the man had been sitting outside of while reading. She paused to let her eyes adjust to the lack of moonlight, gradually making out a narrow band of light at the base of a door across the room. She felt her way past the furniture, then cracked the door, peering out into a well-lit hallway. Seeing no one, she ventured out, hoping she was headed for an exit.

As she tiptoed down the hall, she heard snores behind some of the doors, and realized she was in the men's sleeping quarters. At the first branch, she turned left, hoping that her choice would not lead her deeper into the palace. She kept going, passing door after door without getting any better sense of where she was. From outside, she had not fully appreciated the size of this palace. Afraid that she might not find her way out before the call to prayer woke the household, she quickened her pace, sacrificing silence for speed.

Finally, she rounded a corner and came abruptly on a set of

huge swinging doors. She paused, guessing that she had reached the entrance to the servants' quarters. Entering would be a calculated risk, since it was likely that at least some of the staff were already up and working, preparing the morning meal. On the other hand, with luck there would also be a servants' exit to the outside, a way out. She really had no choice. Cautiously, she pushed the door open—and ran directly into a stern-looking man, who was carrying a tray of fresh fruit.

He eyed her suspiciously. "What are you doing?"

She stepped back, moving out of reach in case he decided to make a grab for her.

His expression soured. "I do not know you," he said in Arabic. "Who are you and what brings you here?"

Thinking quickly, Giselle considered her answer—and the best way to give it. Remembering the way the servants had paused at the door when they'd first brought her inside this palace, and knowing the kinds of secrets that were discussed within these walls, she guessed that Seif and his associates would not risk hiring Muslim servants. No, they would be Israelis as well, although their passports would probably say they came from Lebanon or Egypt.

She arranged a shy smile on her face, meanwhile praying that her conclusions were correct. If not, she was about to give herself away.

"Boker tov," she greeted the man in Hebrew. "I am sorry if I am in the wrong place, but I am new here. Tell me how to find a car and driver; I am to go on an errand this morning." She kept her explanation as vague as possible so that he wouldn't be able to catch her in a false detail.

The man stared at her for a moment longer. Then his shoulders relaxed, although his expression remained stern. "You are badly confused," he replied in Hebrew. "When you return from your errand, ask someone to show you around so that you won't become lost again. And do not speak Hebrew again with someone you do not know. We will pay a terrible price if we are caught."

She nodded, managing to look properly chastised, and switched to Arabic. "I apologize. I will be more careful."

"Good. Now, the servant's exit is down this hallway and to the right. The garage is the large building about thirty meters to the south. And wear your veil once you leave the palace grounds," he reminded her.

Sighing with relief, Giselle thanked him and hurried away before he could think to ask her any questions.

Once outside, she quickly moved out of sight and crouched, making herself a formless shadow among shadows as she determined her next move. The outer wall was about fifty meters away, the only cover a stand of date palms at about the midway point. Staying low, Giselle raced to the palms, then pressed herself against a tree trunk and watched.

Given the nature of the secrets in this palace, there would surely be guards at various intervals along the walls. She waited and watched until she saw one, patrolling slowly from the garage and back, his manner attentive, but casual. A second guard was posted near the front gate, where he leaned against the wall, his rifle draped over his shoulder as he calmly smoked a cigarette. There might be more outside, but she wouldn't know until she got there.

Giselle waited, noting the lightening sky to the east and praying her chance would come quickly. Finally, the second man crushed out his cigarette and returned to his post. Then, silently thanking Raz for her obstacle-course training, she gathered her legs under her and launched herself at the wall, hitting it with a running leap and catching the top with her fingertips.

This was her most vulnerable moment. If either guard happened to glance her way, she would be clearly visible, a black figure dangling helplessly against the white wall. Clinging there, she cursed as the skirt of her cloak tangled with her legs; but finally, she was able to kick free and use her legs to power herself up. She crouched at the top of the wall for a few seconds, looking for more guards. She waited for one to pass, then quietly lowered herself, hitting the ground with a roll. Then she quickly brushed dust off her cloak and hurried off.

❖ ❖ ❖

About half an hour later, the first rays of dawn touched the horizon, and the call to prayer echoed through the streets of Riyadh. Giselle ducked into a darkened doorway, knowing that a woman alone would draw the attention of the men hurrying to worship.

Before the call's echoes died out over the rooftops, the streets, which moments earlier had been devoid of all movement, were suddenly swarming with men. Some were still fastening the buttons of their robes, others adjusting their headwear, having just gotten out of bed.

Their attitudes surprised her. She had expected passion, a fervor bordering on fanaticism. That was what she saw on TV, on Western newscasts dealing with Islamic fundamentalists. Instead she saw weary faces, eyes still glazed with sleep. Islam meant "surrender to the will of God," she knew, and a Muslim was "one who surrenders." The expressions she saw told her that these men surrendered with resignation, a weary acceptance of the burdens of their faith. They reminded her of her father's men, dragging themselves from their bunks at the sound of Reveille.

As these thoughts occurred to her, she began to see these people in a new light, as not so very different from the people she had known all her life. The surprise she felt shed light on her own biases, and she felt ashamed. Her mind had given the word "terrorist" an Arab face, but in truth and in fairness, she realized, a terrorist could as easily be Israeli—or American. All she should have needed to do was look at history to know this—look at the bombing of the Federal building in Oklahoma.

Neither was fanaticism limited to Islam. As Raz had reminded her more than once, Christians, too, had drawn their share of blood. Even though Jesus had called for love, peace, and gentleness among his followers, people calling themselves Christians had perpetuated a long history of hatred, war, and persecution in his name. In the Middle Ages, there were the Crusades; a century ago, the pogroms. Fifty years ago, many Nazis had tried to justify their actions by a few words in the New Testament. Even today, supposed Christians were killing doctors, all in the name of the Prince of Peace. There were extremists and radicals in every nation, in every faith—deranged fanatics who were far outside the mainstream.

She was not alone in assuming that the SOI was Islamic, she realized, although the thought did little to acquit her conscience. The American intelligence community had jumped to the same conclusions. Seif and his followers had understood and exploited this prejudice quite expertly—no wonder they had been able to operate with impunity all these years! Despite obvious inconsistencies, no one had even considered the possibility that the Sword of Islam might be anything but a group of Muslim fanatics.

As the prayer call's final echo dwindled, the streets were still again, the worshipers leaving in their wake an eerie silence. The rising sun glimmered on the horizon, unobstructed by a single cloud, and Giselle suddenly had a new worry, one of a more practical nature. The heat of the day was coming soon, and in this *abaaya*, it would be unbearable. She had a few hours at most to find a way home, or she'd have to find a safe place to hide and wait out the worst of the heat. And every hour of delay was an hour closer to victory for Seif.

"Oh, Lord, I need your help." She was surprised at how easily prayer was coming to her. It was almost like the words just bubbled up from her heart.

Slipping out of the doorway, Giselle began to walk, although her mind was still churning with uncertainty as to her best plan of action. She had no idea how to get back to the airport. That alone was a major problem, since she didn't dare stop someone and ask for directions, out of fear of drawing the outrage of the *Mutawain* for being out alone, talking to strange men. Worse, once she found the airport, she still had no idea what to do next. She had only the small amount of cash Mared had taken from her wallet still stashed away in her bra. It was not nearly enough to buy a plane ticket, and in any event she had no passport, and if her studies were correct, Saudi women traveled alone only with the written consent of their male guardians. Without these documents, she'd never be able to board a plane.

Maybe if she found some Western clothing, she thought, but realized immediately that was even worse. As confining as these garments were, they gave her anonymity, which she'd need once Seif's men began looking for her. Besides, foreign workers needed exit visas to leave the country, so she was still in trouble.

Foreign workers! A plan began forming in Giselle's mind. With one foot still in the Middle Ages, this country depended heavily on a large contingent of Western workers to provide the expertise to run its newly-installed computers, staff its medical facilities, and train its workers. Surely she could find one of these foreigners, who might not be suspicious of a woman alone, and who might even be willing to help her.

With a new purpose, she lengthened her stride, heading in the direction of what she hoped would be the main streets of Riyadh.

❖ ❖ ❖

Vice Admiral Thaddeus Hardy paced the distance from his desk to the file cabinet and back again. "So you have no idea where she is?"

Arn watched him reverse his course again and couldn't help thinking that his old friend had aged several years in the seven days since Giselle had come up missing. "We have a few ideas, but they'll all be tough to pursue," he replied. "We're assuming that the SOI has her. The problem is, in all the years we've been investigating them, we've never figured out where they headquarter. We've been trying to track the operatives we've identified, hoping that their movements might lead us to their base, but so far, they've managed to lose us every time. Apparently they have passports for all occasions, so they can enter a country using one name and turn around and leave using another. Whoever's behind them, these guys are pros. We even spotted one of them entering a secured area in Jerusalem, using a Mossad ID."

"If they're working in Jerusalem, they might be Palestinian," Thaddeus murmured. "Have you checked ties with Hamas and Hezbollah?"

"There are links, but no closer than to the Iranian Mujahadin or Islamic Jihad. Apparently all the major players have done a little business with these guys."

"So you're saying Giselle could be anywhere." Thaddeus paused, then swung his fist heavily into a file cabinet. "By all the saints, Arn!"

"I'm as frustrated as you are, Thaddy," Arn sighed wearily. "We do have one possible lead. For some reason the CIA tipped us off that she was seen in Switzerland. Assuming that the SOI would want to get her out of Europe ASAP, our people reviewed airport security videotapes for all flights leaving Switzerland since the sighting. We have a few possibles. I'd like to have you view them to see if you recognize her." He brought out a tape from his satchel and set it on Thaddeus' desk. "There are several here who look likely, all headed for the Middle East. But they're veiled, so it might be tough."

"What makes you think they're likely?" Thaddeus asked.

Arn shrugged. "Let's watch the tape and you tell me what you think." He wished he could prepare his friend for what he was about to see, but knew better than to try. Anything he said at this point would only compromise Thaddeus' objectivity, and they needed to be as certain as possible of his identification before they could act on it.

Thaddeus nodded and picked up the tape. Arn rose and followed him from the office down the long hall into his living room. "Is Dody around?" he asked, although he already knew the answer.

Thaddeus shook his head. "I sent her stateside to visit her sister. I wanted her out of the way in case the kidnappers were looking for another target."

Arn nodded and kept his mouth shut. Unless Dolores Hardy's sister was Betty Ford, Thaddy was lying to him. But if his old friend wanted to keep his family's problems to himself, that was his business. He'd only brought it up in case Thaddy wanted to talk about it. He sat down on the sofa and helped himself to a nut from the crystal dish on the coffee table.

Thaddeus inserted the tape, pressed the "play" button, and moved to a chair, not taking his eyes from the half-lit TV screen. After a moment, there was a flash of snow, then a scurry of images moving across the screen, which slowed to normal speed. Seen from above, the people seemed casually unaware of the camera, some pausing to rummage through pockets or purses before moving on toward their terminals. Then a man with two veiled women moved into view.

Thaddeus sat forward momentarily, then relaxed. "Neither of them is her," he told Arn as the screen flashed snow again, then cut to a new set of images.

Arn nodded; he already knew. In truth, there was only one real probability on this tape, and he'd put her toward the end. He leaned back, only half paying attention, as his friend viewed the next subjects and again shook his head.

Then it was her turn. Arn's eyes fastened on the screen, but otherwise he was careful not to do anything that might reveal his particular interest in this candidate.

There was something about her; maybe the way she walked with quick steps as if her stride was brought short by an injury or impediment. Or maybe it was the way she seemed to stagger once, and was quickly caught and brought upright by the grim-faced man at her side. Or the way she turned her face up, as if looking directly at the camera and begging it to know her through her veil. Regaining her balance, she pushed away from her escort. He shrugged and let her move away, but kept a firm grip on her arm.

Thaddeus picked up the remote control and rewound, then moved forward again, frame by frame as the woman brought her hands to her face. As the sleeves rode briefly up her arms, there was a glimpse of white cloth around her wrists. He turned to Arn, his expression revealing his horror. "This woman's hands are tied."

"It looks that way," Arn affirmed. "But it doesn't mean it's Giselle," he cautioned quickly. "Women don't have a lot of freedom in Islamic countries. She could just be a runaway wife or daughter being taken home against her will."

"The way she staggers—is she drugged?"

"Possibly," he answered cautiously, although his experts had already confirmed the probability, even down to identifying the substance used. He glanced back at the screen. "What do you think?"

Thaddeus returned his attention to the tape. "I don't know. It could be. . . ." He let the tape continue at normal speed.

Just as she was about to move off screen, the woman stumbled again, nearly falling to her knees before the man caught her. Putting an arm around her waist, he hauled her up again and brought her tightly to his side. Her head turned slowly to stare at him, and Arn could almost see the defiance in her gaze as she tried once more to push away. Then they were gone from view.

Thaddeus reversed the tape again and played this last exchange once more. Then he turned back to his friend, his face more haggard with fear than it had been before. "It's her. I'm sure it's her. The way she juts out her jaw when she's angry . . ." He drifted off, his fists clenching into tight balls.

Arn nodded, fighting to conceal his reaction. "That's a good lead, Thaddy. It helps. We'll take it from here." He rose before his friend could ask for details and reached down to shake his hand. "I hope you don't mind if I get back to work."

Thaddeus rose and walked him back to the office, where Arn had left his coat and satchel. "Keep me posted, Arn."

"You'll know whatever I do," Arn promised, then turned to leave before his friend could see the lie written on his face. He was already holding back—had to hold back, he told himself—to keep Thaddeus from going off half-cocked and tipping his hand before he was ready.

The man at Giselle's side had been photographed by Arn's operatives during a routine security investigation just a week before Giselle's disappearance. The pictures, taken during what appeared to be a chance encounter, showed him conversing in a friendly, perhaps even familiar, manner with Major Raz Chayil.

And until that connection was thoroughly investigated, any questions asked of Chayil might do more harm than good.

❖ ❖ ❖

Akila bint Hakim ibn Rahman considered herself most fortunate among women to be allowed to work in the hospital. Her father, Hakim ibn Rahman, was an enlightened man who studied the Holy Qur'an. In it, he had found no prohibition against women working, and so he had deemed it good and proper that his daughter study medicine. The tenets of Islam decreed that no decent Muslim woman should bear the touch or intimate gaze of a man not her husband. How, then, could such a woman receive medical treatment, unless from a female doctor?

And so Hakim's daughter had been permitted to become an obstetrician. Akila moved unveiled from patient to patient, always careful to keep her eyes modestly lowered from the gaze of their worried fathers and husbands.

Here in the hospital, women were not required to veil, since so much of medicine depended on the ability to look into the patient's face and see her need. This place was Akila's haven from those things she disliked about her country, the rigid traditions of her people which had no true rooting in the Holy Qur'an.

Veiling, for example, was not a requirement of Islam, at least not in the extremes seen here. In other Muslim countries, the teachings of the Prophet (peace be upon him) were taken more literally. He had said only that women should dress modestly, concealing their hair and bodies from men outside their home. It was quite all right to reveal the face and hands. But here, in the protectorate of Mecca, the "wise men" had decreed that all moral laws should be taken, if possible, to additional extremes, so that no blemish should fall upon the Holy City. So women here were faceless shadows, fated to go about in shrouds of black, living fully (if such it could be called) only in the confines of their private rooms.

Things were changing, however. It was coming far too slowly, and not without the notice and protest of religious conservatives, but gradually women were finding a place for themselves. Some taught at the university, educating female students on such subjects as child care and education. If not for female teachers, the young women would have to audit courses via television so as not to offend Allah by interacting directly with male students and teachers. Other women worked in offices, often kept in closets with their typewriters and phones so that they could work without distracting their male coworkers. Still others worked with their husbands at the *souqs*, haggling with the female customers to protect the dignity of all involved.

And some, like Akila, had come to medicine. These women were especially privileged, for here, in this Westernized hospital, things were unusually relaxed. Here, Akila was almost an equal of men. She could walk about freely, no male guardian to protect her, no haze of black veil obstructing her gaze. Here, she could be a doctor whose mind was respected only slightly less than the minds of her male counterparts.

Akila's husband, Adil, passed nearby, heading off to surgery. Their eyes met with a spark of warmth, and he smiled at her in a way that told her that he very much loved her. She glowed inwardly as she felt his eyes follow her down the pristine white-tiled corridor.

Her father had made her a wonderful match in Adil. Theirs was an unorthodox marriage in many respects. First, encouraged by her father, they had actually spent several well-supervised days together before their *Milkah*, or engagement. They had surprised themselves by falling in love. Second, Adil had promised he would have no other wives, nor would he dismiss her should she fail to bear him children.

Of course, *insh'Allah*, if it was the will of Allah, that would soon no longer be a concern, as Akila was three months pregnant with their first child, a daughter. And in this respect, too, Adil was an unconventional husband, overjoyed at the prospect of having a girl child. "She will be educated as you were," he had promised, "and she will marry a man of her own choosing." This radical notion pleased Akila, since so many of her sisters in Islam had been forced to marry men they could not love, men their fathers had chosen with no regard for the tenderness of a young girl's heart.

Akila entered a birthing room and squeezed a young patient's fingers gently before bending to peer between her legs. "Your child is coming soon," she promised, although the birth was still at least an hour away. "This is your first?"

The Bedouin girl nodded, her brow knotted with the agony of a difficult labor that had begun yesterday in the desert. The fourth wife of an aging sheik, she could be no more than thirteen years old—more likely twelve. And as long as her husband remained potent, she would be withered from childbearing by thirty. She and her co-wives, two of whom were also pregnant, were proof to the tribe of his continued virility.

Akila stayed with the girl through a wracking contraction, resolving to ask Adil to speak to the old man. The talk probably wouldn't help, but it would at least make her feel better. And who knows? Some seeds, even planted in the desert sands, could bloom and bear fruit.

Promising to return soon, she left her patient and located a nurse, whom she instructed to stay with the girl and call for Akila when the time came.

She picked up a chart at the nurses' station and made a few comments regarding a patient's medications. She was still writing when a veiled woman wandered in alone, looking around as one lost or frightened. Her *abaaya* was dusty and wrinkled, as if it had been lived in for several days.

"How may I help you?" Akila asked in Arabic, although the woman's bearing suggested that she was not of this country.

The woman turned to her, and through the black cloud of her veil Akila could see her eyes widen at the sight of an uncovered female face.

"You may remove yours as well, if you wish," she told the woman. "No one will bother you here."

The woman nodded, although she made no move to take off her veil. "I need help," she whispered, with only the slightest hint of an accent.

"You are ill?"

The woman paused, then shook her head. "I saw the hospital and hoped I might find someone here. . . ."

"A patient?"

The woman paused. "I . . . I'm an American. I was hoping to find someone of my country here. Someone I could speak with." She hesitated, then spoke again quickly. "I don't mean to offend you, but . . ."

Akila understood. Her father had served for many years as a physician in the house of the royal ambassador in London some years ago. She had spent a year there to complete her studies in medicine, and there were times she would have cried to hear the Arab tongue. This woman had come to a good place, since many doctors in this country were from the West. "I understand," she said, switching to her somewhat halting English. "When you are far from home, sometimes it helps to hear your own language." She glanced at the duty roster posted above the nurses' station. "But I'm afraid the only Americans here today are in surgery at the moment. I could see if we have any patients . . ."

The woman slumped and shook her head.

There was a tinge of desperation about her. Noting it, Akila caught her arm as she turned to leave. "You are frightened. Will you tell me why? If you are concerned for your privacy, I will promise to say nothing, even to my husband."

She saw tears behind the woman's veil. Then the woman bowed her head and allowed Akila to lead her to a vacant examining room.

Inside, the woman hesitantly removed her veil. Beneath it was a lovely face, with round gray eyes and full lips—a Caucasian face, but beautiful even by Arab standards. "How do you stand these things?" she asked, dropping the veil onto her lap with obvious distaste.

Akila smiled. It was the first question she heard each time she met a foreign woman. "One becomes accustomed to it." Seeing the protest in the other woman's eyes, she went on. "In fact, many of our women would be quite offended if you asked them to remove their veil."

The woman looked surprised. "Why?"

"For some, it is a matter of piety. They seek to glorify Allah by repudiating themselves." Akila shrugged. This was not her way, but there were respected women who loved their veils in this manner. "For others, it is perhaps more a matter of vanity. It is quite a grand feeling, you see, to be considered so beautiful that no man may look upon your face without risking thoughts offensive to Allah."

The woman gave her a dubious look, and she continued. "For still others, if their husbands did not demand the veil, they would feel unloved and unprotected. They wish to feel that their husbands are so jealous of them as to demand that they keep covered from the gaze of other men." She smiled. "And I wear my veil in public as a matter of deference to my father and husband, to avoid causing a scandal which might bring them disrespect." She extended her hand in the Western fashion. "My name is Akila. How may I help you?"

The woman accepted her gesture of friendship, squeezing her fingers firmly. "My name is Giselle Chayil . . . Hardy." She slumped again, her expression crumbling as she stumbled over her last name. "I have to get out of your country. It is most urgent."

Akila frowned at the sound of the name Chayil. It was Middle Eastern, of that she was certain. But not Arab. She could not place it, but it felt somehow wrong to hear it, as if it was out of place here. "How may I help you?" Akila asked the woman.

The woman paused. "I'm desperate. I have no passport and only a little money. I know it is impossible, but somehow, I must leave Saudi Arabia."

Akila suspected briefly that the woman was trying to deceive her in order to get money. But her desperation seemed real enough. "Tell me why you must leave, and perhaps I might find a way to help you."

The woman hesitated again. Akila touched her arm. "How will you travel without papers? I will keep your secrets and help if I can."

When the woman finally began to tell her story, it tumbled forth like sand blown by a great wind. Akila found it fantastic, impossible to believe. Spies, terrorists, radical Jews in a country that officially refused to acknowledge that there was any nation but Palestine between the Dead Sea and the Mediterranean— surely this woman was lying. But then there was that name, Chayil. And the look of terror in this woman's eyes as she spoke of being kidnapped and held here against her will.

Such a thing would be easy enough to do, Akila knew. She had heard her cousins speak of such a thing once, of a wealthy Saudi merchant becoming enamored of a beautiful European girl who had refused his proposal of marriage. He had drugged her and placed her in a large trunk, and with enough money to the right officials, his luggage had not been checked. Once she was installed in his *hareem,* he had made her his concubine and refused to let her leave. Fortunately for the girl, her family had some power, and they managed to persuade their government to look into the matter. Eventually, after a near international incident, the man was ordered to allow the girl to return home.

If this had happened to the woman standing before her, there were few laws to protect her. In this country, it would require the sworn testimony of four women to equal that of a single male before the courts. If the man who had kidnapped this woman denied her story and claimed instead that she was his wife or concubine, she would be returned to him despite her protests. Akila took the woman's hands. "I do not know if I believe you, but I can see that you are truly frightened. Come. We will speak with my father," she decided. "He will know what must be done."

After first assuring that someone would know where to find her when the Bedouin girl's time came, Akila helped Giselle to don her veil again and led her to her father's office in the administrative wing of the hospital. There, after also promising to respect this woman's secrets, Hakim listened intently to the story.

He, too, was suspicious. He watched the woman as she told

her tale, and Akila wished that he could see her face as she had. Perhaps that would be enough to sway him.

Finally, he had heard enough. "I cannot believe what you are saying," he decided. "This kingdom does not harbor Jews or terrorists. I believe it is most likely that you married a Saudi man, and now you are finding our ways too constraining. I sympathize, but I cannot part a wife from her husband against his will."

"The man who brought me here is not my husband! Please!" Giselle blurted desperately.

Akila put a hand on Giselle's arm, fearing that her father would mistake her desperation for disrespect. She stepped forward. "Father, I too have heard this story, only I was able to see this woman's eyes as she spoke. She is truly here against her will and truly terrified. Surely that should be cause enough for us to help her. Perhaps you could simply contact her father." She turned to Giselle. "Would that be possible?"

"No," Giselle slumped. "I wish it were that simple, but these people—they have tapped the telephone lines at my father's compound. There's no way to reach him without letting them know where I am."

This response did nothing but firm Hakim's resolve. "I am truly sorry," he told the woman. "But we cannot help you."

"Please, I beg you," Giselle pleaded more calmly. "I am telling you the truth. There is no way I can prove it, but I swear to you by all that is holy, everything I have said is true." She stepped toward Hakim, her earnestness evident in her posture. "Sir, you have a daughter, and I can see that you love her. You would already have sent me away if you didn't. How would you feel if she were in my situation?"

Hakim hesitated, and Akila knew that he was finally sensing the undercurrents she had seen. She waited for his wisdom to guide him.

Finally, reluctantly, he shook his head. "Allah forgive me, for

I sense that your fear, at least, is honest. But I must refuse. If it became known that I had helped a woman escape her husband, there would be a scandal. I am closely connected to the House of Sa'ud, and I will not bring injury to the king by my actions."

Akila wanted to protest, but she understood her father's reasons. There was a growing discontent among certain factions of the citizenry of her country. The poor saw the great wealth of the privileged classes, and they were filled with envy. The pious saw the unfortunate excesses of the rich, and they were increasingly offended. And the activists often laid the blame for every ill upon the royal family's alliances with the corrupt nations of the West, most particularly America. Any scandal, if passions were sufficiently stirred, might spark a protest that could lead to the fall of the royal house. And if that happened, not only would the nation be in turmoil, but Arabs could be terrible in their vengeance. Those of the Al-Sa'ud family who did not make good their escape would be executed most horribly, as might any who had closely served them.

Giselle, too, seemed to understand. Her body slumped as hope left her. "I appreciate your consideration."

With a respectful nod to her father, Akila took her friend's arm and led her out of the office.

Near the exit, Giselle turned and thanked her. "I appreciate your trying to help."

Akila took her hands. "I wish I could have done more. My father is a kind man, but he must be cautious."

Giselle nodded. "I understand. I will find another way." Smiling tightly through her veil, she turned to leave.

Akila watched as the woman walked down the hall, a dark figure much like so many others. But this one walked alone, and there was a caution in her bearing that betrayed an honest fear. As she reached the door, a man entered, and Akila saw her shrink away as he neared, his eyes darting down the length of her body.

The woman's fear was too real to ignore. Akila had seen such fear far too often on the faces of her patients. Too many times she had treated women for terrible injuries, only to watch helplessly as the women were forced to return to the husbands who had battered them. She had seen unwed mothers chained to their beds because, once they delivered, they were to be executed for fornication. She had heard of girls, caught in the embrace of a lover, who were taken by their own fathers into the desert and left to perish.

This woman she could help.

Glancing back at her father's door, Akila turned and dashed after Giselle. "Wait!" She caught up and laid a hand on Giselle's arm, keeping her there as she thought. Finally, she nodded. "My father is correct in that his helping a runaway woman might, if discovered, create a scandal. But I am only a woman. Even if it became known that I had helped you, it would be seen as an act of feminine emotionalism."

The woman stared at her. "Are you sure?"

Akila glanced up to see a nurse hurrying toward her. It was the Bedouin girl's time. She nodded, then turned toward Giselle. "I have never before gone against the wishes of my father." She took a long, steeling breath. "But I will do what I can."

The woman sighed with relief, her veil shifting with the force of her breath. She squeezed Akila's hand. "I don't know how to thank you."

"Come with me." Akila hurried back to the women's ward, where she quickly checked on the Bedouin girl. There was time, but only a little. Telling Giselle to wait, she half-jogged down the hall to the last room in the women's ward. The dormitory-like room was curtained off from prying eyes.

This was where the poorest of Saudi Arabia's poor, the unprotected women, were treated. They had been divorced, most of them, by husbands seeking younger or more fertile wives. Their own blood kin had rejected them as well, and now they

had nowhere to go. They lived in government-sponsored housing, zealously policed by *mutawain* to ensure that they did not
threaten the public morals. An unfettered woman was too great
a temptation to Saudi men to be allowed to live alone.

Akila hated the hopelessness, the despair of this room. Few of
the women here cared if they got well. As used women, without
dowry or great beauty, they had little hope of finding new husbands. Some had children they would never see again, now being raised by the wives who had replaced them. These women
would live and die in a sterile government home, ignored and
unwanted.

She went to the bed of a woman who was recovering from a
suicide attempt. "*As-salaam alaykum, Sitti* Karida," she greeted
the woman with great deference, trying not to notice the irony
of the woman's name, which meant "untouched." "I noticed
when you came in yesterday that your *abaaya* was quite lovely.
Silk, is it?" she asked, knowing that it was not silk at all, but
poor cotton. In admiring Karida's cloak, she had left the woman
no choice. Custom dictated that Karida would have to give it to
her.

Her blatant though veiled request would have aroused curios-
ity or suspicion from most women, but this one only shrugged.
"It is yours. Take it."

Akila looked astonished at the woman's charity, and, as was
traditional, thanked her effusively. "Really? You are most gener-
ous, *Sitti* Karida, and far too kind. A thousand thanks would
not be sufficient for such a wonderful gift as this fine cloak.
Allow me to bring an exchange. It will be a poor substitute for
what you have given me," she added, although Giselle's cloak
was newer and of much finer fabric. "But it will clothe you, and
perhaps with your fine hand for embroidery, you can make something of it."

The woman waved her hand. "Do not trouble yourself.
Insh'Allah, I will die before I have need of another *abaaya*."

Swallowing a lump in her throat, Akila thanked Karida again and took the woman's cloak out to Giselle. "The men of this land recognize their women by unique stitching on their robes. Yours, simply by being plain, is most unusual. If someone is seeking you, you will need to change your clothing." She led Giselle to Adil's office, where he kept in his safe her passport and her travel papers. Inside, she retrieved the items, along with a certain amount of money. "Once I leave, you must lock the door in case my husband tries to enter. Then you will change clothing. Leave your old cloak. I will instruct a nurse to launder it and deliver it to a patient in need."

"Thank you."

Akila waved away her gratitude, lifting Giselle's veil to analyze her features. "No one can say we look alike, but the photo on my passport is poor, and you might pass if no one looks closely." Pressing the travel documents and money into Giselle's hand, she smiled merrily. "The veil, as much as we might hate it, also has its advantages—because of it, many women of this country have managed to travel using others' documents."

Giselle hesitated. "What will happen to you if I'm caught?"

Akila shrugged. "I am unconcerned for myself. But my father will be dishonored as a man unable to control his daughter." Her heart ached at the thought, after all that her father had done to ease her life.

Giselle seemed to understand her feeling. "If I'm caught, I'll say I stole them. And I'll find a way to get these get back to you once this is over." Tucking away the papers, she took Akila's hand. "I don't know how to thank you."

Akila smiled. "There is no need for thanks—charity is a pillar of Islam. This poor help I give you may be pleasing to Allah."

Giselle seemed about to tell her something, but a nurse's tap on the door told her that the Bedouin girl's time was here. She smiled at Giselle and gave her hand a final squeeze. "I must go. When you are finished, go to the nurses' station. I will instruct one of our delivery drivers to take you to the airport." In this country where women were not permitted to drive, the men had made similar "deliveries" before. They would think nothing of this request. "If the van is stopped by the *mutawain,* the driver will claim you are one of his wives. You must not disagree, for he could be jailed or even flogged for sharing a vehicle with an unrelated woman."

Giselle nodded gratefully. "I'll remember."

"I must go now. Peace be upon you, Giselle, and may Allah protect you in your hour of need."

"Shukran jazillan," she heard Giselle call out her thanks as she hurried away.

❖ ❖ ❖

The airport was as Giselle remembered it, bustling with people, elements of the desert blending with the modern age. Making an effort to blend in, she hurried to the counter and purchased a ticket on the next international flight, this one to France.

"You are alone?" the clerk asked, his eyes barely touching her, as if she was somehow contaminated.

Afraid to trust her voice, Giselle nodded, keeping her face down.

The man's face darkened with disapproval. "I must see your travel papers," he demanded, all semblance of respect for decent womanhood gone now as he glared directly at her face through the veil.

The new veil provided by Akila was somewhat thicker than the other, so Giselle felt relatively confident in handing over Akila's passport and the consent form, signed by Akila's husband, which permitted her to travel alone.

She wished there had been time to tell Akila about Jesus. Somehow, she resolved, when this was over, she would find a way.

The clerk took his time reviewing the documents, scowling as if looking for something wrong, some reason to deny her passage. He dared not ask Giselle to remove her veil, so she felt safe enough remaining there, her head bowed under his fierce gaze. Finally, he pushed the documents back across the counter with distaste. "It is not decent for a woman to travel alone without her *mahram*," he chided, referring to an immediate male relative permitted by the Qur'an to act as her guardian.

For a moment, Giselle's temper flared. "My decency is not a matter for your concern," she snapped, then instantly regretted it. To this man, a woman's challenge was unforgivable, and he had not yet sold her a ticket. Softening her tone, she added, "I deeply regret my rudeness, sir. It is worry that makes me so sharp. My husband's dear sister has fallen gravely ill, and my husband could not go to her side. Even though there is no one to accompany me, he has asked me to go that I may be of some comfort to her."

Once again, the veil was serving her, she realized. Bare-faced, her guilty expression at this lie would probably have betrayed her. But even though this man stared at her skeptically, he apparently saw nothing to raise his suspicions. Slowly, his holy outrage dissolved, and he relented. "If you travel on your husband's business, *insh'Allah,* you may be forgiven."

Giselle bowed her head again, this time assuming a subservient posture. "I pray that it will be so."

"Do you have luggage?"

Giselle shook her head, reciting an explanation that she'd prepared as she rode in the back of the delivery van on the way to the airport. "All that I need will be waiting for me at our residence in Paris." She noted with some surprise that this did not seem to bother him.

Nodding brusquely, the man processed a ticket and pushed it across the counter.

"Ma'a salaama," Giselle murmured the traditional leave-taking and hurried away before he could change his mind. Following

the stream of departing passengers, she made her way down the corridor toward the two international terminals.

As they passed through the metal detectors, Giselle realized that the women were being separated into a line, which led to a secluded room. As the men moved on through lines of officials checking boarding passes, and conducting more thorough searches with handheld metal detectors, she realized that the women would be undergoing a similar procedure in a more private setting.

In this private area, Giselle realized that the officials would be female. They could, and would, ask her to remove her veil if anything appeared to be wrong. Tensely, she checked the boarding pass the man had handed to her, wanting to be certain that his suspicions had not caused him to call for a thorough search.

Seeing nothing that looked unusual, she surveyed the area, trying to pinpoint the room's exits in case she needed to leave quickly. Then, taking a deep breath that drew her veil against her lips, she joined the line of black-clad women, which moved into the searching room like a stream of mourners at a funeral.

Inside, she discovered that things were moving along fairly quickly. Uniformed women whose accents suggested they were Yemini approached each passenger with their metal-detecting wands. Once each passenger was thoroughly scanned, one of the women would step closer and run her fingers along the hems of the sleeves and skirt. If nothing was found, the woman was motioned forward, and she passed through a second doorway to rejoin her male companions in the main terminal area. As her turn approached, Giselle removed the last of Akila's money from her sleeve, holding it in her hand, along with her boarding pass and documents, as she approached the women. When her turn came, a third woman, one she hadn't noticed before, took the items from her hand as the other two moved toward her.

The search was over before she had time to worry about it.

One of the women said something brusquely, and, hoping that it was a command to move on, Giselle hurried toward the exit.

"Madam, will you please wait," a voice called after her. The words were polite, but uttered in a sharp, authoritarian tone that made Giselle's back stiffen as she slowly turned back.

Giselle recognized the woman speaking to her as the third woman, and wanted to shout with relief as she realized what she wanted. In her hurry to move away from the searchers, she had forgotten her money and travel documents. She rushed back to the woman, thanked her profusely, then slipped the items into her sleeve and again made for the exit.

She was headed for the boarding line when a man stepped into her path. Mared! The shock was like a dash of ice water. Giselle turned desperately, looking for a way to escape. "No!" she whispered, dodging his hand as it reached for her.

He lunged forward, catching the sleeve of her robe before she could get away and dragging her with him to a corner of the room. Knowing that continued struggles would be fruitless, Giselle stilled, raising her hands in surrender. "OK. You have me, Mared. But if you take me back, your friends will kill me."

He shook his head. "Don't worry. . . ."

"They will, Mared," she argued. "Did you really think they'd let me go, knowing that I can lead the CIA back to the palace?"

He gave her a smile that said she didn't understand. "That won't matter in a few days. If we succeed in our plans, we'll be leaving this place." His grip tightened on her arm as he turned her in the direction he wanted to go. "Now let's go."

She tried again to twist away, but Mared merely continued walking, dragging her along behind him.

Helpless, she came to a decision. She had no choice but to tell the truth. She hurried around in front of him to block his path. "They'll kill me anyway, older brother," she told him in Akkadian, then switched to Hebrew and added in a whisper, "I know who they are."

He stopped abruptly, his expression shocked. "How—"

"Does it matter?" She waited, watching his face. "Decide, Mared. If you take me back, Talman will question me again—this time using his drugs. They'll find out what I know, and they'll kill me. I'm your sister, Mared. Are you willing to let them do that?" His eyes flickered, and she pressed on, her voice growing more urgent. "And what about Raz—what if Talman's right about him? Will you watch these men kill your own brother?"

He shook his head. "They won't kill him, because he isn't going to betray us."

She stared into his eyes. "I'm his wife, Mared. I heard what Talman heard on those tapes he made of us. You don't think he agonizes over the choices he's making? Maybe holding me hostage will keep him in line for now, but what do you think that will do to his future loyalty?"

She went on, desperately seeking a chink in Mared's armor. "And what about these men you're dealing with? When Seif dies, now or later, Talman will be your leader, won't he?" She lowered her voice to avoid being overheard. "The Sword of *Israel*," she said, emphasizing the last word, "may control the future of the Middle East. Do you want a man like Talman to have that much power?"

He had thought of this, too; she could see it in his eyes. With her free hand, she touched his shoulder. "What's so wrong with peace, Mared? I'm a Christian, and you've learned to love me as a sister. You told me that yourself. If you can be the brother of a Christian, can't you be neighbors with a Muslim?"

"No." He raised his eyes, more certain now. "Islam will never come to peace with Israel. It's impossible—a hoax that amounts to murder," he said with passion. "How many Jews will die while we pretend to be at peace?"

"How many are dying now?" she asked gently. "How many will die if your plan succeeds? What lives are you saving by making war, Mared?"

"The lives of future generations of Israel. If we can destroy the Arabs, shatter Islam, we will finally have true peace—peace through power!" He said it with conviction, but his eyes lacked the fire she'd seen before.

"At what cost, Mared? Nuclear war? What kind of Promised Land will you leave your children after Israel drops the bomb on its neighbors? What will happen if a nuclear bomb strikes an oil field—do you know?" She paused, then slipped a hand up to touch his stubbled cheek. "And what kind of peace will you have if you buy it by betraying your own family?"

He stiffened, his eyes fixing on a place some distance away. Then he looked at Giselle again, and the confusion in his eyes resolved. He let go of her wrist. "Go, then. But there are others nearby, also looking for you. If you pass through undiscovered, if you can stop our plans, I'll accept that it is God's will."

Giselle wanted to kiss him. Instead, she nodded and backed away. "Thank you, brother."

"And watch your posture," he added. "You're standing too straight, looking around too much. That's how I knew it was you."

Giselle turned and quickly positioned herself with a group of women who were boarding the plane. As Mared instructed, she kept her head lowered, her eyes on the floor below her, but even so, she noticed the white-clad men who stood near the lines, their eyes casually examining each woman as she passed. Ahead of her, a man noticed, too, and loudly protested this stranger's perusal of his modest wife. The searcher merely shrugged and moved to another vantage point.

Keeping her head lowered and remaining near the woman ahead of her as if she was part of a group, she quietly passed the first man, and then a second. Once more thankful for the all-concealing veil, she finally boarded the plane and was shown to a seat, which a Saudi father politely relinquished so that she could sit in the company of his daughters. He himself took the one last seat, which would have been forbidden to her because it was next to a man.

Several hours later, she was disembarking in France. Most of the women aboard her flight had slipped into the rest rooms upon leaving Saudi airspace, and were now happily clad in Western dresses. These were modestly long and loose-fitting, but nevertheless quite daring by the Saudi standards to which Giselle had become strangely accustomed. Only she, and a woman who looked to be much older, remained in the veil. This garnered her a few curious stares as she joined the milling crowds that moved through customs.

The flight had been long enough to allow her some sleep, which she'd relished, knowing that it might be the last she'd have for many hours. Now refreshed, she found that where her nerves had been dulled by stress and exhaustion during her adventures at the Saudi airport, they were now tap-dancing, causing her hands to shake despite all efforts to still them.

She had managed to slip through security at Saudi Arabia largely because of an ancient system that demanded absolute seclusion of women. Here, however, when the customs officials demanded to verify her identity, she couldn't hope to hide behind the veil. And, as Akila had pointed out, no one could say she looked like the woman in the picture, even though it was somewhat out of focus. Worse, she didn't even match the description, which showed Akila as being four centimeters taller and brown-eyed.

Still, Akila had said that many Saudi women had used each other's papers, so Giselle stayed in line, knowing that any effort to get around customs was probably riskier than going through.

Perhaps it was simply the fact that she'd arrived without luggage during a busy period, but in the end, Giselle was barely noticed. A woman who spoke Arabic asked her to remove her veil, but hardly glanced at the passport as she asked the standard questions. "Where will you be staying? How long do you expect to be in France?" Giselle answered as vaguely as she could, remembering her story about a family emergency, and with a harried smile, the woman returned her documents and she was allowed to pass.

At the currency exchange, Giselle converted Akila's remaining Riyali into French francs. She had just enough left to rent a car and pick up a few items she'd need for the plan she'd formulated during the flight.

❖ ❖ ❖

"Our leader wishes you to know that your wife is well." The words, spoken in Akkadian from the rear seat of a diplomat's limousine, sounded far from reassuring. "We will keep her under guard until our plan has been executed."

Raz clenched his teeth. He had always hated Talman, even more so now. "Let me speak with her."

"That is impossible," Talman answered too smoothly. "But rest assured that she has not been harmed. Your brother watches over her. He is very protective."

Raz wanted to kill the man—probably would have done so had Talman been in his reach. The old man was lying. Did that mean Giselle was dead? "Where is she?"

Talman chuckled—the sound of a jackal growling. "It would be foolish to give you such details, Major. But I will say that she is in one of our safe houses. One with which I am certain you are unfamiliar. She will be all right." His tone softened to a sinister near-whisper. "Although we do wish to learn some things from her."

"She doesn't know anything!" Raz shouted.

"Silence, Major! You will not question your superior!"

Raz took a deep breath, then spoke more quietly. "I'm sorry. But understand me, Talman. The woman is under my protection, and I am holding you responsible for her safety. If anything happens to her, make no mistake. I will see that you pay."

"Do not threaten me, Major." The voice became menacing. "You are to follow the plan. Do so and your wife will be returned to you. Fail us, and we may need her as a hostage."

Helpless with rage, Raz gestured for the limo driver to pull over. Stepping out, he began to walk briskly toward his own car several blocks away, taking deep breaths in order to calm his fury.

"Major Chayil."

The man's voice startled him. He had been distracted, incautious. It was a fatal error for a man in his position. He turned to find two men walking toward him, one of them flashing identification—Office of Naval Intelligence.

"Sir, we must ask you to come with us." One of the men gestured to a nearby car. "It's about your wife's disappearance."

Raz nodded and turned to go with them, hoping that his apparent cooperation would make them drop their guard. As they neared the car, one of the men stepped away, circling round to enter on the driver's side. That was the break he needed.

In a second, the other man was on the ground, unconscious, and Raz was on the run. Glancing over his shoulder, he saw the first man bend to check his partner, shouting into a handheld radio. Within minutes, the area would be milling with agents.

But they wouldn't find him.

It was time to execute a plan that he'd hoped would never be necessary.

❖ ❖ ❖

Eloisa was busy today. Her customers had been more demanding than usual, requiring more of her time. Additionally, several had requested alterations, which she was now tending to. Tonight she would work late to complete her orders.

She barely glanced up when a new customer entered her shop. But, as the vision registered in her mind, her eyes rose again sharply. "Giselle! *Bambina!* I almost did not know you!" Setting aside her sewing, she hurried to greet the young woman, who was strangely dressed in a long black robe. "I have not seen you since your wedding. Where is your handsome husband?"

The look in her young friend's eyes told her that all was not well. "Eloisa, don't you usually close your shop around this time?"

Eloisa glanced at the clock by her work area. "*Sí*, but don't worry. I will be open for you as long as you need. Could I help you find something?"

Giselle shook her head. "No, Eloisa. I'm asking that you close shop for me. Lock the doors, pull the blinds. I don't want to be seen."

In her excitement at seeing her young friend, Eloisa had not noticed until this moment that Giselle's hair was different. It was short, but poorly cut, as if done in a hurry. She had carefully kept her back to the windows while they talked. Her color was high and her eyes bright. Eloisa had initially seen it as excitement, but she now considered that it might be anxiety. And beneath it all, Eloisa could sense that Giselle was also exhausted.

"What is it?" she asked. "What is wrong, *cara?*"

Giselle's eyes filled with tears as the weariness finally overtook her. "Eloisa, I need your help. . . ."

❖ ❖ ❖

A few hours later, Giselle checked her reflection one last time. She drew a deep breath. If anything could get her into her father's villa at Gaeta without being caught, she hoped this was it.

It was something Arlene Riley had said that had given her this idea.

"Wait 'til you get pregnant, Giselle. Nobody will look at your face anymore." Arlene had patted her growing belly, then impishly winked when an attractive man walked by them. But he never noticed. His eyes fell to her stomach and then moved onto Giselle, as if Arlene were no more than a pregnancy.

She had remembered the comment on the flight to France—along with the fact that Arlene often asked Eloisa to make adjustments to her uniforms to make them more comfortable. And once again, Giselle's prayers had been answered; Arlene had in fact just dropped off a uniform at Eloisa's the day before.

Giselle smiled at the way God seemed to have gone ahead of her, preparing every step.

While she had napped in the back room, Eloisa had fashioned a false pregnancy for her, even weighting it so that Giselle's posture would be correct. She had padded the bust and shoulders of the uniform to help Giselle fill it, and then suggested rolling some strips of cotton to be placed inside Giselle's cheeks, adding some roundness there as well.

Eloisa had also recut her hair, giving her a collar-length bob and blunt-cut bangs that somehow made her face seem wider. With a few highlights to change the color, and makeup to modify her coloring, she looked quite different now. Especially when she added the uniform's cap and a pair of dark glasses to shield her eyes.

Still, someone who knew her well might recognize her, and she expected that only the most experienced guards would be guarding the compound today. She stared critically at her reflection, wondering what else she could do that might sell her disguise. Thoughtfully, she patted her stomach as she had often seen Arlene do when the baby was restless.

"There!" Eloisa exclaimed. "That is a good touch. If you do that for the guards at Gaeta, they will never look past your belly."

"Thank you so much, Eloisa." Giselle turned and gave the woman a hug. "I wish I could tell you what was going on. Just trust me that this is more important than you could imagine."

Eloisa patted her cheek. "I do not need to understand it all, *cara*. You've given me the greatest gift I could receive by telling me that you are now my sister in Jesus. And now, if you will do me one last favor before you go, let me pray with you. It is something I have longed to do since you were a tiny one."

Giselle nodded, and the two women moved to a place where both could sit comfortably.

Eloisa took her hand. "*Padre*, Father, we come before you as children. You know Giselle's needs. We seek your will in her situation, and we ask that you watch over her and cause all things to work according to your purpose. Your plan is good, *Padre*, though we do not know it. Help us to follow the path that you set before us. In Jesus' holy name."

The prayer was so simple. Giselle caught her eye. "Eloisa, you know I grew up Catholic. Are you Catholic also?"

Eloisa nodded. "There is still much in my heart that is Catholic. But as you know, one can be in the church for many years, and yet not truly know Jesus."

Giselle nodded. "I've learned that, yes." Somehow, it took more than intellectual assent. There was a difference between knowing and *believing*.

"That is good," Eloisa told her.

"I notice that you didn't pray to a saint or to Mary," Giselle commented.

Eloisa nodded. "When I came to my faith, I found that there were things I had been taught that I could no longer accept. I love the silence and the reverence of the Catholic church, and I am truly blessed when I receive communion. But I find that I no longer need to pray to saints or seek absolution from a confessor. I find that I am God's own child, and that he hears me even though I have no great deeds to commend me."

"Yes, exactly!" Giselle nearly laughed. A few times in the past couple of days, she had wondered if she should be praying to a saint. But she had noticed that it seemed to put distance between her and God. It didn't feel quite right, somehow. She had wondered whether she was mistaken. Now, hearing what Eloisa was saying, it was as if she had heard God himself affirm her feelings.

"I learned many years ago, Giselle, that one may have religion without having a relationship with God. Religion is the church we attend, and all the things we think we must do to make ourselves acceptable to God. And so long as we rely upon those things, we may have moments when we feel deserving, but most of the time we will not. I found in religion that I usually felt that there was a distance between God and myself. Yes?"

Giselle knew what she meant.

"A relationship with God cannot be deserved. We do not earn it, but only receive it because of the cross of Christ. Jesus did all that must be done. Do you understand this?"

The words didn't make sense, not to Giselle's mind. And yet she knew that what Eloisa had said was true.

Eloisa patted her cheek again. "Then you are free! No longer in bondage to guilt and fear and worry that you can never do enough—or worse, to a prideful assumption that you *have* done enough to earn God's blessing. You are simply a child again, and your Father receives you as a child."

Giselle smiled. She hoped to understand it better one day. But for now, just knowing it was true was enough.

Eloisa took her hand again. "God will protect you, Giselle. You are his own now."

ChapterEight

Giselle hesitated at the door, glanced around to see if anyone seemed to be watching, then stooped and retrieved the key from the small ledge beneath the doorstep, and let herself in.

Getting past the guards at the villa had been amazingly easy. Other than requiring her to pass through a metal detector that had been erected as added security, her father's guards had barely glanced at her.

As she'd driven past the compound, she could see that security had been doubled; but here, it pretty much seemed to be business as usual. On one hand, it was a relief. On the other, it was worrisome. What if the slackness at the gate meant that her father was still aboard the *Lamar,* somewhere out to sea? The summit was scheduled for 1300 hours, and she had no idea where it was being held—by the time she found it, Seif would already have done his worst!

Walking into her former home, she felt caught in some strange time warp. Every detail here was the same as it had been the last time she'd visited, proof that it had only been a little more than a week since her last visit. And yet her whole world had changed, and she was no longer the same person. How could everything be so different so quickly?

Heading for her father's office, she made a detour to the living room to see the glow of the sunlight through her mother's gauzy curtains, and the elegant tidiness that her father insisted upon. Would she live here again when this was all over? Somehow, she couldn't imagine it.

In contrast to the rest of the house, the office was a jolt. In the former foyer, now a reception area where Riley usually sat, there were papers strewn everywhere, as if he'd suddenly become so busy that he could no longer take time to file. Frowning, Giselle moved on to her father's door and knocked softly.

"Come in." He sounded exhausted, and for the first time, Giselle realized what he must have been going through. Holding her breath, she opened the door.

Her father stood next to his file cabinets, rummaging for papers, and did not look up. His desk, too, was not what she was used to. There was no mess—no matter what, her father would never tolerate a mess—but things were just slightly off. His blotter was not square, and the papers in his "in" basket were not neatly stacked.

Glancing up, she caught sight of her father and had to suppress a gasp. The lines on his face, which she'd remembered as craggy and masculine, were suddenly hollow and evidence of aging. And had he lost weight? Somehow, he was neither as tall nor as muscular as she'd remembered him.

"Daddy?" she whispered, her eyes filling with tears.

He turned, and the file he'd just retrieved slipped from his fingers. "Giselle? Mother Mary, is that you?"

And then he was holding her, and suddenly she was his little girl again, burying her face against his uniform and trying bravely not to stain it with her tears.

With a last squeeze, he put her away from him, holding her arms as he looked her over. "Are you all right, baby? How did you get here? What happened to your face, your hair?"

She smiled, nodded, and brusquely wiped the tears from her

eyes. "It's a long story, Daddy, and we haven't got time for it now. Please believe me—the SOI is going to try to kill the delegates at the peace summit today!"

He nodded, keeping his grip on her arms as if afraid to let her go. "We know about their plan. Arn's people have everything under control." He studied her face, speaking gently. "Are you aware of your husband's part in all this?"

Giselle took a long breath. "I know he's got something to do with it, but—"

"Don't try to defend him, Giselle," her father warned. "Arn says he's up to his ears in it, and once he knew we suspected him, he disappeared. Arn and I both have people out looking for him, but he's probably long gone."

Giselle tried not to notice the sudden ache in her heart at his words. "What about the summit?"

"It's been moved. We tried to cancel, but the president insists that we go ahead."

She caught her father's arm urgently. "Where?"

She could see him hesitate. She wasn't supposed to know this much. Moving to look him squarely in the eye, she spoke urgently. "Daddy, I probably know almost as much as you do about this. I know that you've been helping with the negotiations, I know that Raz had mapped out plans for several different meeting sites. But what's more important, I know what the SOI plans to do. Daddy, you've got to let me help you!"

He stared at her, shock registering on his face, but then slowly nodded. "The initial plan was to have them meet aboard the *Lamar*, but we have to assume your husband has somehow arranged for the terrorists to board her. I've got a team of men aboard her now, waiting to arrest them if they try. Meanwhile, the only easily-secured site that wasn't on the list of possible meeting places was the embassy itself. We've diverted the delegates there—Raz's marines have been relieved, and I've hand-picked my own people to handle security."

"No!" Giselle couldn't keep the horror from her voice. "Dad, where are the delegates now?"

He looked at her curiously. "They're on their way to the embassy or are there already."

Giselle shook his hands from her shoulders, struggling not to sound hysterical. "Dad, the leader of the SOI is among the delegates. His name is Seif. I overheard him explain his plans. He said he was going to carry explosives under his robes and set them off if something went wrong with the original plan."

Her father's eyes widened briefly, then his face set hard, his expression determined. He reached for the phone. "What delegation is he with?"

Giselle paused. Seif hadn't said, and she could only guess. "Probably either the Saudis or the Israelis."

He hesitated, staring at her.

She nodded at his unasked question. "The SOI is actually a group of Israeli radicals. If you think about it, it explains a lot of things intelligence never understood. Like why they wiped out the Islamic terrorist groups they couldn't control. And where they get their intelligence."

He stared at her as the news sank in. "Giselle, how do you know all this? About the terrorists, and the intelligence?"

"That's a long story, too, Daddy," she answered desperately. "Please, just take my word for it."

He hesitated only another moment, then briskly picked up the phone and started dialing. When the call was answered, he began giving orders. "Get me Arn Killian and Lieutenant Riley out at the embassy command center. I'll take whoever picks up the phone first."

"Daddy, the compound's lines are tapped."

"Not anymore," he assured her. "Arn's men have combed our communications lines with a fine-toothed comb." He returned his attention to the immediate issue. "Can you describe this terrorist?"

She shrugged. "I barely saw his face, but I'd know his voice anywhere." She was relieved to be passing the responsibility to someone who was trained to handle it. Her father would know what to do. He always did.

And yet—this realization struck her with a sudden jolt—neither her father nor Arn, with all their equipment, resources, and expertise, had managed to learn what she knew. For the first time, she saw her father as fallible.

And if things went wrong, Seif and his men would win. The president, the delegates, and the peace process—all of it would blow sky-high in the next few hours. She closed her eyes and prayed that somehow everything would work out.

Her father looked her over, seeming to notice the uniform and fake belly for the first time. "Will this Seif know you on sight dressed like that?"

Giselle glanced at her uniform and shook her head. "I don't think he's ever seen me."

"Good." Returning his attention to the phone, he listened for a moment. "Good work. One more thing, then put him on. I need a helicopter at the villa in five minutes—two if possible."

The admiral waited for a moment, then addressed the new voice that came on the line. "Riley, tell me which delegations have arrived at the embassy. Just Syria? Good. Have your men escort them to the bunker and keep them there. Then I want you to radio the escorts for all the other delegations, except the Saudis and Israelis, and tell them to delay arrival until further notice. Evacuate all nonessential personnel from the embassy, and when the Saudis and Israelis arrive, take each group to conference rooms on opposite sides of the building. No visitors, but don't let them think anything is wrong. Tell them that the other delegations are on their way and offer refreshments while they wait. Keep them calm; tell them the president is handling some stateside business and will be with them momentarily."

Giselle listened, admiring her father's decisiveness. He was right, she suspected, in thinking that Seif would wait to detonate the explosives until he could take as many of the delegates as possible with him. By isolating him, they might be able to buy some time.

After he hung up, the admiral returned his attention more fully to her, inspecting her as if she were under his command. He paused to adjust her insignia and make a minor adjustment to the angle of her cap, then stepped back, seeming satisfied. "You've seen it enough to play the part, right?"

Giselle smiled, saluting smartly. "Yes, sir."

He let her hold the salute for a few seconds before returning it. "Good." He paused. "While we're on the helicopter, you can fill me in on what you've been through."

Giselle smiled. She couldn't wait to tell her father about her experience. But, even more, she ached to tell him all about her encounter with Jesus, and how he had answered her prayers.

"The chopper's coming," he said, hearing the rotors a second before she did. He turned toward the door. "Let's get this thing done."

He opened the door and strode out, the old confidence and authority returning to his stride. Giselle hurried to stay with him, mentally noting the orders he gave her as he walked.

"Stay close to me, pretend to be my aide. Once you see this Seif person, I want you to point him out and then get out. Leave the building and get as far away as possible until I signal the all-clear."

❖ ❖ ❖

To avoid alerting the delegates, the helicopter landed in a park a few blocks from the embassy. A petty officer was waiting with a staff car that took them through the rear gates, so that their arrival wasn't seen.

Riley was waiting at the guardhouse and came running toward their car as they got out. "Sir," he snapped a salute to the admiral. "The two delegations are cooling their heels, just as you said. A couple of the ambassador's people wanted to go in and explain things, but on your orders, we refused access."

"Good work, Riley," the admiral said.

Hurrying ahead to open the door, Riley glanced back at Giselle, and his jaw dropped as he recognized her. "Giselle!" he yelped, rushing toward her to shake her hand. "How did you get here? I thought . . . And what's with the uniform?" He glanced at her father as if wondering if he had realized his daughter was impersonating an officer.

"It's a long story," Giselle repeated.

"I'm all ears," Riley said.

"For the moment, she's my aide. She'll need to get close to the delegates to identify one of the terrorists for us. The man is in there with explosives, waiting to take out the entire peace summit."

Riley stared at him. "Are you sure you want to bring Giselle in here? She could just give us a description and—"

"I'll need to hear his voice," Giselle told him. "Besides, I've come this far. I want to see it through."

"We'll need a firsthand identification," her father put in quietly. "And I have some doubts as to whether even that will be enough to squelch the protests that we'll hear for laying hands on a delegate." He fixed Giselle with his gray-blue eyes. "But I meant it when I told you what to do, Giselle. Once you identify this man, I want you to clear the building. If this thing goes south, I don't want to have to worry about you."

If this thing goes south, nobody's going to live long enough to worry about me, Giselle thought, but she didn't say it aloud. Instead, she nodded and met her father's penetrating gaze. "Yes, sir."

"Arn Killian is on the phone. He wants a few words in private before this thing goes down," Riley broke in as they passed down a long corridor, moving toward the stairs. "He's on his way, but he probably won't get here before the fun starts. He's holding on the secured line in the ambassador's office. I'll need the time to position my men, anyway."

The admiral nodded. "Where's the safest place for Giselle to wait?"

"Assuming you have the delegates in the conference rooms on the third floor," Giselle put in, continuing after she received an affirmative nod from Riley, "my office is probably about as safe as it gets."

Her father nodded. "That's the garden-level row of offices past the east stairwell, third door," he told Riley. "Get a member of the security team to meet her there and stay with her."

"Yes, sir," Riley said, lifting a hand radio from its holster at his belt and quickly repeating the order.

Reaching the stairwell, the admiral halted, turning to catch Giselle's arms. "Be careful," he told her, a worried look in his warm gray-blue eyes.

She nodded. "You, too, Daddy."

After a quick embrace, her father turned and jogged up the steps, taking them two at a time. Giselle watched until he was out of sight, then slowly began her descent to the first basement.

The hallway leading to her office was eerie in its desertion. No secretaries hurrying by with paperwork, no functionaries yelling for quick adjudications, just bare institutional walls with closed doors on all sides. It seemed more cheerless, more stagnant, than she remembered.

She entered her office, trying not to remember that first-day visit from Raz. Or the many visits after their wedding, when his eyes had told her that only his military propriety prevented him from locking her door for a private moment.

Where was he now, she wondered. Already on the way to a hideout somewhere, a place where nobody would ever find him? Already so far away from her that he could never come back, no matter how much she missed him?

At least he was gone. At least he wouldn't have to face arrest—or execution.

She straightened as if the movement could force him from her mind. She had a job to do. Better to think of that, keep her mind focused, her thoughts clear for what she had to do. Better to think of anything else, until she had no other options. Then she would force herself to look into the loneliness ahead and decide how to make the best of it.

A rap on the door interrupted her thoughts.

She unlocked the door and peered out, expecting to find the guard Riley had sent.

It was Gregory Benedetti. He smiled, pushing his way inside and locking the door behind him. "Lieutenant Riley needed someone to come check on you, so I volunteered to stay." He moved toward her, his face a mask of earnest concern. "I heard you had been kidnapped. Are you all right?"

She rounded her desk to put some space between them. Riley may have sent Gregory, but she still felt uncomfortable around him. "I'm fine. . . ."

She was interrupted by the muffled sound of static coming from somewhere on Gregory's person. "What's that?" she asked.

He reached into a pocket and withdrew a small, handheld radio, identical to the one Riley had used. This time the message could be heard clearly. "Ensign Winchell, where are you? Respond!" Riley shouted.

Gregory raised the radio, positioning himself between Giselle and the door. "Sorry, Lieutenant, there's a lot of static down here."

"The admiral says give him another couple of minutes. We'll let you know when it's time to come up."

"Acknowledged," Gregory said, shutting off the radio before Giselle could cry out.

Giselle stared at him, the implications of the situation dawning on her. "Talman said he had another man at the embassy," she murmured. "He was talking about you!"

Gregory smiled tightly. "You're a smart girl, Giselle—too smart. I'm sure I don't have to spell out for you what happens next." Cautiously, he moved toward her.

"No!" There was only one exit. Giselle timed her attack, hoping to catch him off balance and push him aside. She nearly succeeded, but he caught her by the waist and pulled her back, shoving her against the wall with brutal force.

"Talman said that, before you die, I should find out what you know about your father's business." He reached out and touched her cheek. "You should know that extracting information is one of my specialties. And after all the trouble you've been, I think I'll rather enjoy it."

She pushed away his hand, reaching up to strike him, but he just chuckled and caught her wrist, wrenching her arm around behind her so that she grunted with pain. "Please, Giselle, don't insult me by trying out those ridiculous self-defense lessons of the major's on me. The only reason you've gotten away with it so far is that the others underestimated you. I know better than to make that mistake."

She struggled to twist free, but he only applied more pressure, until she thought that her shoulder might pull from its socket.

He laughed at her pained expression. "I did underestimate you once, you know. When we first met, I honestly thought you'd be an easy mark. I had orders to seduce you, to put you in an embarrassing situation and give Talman something to bargain over with your father. But you preferred a man in uniform. The major had the same orders, by the way, once your preference was noted. How does that make you feel?"

Giselle stilled, glaring at him with all the fury she could muster. "But he didn't obey those orders, did he? Instead, he married me!"

Gregory's eyes narrowed. "So you're still in love with him, even after he nearly killed you? You're a fool, Giselle. He married you because Seif told him to. That was better than sullying your virtue, because it gave the SOI an even stronger hold on your father. What wouldn't the old man do for his beloved daughter's happiness?"

"Liar!" Giselle cried, trying again to twist away, ignoring the grinding pain in her shoulder.

"My employers expected great things out of your union— Gili," Gregory spat, twisting her arm brutally as he whispered her husband's nickname for her. "It's too bad the major isn't here to deal with you himself. It might be amusing to watch you realize just how little you really mean to him." Reaching over to her desk, he unclipped the cord from her telephone, then yanked the other end from the wall.

"No!" Realizing his intentions, Giselle summoned a burst of strength and almost twisted free.

He easily brought her back under control. "Wouldn't you rather get out of here before our friend blows up the building?" Pushing her face-down over her desk, he brought her wrists around behind her and tied them roughly with the phone cord. Remembering something Raz had once taught her, Giselle clenched her fists tight as he tied them, buying a little give in the cord.

Keeping her pinned, Gregory began opening desk drawers, searching until he found what he wanted. Tearing off a piece of packing tape, he pressed it firmly over her mouth.

Patting her cheek, he pulled her to her feet. "Then we'll play a little game of Arabian Nights, my little *Sheharezade*. You'll stay alive as long as you have stories to trade for your life."

Catching her by the hips, he tossed her roughly over his shoulder. "Now you won't be any trouble, will you, Giselle?" he asked as he carried her down the hallway. "I know a way out of here— part of a complex of old tunnels left by Mussolini after the second World War. The ambassador uses them when he wants to leave the building without being seen. They're well hidden. I doubt even your father knows about them."

Desperately, Giselle struggled to twist her hands free of their bindings. If Gregory got her out of here undetected, she knew she didn't have a chance. This man was a sadist. He'd enjoy forcing her to tell what she knew—and he'd enjoy killing her when he was finished.

Her efforts met with a measure of success, as the phone cord slipped enough to free her hands. Thinking fast, she shoved against his shoulder, trying to roll off, or at least throw him off balance.

Gregory responded by spinning abruptly and slamming her against the wall with his shoulder, brutally forcing the breath from her lungs. Dazed, Giselle sucked air through flared nostrils, her eyes tearing as she stared at her cap, which had fallen to the floor behind them.

That was it! If she couldn't get away, at least she had to leave a trail! Surely Riley would send someone looking for her when no one answered his radio call. But what could she leave? Her clothing was too sturdy to tear easily. All she had . . .

Her now unbound hands flew to her breast, unfastening the ribbons on her uniform. She had only four and prayed that they would be enough. She let one fall at the end of the hall near the stairwell and another at the bottom of the stairs. The third went down in the darkening hallway leading to the storage area. The last she dropped reluctantly as they entered the archives.

The Great File Graveyard, as Amory had once called it, was dank, so shadowy even with the lights on, that the description had stuck. Giselle pried off her name badge, intending to drop it as well, then realized that it was plastic. The noise of it falling might attract Gregory's attention. But it was all she had left to drop.

Her mind raced wildly, homing in on the only solution. Using the pin on her name badge, Giselle viciously lacerated a finger, squeezing the injury until the blood welled. Reaching out, she smeared it on a nearby box as they passed. It was noticeable, but barely so. Ignoring the pain, Giselle dug in with the pin again, deepening the wound so that the blood dripped liberally from her finger.

Reaching the end of the first row of boxes, Gregory abruptly set her down. Giselle closed her hand into a fist, praying that he wouldn't see the blood. Reaching up, he rapped hard along a poorly-fitted panel of unfinished drywall until it loosened. Then, pushing his fingers through the cracks, he twisted it so that it stood like a slightly open door.

Struggling for balance, Giselle came to her feet and edged away from him, intending to run. But Gregory noticed the movement and caught her arm. "Come on, we're almost there." He tossed her over his shoulder again, bringing her with him through the opening. Giselle grabbed at the drywall, leaving a smear of blood that she hoped would show the way they went. He turned back and replaced the loosened panel, oblivious to the stains.

They were a few paces into the tunnel when a dark blur came at them. Thinking of bats, Giselle flinched, but her muted cry was cut short when Gregory dropped her.

There were sounds of flesh striking flesh, of bone meeting bone. Squinting into the darkness, Giselle could make out two shapes, one larger, more menacing, the other . . .

He grunted as a blow struck home, and Giselle knew his voice as she knew her own. Raz! She flinched as the larger shadow swung at him, a fist connecting somewhere near his head.

The blow seemed to stun him momentarily, and he staggered back a few paces. Furious, Giselle stuck out her feet, tripping Gregory as he followed.

Gregory swore as he dropped to his knees, then caught her foot and wrenched it viciously, causing her to gasp in pain as she felt a tendon in her knee give way. "In case you were thinking of running," he muttered viciously. "You're about to become a widow, Giselle. Please stay and watch."

Furious, Giselle kicked blindly with her good foot, feeling a satisfying blow strike home once before Gregory was out of range. She scrambled to her feet, grunting in agony as her leg nearly gave out beneath her. Leaning against the wall, she ripped the tape from her mouth. Squinting into the darkness, she found Gregory standing alone. A shadow among shadows, he seemed to turn once, twice, as if confused, looking for his prey. And then Raz was on him again, catching him from behind.

Gregory twisted wildly, thrashing at his captor, dashing him against the walls of the tunnel. Giselle felt her way toward them, using the wall for support. Despite the pain, her leg seemed to get stronger as she moved.

She nearly stumbled over something solid. She bent, touched it, and realized what it was—a high-powered flashlight. Thinking quickly, she grabbed it, feeling for the switch. "Raz, close your eyes!" she shouted, flipping the switch and shining the light into Gregory's eyes.

Blinded, he continued to struggle, but Raz anticipated his movements, his hand creeping toward his adversary's throat. Finding it, his powerful fingers dug in, gripping Gregory's neck as the man struggled vainly to pry them loose. In seconds it was over, and Gregory fell limply to the floor at Raz's feet.

Giselle kept the light trained on the limp form on the floor. "Is he . . ."

"He's alive," Raz assured her, raising his hand to his neck to show her what he'd done. "I just cut off the flow in his carotid artery for a few seconds. You'll need him alive to put the finger on other SOI operatives. He's probably the only one of them who'll talk."

She stared at him, part of her wanting to throw herself in his arms, but another part rooted to the spot where she stood. There was so much she needed to ask, so much . . .

His gaze traveled the length of Giselle's body, widening at her apparent pregnancy, then returned to her eyes. There was a long pause, as if he was trying to think of a way to tell her something. Then he abruptly cleared his throat, glancing down at Gregory. "You may want to find something to tie him up with, so we don't have to go through this again when he wakes up."

Giselle nodded, taking the telephone cord, which still hung from one of her wrists. Then suddenly she stopped, her hand creeping up to touch her own throat. She turned to stare at him. "Was that what you . . ."

Her question was cut off by the shattering of the drywall at the entrance to the tunnel. Riley exploded in, followed by several guards. He stopped, staring at the scene before him, then turned to his men. "Someone help Benedetti. The rest of you, take Major Chayil into custody."

"No!" Giselle limped forward, blocking their way. "It was Gregory who brought me down here. He's a member of the SOI."

The men at the entrance parted, allowing her father to step through. He was carrying her cap and ribbons, which he'd picked up along the way. "Giselle, are you all right?"

She nodded, her eyes welling with tears. "I'm fine, Daddy. Raz saved my life."

"What about the blood?" he asked, worry still creasing his brow.

She raised her hands, showing the coagulating blood on her fingertips. "It's nothing. I cut myself to leave a trail so you'd be able to follow us."

"Thank God," her father whispered, suddenly looking terribly old. "I was afraid . . ."

Giselle fell into his arms. "I'm OK, Daddy. You and Raz taught me to take care of myself, remember?"

"Excuse me, Mrs. Chayil," Riley interjected, stepping toward her. "But are you saying that you're certain your husband isn't one of the terrorists?"

Giselle turned, bringing her gaze to meet her husband's.

"Gili . . ." His eyes pled with her to believe it, and every fiber of her wanted to do so. And now she knew—or thought she knew—that he hadn't intended to kill her. He'd intended to knock her out, take her somewhere away from the microphones that he knew were in their apartment, and . . .

And what? She didn't know. Nor could she explain the note, or his terrible fits of rage and guilt, unless he knew he was going to betray her. Mared had seemed certain that he would follow Seif's orders to the letter. And Raz's brother, it turned out, knew Raz far better than she did.

Slowly, painfully, she broke eye contact. A tear traced down her face as she glanced at Riley. "You'd better arrest him," she said softly. Then she turned away, letting her father guide her from the tunnels.

A young ensign was waiting for them at the head of the stairs. "Sir." He saluted her father. "The president and Ambassador Renauld have arrived, and they've countermanded your orders. The president said that holding the delegates was a serious breach of protocol and that he wanted to start a reception line at the main conference room ASAP. He's also ordered us to bring in the remaining delegations. He—"

"Where is he?" Giselle's father demanded.

"Conference room one, sir," the ensign told him.

Taking Giselle by the hand, the admiral took the steps two at a time, half-pulling his daughter up behind him. She struggled to keep up, ignoring the pain in her knee.

Reaching the third floor, he glanced at Giselle, then halted abruptly in the stairwell and reached into his breast pocket. Withdrawing one of the packaged, premoistened towelettes he customarily carried with him for emergencies, he gently scrubbed the blood from Giselle's face and fingers. "I know it's been rough, baby, but you've got to be brave just a little while longer. Make yourself presentable—we don't want to arouse suspicion."

Giselle hissed as the alcohol stung her cuts, but ignored the pain and began plying her father's comb through her tangled hair.

Her father replaced her cap and ribbons and looked her over with a satisfied nod. "You're missing a button, but hopefully no one will notice," he commented. "Stick close to me."

He led her to conference room one, where the president, flanked on one side by Ambassador Renauld and on the other by the secretary of state, was receiving the first of the Israeli delegation. Secret Service agents stood nearby, their eyes flicking sharply over the group, seeming to take in every potential threat. Giselle followed her father, who stationed himself next to the ambassador, so that the delegates would have to pass him before proceeding to the president. He glanced at Giselle, signaling her in so that she stood to one side and slightly behind him.

Giselle scanned each face carefully. She had only glimpsed Seif in Riyadh, barely seeing his face. The only thing she remembered clearly was that he was going bald. She prayed now that the Lord would help her know him when she saw him again.

Her father began shaking hands, greeting each diplomat with a short phrase of welcome, and asking them about their flights. Giselle realized he was drawing them out, making them speak so that she could hear each voice. She edged closer, listening carefully.

The Israelis filed past slowly, then an escort arrived with the Saudis. Some wore *thobes,* some suits, but all, to her dismay, wore the traditional *ghutras,* which concealed the tops of their heads. Giselle scanned their faces, but saw no one she immediately recognized.

The president caught her father's attention, waving him over to speak with the leader of the delegation, a Saudi prince who had provided the military with a good deal of information about Baghdad during the Gulf War. Suddenly alone, Giselle moved closer to the ambassador, listening to his conversations and hoping her father would return to his place quickly.

Then a deep voice cut through her thoughts like a knife. Giselle turned to see two delegates talking quietly as they waited for the line to move. She glanced desperately at her father, but he was still trapped in the president's discussion. Quickly, she moved closer to the men, finding a clipboard on a nearby table and pretending to study it as she surreptitiously glanced at them.

The larger of the two was facing her and occasionally glanced in her direction. His eyes were a deep, piercing brown, framed by prominent cheekbones. His tight, narrow lips gave him a disapproving expression. He wore a thin mustache and goatee, similar to those she had seen on airport photos of the prominent men of the royal family.

Noticing her attention, the man gave her a narrow glare—obviously disapproving of females in military attire—and returned to his conversation. When she heard his voice, Giselle relaxed. This was not Seif.

The second man had his back to her, his robe and *ghutra* obscuring anything she might recognize. Giselle tried to maneuver to a new position to catch a glimpse of his face, but the line moved, and once again he was facing away from her. Glancing at her father, who was trying to extricate himself from the president's side, she moved closer, hoping to hear the man's voice again.

Her eyes followed the length of his arm, and for the first time she realized that he held something in his hand. It was small, about the size of his palm, and cylindrical. His fingers cradled it, his thumb rubbing its side like a worry stone. When she saw the black button on the end, she knew what it was.

A detonator! Desperately, she waved at her father, hoping to catch his attention. At that moment, Arn emerged from the stairwell, followed by Riley and his men.

Seeing them, Seif stiffened, his hand tightening around the cylinder. Realizing she was the only one near enough to stop him before he acted, Giselle dropped her clipboard and moved toward him.

The man with him saw her move toward them, and again glared sharply at her. Seif followed his gaze, turning to face her.

The moment of recognition was electric. Giselle sensed at once that he knew her, and realized that he was about to be exposed. She could almost feel his thumb moving to cover the button.

With a cry, she leaped forward, praying that the shock of her attack would paralyze him for an instant. She struck him hard at a pressure point Raz had showed her, one meant to numb his arm and hand, and heard the detonator clatter to the floor. His companion reached for it, but Giselle brought up her foot, catching him squarely in the chest and sending him staggering. Shoving Seif aside, she dived for the device, coming up with it cradled gently in her hand.

The Secret Service acted quickly, surrounding the president and hustling him into the conference room as two Saudis leaped forward, catching Giselle by the arms. Her father hurried toward them.

The leader of the Saudi delegation came forward, along with Ambassador Renauld. "I demand that this woman be arrested," he said forcefully. "The man she attacked is a respected diplomat and cousin by marriage to our king."

"But he—" Giselle started.

"Silence, woman!" one of the delegates holding her hissed, jerking her arm for emphasis. "You do not speak."

Giselle bit back a retort, realizing that the next few moments would determine the future of the Saudi involvement in the peace process. This was a moment best left to the diplomats.

Ambassador Renauld came forward, his eyes widening in recognition. "I know this woman. This is your daughter, Admiral! I thought she'd been kidnapped!" He turned to her father. "I think you'd best explain this, if you can."

The admiral nodded and approached the men holding Giselle. "Look in her hand," he said quietly.

Glancing dubiously at him, one of the men turned Giselle's hand, revealing the detonator. "What is this?" he demanded.

"I suggest you ask him," Giselle nodded at Seif, who was still prone on the floor, being seen to by members of the Saudi delegation. "He dropped it."

The delegates exchanged glances, then one strode toward Seif and opened his robe, revealing the plastic explosives that were strapped to his chest. With surprised exclamations, the two drew back swiftly, as Arn motioned in his own people. One of them, an explosives expert, quickly disabled the detonator and began removing the explosives, placing them carefully into an armored receptacle that would contain any explosion.

Thaddeus Hardy returned his attention to the delegates. "This man is the leader of a terrorist organization known as the SOI. He intended to detonate those explosives during the peace summit. My daughter was the only one who could identify him."

Stunned, the Saudi delegation stared at their former comrade as he was pulled to his feet by Riley's guard. He glared at them in return. "You deserve death!" he spat in Arabic. "You pretend to have peaceful hearts, signing papers to appease your friends in the West, while all the while, you give money to Hamas for killing Jews!"

The leader of the delegation turned away grimly, waiving his men away from Giselle. He turned to Ambassador Renauld. "I apologize for this man's actions. He was not acting on behalf of our government, I assure you. Since he is one of our people, we would take him back to our country, if you will permit it. I assure you he will be prosecuted to the full extent of our laws."

Giselle was tempted to contradict him, explaining that Seif was in all likelihood an Israeli, but her father's sharp gaze told her to bite her tongue. She almost felt sorry for the terrorist as he was led away; jurisprudence in Saudi Arabia was swift and brutal. She wondered if he would go to his grave with his organization's secrets, hoping that some of his men would avoid detection and manage to continue their work.

"Excuse me, Mrs. Chayil," said a man who had materialized by Giselle's side. "I've been instructed to take you into protective custody." He took her arm and began to lead her toward the stairwell.

Giselle tensed, shaking free of his grasp. "Daddy!" she called loudly, interrupting a quiet discussion with Riley.

The admiral hurried to her side. "What's the matter?"

The man explained his orders again, and Thaddeus waved at his friend and gestured him over. "This man says that you've asked him to take custody of my daughter."

Arn nodded, smiling at Giselle. "I'm sorry. I should have told you myself. After all you've been through, I should have realized that you wouldn't want to go anywhere with a stranger."

"Where are you taking her?" her father asked.

"To the Security Unit."

The admiral stared at him. "You'll do no such thing! Take her to the villa."

Arn shook his head. "Sorry, Thaddy, but this one's my call. She has to be debriefed, and besides, the Security Unit is the safest place for her, at least until we track down all the SOI operatives in the area."

"But I don't want to go!" Giselle protested, remembering the squat little building with its tiny, airless cells and thick steel doors.

"I'm sorry, kiddo," Arn told her, gesturing for his man to come forward again. "You don't have a choice on this one."

She glared at him, tearing her arm free of the man's grasp again. "It seems I haven't had much choice in anything lately."

Her father put a comforting arm around her. "Just a little while, Giselle. Tell these men what they want to know, so they can do their jobs. Arn's right—the Security Unit's the safest place for you until things settle down." He gave her a hug, tickling her chin with his finger. "The president says he wants to press on with the summit. He says it took an act of God to get all these countries to send people, and he's not about to postpone and give anyone time to reconsider. So I'm afraid Arn and I are stuck here at least until the team finishes checking the rest of the building. Once everything's in order, I'll be by to visit you."

Arn's man took her arm again and began to lead her away. Resigning herself to the contact, Giselle stared over her shoulder at her father until they were out of sight.

*Chapter*Nine

Giselle sat on the corner of her cot, hugging her knees and trying not to count the hours. For three days they'd kept her here in this miserable little cell, barely giving her a chance to rest between interrogations. They were trying to wear her out, she knew, make her break down from exhaustion and tell them everything.

It seemed everyone wanted a piece of her—Naval Intelligence, Defense Intelligence, the Secret Service, and a few agencies she'd never even heard of. She had borne it with reasonable tolerance for the first few rounds, but now she was fed up.

Why did they keep asking the same questions, over and over and over again? Why wouldn't they tell her what was going on outside this room? Had the peace summit been successful? Had the terrorists been caught?

And mostly, what about Raz? She was desperate to know what had become of her husband. But every time she asked, they just shuttered their eyes and asked another question. Even her father wouldn't say.

She wanted this over! She wanted to walk out of this cell and demand information. And, more than anything, she wanted to talk to Raz. Had he ever loved her? Was he going to prison? Was any part of him the man that she'd thought she married? The questions slipped up like silent predators, to gnaw at her in this terrible isolation.

She thought of praying, but it seemed like God was no longer listening. What was wrong? What was so different from a few days ago, when everything she asked was answered so quickly?

"God, please! What have I done wrong?" she asked the light above her bed.

She sat upright at the sound of keys turning in the iron door. Maybe this was it! Maybe they were finally letting her go!

The door opened, admitting a man she'd never seen before. He carried a chair with him, which Giselle had learned was not a good sign. He intended to be here for a while. She slumped back against the wall, returning to her original position. "What do you want?"

He took his time answering, scooting the chair up close so that his knees touched the side of her bunk, and leaning forward to scrutinize her. There was nothing friendly in this invasion of her space. In fact, from his frigid blue eyes and steel mask of a face, Giselle guessed that the intent was to intimidate her. If so, he underestimated her weariness, because she was much too numb to be bullied successfully.

"I'm Special Agent Corridan—CIA," he said at length. "I'd like to ask a few questions."

She met his gaze silently.

"I've read the transcripts of your previous statements. There are a few things that don't seem to add up." He made it sound like an accusation.

She maintained her silence. One of her first interrogators had used silence to make her nervous. It had worked—until she'd realized what he was doing. Now she enjoyed reversing roles. If they wanted to ask her questions, they could just ask. But if they were going to try to manipulate her feelings, she didn't have to play.

The silence drew thin, then snapped. The man cleared his throat. "If you're afraid of incriminating yourself, we're willing to offer you immunity for anything you might have done. After all, you eventually did the right thing and kept the delegates from being killed."

Giselle raised an eyebrow. "Are you accusing me of something?"

"At the moment, no," he replied. "But we could charge you with withholding information."

She sighed. "Look, whatever your name is—and don't bother reminding me, because I'm too tired to care anyway—I haven't done anything wrong."

His gaze didn't waver. "Our informants tell us that you were with Mared Chayil willingly, and both of you were very actively trying to avoid apprehension."

She paused, digesting what he had unwittingly told her. "So the Arab was one of *your* people!"

The man's face remained impassive, but his refusal to answer confirmed her speculation. Giselle shrugged. "Well, if he'd bothered to identify himself that first day, I might have gone with him."

"You didn't give him much of a chance."

"I had reason to believe he was with the SOI."

"Why?"

"Because . . ." She stopped herself, took a deep breath, and measured her response. "Maybe I was just overly suspicious of strangers. I was almost kidnapped by terrorists once before." She tried not to wince at the memory—at the time, she'd thought Raz was the terrorist. Could she have been right after all? She still wasn't certain, but a small voice inside her said no. Which was why she now refused to incriminate him.

Had it been necessary to save lives, she'd have told everything, about the note, about Raz's odd and frightening moods—even about the terrifying fight they'd had the night she'd learned his secret. But now, there seemed to be no clear need to do so. If Raz was guilty, surely there would be evidence enough to prove it without her input. Whatever he'd done, hers would not be the voice that damned him.

The man abruptly switched subjects, as if hoping to throw her off guard. "Were you with Mared Chayil willingly?"

"Yes. Before I knew he was with the SOI, I was with him willingly."

"So evidently you trusted him. He was your husband's brother. Had you met him before?"

"I thought you said you read the transcripts," she said, no longer bothering to conceal her impatience.

He shifted abruptly, kicking the bed with a startling brutality. "Why are you lying, Mrs. Chayil?"

"I'm not lying," she retorted, starting to rise. He pushed her back down, and she glared at him. "If you know anything, Agent whatever-your-name-is, you know that manhandling me is a very bad idea. You know everything I do. Go do your job and leave me alone."

He shook his head. "If we knew everything you did, I wouldn't be here, Mrs. Chayil. Why won't you tell us what you know about your husband's involvement with this organization?"

"What makes you think I know anything?"

He smirked. "Are you trying to tell me that you lived with him for three months and never realized anything was wrong? Are you trying to tell me that those terrorists, as they discussed virtually every aspect of their plan while you listened, never mentioned his name?"

"I'm trying to tell you the same thing I've told everyone else. I don't have to answer any questions about Raz. He's my husband. I invoke marital privilege." She recalled the term from one of the classes she'd taken at Georgetown University, regarding American jurisprudence.

He leaned forward so that his face was only inches from hers, and pierced her with his gaze. "Are you saying that you have information that could incriminate him?"

She smiled back at him. "I'm not saying anything at all."

He straightened, taking a deep breath. "Have it your way," he told her, then turned and rapped on the door.

❖ ❖ ❖

Agent Corridan drove until he was several hundred yards from the compound. Then he reached into his briefcase and retrieved a sat phone. Dialing the number, he raised the device and spoke briskly. "We can relax. She clearly doesn't know anything. She's afraid he's guilty."

"That is good," came a voice in response, thick with an Arab accent. "Return to base."

❖ ❖ ❖

Giselle was just lying down for a nap, when the door opened again. This time she just rolled to face the wall and ignored it. "Whoever it is, I'm not saying another word until I get some rest," she called.

"Hi, baby." Her father sat on the bed beside her. "I just came to see if I could do anything for you."

She smiled at him. "Just get me out of here, Daddy."

"I wish I could, Giselle, but it's out of my hands." He patted her shoulder. "But it's only for a little while longer, they tell me."

She rolled away again, trying not to show her frustrated tears. "They said that three days ago. Am I under arrest? Aren't there laws that say they can't keep me without charging me with something?"

He rose and began pacing, the size of the cell allowing him only two shortened strides in each direction. "They say you're not cooperating, Giselle. Why would they say that?"

"I don't know."

"Arn seems to think you know more about Raz's involvement than you're saying. Are you protecting him?"

She dropped her eyes, and he read the expression on her face. "Giselle, why?" he exclaimed. "Why is everyone protecting that traitor?"

She shrugged. "He's my husband, Daddy."

He paused, gazing down at her. "He doesn't have to be. I've spoken with the Monsignor. Since you two were never married in the church, there's no problem with your getting an annulment."

"Annulment!" The word stunned her. She sat up. For some reason, her marriage meant more to her than it ever had before. Maybe it had to do with her newfound faith in God. But for whatever reason, right now, the thought of ending it was intolerable. "How could I want an annulment, Daddy? I still love him!"

He sat again, taking her hands in his. "You love the man you thought you knew. I liked that man, too, Giselle. But that wasn't who he really was—not if he was aiding and abetting terrorists!"

She turned away, brushing at the tear that slid down her cheek.

He stroked her hand gently. "Maybe it's too much to ask for you to get over him so quickly. But you will get over him, I promise. As far as I'm concerned, the sooner that man is out of our lives, the better."

She didn't answer, knowing it would do no good. Once her father made up his mind about something, there was no point trying to change it. Besides, she wasn't certain that he was wrong.

"Your mother's coming home tomorrow," her father told her, changing the subject.

"How is she?"

He grinned. "We had a long talk on the phone last night. She sounds better than she has in years, Giselle. She was like the woman I married."

She smiled, fighting the pang in her own heart. "You sound like a man in love, Daddy."

He took her hand. "You'll love her, too, baby. You don't remember the way things were, but we were a real family then. It can be like that again. When they let you out of here, you'll come home and stay with us."

Giselle dropped her eyes, trying not to show how much the idea hurt her. "I'm looking forward to seeing Mom," she murmured. "But right now I'm very tired, Daddy."

He nodded, releasing her hand. "I'll let you rest, then." Standing, he crossed to the door and rapped, then turned back to her. "Don't worry, Giselle. I'll take care of everything."

She forced a smile. "I'm not a child anymore, Daddy. You don't need to protect me."

"Maybe not," he agreed reluctantly, "but you're still my little girl."

❖ ❖ ❖

A few hundred yards away, Arn Killian sat in the makeshift office he'd arranged in his quarters, surrounded by piles of reports from his agents in the field. Committing a report to his prodigious memory, he placed it in the shredder and started a new one.

"Blast," he muttered, reading rapidly. His team in Egypt had managed to track down Talman and two others, but Mared Chayil remained at large. They had spotted him at the airport, apparently about to catch a flight to Lebanon. But as they moved in, a group of men who had surrounded Chayil whisked him away before anyone could react. Arn's operatives recognized one of the men as a CIA agent they'd worked with on an earlier operation. But when they'd contacted the CIA office in Cairo, their inquiries were met with flat denial.

It made no sense—no more than the order he'd received,

straight from the Pentagon, before his agents had gotten a chance to question Raz Chayil. He had been instructed to order the major's immediate release. No further action was to be taken against him, nor was he to be questioned. All evidence against him to date, most of it circumstantial anyway, was to be shipped to the Pentagon, where, Arn was sure, it would quietly disappear.

"What's going on?" His mind echoed Thaddy's shocked query. "Why are they protecting these people?" It galled him almost as much as it did Thaddy to let that traitor remain in the service as if nothing had happened. And yet the decision had been made.

It didn't make sense. Unless . . .

There was a knock at his door. He called out, and a member of his local team entered. "We just finished with the admiral's office."

Arn nodded. After reading the reports detailing Giselle's admission of eavesdropping, he'd immediately told Thaddy to move to a new location and sent his people to take a look at the office. Not that he didn't believe the kid, but it always paid to verify stories. "What did you find?" he asked.

The man sat, making himself comfortable. "We found the tile she was talking about, but the airspace surrounding the sprinkler pipe was filled in. Somebody went in with that fast-hardening foam. We dug around a bit to see if the hole went all the way up, like the girl said. It did—once." He reached into his pocket. "And look what else we found." Grinning, the man produced a tiny, wireless microphone. "It was tucked nice and neat against the pipe."

Arn took the device and examined it, then closed his fist around it. He knew the technology and who had developed it. The CIA again!

Dismissing his operative, Arn closed his eyes, pondering the implications of this latest find. So the CIA had been tapping Thaddy! He had no doubt who the real target of their interest was. It was no secret in intelligence circles that Arn and Thaddy were friends, and that they were in regular contact.

It wouldn't be the first time that the members of one intelligence agency tracked the activities of another. Clearly, the CIA felt he had information he wasn't sharing—or they had their own secrets, and they wanted to know how close Arn was to learning them.

That last thought resonated in his mind. There was something there. . . .

His mind tracked to the hole in Giselle's story, uncovered by this latest find. Reaching into the cavernous bottom drawer of his desk, which was filled with narrow boxes of neatly-labeled tapes, he readily found the tape he wanted. Flipping it into his tape recorder, he performed a feat that never failed to impress his operatives, forwarding the tape to almost the exact part of the interrogation that he wanted to hear:

Q: So you eavesdropped on your father?

A: I didn't realize how dangerous it was. I just did it to feel close to my dad. He was always working. It was the only way. . . .

Q: How long did this go on?

A: I discovered it the first time we were stationed here, when I was about eight. Then when we lived in the villa, both times.

Q: When was the last time you listened?

A: Last spring, shortly after I came home from Yale.

Q: Was that before or after you began seeing Raz Chayil?

A: Before, just a few days before we started dating.

Q: Why did you stop eavesdropping?

A: (Pause) I guess I just realized it was wrong for the first time.

Q: How did you come to this realization?

A: (Pause) It was something Raz said to me—something he said in passing. Just a casual comment, you know? But it made me think. . . .

Arn rewound the last section twice, then smiled. Suddenly, a lot of things were beginning to make sense.

Picking up the phone, he rapidly dialed his man in charge of investigations at the embassy. "Listen," he said when the operative picked up. "That business you found over at the embassy, is it still intact?" Receiving an affirmative, he grinned. "Tell them to leave it. I'll be out to have a look in a couple of hours."

❖ ❖ ❖

Giselle had another visitor. This time it was Arn, and he came bearing gifts. "I brought you a change of clothes, Giselle. I'll bet you're sick of what you're wearing."

She shrugged. The gray coveralls they gave her every day were ugly, but functional. They were the least of her complaints. "I'm sick of everything about this place. When can I leave?"

He grinned. "We're ready to cut you loose right now."

Giselle stared at him, unable to believe it.

He smiled at her. "Get changed, Giselle. The door will be unlocked when you're finished. I'll be waiting for you outside."

As soon as he left, Giselle hurried to the door and tested it. As Arn had promised, it was unlocked. She hesitated, feeling like an animal that had become accustomed to its cage. Why was this suddenly so easy?

Shrugging off her doubts, she changed quickly and hurried out to join him.

He was waiting just outside her cell. Taking her arm, he escorted her quickly down the row of cells, through the outer office, and outside.

It was nearing dusk outside. Giselle blinked at the sky, feeling disoriented. In her cell, she had believed it to be midday.

Arn guided her to a jeep, helped her in, then went around and got into the driver's seat. "By the way, your husband's been released—lack of evidence. He's confined to quarters out at the embassy at the moment, but there are no charges pending. You wanted to know."

Giselle gratefully brushed a kiss against his cheek. "Thanks for telling me." Lack of evidence. Did that mean he was innocent, or just that they couldn't prove his guilt?

Arn was watching her face. "If you want to see him, I'll take you. Thaddy will kill me, but it's your call."

"I want to see him," Giselle confirmed, watching the satisfied smile that crossed his face. "But why would you offer to take me?"

He started the jeep and backed out of the parking area. "It's the least I can do, after all you've been through."

She stared at him—this accommodating attitude was a far cry from his frustration and annoyance when he had questioned her for several hours yesterday. "You're in a good mood," she commented.

"I just managed to put a few things together is all—and I love it when that happens."

"What things?" she demanded.

He winked at her, putting a finger to his lips. "You know better than to ask, godchild of mine."

Giselle rode in silence until they had left the compound. Then she glanced at Arn. "Can you tell me how the summit went?"

He nodded. "Once we got everyone settled down, things went well enough. There's still a long way to go, but the president got some agreements that look very promising. I guess we'll see if anybody sticks to them."

"That's good." She settled back in her seat, enjoying the ride. She couldn't believe she'd ever taken the beauty of the Italian landscape for granted, the lush greens, the blue sky—the azure waters. "What about the SOI?"

Arn rolled down his window, gesturing for her to do the same, if she wanted to. "I'm sure the fresh air feels good after three days in that cell."

She nodded, letting herself relax and enjoy the feel of the wind against her face.

"Between my people, the CIA, and Mossad, we think we have most of them in custody."

"Mossad is cooperating?" Giselle repeated, surprised.

Arn nodded. "From all I can tell, they were appalled when they found out what had been going on in their own playground. They moved on the information very quickly. In fact, they've already cleaned house. From what we're hearing, the SOI operatives who've been caught in Israel haven't fared very well. A few have lived to talk, but . . ."

Giselle tensed. "What about Mared?"

Arn shrugged, glancing at her briefly. "He's still out there. We may never catch him."

Giselle watched his face. His expression was too carefully guarded for that to have been a casual comment. But from the set of his jaw, she could tell that he wouldn't elaborate. So she relaxed again, leaning back in her seat and closing her eyes. "How did all this get started—or do you know?"

"The Mossad has shared some of its background information with us. From what they've told us, the man you knew as Seif—his real name is Gideon Napthali—was in the Mossad himself. Fairly high up in the chain of command, he was running a string of operatives who were working to infiltrate Palestinian terrorist operations. At some point, one of his people happened to question the real Seif—a Saudi merchant suspected of bankrolling Hamas. The man noticed that Seif bore a striking resemblance to his superior, and he mentioned this in his report."

Giselle opened her eyes. "So Seif—I mean, Napthali—was an impostor?"

Arn nodded. "Shortly after this report was filed, the real Seif was taken to a Mossad detention facility for further interrogation—and that's the last anyone saw of him. From there on out, near as anyone can tell, Napthali took over Seif's life. He managed to get a strong foothold in Hamas, and then began placing his people in several other Palestinian operations. As his power base grew, he began to realize what he might be able to do. His focus changed from information gathering and arrest to infiltration and control—you know the rest. The guy was brilliant, if you can be both brilliant and totally deranged."

Giselle nodded, wondering how Mared and Raz had gotten caught up in it.

They rode in relative silence for the rest of the way, Giselle lost in her thoughts and Arn apparently in his. As they neared the embassy, Giselle felt her impatience to see her husband growing. Soon, she promised herself. Soon she would know whether the man she married was fact or fiction.

As they entered the embassy compound, Giselle brushed a hurried kiss against Arn's face. "Thanks again, Arn," she said quietly. "I hope this doesn't get you in too much trouble with Daddy."

He nodded. "I'll handle it. Now go on with you. I'm sure you and your husband have a lot to sort out."

Nodding, she stepped out of the jeep and hurried to the apartment. There were no guards. Raz was merely under orders to stay inside. Briefly, she wondered whether she'd find him there, or whether he'd already taken advantage of a chance to flee.

Finding the door open, she slipped quietly inside and hurried to the bedroom. He was there. She could almost imagine he was waiting for her, until she saw the suitcase on the bed.

"Where are you going?" she asked, stopping just inside the door.

He glanced up at her, and for a moment time stopped. She wanted to run to him, but something rooted her in place.

A pain filled his eyes, piercing her like a knife. "I've put in for a transfer. I'll be gone as soon as the order comes."

She swallowed hard. "Where to?"

"Anywhere. Away from here." He returned to his packing. "If you want your things, come back tomorrow. I should be out by then."

"I can't leave," she whispered. "Not without knowing. Please, Raz. I have to know."

"What do you want to know? Whether I lied to you? Whether I used you? You already know that I did." He turned away, busying himself at the chest of drawers. "Do you want to file for a divorce or shall I?"

She stared at his rigid back. "Is that what you want?"

He shrugged. "It's for the best."

"Is it?" The words caught in her throat.

He braced his hands on the chest of drawers and took a long breath. "You'll never be able to trust me again. Why should you? I can see it in your eyes. What did you come here for? Whatever you want, I'll give it to you—a divorce, alimony, whatever you think is fair. Just go, before . . ." He broke off, choking back the words. "Just go, Giselle."

"Raz . . ."

He stiffened. "Just go, Gili. I want you to go."

She stared at him for a long moment, unable to believe what he was saying. Then, stifling a sob, she turned to leave.

He caught her at the front door, slamming it shut again before she could exit. He had her backed against the wall, but couldn't meet her gaze. "I'm sorry."

All the lies. . . . A part of her wanted to scream at him, to hurt him the way he'd hurt her. But a greater part was glad that he'd stopped her from leaving. She reached up to touch his face, letting the tears fall. "Tell me, Raz. Who are you? Please! I can't bear not knowing."

Her touch brought his gaze up to meet hers. Seeing no accusation there, he nodded. He raised a hand to brush at her tears, and without meaning to, she flinched away.

He looked pained by her reaction. "Where should I start?"

Giselle forced a smile to cover her growing anxiety. What if he told her he was guilty? What if . . . ?

She stopped herself from thinking. "From the beginning."

He caught her hand and led her back into the living room, sitting with her on the sofa. "In that case, you need to know something about my family. My parents weren't just Israeli immigrants—they were both agents of Mossad."

Giselle nodded, too numb by now to be shocked by anything. She remembered what Arn had told her father years ago. Raz's father worked at a swank Washington psychiatric facility, and his mother was a press agent for a senator. Both were probably perfect occupations for agents seeking information.

Raz shrugged and went on. "I guess you could call it the family business. When Mared came of age, he returned to Israel and joined Mossad as well."

"But not you?" Giselle queried. She couldn't be sure of anything.

"Not me. Maybe it was because I never lived in Israel, but I loved America. All I ever wanted was to be a marine. Maybe I felt guilty about what my parents were doing and wanted to give something back. I don't know. My father didn't approve, but Mom put her foot down. She did all she could to help me, even getting the senator she worked for to give me a nomination to the academy.

"Shortly after that, my father was killed in a terrorist bombing. Mared came home for the funeral. We didn't realize it at the time, but that is when he was identified as a Mossad operative. When he was spotted in an American airport, the alarm bells rang all over Washington. They searched his luggage, and something he was carrying gave them their first real lead on the SOI. Within a couple of weeks, the CIA was checking out every member of my family. They found out about Mom's activities, but they didn't arrest her. Instead, they came to me. They told me they would arrest her, try her for treason. They showed me photos of Ethel Rosenberg in the electric chair for giving American secrets to Israel. If I didn't do what they said . . ."

Giselle watched his face, digesting what he was telling her.

Raz continued quietly. "They wanted me to let Mared recruit

me into the SOI. Over the years, they helped me position myself so that I was of increasing value to the SOI."

Suddenly, the wild mood swings that had so baffled her through their marriage made perfect sense—the rage, the anguish. With every step he took to protect his mother, he was betraying his brother!

"Then I was assigned to your father's command. Mared contacted me one day and told me the SOI had a plan that would bring me to the admiral's attention, make me a hero. I swear, Giselle, I didn't know what they had in mind until it started happening. By then, I had no choice but to step in." He stared at his hands. "I'd never killed anyone before—even though they were terrorists, knowing that they had been set up made it all worse."

Giselle winced, remembering the violence of that day. "The whole thing—even the day we met . . ."

He nodded, his eyes fixed on her face, gauging her reaction. "But I didn't know that until it happened. I swear it, Gili. I didn't know what they had planned."

"What about our marriage?" she asked, dreading to hear the answer. "Gregory told me you were ordered to marry me."

He nodded reluctantly. "It's true. First they wanted me to seduce you. Later on, when they saw how close we were getting, they told me to marry you. They wanted me to get in tighter with your father."

Giselle tore herself away from him, coming to her feet several paces away. She stared at him as his words sank in, then slowly turned away.

"Forgive me, Gili," she heard him beg.

Brokenly, she began walking toward the door. Everything seemed to be going in slow motion, as if through water. She couldn't get away quickly enough.

He caught her as she reached for the doorknob, turning her to face him and pulling her into his arms. "I'm sorry," he whispered against her tear-streaked cheek. "I'm sorry."

"No!" she sobbed, pushing against him. "Let me go. Just let me go."

He tightened his embrace and held her until she stopped struggling. Then he caught her chin and waited for her to bring her eyes up to his. "It didn't matter, Gili," he told her earnestly. "By the time I got those orders, I'd already decided for myself. I loved you. I still love you. You're the only real thing in my life, Gili."

Wild with pain, Giselle struck him with her fists, pounding hard against his shoulders as she sobbed. He did nothing to stop her. "I love you," he whispered as each blow landed. "I love you. I love you." When she was finally spent, she gripped his jacket in her clenched hands and wept softly. He cradled her against his shoulder, rocking her gently until she quieted. Then, tipping her head back, he stared down into her eyes. "I do love you, Giselle. What can I do to prove it to you?"

She stared at him, at the anguish in his eyes, the grief in his expression, and she knew that, no matter how they'd come together, she couldn't let him go. "Don't leave me," she pleaded softly. "Wherever they send you, take me with you."

He caught the back of her head in a firm hand and took her mouth in a kiss that rent her soul and put it back together whole. Fiercely, she threw her arms around his neck and kissed him back.

They had a long way to go yet, a lot of wounds to heal. But with God's help, Giselle was suddenly certain they could work it out.

❖ ❖ ❖

Later, Raz held her on the sofa, staring at the beautiful, trusting woman who was now asleep against his shoulder. He smiled and pressed his lips to her hair, filling himself with her scent. "Maybe it's about time we took that honeymoon," he whispered when she stirred.

She smiled, brushing her forehead against the stubble on his chin. "Let's leave right now. Make them come looking for us."

He took her hand, bringing it to his lips and nibbling on her fingertips. "Your father said you wanted an annulment."

She pinched his arm hard, causing him to wince. "What did I say about talking to Daddy without me in the room?"

He grinned, remembering. "So you never—"

"Never!" Running a finger down his chin, she snuggled tightly against him. "You?"

"Never," he vowed solemnly.

"Semper Fi," she sighed, closing her eyes contentedly.

Careful not to disturb her, he slowly reached to the back of the sofa and took hold of something. With only a little effort, it came free in his hand, and with a quick, crushing squeeze, it was destroyed. He brought his hand back up and looked at its contents. In his palm lay bits of metal and plastic, crushed beyond recognition.

Smiling at the remains of the tiny microphone, he turned his hand and let them fall soundlessly to the floor, where he ground them further with his heel.

He returned his attention to his now-sleeping wife, kissing her hair again, then resting his head against hers. Never again, he promised her silently. Never again.

❖ ❖ ❖

Arn Killian sat quietly in Gregory Benedetti's office as static filled the room. Reaching under the desk, he slid back a concealed panel and removed a tape, which he placed in his breast pocket. He had what he needed, and he knew it was a gift from Raz Chayil. He knew, too, that such a gift would never come his way again.

Smiling, he began to dismantle the listening device.